COLD EVIDENCE

RACHEL GRANT

JANUS
PUBLISHING

Flashpoint

Tinderbox

Catalyst

Firestorm

Inferno

Romantic Mystery

Grave Danger

Paranormal Romance

Midnight Sun

Writing as R.S. Grant

The Buried Hours

This one is for Darcy Burke,
Critique partner, late-night IM sanity checker, and dear friend.
I don't know how I'd navigate these murky waters without you.

Chapter One

Strait of Juan de Fuca, Northeast of Neah Bay, Washington
September

Undine Gray fluttered her fins, swimming slowly upward to the decompression stop with one hand gliding along the anchor line. She spotted her destination, a bucket tied to the line, and floated up the last five meters. She and her dive partner, Yuri, had each deposited a book in the pail for reading during the twenty-minute decompression stop.

She set her dive computer to alert her when it was time to ascend again. Now that she was within radio range of her team on the dive boat above, she pressed the button on her full-face radio-equipped mask. "Undine to *Petrel*, had to abort dive due to trouble with my tank. At decompression stop now. Send oxygen. Over."

"Sorry to hear that, 'Deen. It checked out before you dove," Jared said and added a few curses before he released his radio button.

"I know. Not your fault. Over." But it was a serious

problem that her fifteen minutes of bottom time had to be shortened to less than five. Given the depth of this dive, the surface interval required meant she wouldn't be able to dive again until tomorrow. They'd just lost an entire day from their tight schedule. Maybe she shouldn't be so pissed at Yuri. "Yuri's tank was fine. He refused to abort. I ordered him to surface—this goes against every protocol he agreed to—but with my tank leaking, I couldn't afford to waste a minute arguing and had to leave him. He said he'd locate the datum we dropped yesterday and hook up the permanent buoy line, then surface. He should reach the decompression stop in five minutes. Over."

"Gotcha. I'll talk to Yuri. If he pulls something like this again, he's fired," Jared said. "Over."

"Good. That's what I told him. Removing the full-face mask to switch to pure oxygen. Going radio silent. Over."

"See you on deck in twenty, 'Deen. Over."

She slipped off the full-face mask with the built-in radio and regulator and fitted the pure oxygen regulator attached to the boat via a long hose over her nose and mouth. Then she donned her regular dive mask, cleared it, and blinked the salt water from her eyes. With twenty minutes to kill and no longer in the dark deep, she switched on her flashlight and plucked a book from the bucket and chuckled at finding a Tom Clancy Cold War-era spy novel. Surely her Ukrainian dive partner had already read all of Clancy's books by now? But then, compression-stop reading was more about passing the time than getting engrossed in a novel, and once a paperback book had been immersed, there was no letting it dry out to read on land. Perhaps she should have brought an old favorite as Yuri had, instead of a new romantic suspense novel; then she could just reread favorite scenes as she waited for the nitrogen buildup to release from her bloodstream.

Five minutes in, her computer beeped, reminding her

that Yuri should have joined her at the decompression stop by now. A glance into the dark depths revealed no faint glow from below, and unease settled in her gut. Yuri had said he would ascend after he located the anchor base for the permanent buoy. If he didn't find it within five minutes, he'd promised to abort and surface.

She gripped the mask with the built-in radio. After a moment's hesitation, she switched back to her scuba tank so she could talk to Yuri. At this in-between depth, the radio should reach both the bottom of the strait and the boat on the surface.

She cleared the mask, then said, "Yuri, man, where are you? Over."

Silence.

The team on *Petrel* would have heard her, but they wouldn't muddle Yuri's response by chiming in.

She glanced at her air tank. Dare she risk descending again? Yuri could be injured or stuck. If she descended again now, she would be pushing her tank to the limit. But there was an oxygen line at the decompression stop. She didn't need to save air for that.

"Yuri?" she said again. "Say something. Anything. If you need help, I'll come get you, but I don't have enough air to mess around. Over."

The weather had been calm today, and the slack tide provided the perfect window. This should have been a piece-of-cake bounce dive even though it was deep, but her gauge indicated a too-rapid loss of air when she'd reached one hundred and ninety feet. She'd had no choice but to abort. She had over a thousand hours of bottom time—more than most divers twice her age, and far more than the middle-aged salvage specialist, but he refused to acknowledge her expertise because she was Stefan Gray's daughter, and he wasn't a fan of the marine biologist who'd gone Hollywood to fund his research institute.

One thing Yuri didn't understand was her father might be a celebrity underwater explorer, but the man was a scientist first, last, and always, and he was probably the most experienced and knowledgeable scuba and technical diver on the planet. As his daughter, she knew diving almost better than she knew walking. Her screwing up a dive was akin to Neil Armstrong's kid not being able to find the moon in the night sky.

Yuri's refusal to ascend with her was a small, stupid rebellion, and now it was one that could cost both of them their lives, because she had to go after the old fool.

She addressed the team on *Petrel*. "I'm going to find Yuri. Send Loren down with a tank for me. If Yuri has to ascend quickly, I'll inflate his buoyancy compensator vest, but I'll stay down so I can decompress. Radio the Coast Guard. We might need an airlift to a hyperbaric chamber for him or both of us. Over."

"Copy that, Undine," Jared said. "A NOAA vessel isn't far off our starboard. Maybe they can provide assistance. Loren is radioing them and alerting the Coast Guard we are a team of Navy contractors with a civilian diver who has failed to—"

His words cut off. A second later, the line in Undine's hand went slack. She pulled on the rope as she looked upward. A giant flash lit the surface, piercing the dark water above her head. A wave pulsed downward, sending Undine spiraling through the gray depths.

She lost the flashlight. The book. The bucket. The anchor line. Everything was gone as she tumbled end over end in an underwater current with the power of a fifty-foot breaking wave. There was no up, no down. Just water, which broke the seal on her mask and flooded her sinuses.

She had no idea how far she'd been tossed or even her

depth. It was far too soon for her to surface, but one hand found the strap for the heavy air tank, while the other found the pull cord for her buoyancy compensator vest.

She released the tank and tugged the cord, then shot to the surface.

*L*uke Sevick reacted instinctively and slid his arm around the rail mounted to the dive platform and gripped his wrist, bracing himself for the sudden wave triggered by the rapid series of explosions off the port side. Frigid water sluiced over the low platform of the research vessel, drenching him. His body lifted and his chest slammed into the side as the boat rocked, but his grip held and he remained on the platform instead of being tossed into the icy strait.

The biologist to his left wasn't so lucky. Henry was swept over the edge as smoothly as a poached egg slides from a pan.

Shit. This was supposed to be a calm day out at sea. None of the crew had donned their survival suits. Stupid.

He braced for a second wave. After the drop, he grabbed the nearest life buoy and tossed it to Henry, then he climbed to the upper deck and hurried to a lifeboat. He had only a few minutes to fish the man out before hypothermia would get him. Plus, they needed to see if there were survivors from the boat that blew up.

What the fuck was that? He hadn't yet begun to wrap his brain around the explosion. He'd barely had time to react to the resulting waves.

He pulled back the cover of the lifeboat and jumped inside just as two others reached the rail. "Joan, lower us down! Martin, you're with me." They were all trained for water rescues, but Martin was a stronger swimmer, and as a former SEAL, Luke was the most experienced with this sort of thing. It was an easy call to make.

The boat dropped. Martin grabbed the loose bowline, while Luke took the helm. He started the engine within a second of hitting the water and set a course for Henry, who, thankfully, had caught the floatation device. A hundred meters beyond Henry, he caught a flash of orange in the water. A life vest?

Could someone from the wreck have been thrown that far?

"After we grab Henry, we're checking out the wreckage. I see orange at twelve o'clock," he shouted over the roar of the motor.

"There was a diver-down flag by the boat. I heard over the radio they're out here for that Navy salvage project," Martin shouted back.

That explained the dive setup he'd been admiring before the boat blew to hell.

Luke steered the craft to Henry's side, and Martin scooped the man from the water.

"Hold on!" Luke shouted. He gunned it, aiming for the fleeting orange that dipped and bobbed in the unsettled water.

Odds were anyone on that boat was fish food, but he had to try.

He slowed. As the boat neared the debris field, the figure took form. It was a body, a woman from the shape. She was faceup thanks to her BC vest, wearing a dry suit.

A diver, as Martin had suggested. If she hadn't been *on* the boat, she might have a chance.

He and Martin pulled her into the lifeboat. He laid her flat on the bench seat and pulled off the full-face mask. Water poured out. Hell. How long had she been without oxygen?

She still had a pulse.

"Shit," Martin said, "She's bleeding from the ears. Popped eardrums. Probably bent. You good with rescue breathing?"

Luke nodded.

"I'll radio the Coast Guard and tell them to get their chopper ready. She needs airlift to a hospital with a hyperbaric chamber."

"Do it," Luke said as he checked her airway and tried to inflate her lungs. Nothing. He gave her abdominal thrusts, then turned her to the side as she vomited seawater.

He pressed his mouth to hers and gave her breath. Her chest rose. He filled her lungs again as Martin gunned the engine, steering the small boat toward Coast Guard Station Neah Bay, which was less than two nautical miles away.

Another lifeboat had launched from their NOAA vessel and was headed for the debris field, likely to search for more survivors. They would do the same as soon as this woman was loaded on the Coast Guard copter.

She vomited a second time, then her chest rose of its own accord. She was breathing. He wasn't ready to cheer, though. She could yet suffer a stroke—if she hadn't already.

He lifted one eyelid, then the other. Bloodshot with uneven dilation. At the very least, she suffered from external ear squeeze, but the fact that she was unconscious indicated an air embolism.

She needed to be kept flat and warm. No point in removing her dry suit until they had her at the station and could wrap her in heated blankets for the airlift.

He studied her face as her breathing evened out. There was something familiar about her, but the creases around her cheeks and eyes from the mask and bluing of her lips made it hard to tell. She could just have one of those faces.

Martin had mentioned the Navy, and he knew a lot of people in the Navy diving realm. Water-based ops had been his SEAL team's focus. It was possible he'd met this woman at some point.

He swept the end of her dark, wet braid off her chest, revealing a name emblazoned on her dry suit: *Gray*.

His stomach dropped as his gaze returned to those blue lips and wide cheekbones. There was a family named Gray who was synonymous with scuba diving and underwater research. So deeply entrenched was the family business, they had custom-fitted dive suits with the family name emblazoned on the left breast.

And underwater explorer Stefan Gray's daughter, the pretty water nymph, Undine, was the woman who'd fucked up his life twelve years ago.

Chapter Two

The pressure in Undine's skull was unbearable. A vise closing in on her temples. She was vaguely aware of being moved. Cool air hit her skin as her dry suit was sliced open and pulled from her body. Warm blankets pressed around her, and she let out a soft purr, then settled into oblivion, escaping the pain.

She dreamed of Luke Sevick, first his smiling face that had made her teenage heart swoon, transforming into the red-faced anger of their final meeting. Shame and longing settled in her belly, even in sleep. She hated dreaming of Luke, hated the way it made her feel about herself, the deception she could never erase.

But dreaming of him was inevitable, like the sunrise. Usually the dreams came when things were going well, her subconscious kicking her in the teeth and telling her she didn't deserve success or happiness.

Trina—the only friend Undine had dared share the story with—thought the dreams were a sign Undine pined for him, but she knew the truth. The dreams were her secret scarlet letter. She was the reverend in that old book, the one who bore a hidden stigmatic letter on his chest, remaining silent while his partner in sin, Hester Prynne, was forced to bear hers publicly.

She got off scot-free from their indiscretion—which had been entirely her fault—while Luke lost everything that mattered to him.

She drifted into consciousness, took in that she was in a hyperbaric chamber, then unwillingly retreated back into the dream world where she revisited her greatest shame.

Luke, laughing as they sat by the campfire on the beach, his arm draped casually around her. The feel of her heart rate kicking up as she realized he was about to kiss her. Not just their first kiss, but *her* first kiss. Ever.

And he didn't know. Couldn't know. Because he thought she was an experienced nineteen-year-old.

The *only* good thing about dreaming about Luke was she always recognized it was a dream. Her subconscious couldn't fool her, because no way in hell would Luke Sevick ever be a part of her life again.

She only wondered why he visited her dreams today. He was a harbinger that things were going too well, but she had the unsettling feeling that wasn't the case now. Hazy images of pain, shock, and tumbling in the sea came to her in the lucid dream. She couldn't remember what happened but had the distinct feeling it wasn't good.

She pushed at the edges of sleep, grabbing on to consciousness. Pain pierced her temples. Her joints ached. She slowly opened her eyes to a blurry, bright world. Again, she recognized the insides of a hyperbaric chamber.

I have the bends?

She never screwed up diving. She was a damn encyclopedia of dive safety. Hell, she'd been teaching safety classes since she was sixteen, working at her father's institute. That was how she'd met Luke.

What happened?

She closed her eyes against the bright light and tried to focus on something other than the pain in her skull. The line to the surface snapped, a light flashed, and the sensation of tumbling rocked her. She coughed at the memory of water invading her mask, forcing its way into her mouth and nose.

She opened her eyes again and realized someone was in the room. Whoever it was had moved to the side of the chamber. Slowly, she focused on the face that gazed into the chamber window.

She blinked. Once. Twice. She must be dreaming. This wasn't possible.

The man's gaze fixed on hers. His eyes narrowed. "Hello, Undine," Luke Sevick said.

She closed her eyes and prayed this was yet another Luke nightmare.

✳

"Chicken." The word slipped from Luke's lips. Jesus, he was kicking a wounded woman when she was down. What sort of asshole was he?

But he was pissed. Angry that he'd spent the last several hours worried about the bitch who'd ruined his life for a teenage lark, angry that his heart had been ready to explode when he realized she might die, angry that any part of him had the capacity to care about her. Angry that in a few hours he might come face-to-face with her father for the first time in the dozen years since the man had withdrawn his scholarship, destroyed Luke's professional dreams, and tried to have him sent to prison.

When the prosecutor refused to file statutory rape charges, Stefan Gray had sworn Luke would never get a field research job in marine biology, and he'd promised to tell administrators the whole ugly story if Luke so much as applied for a job teaching high school.

Dr. Gray didn't give a crap that Undine had lied about her age and had been damn convincing. She'd been taking college courses and was teaching at the institute; Luke had every reason to believe her when she claimed to be nineteen. But even then, he wouldn't have touched the premier marine biologist's daughter, except she'd pursued him with a single-minded, guileless sweetness, seducing him with the wonders of the ocean and knowledge beyond her years of the sea that abutted the Monterey, California institute that was her home.

At twenty-two, he'd been helpless to resist her allure.

As a result he'd lost his job, his scholarship, and his future.

Dr. Gray didn't hold her responsible, because Princess Undine could do no wrong in her father's eyes, and seducing one of her father's too-old-for-her employees was definitely wrong.

Dammit. This was not the time to be reliving the nightmare that had changed the course of his life. He'd found purpose in the Navy and made a home on the SEAL team that focused on dive-based operations. When a minor injury meant he could no longer serve as an active duty SEAL, he'd dug out his old bachelor's degree in marine biology and applied for a transfer into the National Oceanic and Atmospheric Administration's Commissioned Officer Corps. He was still in the uniformed service, serving his country, working in the field he'd loved and lost.

And there was nothing Stefan or Undine Gray could do to take it away.

The door opened. He glanced over to see the captain of the NOAA vessel he'd been on when the explosion occurred. "How is the patient?" Capt. Hogarth asked.

"She woke a bit ago, but didn't speak." However, after seeing the recognition in her eyes he suspected she'd played possum. It had been several minutes before her breathing evened out to a sleep rhythm.

"The Navy confirmed she's Undine Gray. How did you recognize her?"

"I worked for Dr. Gray a dozen years ago and met her then."

"The big man is supposed to be here in a few hours," the captain said.

Luke tried to suppress a grimace.

"He'll likely wish to thank you in front of the television cameras."

"Gray does everything in front of cameras these days, but I have a feeling he'll forgo them this time." He allowed himself a cynical smile.

"Out of respect for his daughter's lost team. I suppose you're right."

He considered his reply carefully; no matter how unwitting he'd been, the shame over his part in the brief, abhorrent relationship with Undine remained with him even now. "More likely because we parted on bad terms. He doesn't like me, and I…have no fondness for him." *Or his daughter*. He left the last part unsaid. His skipper would never believe him, given that he'd insisted on accompanying her to the hospital. He cleared his throat. "How many were on the boat that blew up?"

"The Navy has confirmed six including Ms. Gray. Four were contractors. One of the victims, Jared Cornish, was the owner. The Navy had leased *Petrel* from him for a salvage operation that was set to begin next week with Navy divers. Three of the crew were Cornish's employees. One victim was civilian Navy—the Public Affairs Officer from Bremerton. Ms. Gray, also a civilian, works for Naval History and Heritage Command in DC."

"NHHC? She's an historian?" That was a long way off the career path she'd been destined for once upon a time.

"She works for the Underwater Archaeology Branch. Get this, her boss is the US attorney general's wife."

He vaguely remembered hearing that fun fact after Mara Garrett, who'd been a Joint POW/MIA Accounting Command archaeologist, had made worldwide headlines by facing down a North Korean firing squad. His SEAL team and JPAC were both based on Oahu, and he'd lived there at the time. To the best of his knowledge, he'd never met Mara Garrett, but had served with several men who had.

He kept his gaze fixed on Undine. She'd been the only survivor of the blast. He didn't relish being the person to tell her, but someone who knew her should deliver this news. As far as he knew, he was the only such person for a thousand miles.

"What's the word on the investigation into the explosion?" He knew it was far too soon for anything but speculation, but still, he hoped to hear it was all a horrific accident. Because even though twelve years hadn't diminished his anger, the idea that someone had sabotaged Undine Gray's boat triggered a protectiveness he had no business feeling.

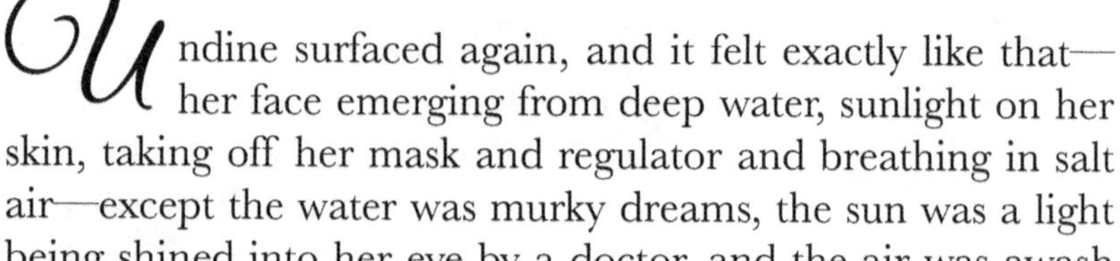

*U*ndine surfaced again, and it felt exactly like that— her face emerging from deep water, sunlight on her skin, taking off her mask and regulator and breathing in salt air—except the water was murky dreams, the sun was a light being shined into her eye by a doctor, and the air was awash with the scent of antiseptic cleanser.

"Pupils look good," the doctor said. He smiled.

Or at least she thought he did. She was slightly blinded by

the light. She blinked several times, then tried to focus again. This time his smile was clear.

"Ahh. Good. You're awake. How are you feeling, Ms. Gray?"

His words were muted. That combined with the pain suggested she'd burst her eardrums on the fast ascent. A glance around the room, though blurry, showed she'd been removed from the hyperbaric unit while she slept. She was in the same room, resting on a gurney next to the unit. She cleared her throat. Her voice came out harsh, raspy, like she still had salt in her throat. "Like my head's in a vise."

His grin widened. "Speech is good. Facial muscles moving in tandem. No signs of stroke. Excellent."

She supposed that was good news, but the events of—this morning? Yesterday?—were at the forefront of her aching brain. "Yuri. Is Yuri okay? And the others. On *Petrel*. Are they…here?"

Movement behind the doctor caught her attention, and she shifted her gaze to see Luke, proving that part of her dream hadn't been a nightmare after all. The doctor shifted so she could see him better. "I assume Yuri was the other diver? I told the Coast Guard investigators to search for another diver, that you'd never dive alone."

She nodded, feeling tears gather in the corners of her eyes. He'd said search. Not rescue.

It's too late for rescue.

"I'm sorry, Undine," Luke said softly. "You're the only survivor."

The doctor stood. "We need to finish the exam, but I'll give you a moment."

"Thank you, Doctor," Luke said. After the door closed behind the physician, he turned to her. "I hope you don't mind, I asked to be here when he woke you. I figured you'd have questions, and this news is best delivered by someone you know. Even if that someone is me."

"Thank you," she said, utterly touched that he'd accepted the responsibility, in spite of the fact that he must hate her for what she'd done all those years ago. All at once, Sandy's smile flashed in her mind, a memory of the Navy Public Affairs Officer's grin as she called Yuri on his blatant sexism or delivered a surprisingly clever pun.

Sandy was gone. As were Jared, Yuri, Loren, and Scotty. Gone.

In a flash of light, the space of a few heartbeats, they were gone.

They could have been dead before she reached the surface.

Grief and shock hit her with the force of a breaking wave. She sat up and hugged her knees, burying her face as sobs racked her body.

Luke let out a soft curse. Arms encircled her, and she was lifted from the gurney. He turned and sat on the mattress, cradling her on his lap.

She wrapped her arms around his neck, tucked her face against his shoulder, and cried, thankful for the encircling arms, no matter who provided them. He said nothing as he stroked her back, and for that she was grateful as well. She didn't want to be quieted, didn't want details. She just wanted to know she wasn't alone.

When the first wave of sobs quieted, Luke's arms loosened, but he didn't release her. "Your dad is on his way. He'll be here in a few hours. I don't intend to be here when he arrives."

She took a deep breath. "That's probably for the best. But...you're the one who saved me, right?" She must have glimpsed him in the rescue. That was why she'd dreamed of him. "He'll be grateful."

He nodded in answer to her question. "Honey, your father will never be grateful to the man who seduced his little girl."

She cringed at that. They both knew she'd been the instigator. She'd been sixteen and believed herself mature and worldly, only later recognizing what a selfish child she'd been. That first year after she'd ruined his life, she'd sent him letters, apologizing. Each one came back, unopened, with "addressee unknown" written across the front in Luke's bold scrawl.

She slid off his lap, unable to utter the apology he probably still didn't want to hear. This wasn't the time for this conversation. Five people she'd worked with had died. Nothing else in her sorry past mattered. "How long has it been since…the explosion?"

"Seven hours."

"The families have been notified?"

He nodded. "The Navy handled that."

She swiped at a fresh wave of tears. "I've only known them for six days. Well, Sandy and I exchanged emails since August, planning the excavation setup, but we didn't meet until I arrived here late last week. I know she's married, but I don't even remember her husband's name." She focused on this detail, searching her conversations for a reference point. It seemed wrong that she couldn't put a name to the most important person in Sandy's now-ended life.

A knock on the door was followed by the doctor stepping back into the room without waiting for permission. "Ready to finish the exam now?"

She nodded.

"I'll leave you alone, then," Luke said. He slipped out the door before she could respond, and she wondered if she'd ever see him again.

Chapter Three

*L*uke was tempted to make his escape. He was done. He'd delivered the news. He owed nothing to Undine or her father. He was in the corridor, heading to the front door of the hospital when something stopped him. Loyalty to the Navy in which he'd proudly served?

Maybe.

A strange jolt in his gut at having seen the very adult woman Undine had become?

He hadn't seen a trace of the girl he once knew. Far from it, he saw a woman he'd never met. He neither liked nor disliked her in the same way he didn't have an opinion on the tellers at his rarely visited bank. But she wasn't a stranger, and they did have a past. A poisonous one that had shaped his postcollege adulthood.

She had almost died today. She *would* have died, along with her coworkers, if the NOAA research vessel hadn't been in the right place at the time of the explosion. Hell, he might not have spotted her in time if Henry hadn't been swept overboard.

Fate. Chance. Destiny. All had conspired to save her.

Bullshit.

It was nothing but dumb luck.

But still, stranger or something else, it had felt wrong to leave her with only doctors and nurses for company and comfort. Now she was out of the woods, having escaped her ordeal with a mild concussion and two busted eardrums. He could leave.

He *should* leave.

Due to the dramatic explosion, military involvement, and that the sole survivor was a celebrity scientist's only child, the press had parked outside the hospital. Capt. Hogarth had warned him more were arriving with each passing hour.

The brass within NOAA wanted Luke to make a statement to the press. He and Martin were to be made into heroes for doing what anyone in the same circumstance should do. He was happy to give Martin his moment, but for himself, he knew his SEAL background would be trotted out and lauded in ways that would make him uncomfortable. He'd never courted the limelight and had appreciated that his SEAL team had largely flown beneath the radar, rarely garnering media attention or mention. The way it should be.

The last thing he wanted was to be called a hero for doing nothing more than what was expected. And he sure as hell didn't want the press digging into his past with Undine. He'd been assured when the prosecutor refused to file based on Undine's sworn statement that she'd lied very convincingly, that there would be no public record of the incident. In the prosecutor's view, Luke had committed no crime, even though a law had been broken.

A strange legal gray area that had saved Luke from serving time and having to register as a sex offender, but which had angered Stefan Gray to the point of exacting the only revenge he could: utterly decimating Luke's prospects in his chosen field.

Now Luke stood in the hallway in indecision. Keep Undine company until her father arrived, or get the hell out while he still had a chance?

What would he do if it weren't Undine Gray who sat alone in a hospital room? What if it were some other woman who'd survived an explosion that killed five coworkers?

He'd stay by her side.

He turned back for the waiting area adjacent to the hospital's recompression unit, nodding to the security guard at the door. Would there be security to keep out reporters when she was moved to a regular room? She was in no condition to answer questions about her dead coworkers or describe the trauma she'd been through, and he hated the idea of her being the victim of an ambush interview.

Pictures of the rocky coastline decorated the waiting room walls. Seals sunbathed and otters played in the surf. Usually he'd zero in on the marine life, but tonight he found he was drawn to a picture of a sunken ship covered in barnacles.

Underwater archaeology. Never in a million years would he have guessed that was where she'd end up. She'd loved marine biology as much—possibly more—than he did. At sixteen, she'd been the deserving heir apparent to her father's institute. So much so that it had been easy for her to pass herself off as nineteen. She'd served as both dive instructor and researcher, and had been enrolled in senior-level biology courses at the local university. Her knowledge of aquatic life had surpassed his and the other new researchers.

What was it about archaeology that had captured her sharp mind? Perhaps for her, underwater was underwater. She didn't care if she was studying fish, plants, or shipwrecks, just so long as she was under the sea with all the other merfolk.

Her name, he knew, translated to mermaid, or sea

nymph, depending on the source. The perfect name for Stefan Gray's daughter.

"The doctor has finished the exam, Lt. Sevick. You're free to join her."

He raised a brow at the nurse. "She wants to see me?"

"She requested you, if you hadn't left."

He nodded and thanked the man, then pushed open the door.

She gave him a tentative smile. "I didn't think you'd still be here."

He shrugged. "I considered leaving."

Her gaze dropped to her bare feet, which dangled over the side of the gurney. "I wanted to ask…about the explosion. Did you…see it?"

He nodded. "There were at least two explosions, from the sound. One burst followed by another."

"The boat, how…what…was it completely destroyed?"

He nodded. "There's a chance it was deliberate. The second explosion might have been the fuel tank. Whatever it was, it was big."

Her eyes widened and her jaw dropped. He had a feeling she'd been caught on the word "deliberate" and blanked out from there. He mentally kicked himself for saying it. He'd had a lot of hours to think while waiting for her to be pulled from the hyperbaric unit. Too much time, probably.

"You think my team was…murdered?"

There was no point in denying it. "It's possible."

"I was at the decompression stop at the time of the explosion. The shock wave knocked me clear of the sinking debris."

"You were incredibly lucky."

"If I'd been at the bottom—at a hundred and ninety feet —I still might have survived. The drift as the boat sank would have left me clear. I was *supposed* to be at the bottom. I aborted the dive because my air gauge was on the fritz. I couldn't trust it."

He frowned at her. "Your gauge was on the fritz? Since when do you dive with faulty equipment?"

She pursed her lips. "Everything checked out on the surface."

The fact that *her* equipment, of anyone's, had failed made him suspicious. "It would have to. Everyone who knows you knows you inspect everything twice and leave nothing to chance. The fact that you had a bad regulator today of all days, is…disturbing."

She rubbed her arms, looking so scared and vulnerable, but his comforting duty had ended when the tears stopped flowing. No way in hell would he touch her again.

"Listen, Coast Guard and Navy investigators are eager to interview you. Be sure to tell them how careful you are, how experienced you are with diving."

She nodded. "The doctor said they'd be here soon."

He saw his opportunity to escape before her father arrived. "If you don't want to be alone, I'll stay, but otherwise I should go." He wasn't abandoning her. It wasn't *his* job to protect her from the press. That duty should fall to her father, or boyfriend, or husband.

He didn't bother looking for a ring. Most divers didn't wear them. And frankly, he didn't want to know. It didn't matter to him one way or another.

"I—I think it would be best if you go. I'll be fine. I just wanted to thank you…for saving me."

He gave her a sharp nod. "Have a good life, Undine."

Chapter Four

Port Angeles, Washington
Six Weeks Later

Undine stood outside Luke's apartment, her stomach in a knot. She shouldn't be here. She should be on a flight back to DC, returning to the job and life she'd built. Or, because she had another month left in her leave of absence, she could fly to Monterey and go diving on some of her favorite kelp forests.

Except that was the problem.

She couldn't dive.

She took a deep breath and knocked on the door. A moment later, she heard footsteps. She faced the peephole, offering a tentative smile, and held her breath.

She didn't really expect him to open the door. She braced for the sound of retreating footsteps.

After a long moment, the dead bolt clicked and the door opened. Luke leaned casually against the frame, his brow furrowed in question. "Undine. What brings you here?"

He was bigger—more muscular about the shoulders and

chest—than he'd been at twenty-two. She'd read the news reports that followed her rescue and learned he'd been a Navy SEAL. An injury had taken him out of active duty service with the SEALs but hadn't prevented him from transferring to NOAA's Commissioned Officer Corps, where he was now a lieutenant, finally using his marine biology degree. She'd seen a picture of him in his Navy uniform and had been reminded of how her infatuation had begun. She'd thought him handsome twelve years ago, but if anything, she found him even better looking now with lines of experience etched into his features.

"I—I have a favor to ask."

His eyes flattened. "Ballsy move."

She shrugged. "I've always had more courage than brains." She cocked her head. "Is this a bad time?"

His nostrils flared as his blue eyes studied her intently. Finally he said, "You can have ten minutes." He gestured for her to enter.

She stepped inside, noting a pile of shoes by the door, reminding her that in the Pacific Northwest, people often removed their shoes to avoid tracking mud into homes. She'd slipped off one sneaker when her gaze landed on a pair of high heels. She flushed, embarrassed to have intruded. "Do you have company?"

He glanced at the shoes, then shook his head. "No," he said, offering no further explanation.

Not that he should. It was none of her business. She hoped he did have a girlfriend. That he was happy. He deserved it. She toed off her other sneaker and followed him into the living room.

His apartment was on the fourth floor of a waterfront condo building. His front window had a sweeping view of the strait. It was only five p.m., but in early November, that meant the sun had set and it was nearing full dark. Shadows fell over the strait, but lights along the waterfront broke the darkness and gave her glimpses of the turbulent Salish Sea.

She shuddered and reminded herself the wind would lessen tonight. Tomorrow would be a calm, clear fall day all along the north coast. Slack tide would be just after two o'clock at Neah Bay. She turned to face Luke and swallowed against the sudden rush of emotion. "I heard you assisted the investigative team and dived on *Petrel* to collect pieces of the wreck."

He nodded. "Once, when the Coast Guard was short a dive partner. Given my background and dive experience, it made sense."

He probably had more dive experience than most of the Coast Guard divers combined, which was why she was here. "Do you agree with the finding that it was an accident?"

He shrugged. "That's not my field."

"In the hospital, you said it could have been deliberate. You were concerned because my equipment failed at just the right—or wrong—time."

"I was just running off at the mouth. Speculating."

"But you've worked with explosives. And boats. I read that in the news accounts online."

"Yeah, I've planted my share of explosives on hulls of boats." His wide shoulders rose and fell again. "But they found no evidence of an external explosive."

"My tank wasn't found. What if it had been sabotaged, like you suggested?"

"Yuri Kravchenko was never found either. There was a lot of shit that was never found. It's a deep dive, located near a treacherous stretch of coastline. Things get lost. Hell, *Petrel* and the Navy sub probably aren't the only boats down there. It was dark, cold, and deep. The current silted over much of the debris within days of the blast. I didn't even see the Navy sub you were supposed to be diving on."

"Which brings me to why I'm here."

"You have a favor to ask," he said, his voice guarded.

"Yes. With the investigation complete, I want to dive on the site. I need to see it."

"And why are you telling me this?"

"A few days ago, I hired a boat and a dive partner for just that purpose, but when the time came to get in the water I—I—froze. I couldn't do it." Her breath became short and she felt the same panic infuse her again. She might as well be back on the dive platform. "Now I'm afraid that if I don't dive again—*there*—that I'll never have the nerve to dive again."

"You need to get back on the horse."

"Yes."

"And you want *me* to be your fucking saddle."

She met his angry gaze. "Yes," she whispered.

*L*uke couldn't quite believe her audacity in asking this of him. She wanted him as her *dive partner*. The last time they'd donned wetsuits together, they'd ended up on a private beach next to an aquatic preserve, where unbeknownst to him until he was mid-deed, he'd taken her virginity in the one and only time they'd had sex. She'd planned it all, right down to bringing condoms in her ditty bag, which weren't standard issue in the institute's dive kit.

"*No*," he said. "Absolutely not."

"With a strong dive partner, I might not panic again. I know I'd feel safer with you."

"While you're the last person I'd feel safe with."

"Dammit, I'm twenty-eight years old!"

"Yeah? Show me your ID."

She flinched.

Good.

"I deserve that. And so much more." She shook her head. "Listen, I know you probably still aren't ready to hear my apology—"

"Let's get one thing straight right now. You can be sorry all you want, but I don't want to hear nor do I have to accept your apology, and I sure as hell don't have to forgive you."

"I'm not asking for your forgiveness. I'm asking for your help." Her voice shook with emotion, and damn if that didn't give him pause. "You were a SEAL. You probably have as many—even more—hours in the water as I do. And you've been *there*. At the wreck site. I can't think of anyone I'd feel safer with. I had a panic attack, and now I'm scared as hell that the one thing I'm good at, the one thing I know better than breathing, is the one thing I'll never be able to do again, because I'm terrified."

He felt a small, bitter twinge of schadenfreude. "Well, maybe then you'll know how I felt twelve years ago." The moment the words were out of his mouth, self-loathing settled in. He didn't wish that feeling, that fear, on anyone. Not even Undine Gray.

She closed her eyes and took a deep breath. "I know I deserve that too. I tried to get my father to back down. I really tried."

"And maybe, just maybe, you should have considered your father's reaction *before* you put me in that position. In another state, I would have been sent to prison. I would've been forced to register as a sex offender." California law allowed a defendant to present evidence that the victim had lied about their age.

Tears flowed freely down Undine's cheeks. "That's my biggest regret, that I never considered the consequences to you." She swiped at her cheek. "You're right, you're the last person I should ask anything of. I just... I'd hoped... We were friends once, before I fucked up your life, before I got so wrapped up in my stupid, girlish belief that you were *The One*, and that *True Love* made what I did okay."

"We were never in love, Undine. You had a crush, that's all it was."

"I know that now. Believe it or not, I *did* grow up."

"And yet you're still here, in my living room, asking *me*, of all people, to help you."

"I am. And I'll listen to every angry, nasty thing you have to say to me, because I deserve it. The fact remains that we *were* friends, and I've missed that friendship."

"I haven't missed you at all."

He had to give her credit for facing his bitterness head-on. She flinched, but she didn't cower or back down. She didn't walk away.

Could he do what she asked, take her to the deep? He couldn't think of a single reason why he should. He sure as hell didn't *want* to. But still, he must be a sucker, because he found himself saying, "When?"

"Conditions should be perfect tomorrow afternoon. I've arranged for a boat."

Tomorrow he was supposed to head to the research housing out at Neah Bay, where he would spend the rest of the week monitoring a pod of orcas and seal activities as part of his ongoing research into the effects of sonar on marine mammals. The site of the explosion was in the strait, just two miles north of Neah Bay. He didn't even have a handy work excuse to say no. "Cancel the boat. I can get us the best dive skipper in the region."

Her eyes widened. "You'll do it?"

He met her gaze. "I know you're used to being the dive master, but so am I. If I take you down, I'm running this show. Period. If the water is too rough, we bail. If you show any sign of panic, we're outta there. Got it?"

She nodded.

"Where are you staying? I'll pick you up at oh-seven-hundred."

She gave him the name of her hotel, then added, "But I have a rental. We can take separate cars."

"No. You're riding with me. That'll give you two hours to convince me I'm not making a mistake in helping you."

Chapter Five

$\mathcal{U}$ndine settled in the passenger seat of Luke's SUV. He handed her a cup of coffee after she buckled her seat belt, then he passed her a second paper cup filled with sweetener packets and tiny containers of creamer. "If I remember correctly, you like lots of sugar and cream."

A small, inappropriate bubble of laugher attempted to break free. She managed to contain it to a snicker.

"What's funny?" he asked.

Dare she tell him? Ah, why the hell not? He already loathed her. Nothing she said would change that, and it was a relief that neither of them were pretending they didn't share a bitter history. "I was never a coffee drinker—before—but I figured a nineteen-year-old would drink it. So whenever I was with you, I had coffee. But I *hated* it. That's why I put in so much cream and sugar."

He grunted. The sound might indicate mild amusement. She couldn't be certain. "And now?"

"I'm more of a tea person. But I do drink coffee with a little cream."

"Put the sugar in the glove box, then. Joan will use it."

She wanted to ask if Joan was the owner of the high heels, but restrained herself. None of her business.

Port Angeles was five miles to the east by the time she worked up the nerve to ask the question that had nagged her from the moment she was lucid in the hospital. "Are you happy, Luke? With where you are now?"

He was silent for a long while. Finally he said, "As much as I want to say no just to hurt you, it would be a lie."

She swallowed at that. "You still want to hurt me."

He glanced sideways. "Not physically. Never, ever physically. But yeah, for a lot of years, I wanted you to be punished like I was."

She'd had to create her own punishment, to come up with something that felt equal. But now wasn't the time to tell him that. He was still too raw. And he might not give a damn or think it was enough. No, best to keep her hair shirt private. "But you're happy now."

"Yes. Very."

"How long have you lived in Port Angeles?"

"A year. I was stationed here after I finished my three-year stint of sea duty for the NOAA Corps."

"Before that, you were a SEAL." He'd had two intense careers in the twelve years since she'd known him.

He nodded.

"Do you know the guy who shot bin Laden?"

He rolled his eyes. "You're not even original asking that."

"I figured it was the requisite question."

"I don't know him, and I'm glad I don't. He broke the oath of silence we all agree to. A lot of SEALs feel betrayed."

She nodded. She was well aware of that. She did work for the Navy, after all. Trina, her coworker and one of her closest friends, was engaged to a former SEAL. She'd ask if Luke knew Keith Hatcher, except she'd already questioned Keith, who'd told her no. Keith had been based out of Norfolk, while she'd learned Luke had been in Hawaii.

"How long have you worked for the Navy?" he asked.

"I got the job a few months after I finished grad school, going on four years now."

"You have an MA?"

"Yeah. Texas A&M. Nautical archaeology."

"You like it? The field and the job?"

"Yes to the field." She wouldn't elaborate now on why she'd ended up in archaeology, so she focused on the second part of his question, and smiled, thinking of the friends she'd found in her coworkers. "I love my coworkers, sometimes find my boss creepy, but I enjoy the job. These last six weeks, though…it's been a little tough."

"Creepy boss? Isn't the AG's wife your boss?"

She let out a sharp laugh. "Oh God. No. I mean, she is, but that's not who I meant. Mara's cool. Best boss I've ever had and also a good friend. No, I meant the Navy's under-water archaeologist, the head of UAB—the Underwater Archaeology Branch. Technically, he's under Mara, but they're the same pay grade and he's sort of got his own little fiefdom. I'm pretty sure he thinks he's *her* boss."

"And how is he creepy?"

She shrugged. "He just makes me uncomfortable. But he's never actually crossed a line. So I deal. Erica is just below him in the hierarchy. She watches out for me."

"When are you going back?"

"I'm not sure. I'm on leave now and have another month if I want it. Plans to excavate the sub have been put on hold indefinitely. I was thinking of going back after this dive. Later this week." She touched her ears. She'd been in a fog that first week in addition to having busted eardrums. It was safe for her to fly now—and had been for the last few weeks, but she hadn't been ready to return to DC. She'd been waiting for the determination of accident or sabotage. Trina believed that was just an excuse, that Undine was reluctant to leave without seeing Luke again, but she couldn't really credit that theory.

Yet here she was, riding in an SUV with Luke Sevick. Although, that was because she'd fixated on diving on the wreck one more time. It hadn't been an excuse to see Luke. Definitely not. She'd tried to dive, and failed.

And the panic attack had scared the hell out of her.

"Tell me about the sub. The one you were supposed to bring up. It was only mentioned briefly in the press about the accident."

"That's because the Navy wanted to downplay it since it will remain *in situ* for a while yet. It's far too deep for recreational diving, but there are a few unethical salvage divers out there who follow the news a bit too closely. There isn't anything strategic about this sub, but it has human remains we want to recover."

"It's the USS *Wrasse*?"

"You know the story?"

"Not really, just that it was a really old sub that went down on its swan song cruise in the fifties or sixties."

"Actually, it wasn't the swan song. Or, it wasn't supposed to be. The original account of the incident was somewhat muddled because *Wrasse* went down in the middle of the Cuban Missile Crisis. Given the heightened tensions and what was seen as the vulnerability of the strait to invasion via Soviet submarines, the Navy feared the sinking would be blamed on Soviet saboteurs, which would further incite the factions who wanted to invade Cuba." She gazed out the window, watching the north coast of Washington pass by as she settled into this neutral and safe topic.

"So what really happened?" he asked.

"My friend Trina—she's an historian at NHHC—

researched it, because the Cold War is her specialty, and the true account was deeply buried among the formerly classified documents relating to that period, even though the sub itself was a pre-World War II Mackerel-class submarine. Commissioned in forty-one before the war, it patrolled the Pacific coast for most of the forties. It was decommissioned in fifty and sat in the Bremerton mothball fleet for a dozen years before the Navy decided to have it towed out to the Pacific for a sink exercise drill."

"It sank before they could use it for SINKEX?" Luke asked.

"Yes, it was going to be targeted with missiles, a demonstration—for the Soviets—of how accurate our defense systems were."

"Good timing with the Cuban Missile Crisis going on."

"But that was also the problem. SINKEX was scheduled for October twentieth, smack-dab in the middle of the crisis. Seven members of the sub's former crew had gathered to say good-bye to her, including her first captain, who'd joined the Navy at the end of World War I and retired an admiral after World War II. They were granted a ride on the tug that was towing the *Wrasse* to the Pacific for SINKEX, when the tug crew received a summons to hurry to Alameda for picket duty. We were on the brink of nuclear war, and the Navy was slated to be the first wave of defense. All hands were needed.

"They were in the strait when the orders came in, but they had this contingent of retired sailors aboard, including the admiral, and a sub in tow. According to the written account, that was when the old admiral got it in his head that they could help the Navy out by piloting the sub to the marina at La Push out on the Pacific coast—as that was close to where they'd planned to conduct the original exercise—allowing the Navy to dispose of the sub, either through SINKEX or scuttling, when they had more time. That would relieve the tug crew to race to Alameda, *and* get the retired sailors and ancient sub off their hands.

"The seven retired Navy guys were eager to go for one last sail on the sub, according to a sailor who recorded details that never made it into the tug's log book—it's that account of the incident that Trina managed to find in the classified documents. The mothball fleet commander's account was somewhat different, but then, it really isn't clear if he authorized or even knew what was going on in the strait at the time.

"In Port Angeles, they fueled up the sub and hooked up the radios, but there was no sonar or radar—which was fine because it was supposed to be a surface cruise only, about a hundred nautical miles to the port at La Push."

"And this is where the story turns tragic," Luke said.

She nodded. "They were near Sekiu when *Wrasse* dove for no reason. No distress call. No nothing. They just went down—but it was controlled. They stayed at periscope depth for several minutes before the sailor on the tug lost sight of them. The tug captain tried to hail the retired admiral. The response was complete silence. They don't know if the radio failed or if there was some other system failure, but the fact that the dive was controlled was odd. They waited for the sub to surface, and it never did. It was the last anyone saw of the USS *Wrasse* and her seven-man complement."

They'd reached a stretch of roadway that ran along the southern edge of this expanse of the Salish Sea, which was the official name of the intricate network of coastal waterways that included the Strait of Georgia in Canada, Puget Sound, which divided the bulk of Washington from the state's two largest peninsulas, and the Strait of Juan de Fuca, the common name of the body of water to her right. Soft waves of low tide lapped at the shore. It was a beautiful, crisp, early

November day, probably not much different from the late October day in which *Wrasse* disappeared.

"After the crisis was over, the Navy searched for the sub, but given the depth and width of the strait, it was impossible. Mackerel-class subs were the smallest from that era, not like the giant ones we have today that would be hard to miss, and all they had was a starting point. They had no idea how far *Wrasse* traveled underwater, and no clue why she sank. The sub had more than enough fuel to get them all the way to La Push, but they were blind down there without sonar."

"How did you find it now?"

"About two years ago, a large piece of metal got caught in a fisherman's net. He shredded the net bringing it up and then tried to sue the Navy for the damage. They sent out a few divers to see if it really was a Navy vessel, and they found more of the wreck. It fits the time period and sub class. We're ninety percent certain it's *Wrasse*. Our job was supposed to be to confirm it, map it, and work with divers from the Joint POW/MIA Accounting Command to determine if we could recover the remains for reburial. All seven men who died were career Navy, and their service ranged from World War I to Korea."

"What's going to happen now?"

"I think NHHC will try again next spring." She shifted in her seat, her belly turning sour at the idea she might not be able to complete the project, not because the Navy wouldn't let her, but because she was chickenshit and would never dive again.

Who would she be if she didn't have diving?

"Does the Navy know you're planning to dive there today?"

"Erica and Mara know."

"Who is Erica? You mentioned her earlier."

She shifted her gaze from the coastline back to his profile, which she'd been avoiding looking at mostly because she was uncomfortable with the fact that she found him attractive. She would never act on it. Finding him easy on the eyes was a far distance from actually desiring him, and her feelings for him were long since dead and buried. But still, he would slam on the brakes and kick her out of the car if he knew she even entertained the notion that his thick brown hair looked good in that short cut, and his eyes had always made her think of an Atlantic blue tang. So much so that she'd given away the ones in her home aquarium not long after she'd ruined his life. But then, the only reminder she'd kept from her time with Luke was a sand dollar collected from the beach where she'd lost her virginity.

"Undine?"

She shook her head. "Sorry. I was just… Never mind. Erica Scott is another underwater archaeologist at NHHC. You might have heard of her. She played a role in that scandal years ago—the one that involved all the money and artifact smuggling from Iraq."

His brow furrowed, then finally he said, "Erica Kesling? I guess she married the senator's stepson."

Undine nodded. "I was a bridesmaid at their wedding last spring. This dive was supposed to be her project, but she's six months pregnant, so UAB sent me." She settled back in the seat and fixed her gaze on the road ahead. "She came out here for a week, to be with me after the accident. I couldn't fly home because of my ears and was pretty much a wreck."

"I thought your father was with you."

"I sent him back to Monterey as soon as Erica offered to stay with me. My dad and I… We don't get along like we used to."

He was silent at that. Did he really believe she and her father could pick up their close relationship after what Stefan had done to Luke?

Her parents had divorced when she was six, and her mother hadn't batted an eye at granting Stefan full custody. She was tired of the travel and the responsibility. She'd moved to landlocked Arizona and acted put out when Undine visited for one measly month each year.

As a result, she'd bonded twice as hard with her father, and he'd lavished her with enough love to make up for two parents. Their once-close relationship had shattered when she was sixteen, but the rift was one-sided. She couldn't forgive her father's actions toward Luke. He'd wanted the man to go to jail and had tried to make it happen. There was no forgiving that.

"After Erica left, Trina—the Cold War historian—took her place for a week."

"Good friends to drop everything for you."

"The best." Growing up around the world as she had, she'd never had friends her own age. She'd been younger than her peers in college and grad school and was at the young end of the spectrum among NHHC employees, but for the first time, she had women friends she was close to, and they were a precious gift, making her realize exactly how lonely she'd been. For a brief time, Luke had filled that lonely gap, but that…hadn't been fair to him.

Okay, that was an understatement.

There was a certain degree of responsibility Stefan had yet to own. She'd spent much of her childhood and adolescence on boats, traveling the world, and her dad never provided opportunities for her to socialize with other children or teens, so she'd taken on the role of adult, just to fit in. She'd been desperate for attention from the opposite gender, and boys her own age didn't pass through her orbit with any regularity. Her father had never acknowledged his role in the ugly outcome.

"I don't know what I'd do without them," she continued.

"They both work for NHHC, so getting the leave approved wasn't a problem, but blowing vacation time to hang out with a friend who was a complete wreck—I owe them huge."

"Your dad…" Luke said, then cleared his throat, "he, uh, called me."

Her spine went rigid. "He did?" She curled a hand into a fist. If her father said anything even slightly rude to Luke, she didn't know what she'd do. Their relationship was strained enough as it was. "What did he say?"

"He thanked me for pulling you out of the water, then hung up. I gathered it pained him to make the call and figured you'd put him up to it."

"No. I would *never* ask Dad to call you." She pursed her lips. "Maybe it's a NOAA thing. He really wants in on some research NOAA is doing in the Galapagos, and I gather he's losing influence there because of his stupid reality show."

"What the hell is up with that? *Sink or Swim* has brought his credibility as a scientist to an all-time low."

She shrugged. "Underwater research is expensive, and documentaries don't bring in the big bucks like they used to, whereas reality competition shows make stupid money. But yeah, I hate that show and told him it was a dumbass idea."

They eased into a companionable silence as the coastal road passed beneath the wheels of his SUV. What would it be like to really be friends with this man, if she hadn't screwed up so horribly when she was still too young to know better?

*L*uke focused on the road ahead, trying to ignore the irritating tug in his gut. He couldn't fathom how he could feel any sort of attraction to her; therefore, this couldn't be attraction. It must be some heretofore-undiscovered form of sympathy. He felt sorry for her ordeal, which inhibited his anger triggers, and unable to feel or process the anger that usually accompanied thoughts of her, he was vulnerable to other emotional reactions to her physical presence, like noticing her warm smile when she spoke of her friends.

Undine's wide cheekbones, full lips, and green-brown eyes were pretty, but when viewed dispassionately, he'd place them at the unremarkable end of the spectrum. When she was younger, long days in the tropical sun had given her hair natural highlights, but now it appeared she spent far less time outside on the water and her long, straight hair was dark, glossy brown. Pretty, but again, nothing out of the ordinary.

He supposed it had been her personality that gave her looks an extra spark. Her light, flirtatious nature had a magical quality that had, over time, transfixed him. He wondered if she still had that power, if her charm and wit could enthrall him into seeing her as a great beauty again.

Her personality was subdued now—understandable given both her situation and their history—but would she bloom into the orchid he remembered? Dare he risk spending time with her to find out?

He again asked himself what he was doing with her now, and all he could think was that in spite of everything, he couldn't turn his back on her plea. He understood the hazards of PTSD. But it was also possible some spark of their friendship hadn't been extinguished as he wallowed in anger.

Or maybe he was just tired of being angry and seized on the chance to let it go. Maybe taking her on a dive would grant him freedom from the ugly emotion that had claimed too much of him over the years.

And maybe he should stop trying to psychoanalyze himself and focus on the damn road.

He'd spent the last fifteen miles trying to justify the fact that last night he'd had sexy dreams about her.

In the past, sex dreams featuring Undine Gray had left him filled with shame, revulsion, and horror. He'd wake in a sweat and immediately need a shower. Hard to explain if a girlfriend was sleeping over. But those dreams had Undine frozen in time, forever sixteen. She was now very much a woman, and a pretty one—maybe even remarkably so if he would stop lying to himself—at that. Last night's dream had been different from the nightmares he'd suffered in the past. The subconscious encounter had featured the woman who'd brazenly asked for his help yesterday. He'd woken with a hard-on instead of in a sweat, and then cursed himself for agreeing to take her diving as he waited for dawn.

He could psychoanalyze himself from Port Angeles to Neah Bay, but the end result would still be the same: he was attracted to Undine Gray.

If he acted on that attraction, he'd have to be the biggest dipshit on the planet, because even though she'd grown up, if they engaged in consensual, recreational sex, he didn't doubt that once again her father would find out and come gunning for him with both barrels. Even though there was nothing legally the man could do, he was still the world's preeminent marine biologist and Luke had finally returned to the profession.

He had too much to lose and wouldn't risk it for a blowjob. She wasn't *that* tempting.

A question that had bothered him for the last twelve years came to the forefront of his mind. "How did your father find out about us?"

She pulled her legs up onto the seat and wrapped her arms around them. "I don't know. I asked, but he wouldn't say. My guess is someone at the institute told him."

"We were careful." He hadn't known her age, but she was the boss's daughter. When it became clear something was developing between them, even before their first kiss, they'd agreed to be discreet. His need to protect his job had played right into her seductive plans.

"We were. But we still flirted."

"Sweetheart, you flirted with *everyone*." The endearment slipped out. He asked himself if he regretted it and didn't have an answer.

"True. But with you…I was different." He glanced sideways, catching her smile as her eyes lit up with a hint of mischief. "Really, it's *all* your fault."

Her sheer audacity triggered a sharp, surprised laugh. "*My* fault?"

"Totally. You showed up at the institute with your movie-star-handsome face, that ginormous brain, and that passion for the sea. And then you had to go and *notice* me. You listened to me like I was important. I took one look at you, and I just…wanted."

"Honey, we all noticed you." Another endearment. What was wrong with him?

"Yeah, but you were different. Your gaze didn't skip over me as the boss's daughter. Someone to give token, even condescending attention because I was Stefan Gray's progeny. You actually talked to me about our research—as if *I* was the expert."

That startled him. "But you were."

"True. But no one else recognized that." She unfurled her legs, no longer holding herself in a tight, defensive ball. "When you asked me how old I was and I realized you didn't know…I feared the only reason you were showing me that respect was because you thought I was older. When I told you I was nineteen, it wasn't because I had plans to seduce you, it was because I didn't want to lose that respect. I didn't want your gaze to skip over me like the others. I grew up on my dad's boat and at that damn institute, and I was so damn lonely. I didn't even know how lonely I was until you filled the void."

He'd never imagined she could say something that would make sense of her actions, or that would cause his heart to soften, but then, in all the intervening years, he'd never once tried to understand Undine's perspective. For the first time, he realized that maybe he'd done her a disservice in turning a blind eye to her role at the institute.

He cleared his throat as he tried to regain his equilibrium. He'd been so clear in his opinions of her. So set in his version of the facts, forgetting that facts were open to interpretation. He could be a crappy scientist at times. "Thank you for telling me that," he said.

He reached for the knob on the radio and turned up the volume on a Canadian station that played mostly Rush and Bachman-Turner Overdrive, effectively cutting off further conversation. Fifty more winding miles to Neah Bay, and he was already reevaluating everything he thought he knew about her.

Chapter Six

The boat Luke had arranged was skippered by Ray Ferguson, a Makah tribal member who ran a charter dive business for tourists. He occasionally hired out to NOAA for deeper, longer technical dives and had been on Undine's list of approved contractors to work with the Navy, but he'd had surgery in September and had been unavailable to hire out for the dives on *Wrasse,* and last week, he'd been out hunting when Undine sought a boat for her dive, forcing her to hire a skipper and dive partner with less deep-water experience.

A calm settled over her as she gripped Ray's hand and climbed aboard his boat. She didn't know if it was the seasoned skipper, the clean, well-maintained boat, or her former-SEAL dive partner, but she didn't think she'd suffer another panic attack today.

Luke handed her his tank. She set it out of the way on the deck as he climbed aboard carrying the bag that held his wetsuit and fins. Her equipment had been lost or destroyed in the accident, but she'd been assured Ray had equipment she could rent. Until last week's failed dive attempt, she'd never used rental equipment before, and was possibly more uneasy about that than any other aspect of this dive. It was a simple fact that when it came to scuba, she was spoiled.

The weather was perfect, a crisp, sunny fall day. The kind of day Washingtonians claimed never happened outside of summer, but she'd spent enough time in the Pacific Northwest both last month and during her nomadic childhood to know the truth.

Luke officially introduced her to Ray, adding, "Ray's the best dive skipper on the north coast."

The middle-aged Native American smiled, revealing deep dimples in both cheeks. "Still a suck-up, I see."

Luke laughed. "No. Smart. Always be nice to the man who controls the oxygen line."

Undine flinched, reminded of Jared, but she covered it. She didn't want Luke to get any hint she was uneasy about the dive.

"True," Ray said and turned to Undine. "Before you get suited up, I want to go over the chart with you to get a fix on our destination."

"Certainly."

The chart was laid out on a table in the main cabin. She leaned over it and studied the sea floor contours. She knew this chart so well. She'd marked up the one on *Petrel* with the limited information she had on the sub wreck, dots on the map indicating where pieces of *Wrasse* had been found.

This chart was blank. A do-over. But not for five other people. Loren, Scotty, Jared, Yuri, and Sandy would never get a do-over again. She sucked in a deep breath.

A hand gripped her shoulder with a comforting squeeze. She looked up to meet Luke's Atlantic-blue-tang eyes. "You okay?" he asked.

She nodded and faced the chart again, then traced a contour line. "The first piece was found in this area." She slid her finger south three inches. "But we found what might be the intact hull in this area." Another inch east. "And this is where Yuri and I were supposed to set the last anchor line." She met Ray's gaze. "This is where I want to go."

Luke stared at the depth marker for a long moment, then slipped onto the bench seat. "Okay, we'll drop anchor and do a simple bounce dive. We don't have mixed gases, so we can't stay long. We'll have one decompression stop on the way back up, where we'll switch from scuba to a pure oxygen line from the boat." He glanced up at Ray. "Do you have a radio mask for Undine so we can talk underwater?"

"Yes."

"Okay, then. Let's do this."

While Ray piloted the boat out of the bay and into the strait, Undine inspected the dive equipment. Everything was in good order, but unfortunately, Ray didn't have a dry suit in her size. She'd have to go with a wetsuit. She'd be cold as hell for the first minutes, until her body heated up the water in the suit.

But she could do it. She *would* do it.

Wetsuit in hand, she went into the cabin to change. She had the tight suit over her hips when her heart began to race. She paused, placing her hand on her chest, and took several deep, slow breaths. She had to get this under control. If Luke saw her like this, he'd abort the dive, and he wouldn't give her another chance.

Deep breath. In through the nose. Out through the mouth.

In the back of her mind was the knowledge that Luke would be right to cancel the dive if she couldn't get herself under control. It would be stupid to risk her life and terrible to risk his.

Is this PTSD?

Both Trina and Erica thought so. They had encouraged

her to return to DC, seek therapy, and take it slow. They believed she'd dive again, that she didn't need to force it now.

But she wanted the quick, easy fix. Rip the bandage off. Face the demon head-on. She feared if she left Washington without completing this dive, that therapy wouldn't work, her diving days would be over. It was irrational. Possibly stupid. But it was the battle she'd fought in her mind these last weeks, and her gut, her instinct, every indefinable drive in her brain, said she *must* do this. It was a compulsion.

So here she was.

Footsteps creaked on the steps. "Undine?" Luke asked. "You okay?"

With another breath, she pulled the suit over her hips and slipped her arms in the sleeves. The rental suit lacked the long cord that made it possible to zip herself. "Fine, but I need help with the zipper." She pulled the curtain aside and presented her back to him, lifting her hair, which she'd braided for the dive. "Please?"

Given the necessary tightness of the suit, zipping was a slow, two-handed job. She felt his warm breath on the back of her neck as he held together the sides with one hand, and inched the zipper up with the other. His touch on her bare skin triggered a new sensation that ousted all anxious thoughts of panic and PTSD from her brain.

She focused on her breathing, but not due to panic. Good Lord, if he knew he affected her in this way…it was all over.

This is work. Nothing but a job.

But she damn well knew that if Ray were the one zipping her in, she wouldn't be so affected. The sad, horrific truth was Luke Sevick turned her on. She didn't see the man he'd been at twenty-two, she only saw the man who'd waited for hours in the hospital so he could tell her the worst news she'd ever hear. The man who'd agreed to help out the woman who ruined his life for no good reason except that it was the humanitarian thing to do.

Her limited experience with Luke Sevick, former SEAL and current NOAA lieutenant, showed her there was a lot to like and admire.

Which was a huge problem.

He finally got her zipped up and stepped back. She released the breath she'd been holding and hoped it just appeared she'd been sucking in her belly to aid him. She dropped her braid and turned, the words thank you on her lips, when she caught sight of his chest, and air whooshed out of her lungs, rendering her speechless.

He'd pulled his wetsuit over his legs, but the top half remained bare, folded down at the waist, leaving his torso and shoulders exposed to her eager gaze. He was cut, sleek and muscular with broad swimmer's shoulders and massive biceps.

She coughed and tried to regain her composure. A smile played about his lips, and she gave up playing it cool. "You've, um, packed on a bit of muscle since I saw you last."

"Job requirement with the SEALs."

She laughed. "Right." Working for the Navy and hanging out with Trina and Keith, she'd met her share of former and current SEALs and some, like Keith, were thick and muscular, but others had more of a sturdy build—strong, solid, but not sculpted like Luke. But then, he'd been on the team that focused on the water-based missions, so it made sense he was built like an Olympic swimmer meets bodybuilder. "It, uh, looks good on you."

Her fingers itched to touch him, as if he were a sculpture that required hands as well as eyes to take in the beauty. The craziest part was he seemed to be enjoying her frank admiration. He wasn't repulsed or angry. He chuckled and crossed his arms, then turned in a slow circle, allowing her to appreciate his muscular back.

His back. Holy shit, he wasn't just a work of art, he was a frigging masterpiece. It was too bad the top half of his wetsuit hung over what was probably a spectacular ass.

He flexed his shoulders, and his back muscles rippled—a visual symphony. She rolled her eyes at the over-the-top display. "Sheesh, Sevick, do you think you're auditioning for a Men of NOAA calendar?"

He turned to face her. "I should. They'd easily give me a whole season."

She'd buy it if he were all twelve months.

She grinned up at him, stupid happy that he was being *nice* to her. Maybe he was even flirting a little bit. Not that flirting, in and of itself, meant anything. Undine was a pro at the meaningless flirt, the teasing compliment that invited light attention but nothing more. This was akin to that, telling her he'd softened toward her.

It didn't mean he was attracted to her, or even that they could be friends. But maybe, just maybe, he didn't hate her.

Hate was a strong word, and a stronger emotion. Being on the receiving end of his hatred was painful, and it had been even worse knowing she'd earned that animosity. She'd carried his hate, that stigmatic scarlet letter, for twelve years—and had expected to bear it for the rest of her life.

"Summer, I hope," she said, flexing her flirtation muscles for the first time since the accident. "It would be a shame to cover that up with a Santa suit."

He grinned. "I could just wear the hat."

She shook her head. "It might be hard to find one big enough for..." She dropped her gaze to his crotch and lowered her voice. "Your ego."

He tilted back his head and released a full laugh that rocked his impressive shoulders and stretched his abs. But even more than the perfection of his body, she enjoyed what it did to his face. His eyes lit, and deep grooves in his cheeks widened his smile.

Warmth flowed through her at the knowledge she could still make him laugh. "Finish suiting up, big fella. The water is cold as hell, which should shrink up your ego just fine."

He chuckled and pulled on the top of his suit. His was a newer, high-tech suit that zipped at the collar, so he required no assistance.

She set about donning her booties, hood, and gloves. Every millimeter of skin would be covered. The Strait of Juan de Fuca was too cold to mess around.

She returned to the deck to see they neared the dive location. Something had happened in the silly exchange with Luke. She faced the water, a new calmness radiating from her center.

She was no longer afraid.

✻

The first minutes of a dive in cold water in a wetsuit were always hell. Dreading submersion didn't mean Undine was suffering from panic, it meant she was human and knew exactly how much the coming minutes would suck. She took a slow breath and slipped off the platform into the strait. The icy water filled the suit, and she questioned her sanity and vehemently cursed the sea for not being tropical.

Naturally, Luke laughed at her. "Well, Gray, at least you're too cold to be scared."

"I'm too cold to think of a pithy reply, so piss off."

"That's one way to warm your suit."

She snorted. The dreaded shot of cold water rushed to the small of her back and climbed up her spine. "Jesus. I swear the water is five degrees colder than it was in October."

"Actually, it's slightly warmer at fifty-three degrees. You were spoiled in your dry suit. Now, if you're done whining about the temp, we can get started. Ready?"

"Easy for *you* to be sanguine. You've got a fancy wetsuit with the extra thermal layers. Mine's an old-skool rental." She turned to Ray on deck. "No offense. I'm grateful for the rental. I'm just freezing my tits off."

The skipper laughed and waved her off. "The high-end European suits like your boy has there are too expensive for me to stock."

Her boy. As if. Ray Ferguson needed glasses if he thought there was anything between her and Luke.

"Time for a mask check," Luke said.

She secured the full-face mask that would make it possible for them to talk, and gave him a thumbs up.

The equipment checked out, and down they went. Following Luke's fins into the cold dark felt strangely like old times. Except he'd only been at the institute for three months, so they'd dived together a scant number of times.

She kept him in the bright beam of her headlamp, noticing that his ass was indeed as fine as she'd suspected. It really wasn't fair how damn good he looked.

After they'd descended about thirty-five feet, his baritone voice spoke directly into her ears. "One atmosphere down. How are your ears, 'Deen? Over."

"Clearing fine. No pain. Over." Her burst eardrums had healed, but she needed to be gentle clearing them as she descended. If at any point she couldn't clear, they'd have to abort or she'd risk seriously damaging her hearing.

"Keep me posted. Take no chances, you got that?"

"Copy that. I promise. Over."

He was silent for a moment, then said, "And how is the rest of you? You feel okay? Over."

It was cold, dark, and there wasn't a single fish or pretty

piece of coral to see at this depth, yet the enveloping sea felt like an old friend. She was no longer chilled, but that wouldn't last as they neared the bottom. But for now, she felt pretty damn good, and told Luke that. Then she added, "Thank you. For this."

His response was slow in coming. When he finally spoke, even the tinny radio couldn't keep the warmth from his deep voice. "You're welcome. It's hard to say no when a water nymph begs you to return her to the sea."

She laughed at his reference to the meaning behind her name. "Does this mean I need to give you a boon from the treasure chest in my grotto?"

"I believe it does."

She smiled and again cleared her ears as they'd dropped another atmosphere.

Finally they neared the bottom, and she turned on her spotlight and scanned the floor, searching for the anchor they'd dropped that last day, just to have a reference point. Everything was different. The explosion and resulting debris had churned everything, as had a few storms in the intervening weeks. The pieces of the Navy sub that had been cleared were likely buried again.

They'd discussed their dive protocol earlier, and as planned, Luke tied a thirty-meter rope, knotted at five-meter intervals, to the anchor line, which would act as a dog leash so they wouldn't lose their position relative to the boat. Visibility was good at the surface—fifteen meters easy—but down here, it was dark, and with spotlights, the range was half that distance at best.

They had dive computers and each other, but there was nothing simpler than having a line to follow back to the boat, so for the quick bounce dive, Luke had opted for simple and safe.

Holding the line at the first knot, Undine swam in a

circle, examining the floor. She then extended the radius another five meters by moving to the next knot on the line. Beyond the spotlight beam was murky darkness.

Twenty meters out, she came across a piece of debris that likely came from *Petrel*. She looked toward Luke, who swam three meters away, but she couldn't see more than the dim outline of his yellow mask.

"You okay?" he asked again.

"Yeah. I just…for some reason I thought they'd collected most of it."

"It's too deep. They searched for remains and only collected what they needed to determine if it was an accident or not."

She nodded, feeling foolish. She, of all people, knew how difficult it was to document a site this far down. But for some reason, because it was an investigation, she'd thought this would be different.

But then, the explosion that destroyed *Petrel* had been deemed an accident. The blame had fallen on Jared's faulty maintenance and handling of an oxygen tank.

Something looked odd up ahead, but it was just out of reach of her flashlight. She swam forward with a quick burst of speed and grunted as she reached the end of her leash.

"You want to be set free, Fido?" he asked

"Woof, woof," she replied.

He laughed. "I thought it was one bark for yes."

"One is no. Two is yes. I'd flash puppy dog eyes at you, but since you can't see my face, that would be a waste."

"I'll hold the line. We can run another line between us to increase your range."

"I suppose that makes me your bitch?"

He let out a bark of laughter. "Is that an offer?"

"Oh no, Sevick, you want a piece of this, there can't be

leashes or dog collars involved." Had she really just said that to Luke?

"Okay, then," he said. Was his voice a bit husky? Hard to tell with the tinny radio.

She turned toward him and realized his flashlight beam was scanning her butt. "Are you checking out my ass?"

"Why not? You checked out mine on the dive down." He handed her another yellow rope that would grant her another ten meters, and took the end of the original line in his other hand. "What did you think, by the way, A or A-plus?"

She laughed. "So much for your ego suffering shrinkage." She looked into the darkness beyond her spotlight. "Something looks weird up ahead. I'm going to check it out."

"The view's just fine from here."

She paused again. That didn't sound like Luke. Well, it did, but his words—the whole conversation, really—seemed a little strange since he was directing it at *her*. "Luke, are you narked?"

"I don't get narked. I was a SEAL."

"Bull. Everyone gets narked now and then. Even muscular, handsome SEALs. And you wouldn't be checking out my ass if this weren't a five-martini dive." The general guideline was that each atmosphere descended after the first was the equivalent of drinking one martini. Nitrogen narcosis could be relatively harmless in shallow dives, but down here, it could be fatal. "Let me check out this thing, then we'll go up."

"Honey, I'm a guy. I'll check out an ass as sweet as yours anytime, anywhere."

"Fine, but you wouldn't tell *me* about it. You are totally narking." She swam forward and ran her light over the floor. She gasped. "Luke, during the investigation, did anyone use an undersea cable trencher to excavate—to clear large swaths of floor?"

"No. Why?"

She needed his eyes, but he was literally at the end of his rope. However, the leash was an overabundance of caution for the quick bounce dive because visibility was limited at this depth. They still had their computers and were both experienced divers. But he could be narked. She swam back to him. "How many fingers am I holding up?" She raised a gloved hand.

They were face-to-face at the bottom of the sea, and he met her gaze in the wash of the spotlight. "Two. I'm not narked."

"Good. Let go of the line. You need to see this." She led him to the cleared area, where a bowl-shaped depression had been cut into the sea floor. "See this? I've excavated with a cable trencher before, and this is exactly what it looks like. Someone's been digging here. Recently. Very recently."

Chapter Seven

Luke wasn't narked, but he probably should have claimed he was. Shit, what was he thinking flirting with her like that?

He hadn't been thinking, he'd just been enjoying. Her ass. Her company. The synchronicity of diving with someone who moved through water with the grace of a mermaid and had a sharp wit that repeatedly caught him off guard.

Her blatant admiration when she'd studied his body had been a complete turn-on and had burst open a mental door he'd intended to keep locked. Now he couldn't look at her without feeling a jolt of lust, and the way her ass moved as she executed a smooth dolphin kick was damn sexy. Watching her swim made him want to take her home and screw her brains out.

Being inside her hot body after this expedition into the cold deep would be a sensory indulgence. Decadent, hedonistic joy.

Shit. He really wished he were narked.

He was lusting after Undine Gray, of all women. Except…she wasn't the Undine he knew once upon a time. It was more like he'd just met a woman who vaguely resembled someone he used to know, and he was curious.

Well, maybe not so much curious as sporting wood. In fifty-frigging-degree water. Okay. Maybe not literally sporting wood. Mentally. Metaphorically. And when he got out of the cold-as-fuck water, magnificently.

He needed to get his head—the one on top of his shoulders—back on the job. He swam the perimeter of the cleared area, Undine at his side. She kept him close, like a mother dolphin—or a mermaid—protecting her offspring. Sweet, the way she did that, worried that he was narked. But he wasn't, even if he should tell her he was.

"This is weird as shit, Undine," he said, addressing what really mattered.

"Who could have done this?" she asked. "With the investigation, a lot of people know the boat location, but details of the sub were kept to a minimum. And we hadn't even explored this area yet."

"Maybe one of the investigators found something and they came back to get it," Luke suggested.

"What on earth could they find here? It's not like the sub was full of gold. There's no record of any ship loaded with treasure being lost in this area."

He ran a gloved hand through the silt berm that formed a ring around the excavation. "Take a picture. I'll contact the Coast Guard investigators and ask if they know anything about this."

"Okay."

After she photographed the seafloor, she led him back to where they'd dropped the line. He used his spotlight to search for the yellow rope. He spotted it and reached for it. His thickly gloved fingers sank into the soft silt as he tried to grab it. Slight loss of motor control. Expected, but a good indicator that they were nearing the end of their allotted time.

His hand brushed against something under the silt as he got his fingers to obey his mental commands. He reached down for the object. Could be a rock, but the light had caught something rust colored. He brushed off a four-inch-wide piece of oxidized metal, finding an edge.

"What have you got there?"

"Not sure. Part of the sub?"

"Complete, whatever it is. No jagged edges." She pulled out a knife and poked at the silt until she found another edge. They had a corner. Between them, they cleared all four sides and pulled it from the sea floor. It was a small, corroded metal case the size of a laptop, or, more accurately for the time frame in which it was lost at the bottom of the sea, a typewriter or portable record player case.

"Do we leave it here?" Luke asked.

"I'm authorized to collect diagnostic artifacts from the sub. With electrolytic reduction, we could open this and see what's inside. It falls within the purview of diagnostic pieces."

"Well, then, I guess this is my boon." He slipped the box into a mesh bag and grabbed the rope, leading her back to the anchor line.

They left the wreck and swam upward, using the anchor line as their guide. They removed the full-face masks and switched to pure oxygen provided by a hose from Ray's boat at the decompression stop. Unable to speak without the masks, they passed the twenty minutes in silence.

He watched Undine carefully, searching for signs of stress or anxiety. This was the point at which *Petrel* had exploded.

She didn't look happy, but she also didn't look like she was about to lose it. The woman had guts. It had taken a steel spine to approach him to take her down, but he understood why she did it. Hell, it was probably part of why he said yes. He doubted there was another person on the north coast who had as much dive experience as he had. She could relieve at least one anxiety by lining up a strong dive partner. He just happened to be her best choice.

And here he was with Undine Gray back in his life.

And he didn't hate it. Although he should. He really should.

An hour from now, they'd be back on shore. He'd drop her at her rental cabin, and he'd go to the research housing east of town. Another researcher was driving to Port Angeles tomorrow and had already agreed to drive her back. Luke didn't even have to spend another two hours in the car with her. For the second time in his life, all association with Undine Gray would be severed.

It was what he should do. What he needed to do. He had a job and a life and didn't want his messy past to interfere with his pretty damn good present. And yet he wondered if he'd be able to walk away from her, or if this pull of attraction would prove he was a glutton for punishment.

Because no way could anything happen between him and Undine without opening them both up to a world of pain.

*L*uke's SUV pulled up in front of Undine's rental cabin near the edge of town. It was one of ten identical units in a row that ran in a perpendicular line to the main road that separated the town from the bay. Since salmon season had ended in late September, only a third of the units were in use on a Monday night.

Luke grabbed her large suitcase and the case they'd taken from the wreck from the back of his SUV while she collected the cabin key from the rental office next to the road. After she unlocked the door, he carried the items inside and set her suitcase on the bed. "What do I do with this?" he asked, holding up the rusted case.

"Just set it on the table. I'll get a cooler from the general store and keep it wet with seawater overnight while I figure out where and how I'm going to do the electrolytic reduction."

He placed the item on the small corner table, then leaned against the open doorframe.

"My boss is probably going to ask me to dive on the *Wrasse* again," she said, "to document the extent of the digging. Are you available for another dive?"

After a long pause, he finally said, "No. I have work to do here in Neah Bay. No time."

She nodded. She took a deep breath, bracing herself to say good-bye to Luke Sevick for the last time. She pushed out the air from her lungs through her nose, like she was underwater and needed to clear her mask. "I understand," she said. The sad truth was, after the banter underwater and the surprising chemistry they'd shared, she was unprepared for this good-bye. He'd awakened her libido, and she was certain he felt the hot undercurrent too. "Luke, do you have plans for dinner?"

He turned in the doorway and faced out, toward the trees and empty campground across the parking lot. His beautiful wide shoulders shrugged. His muscles were hidden now under a dry NOAA sweatshirt, but she knew what treasures the baggy garment hid, and that was all she saw when she looked at him—the world's most spectacular biceps. Muscles she wanted to trace with her lips before she pushed him on the bed and took him deep. "I haven't really thought about it." He turned to face her. "Are you asking me to dinner?"

The town had only three restaurants, one of which was really just a minimart that sold pizza by the slice. Given the limited choices, dining together would be expedient and wouldn't resemble a date, even if that was what she wanted it to be. "Yeah," she said. "I guess I am. As a thank-you, for helping me."

His gaze shifted from her eyes to her mouth, then dropped lower before bouncing upward with lightning speed. "No need to thank me."

She flashed what she hoped was a winning smile, but guessed it fell short. "But I'd like to anyway."

He frowned. "I don't think that's a good idea." He sighed. "You seem like a nice person, Undine. I actually enjoyed today—which was a surprise. Maybe, if we didn't have history, we *could* be friends. But the truth is, for me, you'll always be the girl who fucked with my life."

His words shouldn't sting so much, because they were true, but still, she felt the bite. "So you *were* narking earlier."

"No. For a minute there, something just…clicked between us, and I allowed myself to forget and enjoy. And I shouldn't have. I'm sorry."

"No need to be sorry. Thank you for your honesty. Good-bye, Luke."

He nodded. "Take care, Undine."

She closed the door behind him and leaned against it, listening to the sound of him driving out of her life.

Chapter Eight

"I'm sorry, Greg, we didn't have time or visibility to look for trencher tracks. The clearing was so unexpected. I wasn't prepared." Undine sat at the tiny table and glared at the half-eaten slice of pizza next to the computer as she spoke to her boss, Dr. Greg Mulholland, director of the Underwater Archaeology Branch of Naval History and Heritage Command, on a Skype call that kept cutting out due to the weak Wi-Fi. Her cabin was too far from the office to maintain a strong signal. She'd forgotten to buy a prepaid cell phone for this short trip to Neah Bay, which had only one cell phone tower and her carrier didn't own it.

"If you think we've got an SMCA violation, we've got to pursue it," Greg said, referring to the Sunken Military Craft Act, which was enacted in 2004 to protect all underwater US military vessels, which could be hazardous, historic, fragile, contain military secrets, and/or, as with USS *Wrasse*, gravesites. "But there is no way the Navy will be able to get a team of divers out to inspect the wreckage any time soon. Not to mention that we need to identify *who* is digging on the sub." He paused. "You're *certain* no one used a trencher to investigate the explosion?"

"No. Verifying that is next on my to-do list. But even if they did…the excavation was recent. Like two days ago recent. The sea is active out there, so close to where Juan de Fuca meets the Pacific, and there was a storm five days ago that would have churned the sediment."

"I'll make some calls, Undine, but in the meantime, do you think you could dive again? Get a better scope of the scale of the excavation? Hell, if you could photograph tracks from the cable trencher, we might have something to go on."

Undine dropped her head into her hand and massaged a temple. It was nearly six in the evening, and the wind had started to kick up. She slid off the stool and opened the cabin door. A glance to the left gave her a limited view of the sheltered bay. This time of year, it got dark early in Washington, and the sun had set an hour ago. Rigging clanged and boats rocked in the glow of halogen marina lights.

A long spit protected the bay from the strait, but beyond the arc of the breakwater, large waves were likely forming in the Salish Sea. She leaned back inside the cabin and projected her voice toward the computer. "The weather isn't cooperating. According to the forecast, it'll be two, maybe three days before the water is calm enough for another dive."

"I realize that today's dive was on your own time and expense, but if you can do another one, I'll see if I can get financial to get you travel orders with a job order number. Then we can pick up your lodging costs and you'll be covered by the department's insurance for the actual dive."

"That would certainly help, but there's another problem. I need a dive partner, someone who can handle that kind of depth with scuba. According to Navy regs, it should be a technical dive, but we don't have the setup for mixed gases. *Petrel* was the best-equipped dive boat in the region, and it's gone. The nearest boat with the proper equipment is probably my dad's, which I think is somewhere along the Oregon coast right now. But the Navy can't afford to hire *Nereid*, not for something like this, and my father can't afford to let us use her for free."

"What about the man you dove with today, Lt. Luke Sevick?"

"He's not available," she said.

"If it's a work conflict, I can contact his supervisor at NOAA. We're both federal agencies. We might be able to borrow him."

"No," she said sharply. Too sharply.

"Why?" Greg paused. "Is something wrong? Was he a… problem? If he was at all inappropriate—"

"No! No." Oh God, the last thing she needed was for Greg to insinuate Luke had sexually harassed her to his superiors at NOAA. "No. He was fine. Great, actually, to help me out. I just don't think he'd appreciate being jerked around when he has a job to do. He agreed to take me down once as a favor. I can't ask more from him."

"You aren't asking, I am. This is a Navy project, and unauthorized excavation of the *Wrasse* is rather serious and needs to be investigated. He's there. You're there. He's more than qualified for us to get a waiver from SecNav to exceed the depth limits for scuba if he's your partner. He's the perfect solution."

She closed her eyes. Greg was right. But asking Luke for another favor was out. He'd made it clear he was done. He never wanted to see her again, and she never again wanted to face the judgment in his eyes.

Twelve years hadn't diminished her guilt. She didn't need to add his ongoing condemnation to her already full plate of self-recriminations. "I'll see if I can find a dive partner. There was a guy with the Coast Guard, who tried to take me out last week." She refrained from telling Greg she'd had a panic attack. She didn't need that in her work file. "He might be available. If not, Ray, the skipper, might know someone."

"But you've already identified the perfect partner, and it would be faster if I contact NOAA. Speed is an issue here."

"I said no, Greg, and I mean it. Officially, I'm on leave. *I don't even have to do this dive.*" She couldn't believe she'd just spoken to her boss that way, but she absolutely could not let Greg Mulholland pull strings to get Luke back in the water with her. Luke would think she was behind it, and whatever small peace there was between them would be utterly gutted.

"Someone from the Underwater Archaeology Branch needs to check out the disturbance to the *Wrasse*. Erica can't dive because she's pregnant, and Cressida hasn't gone through Navy dive school yet, so we can't get a waiver for her to use scuba at that depth. That leaves me as the only other UAB diver who qualifies. If I have to, I'll fly out. I can be your dive partner, but it would be more cost efficient and expedient if I could get NOAA to lend us Sevick."

Undine stiffened. The last thing in the world she wanted was to be stuck in tiny Neah Bay with her boss. "I'll do it, but give me time to find a dive partner before you force the job on Luke. I'll get working on that right now, actually. Thanks." She closed Skype before he could reply.

Shit. She'd just essentially hung up on her boss. It was entirely possible her days at UAB were numbered. She felt nauseated and wasn't sure which was worse, that she'd just pissed off her boss, or that she'd have to dive again on the *Petrel* and *Wrasse* wrecks with—or without—Luke Sevick.

She considered calling Erica just to have someone to talk to, but Erica was second in seniority in the branch, and complaining to her would put her in a difficult place. When Erica stayed with her after the accident, Undine had finally told her about Luke, so she'd understand why Undine didn't want Greg to force another dive on him, but as a supervisor in UAB, Erica would also understand Greg's reasoning.

No, best to reach out to Trina, who could listen as a friend, not a boss. She used Skype to call Trina's home phone and hoped the Wi-Fi wouldn't cut out.

Trina's boyfriend, Keith, answered. "Hey, Undine, what's up?"

"Hi, Keith. I wanted to whine to Trina a bit about Greg, men in general, and maybe former Navy SEALs in particular. Is she home?"

Keith, also a former SEAL, laughed. "They can't all be as perfect as I am, doll. And you know Trina loves to listen to you whine, but she's out. Wine-tasting night with Mara, Cressida, Isabel, and Erica."

"Oh, man, I forgot it's first Monday. Now I'm homesick." For the last few years, on the first Monday of the month, Undine had met with her NHHC coworkers for girls' night. It had started out as a book club, but at some point, they'd ditched books in favor of pinot noir. Sometimes they went out for wine or beer tasting, but usually they gathered at one apartment and prepared a fancy meal to go with the evening's drink selection. The conversation was lively, intelligent, and always a blast. A year ago, they'd welcomed Isabel Dawson, Senator Alec Ravissant's fiancée, to the group, and in September, former intern and new UAB permanent hire, Cressida Porter, had joined the fun.

"You should call," Keith said. "They booted Lee out—he and Alec are here—and are hanging out at Erica's tonight. They can put you on speakerphone, and it'll be like you're with them."

"Thanks, I'll consider it."

"The former SEAL you want to complain about, is he the one you asked me about before? Luke Sevick?"

"Yeah. But it's no big deal. He's a good guy. I'm the one who screwed up."

"I should probably tell you that Trina...*might* have nagged me to tap some sources for information on him."

Undine's belly flopped. First Greg, now Keith. Was everyone going to get up in Luke's business because of her? "What did you do?" she asked in a guarded voice.

"Just a simple inquiry."

Undine felt a flush coming on. "You didn't...you didn't mention me, did you?" Jesus, if Luke somehow got word she was checking up on him. *Stalker much?*

"Lord, no," he said. "It was all aboveboard. I listed him as a potential recruit for Raptor, which means we do a preliminary background check," Keith said. "Trina was most interested in his service record."

"She still thinks I'm hung up on him."

"Maybe. Probably."

Undine closed her eyes and shook her head, wondering if Trina was right. She couldn't resist asking, "So, he looked good on paper?" Not that it mattered. It couldn't matter. She was out of his life for good, no matter what crap Greg might pull.

"Let me put it this way: If I didn't want to hire him before, I do now."

The idea of Luke moving into Undine's inner circle of friends in DC brought another wave of nausea. "Please don't."

"Don't worry, doll. Trina would kill me."

"I'm not sure how I feel about Trina asking you to check up on him."

"I told her you'd be pissed. But she asked me to do it because she loves you and is worried about you."

That quickly, tears came to Undine's eyes. Trina had been such a good friend to spend a week in Port Angeles with her after the accident. "Tell her I love her too. I'm not going to call and interrupt girls' night. I'm too much of a Debbie Downer right now. I won't spoil their fun."

"You know they won't mind."

"I do. But I still won't call."

"Okay. Take care, 'Deen."

"You too, Keith."

She ended the call and stared at the computer screen. She wouldn't be surprised if her friends tried to check in on her, and she really didn't want to bring the group down. Erica would get a full briefing on the *Wrasse* project from Greg tomorrow anyway. She closed Skype and her laptop. They wouldn't be able to reach her if she wasn't online.

She swiped at her eyes, berating herself for being so upset about…everything. She'd seen a piece of *Petrel* underwater. Greg had threatened to fly out and make her dive with him. And Luke…he'd turned out to be a hot, amazing man—and he couldn't look at her without resentment.

She just wished the last item didn't bother her so much. It was understandable to be shaken by seeing a fragment from the explosion that had killed five people and almost killed her. And Greg had been a source of unhappiness at work for a long time. But Luke… Dammit, she could have gone the rest of her life without facing his condemnation again and even longer without feeling an intense pull of attraction for a man who'd spent the last twelve years hating her.

*L*uke paced the small house, wound tight and not sure why. Well, okay, he knew. He just didn't like it. How could the hurt in Undine's eyes gut him when he had every right and reason to say what he had and cut the ties between them? Thank goodness Carlos had gone to dinner, leaving Luke alone in the small house owned by NOAA, which was available to employees when they visited Neah Bay for work. He didn't want to answer Carlos's abundant questions about Undine Gray, and he definitely didn't want to discuss the woman's father with the starstruck NOAA ichthyologist.

Carlos was totally jazzed about driving Undine home tomorrow, excited to have the chance to meet the big man's daughter. Luke should be grateful he was willing to provide the service instead of disappointed in his decision to pass her off on someone else. He was in Neah Bay to work. Period.

His cell phone rang, and he seized it like a life buoy. Caller ID showed it was the investigator from the Coast Guard returning his call. "Hey, Luke, thanks for your message. I contacted all the agencies that had a hand in the investigation of the *Petrel* accident, and no one's dived on the wreck since the case was closed."

"Did you find out if anyone used a cable trencher to clear sediment during the search for pieces of the boat?"

"No trenchers were used. Something like that would have tossed all the small pieces we were trying to find. I can see how it would be good for clearing the hull of a big submarine, but it would be useless for our investigative purposes."

"Does the Coast Guard have any concerns or jurisdiction over the recent digging?"

"I'll pass the info up the line, but given that the evidence collected indicated the explosion was an accident, I doubt it. There's just not much we can do. The wreck isn't within the Olympic Coast National Marine Sanctuary, so there aren't any restrictions from NOAA or on our end. The Navy, however, will have issues. They retain sovereignty over all sunken vessels, and my understanding is *Wrasse* holds human remains. Ms. Gray will need to report it to her boss. They'll take the lead on any investigation into the digging. But I can't imagine they have the resources to do much right now."

Luke thanked the man and hung up. Undine had said she'd call her boss, but he needed to tell her the clearing was not part of the investigation into the explosion. It was unsettling that someone had been there so soon after the explosion. At a hundred and ninety feet, it wasn't the kind of dive a person did on a lark. The digging made him uneasy about that "accident" determination.

But what would anyone want with a US submarine built prior to World War II that had been stripped of everything nonessential and scheduled for SINKEX before accidentally sinking? At the time she went down, the sub hadn't contained valuable technology or secrets.

There was no logical reason for anyone to dig there, and even less reason for anyone to swim in that part of the strait. It wasn't a recreational dive with pretty fish or corals to look at. It was deep, difficult, and dangerous. So why would someone go down there, and with a trencher no less?

Something was going on, and he'd lay odds it had everything to do with the explosion.

His phone rang and he answered without checking caller ID. Big mistake. "What the hell are you doing sniffing after my daughter again, Sevick?"

Luke pulled the phone away from his ear and checked the number. Central California area code. *Shit.* "Stefan," he said, with false cheerfulness. "How great to hear from you again so soon."

"Cut the crap, Sevick. Why are you demanding the Navy assign you as my daughter's dive partner? Are you so hard up for work that you need to manipulate a woman who's been through hell?"

"What are you talking about, Stefan? I dived today with Undine as a favor to her, so back off."

"You dived with her, today?" Stefan paused. "You are a special kind of asshole to take advantage of her right now."

"I don't have a clue what you're talking about. I dived with her after she begged me to take her down. She has PTSD and was afraid to dive again. She wanted a strong partner. I helped her. Period."

The big man was silent for a moment. "My daughter has PTSD?"

"Of course she does. Five of her coworkers died. *She* could have died. What sort of rock do you live under?" Luke would never understand Stefan Gray.

"I just got a call from Greg Mulholland, her boss at NHHC. Greg wants me to use my connections at NOAA to get them to assign you to work with Undine until they know what's going on with the *Wrasse* wreckage. Clearly, Greg doesn't know shit about your history with Undine or he wouldn't have asked that of me."

"My history with Undine doesn't matter anymore. It's time for you to catch up, Stefan."

"Your history with Undine matters to *me*."

"You can bitch all you want, but your opinion is irrelevant in this equation." Luke decided he'd had enough and hung up on the man he'd once worshiped.

He stared at his phone.

Shit. Stefan Gray had just called him. The man ranked number one—even ahead of Undine—on his list of people he'd hoped never to speak with again. It appeared that, because Luke had said no, Undine was pushing for NOAA to force him to dive with her again. He hadn't expected that of her, but then, what did he know about Princess Undine, except that she was used to getting her way?

It was a sad fact of his life that she always got what—*and who*—she wanted.

Well, Luke had no intention of being jerked around by the princess. He would never again be one of her subjects.

Chapter Nine

The cabin was too small to pace, and if she stayed inside much longer, she might lose it. The day had been an emotional roller coaster that included Luke's flirting and resentment. She was wound up, frustrated, depressed, and angry—the full spectrum of her least favorite emotions. It was dark out, but Neah Bay was the kind of town where a woman could safely run at night. She grabbed her running shoes. She needed the exercise. To move. To feel the burn. Anything to shut down her thoughts. Physical pain to replace mental.

A gust of wind slapped her as she stepped onto the porch to stretch. The storm was ahead of schedule. She was lucky they'd completed the dive without being hampered by the weather. At least the storm would buy her a few days to find a dive partner.

She took off down the sidewalk that paralleled the main road, running full bore with the wind at her back, saving nothing for the return trip. She decided to run the length of town, then head down the spit access road. She could run along the beach on the other side of the breakwater. This time of year, she'd have the entire north coastline to herself.

She couldn't run away from her anxieties, but that didn't mean she wouldn't try.

She was as graceful on land as she was in the water. Luke shut off the engine of his SUV and watched Undine disappear down the road, her sleek, lithe body moving in perfect synchronicity. It was a cold night to run in yoga pants and Lycra top, but she ran with speed that would generate enough heat to see her through.

He hated that he found her sexy, even now.

He hadn't wanted to see her again—ever—but his calls to her cell phone had gone straight to voice mail. She probably didn't have the right service provider for Neah Bay, leaving him with no choice but to drive to her cabin. He'd arrived just in time to witness her taking off down the sidewalk.

Follow, or wait?

She had a head start and was fast, but he was faster. And he too could use a run.

He put his SUV in gear and pulled out onto the main road. She'd already reached the small waterfront playground. He watched to see if she would turn toward the breakwater or away, into the town's small residential area. A mutt that was at least half black lab approached her and sniffed at her hand, keeping pace as she passed the senior center. The rez dog was one of two that hung out on the waterfront. The friendly hound had joined Luke on a few runs in a similar fashion, giving up only when he realized Luke wouldn't toss him a stick while running.

Undine turned for the breakwater access road, and Luke

made his decision. He pulled into a parking space next to the playground. He would catch up to her on the spit.

He slipped on his running shoes. After a token stretch, he took off down the road after her. She was too far ahead for him to catch sight of her along the dark curve of the access road.

He finally came out of the woods at the start of the breakwater, but she was nowhere to be seen. She wasn't running down the spit. She must have dropped down onto the beach outside of the protected zone.

He turned left, crossing over sea grasses to reach the beach. A thin strip of sand hugged the hillside. The rising tide covered the majority of the jagged rocks that littered the sand, giving the beach a deceptively friendly appearance.

It took a few moments for him to catch sight of her pale, skintight top in the moonlight as she jogged the narrow stretch of sand. He put on a burst of speed and closed the distance between them as she neared the end of the beach, where cliffs met rocks and sea.

He didn't want to scare her by appearing in the dark without warning, so he shouted, "Undine!"

She glanced back and saw him, then dug in for more speed, heading for those treacherous rocks. "'Deen! It's Luke!" he shouted, just in case she hadn't recognized him in the darkness, but he figured she knew exactly who chased her. She probably didn't want to deal with him, given that she'd screwed him over yet again.

He let her gain for a moment, then released a burst of speed of his own, quickly catching up to her. He was on her heels. "'Deen," he repeated, a sharp edge to his voice.

Her body tucked to release more speed, but she didn't have any left, and she slowed with a small stumble. He was close behind her, and his toe tapped her heel. He caught her waist to prevent her fall, but he was forced to slow too soon and couldn't recover. He went down, taking her with him, but he rolled, his arm around her waist. Cushioning her as his shoulder hit the sand.

They tumbled sideways, coming to a stop inches from the high water line of the unfettered surf, his body on top of hers. Exhilaration coursed through him. His senses ran high. The hard, fast run. The unintended tackle. Having Undine's sleek body pressed against his as he sheltered her from the chill wind. The threat of the rising tide and crash of waves that lapped at the shore just feet away.

He was angry and turned on, and Undine Gray was the cause of both. He straddled her waist and grabbed her arms, pinning her wrists above her head with one hand. Her body paralleled the shoreline, and the slow, reaching wave threatened to soak her.

She stared up at him, her big, beautiful eyes wide with shock. Her chest rose rapidly as she panted from her hard run. Then her breathing changed, and the moonlight showed dilated pupils.

She was as turned on as he was.

"I hate it that you said something to me today that made me question my judgment of you, then you turned around and did exactly what the old Undine would have done." He wanted to lean down and dip his tongue into the hollow of her collarbone, to taste the salt of her sweat. "I hate even more that even after you've screwed me over *again*, I want you. I hate that I want to slide deep inside you. To taste you. To feel your heat."

"Yes," she said in a whisper. Her hips bucked upward, pressing herself to him in the only way she could.

He buried his face in her neck, taking in the scent of her as his heart rate kicked up. It had been a ridiculously long time since he'd been this ramped up for someone, and he'd never ridden the fine line between anger and lust before.

It was intense, this feeling. An adrenaline rush very different from what he'd experienced in combat. Her swimmer's body turned him on in a way he'd never expected from a purely physical attraction. And that was all this could possibly be—straight-up physical lust—because there was no way in hell he was falling for Undine Gray again. Ever.

"Either kiss me, or let me up," she said. "The sand is frigging cold."

He grinned and leaned over her. Pinning her chest with his, trapping her under his weight. "It's about to get a lot colder," he whispered.

The slow, reaching wave licked her side and his leg, and she squealed at the shock. "Oh my God, the water is liquid ice!"

He laughed and rolled her, planting himself in the surf with her above him. No way was this ending before he got his kiss, even if it meant he was the worst sort of fool. "Is this better? Now my ass is the one freezing."

She straddled him. Further copying his action, she took his hands and pinned his wrists above his head. A wave crashed, and from the roar of it, he didn't have to look to know this one would climb the sand and swamp them. She waited until the frigid deluge was a certainty, then flashed a wicked grin and pressed her mouth to his. The water reached him as her tongue slipped inside his mouth. He couldn't help but gasp at the shock of the cold even as the kiss filled him with heat.

She laughed against his mouth as water splashed over them both. Salt sprayed his eyes and seawater seeped past the seal of their lips. He ripped his hands free from her grasp to capture her face, preventing her from ending the scorching, ice-water-invaded kiss.

The sea retreated, and still he kissed her. His tongue slid

against hers, the hot, salty kiss worth every discomfort and chill.

He felt her chest shake against his, recognizing the laugh she held in as she sucked on his tongue. With his cradling hands, he lifted her mouth from his as he rocked his hips upward, pressing his erection into her straddling crotch.

"Wow, Sevick. That was pretty damn hot for being so fricking cold."

Shit. What was he doing? And why did he want to keep on doing it? "I don't know what's worse, that you're steamrolling me into working with you, or that your dad is getting up in my business trying to prevent it." And then, because he was a dumbass masochist, he pulled her head down for another kiss.

His tongue stroked hers as he rolled her again. He pressed her back into the sand, and another wave splashed against them. She gasped at the cold even as she wrapped her legs around his hips, locking him in the cradle of her thighs, kissing him with matching fervor.

The water retreated, and he felt her body shiver with cold that finally exceeded the heat of their mouths. He ended the kiss.

"I'm n-not trying to f-force you to work with me," she said after catching her breath.

Luke stood and pulled her from the sand. "Then explain to me why my boss called me right after I hung up with your dad and said I might be relieved of my duties for NOAA so I can work with you and NHHC?"

She was drenched and trembling. He pulled her into his arms to block the wind. This was wrong on so many levels, but he'd started it, and he could hardly leave her exposed to the chill air.

It didn't help that she felt so damn good in his arms.

"Th-that was my boss. I told him n-no. Not to ask you.

He insisted, but I asked him to give me a few days t-t-to line up a different dive partner." She pressed her face into his chest. "M-my dad called you?"

"Yes."

"Shit, Luke. I'm s-sorry. Really. I told Greg no."

He wanted to kiss her again and warm her with his body. Instead he said, "Let's get you back to my SUV. We can run the heater and talk." And he could use the walk in the cold wind to get his head on straight, as far as she was concerned.

If it were light out, they'd be quite a sight, coated as they were in sand and salt, their clothes flecked with bits of decaying bull kelp and eelgrass.

She was soaking wet, and the wind was cruel. They had a half-mile trek to his SUV, and he had no coat or anything dry and warm to offer her. "You up for a run?" he asked.

She nodded, her teeth chattering. "Yeah."

"Good. You set the pace."

She took off. Her muscles quickly heated, and she gained speed as she ran down the wooded roadway. Again, he trailed behind her, watching her lithe form, baffled as to how he could want her even now.

They reached his SUV, and he turned on the heater. He stared out over the bay as she settled, shivering in the seat next to him. "Let's get one thing straight," he said, keeping his gaze on the water because he didn't seem to have control when he looked at her. "Your lie fundamentally changed the direction of my *life*. I had to own my part in it —I was twenty-two and had sex with a sixteen-year-old girl. I wanted you, and I acted on that desire, but after I knew the truth, I wanted to bleach my brain of the memory. I was horrified and ashamed. I never would have touched you —never would have even *wanted* you—if I'd known the truth."

She rubbed her arms. The vent blew out cool air, making

the cab even colder. "I know. For what it's worth, I'm sorry. I've always, always been deeply sorry."

"Dammit! I don't want to hear your apology. I've *never* wanted to hear your apology."

Because then I might have to do something about it.

She reared back at the anger in his voice. She'd be shocked to know how much rage simmered inside him.

What was wrong with him that he wanted to screw her, but he still wasn't ready to hear her apology? He'd been so caught up today in the thrill of being with someone who shared his passion for the sea, who was smart as hell, and who made him laugh. Deep down, he'd probably always carried Undine in his mind as the type of woman he wanted…if only she were older.

And now, here she was, older.

And damn him for being a chump, but he wanted to fuck her. "I won't dive with you again. Sorry, but Princess Undine won't get her way this time."

She flinched. "I told Greg no, Luke. Fight fair. Don't hold me responsible for something I had no control over."

"Fine. I'll accept that you didn't *set out* to fuck with my life again, but you will acknowledge that was the end result."

She gave a sharp nod.

He put his SUV in reverse and pulled out into the main road. He'd drop her at her cabin and go back to his place and jack off if he had to. A minute later, he parked in front of her unit and grunted out a good-bye as she slipped from the vehicle.

Her wet jogging shirt was plastered to her body and the headlights revealed the goose bumps on her skin. She fumbled in her pocket for the key, but it appeared her fingers were numb.

Shit. He shut off the engine and climbed out. He'd get her inside, make sure she got warm, then he was out of there.

Surely he could control himself for five lousy minutes.

He met her on the porch and slipped his hand into the small zippered key pocket on her pants to grab her key.

She met his gaze, her big brown eyes full of surprise. "Thank you." She leaned into him as if seeking warmth. He pulled her against his chest as he reached for the lock, key in hand.

The press of her body against his as she shivered overwhelmed his control. She smelled like the sea and he wanted nothing more than to warm her from the inside out. He had to taste her again. He pinned her to the door and slid his tongue between her lips. Her arms circled his neck, and she kissed him back with the same heat she'd given on the beach. He worked the key and her mouth at the same time. When he had the dead bolt unlocked, he wrapped an arm around her waist and lifted so she wouldn't stumble when he pushed the door inward.

He carried her inside and slammed the door behind him. He set her down and ended the kiss so he could lock the dead bolt. "Strip. We need to get you into a hot shower."

"You first," she said.

He leaned his forehead against the door as he considered her clear invitation. He should walk right now.

He faced her and was about to say as much, but she was trapped trying to pull off her wet, tight jogging top with built-in bra. She had the garment wrapped over her head and shoulders, leaving her breasts exposed to his gaze and touch.

Unable to resist, he leaned down and licked one salty peak and then the other. He cupped both breasts in his palms and stroked her nipples with his thumbs.

Oh Jesus. He couldn't walk away now. Not unless she called a halt.

She groaned and said, "Help me out of this thing. I want to touch you."

Okay, she wasn't putting on the brakes.

He freed her from the shirt, then whipped off his own before pulling her to him so her chilled skin pressed to his. "God, you're beautiful." He kissed her, sliding his tongue deep into her mouth. This was so wrong, but he was going to have her. Here. Now.

She kissed him back and ran her hands over his chest, moving to his hips and down to cup his butt. "I'm going with A-plus for your ass," she said against his lips.

He laughed. "Wait until you see my...*ego.*"

She made a sound that was somewhere between a laugh and a groan and slipped her hand inside the front of his damp jeans and stroked his erection. "Ah, fuck, but I want this," she said.

He didn't need any more encouragement. "Get naked. Now." He followed his own command and stripped. He grabbed his wallet and plucked out a condom, then met her gaze.

She was beautifully naked. All sleek muscles and curves. He wanted to lick every inch of her. But he wouldn't lie to her about where this was going or what it meant. "This means nothing, Undine. I don't accept your apology. This is simple proximity and lust. You have a problem with that, this ends now."

She nodded. "Just shut up and fuck me." Then she smiled and dropped to her knees before him. "Or better yet, put your cock in my mouth."

Jesus. This wasn't the response he'd expected. But then, she likely harbored her own cauldron of pent-up emotions. That thought would give him pause, except she didn't wait for permission and licked the underside of his cock from base to tip, then took him deep into her throat.

"Holy fuck. *Undine.*" Her name was a prayer. Or a wish. Or a thank-you to the multiverse that he existed in this here and now that included Undine Gray's hot mouth on his hard prick.

He watched her through slitted eyes, his pleasure sensors nearly overloaded with the sensation of her tongue running up and down his cock as he feasted on the sight of her lips wrapped around him. The suction and slide. Her beautiful lips. Her hooded eyes. And adding to the intensity was her soft moan that told him she enjoyed sucking on him as much as he enjoyed the sucking.

She cradled his balls with one hand, stroking underneath, while her other hand wrapped around the base of his cock and added to his pleasure. Christ, she was about to make him go off like a firework with a short fuse.

He pulled back, sliding out of her mouth. "Careful, babe. I don't want this to end too soon."

She met his gaze and ran her tongue over her lips. "I want to make you feel good."

"You already have. Your mouth is so fucking hot. But we can both get there when I'm deep inside you." He pulled her to her feet and slid his fingers between her thighs. She quivered as he stroked her clitoris and let out a gasp when his fingers dipped inside her slick heat.

She was wet and ready for him. He groaned. "I need you on my tongue." He scooped her up and tossed her on the mattress, then spread her legs and licked her. She bucked against him, and he chuckled, then dipped his tongue inside her. He pressed his thumb to her clit as he fucked her with his tongue, loving the taste of her wet, tangy arousal.

He grazed her clit with his teeth, and she came off the bed with a jolt. "Get your cock inside me, Sevick. *Now.*"

He chuckled and stroked her with his tongue some more. Her body curled around him, cradling his head at the juncture of her thighs, and he figured that was pretty much the best place in the world to be.

"Shit, Sevick. You're going to make me come. Dammit, I want you inside—" She gasped, and he felt her shudder as she slipped over the edge, her body quaking with the power of her orgasm.

He pressed his tongue to her clit, holding her there as she thrashed. When she reached the end of her tremors, he scooted back and searched for the condom. He spotted it on the floor and climbed off the bed to grab it.

He wiped the moisture of her from his chin as he stared at her, splayed on the bed. A feast for eyes and body. She smiled at him, her face relaxed and her eyes slitted. She curled a finger toward him and slid to the edge of the bed. "Before you put that condom on, bring your cock over here."

He wasn't one to pass on a summons like that, and slipped his penis into her inviting mouth. She brought him to the edge of orgasm so fast, he was nearly blind with the intensity.

He stepped back before she could push him over the edge and rolled on the condom. He climbed on the bed and settled between her thighs, his erection ready at her vagina. He lowered himself until they were chest to chest and kissed her. He explored her mouth with his as he shifted his hips and in one smooth thrust, buried himself deep inside her.

Her tight heat encased him and felt every bit as good as he'd imagined. Better even.

She felt so good, the way she wrapped her legs around his hips and gripped his ass. She kissed him deeply and made sexy moaning sounds against his lips. She tasted sweet and salty and smelled like sand, sea, fresh air, sex, and Undine. His four favorite scents with one new addition.

He opened his eyes and lifted his mouth from hers so he could watch her face as she neared a second orgasm. Every thrust brought him closer to release, and with all his senses fully engaged, this one would be powerful.

She crested, and her moan pushed him over the edge. Pleasure swamped him, and he couldn't hold back a curse as he pulsed inside her. His orgasm was hard, lasted longer than usual, and was blinding in intensity.

Holy hell. He should have known it would be like this with her. After all, she was the ultimate forbidden fruit, the one woman he should avoid at all costs. So it would stand to reason that fucking her would be the ultimate dirty pleasure.

He stared down at her, still inside her body. His heart rate was nowhere near normal, but heading in that direction. Her eyes were closed, and a soft smile played about her mouth. Oh God. That mouth. The one that had been wrapped around his cock.

The one he wanted to see wrapped around his cock again and again.

He didn't know who he'd been fooling when he tried to convince himself he didn't find her attractive. She might not be supermodel gorgeous, but to him? She was utterly beautiful, this woman who'd just returned to his life with a vengeance.

What the *hell* had he just done?

He'd had sex with Undine Gray.

He slid from her body and climbed from the bed. He made a beeline for the bathroom, where he cleaned up and disposed of the condom. He splashed water over his face and found it hard to meet his own gaze in the mirror.

Due to the accident, she was vulnerable, but he'd taken advantage and had sex with her.

Willingly or not, she was messing with his career again, and he'd had sex with her.

He was back on the radar of her asshole father who'd ruined his career once, and he'd had sex with her.

He'd ask himself what the fuck he was thinking, except he'd have to have a brain to think, which obviously he didn't.

He swallowed cold water directly from the faucet. How could he let himself be drawn in by Undine again? And yet, he couldn't blame her. This was all on him. He was both asshole and fool and so completely fucked.

He stepped from the bathroom.

She was still sprawled on the bed. She smiled at him. Nothing tentative. She was the picture of sexual contentment, and he felt a flash of pride at being the cause.

Too bad he was also about to be the source of anger and hurt. He plucked his damp jeans from the floor and pulled them on. A glance in her direction showed her expression had gone from languid to guarded.

He pulled his wet T-shirt over his head. It was cold against his skin. He deserved the discomfort.

He sat on the edge of the bed to slip on his shoes. She sat up at that point. "You aren't even going to say anything? You're just going to leave?"

He shrugged. "There's not really anything to say, is there?" He grabbed his wallet from where he'd dropped it on the floor and met her gaze. He was thankful to see anger. He'd have a hard time walking away from hurt.

"You might have an A-plus ass, but you're also a grade-A asshole."

He shrugged. "What can I say? I'm the best at everything." He opened the door and stepped outside. He didn't have it in him to say good-bye to her one more time.

Chapter Ten

For two days, rain fell in sheets across Neah Bay. The potholes that littered the parking area in front of Undine's cabin had turned into lakes, with rivers of mud that ran in between. She sat on her porch, dreading Luke's inevitable arrival but knowing he'd show up today just the same.

She hadn't seen or spoken with him in the two days since he bolted after sex. Two days during which she'd negotiated with her boss over when and how she'd dive again on the *Wrasse* wreckage. Twenty minutes ago, she'd been given the final word: Lt. Luke Sevick was being lent to UAB for an indefinite period. He was hers to command until they'd documented the digging and potential looting of the Navy submarine.

Luke would have no say in the matter. NOAA had long been seeking action from UAB around some Navy vessels that needed cleanup in two marine sanctuaries. A deal had been struck, and Luke was part of the trade. As soon as Greg delivered this news, Undine had parked herself on the porch to await his furious arrival.

She'd had nothing to do with the negotiations. Had, in fact, been actively seeking another dive partner. Lt. Parker Reeves, the Coast Guard officer who'd accompanied her on her aborted dive attempt a week ago, had agreed, but he was being relegated to backup aboard Ray's boat, as he wasn't as experienced as Luke, and the Navy really wanted the former SEAL for the dive. But still, she had no doubt Luke would blame her. Another sin to lay at her feet. It was a special touch that officially he would be working for her.

Oh, irony.

She'd be amused if she weren't so damn angry—at Luke. At Greg. At her father. The trifecta of men who could and had hurt her the most.

She wasn't angry she'd had sex with Luke—she'd wanted him and had enjoyed every moment of the encounter. But she was hurt by the way he'd walked out, and mad at herself for wanting—even expecting—more from him.

Instead of waiting for Luke to show up now, she would attempt to track him down, but she didn't have a car. She'd spent the last two days stranded as the storm raged. She never should have agreed to return her rental car in Port Angeles, but money had been tight and it was an expense she could cut.

Neah Bay was a small town—she could walk from end to end in less than twenty minutes—but walking in cold November rain got old fast. At least the grocery store was next door, and the biggest restaurant was just across the highway. She hadn't starved in her isolation, but there'd been precious little to entertain her.

Two days ago, she'd walked to the Makah Cultural and Research Center. The curator had agreed to let her set up an electrolytic reduction tank in the museum's curation facility for the case she and Luke had collected from the wreckage.

That task complete, she'd spent an hour touring the

museum and hoped that before she left Washington, she'd make it out to the beach at Ozette to see where the village archaeological site had been located. She'd done little terrestrial archaeology as an undergrad, and the digs she'd worked on had been historic sites, so she was out of her depth, but she still found the subject fascinating. The Ozette site, considered the American Pompeii due to the incredible preservation, was a Makah village that had been buried by a mudslide around five hundred years ago. It was a rare and detailed glimpse into the precontact period of the Pacific Northwest. Plus the thousands of artifacts collected from the village were just plain cool.

Ozette was on the Pacific coast, south of the northernmost tip of the contiguous United States at Cape Flattery. It was just over twenty miles from Neah Bay to the trailhead, about an hour-long drive given the winding road. She'd have made the trek during her last two down days, but she didn't have a car, thanks to Luke, the grade-A asshole.

She wished he'd get here so they could hammer out the details of their dives. She wanted them done and behind her, so she could go home. She'd settle back into her life in DC and happily never see him again. But she'd decided to stay on in Neah Bay and see this through, because she owed it to the people who died on *Petrel* to get in the water and look for answers, even if that meant diving with Luke.

At last, Luke's mud-splattered SUV pulled into the parking lot. He took one of the potholes head-on, and a sheet of water sprayed out. If he'd been at a slightly different angle, it would have drenched her on the porch.

Yeah, he might be a little bit pissed. Bully for him.

He sat in the cab of his SUV, staring at her. A scowl settled so deep across his features, she was reminded of the childhood whispers that if you held your face in a certain way too long, it would freeze in that position. Finally, he climbed from the cab and stood in the rain in front of her porch, demonstrating he'd rather get soaked than stand too close to her.

"If I have cooties, Sevick, it's safe to say I caught them from you."

His features softened, one brief flash of amusement, then the scowl returned. "Ms. Gray, I may have been your first and even your last lover, but I'm going to venture to guess I'm not the only man you've screwed."

No. But as in everything, you were the best.

She refrained from making that observation; it would only feed his enormous ego. "At this point, it doesn't even matter if you don't believe me, so I'll only say it once. I had nothing to do with you being forced to work with me. I did what I could to stop it. It turns out what I could do wasn't much."

He stood in the rain, silent and glaring. Finally, he gave a sharp nod. "I believe you."

"I'm curious… Why?"

"Because I can't imagine you wanting to dive with me again after the way I left the other night."

"Is that why you did it? Why you screwed me, then bolted?"

He shook his head. "No. I didn't have an ulterior motive. And we had an agreement that it meant nothing."

"True. I guess I'm just old-fashioned and expect at least one post-sex kiss before the kiss-off."

He shrugged. "I'm not one for useless gestures or fake sentimentality."

"Apparently." She cleared her throat. "So how are we going to do this? You, working for me?"

He stepped up on the porch and planted himself in front of her, looming, his shoulders wide enough to block the sun —if such a thing existed on this sloppy, wet day—his stance pure intimidation. "Let's get one thing straight right now. *I am not working for you.*"

He'd miscalculated, clearly, because standing as he was, his crotch was level with her face, and all she could think of was how beautiful his body was when she took him in her mouth. Her breathing turned shallow, and she licked her lips —unintentionally. She didn't even realize she'd done it until his jeans bulged with a growing erection. She flashed a defiant grin. "Parts of you work for me just fine."

He leaned down and braced his hands on either side of the flimsy deck chair. "I never said I didn't want to fuck you again. I'll take you here and now if you want, and it will mean exactly as much to me as the other night did, which is to say, nothing. The fact that my body responds to you is simple biology."

She was tempted to take him up on his cold offer just to prove him wrong. Instead, she got a grip on her emotions and tapped his chest, pushing him back. Once she had room, she stood. "Get over yourself, Luke. This isn't about us. This is about *Wrasse* and *Petrel*. The only reason I'm willing to dive there again—either with or without you—is because we need answers. Did you read the report on the accident?"

He gave a sharp nod.

"What did you think of it?"

He shrugged. "It was the best they could do with limited information."

She'd have to take his word for it. For herself, she hadn't been able to read the report. Every time she tried, she'd gone back to that moment when the anchor line snapped and she'd looked up to see a flash of light at the surface. She couldn't remember without holding her breath. Without feeling suffocated. Without trembling. Without losing her shit.

She'd asked Erica to read it and share the pertinent details. As a result, Undine knew the basic facts: There'd been a problem with the oxygen tank, the one that was attached to the hose that had fed her pure oxygen during her decompression stop. She'd breathed from that tank until she'd donned the full-face scuba mask again so she could radio Yuri.

Pieces of the tank had been recovered, enough for investigators to determine the first explosion—the investigation also revealed there had been three explosions in rapid succession —started at the cylinder valve. Investigators believed the explosion was caused by the use of an O-ring and gasket that weren't compatible with pure oxygen and a pressure-adjusting screw that wasn't completely unwound.

Three tiny pieces—they would fit in one hand with plenty of room to spare—had destroyed a forty-foot boat and killed five people.

Jared had changed the cylinder that last morning. The first time a new cylinder valve was opened, it was always vital to make sure the regulator outlet valve was closed. For whatever reason, Jared didn't fully unwind that one screw when he turned on the oxygen for her decompression stop. That the explosion didn't occur immediately was lucky for Undine. But when he closed the valve after she switched back to her scuba tank, the uneven pressure likely leaked oxygen, which reacted to the gasket and O-ring made of an incompatible elastomer, triggering the first explosion. The blast set off a second, adjacent oxygen tank, which, from the boat fragments collected, appeared to have shot through the deck and ignited the boat's fuel tank, triggering the third explosion.

The anchor line Undine had been holding ran next to the oxygen hose. The line snapped with the first explosion. Jared had probably been closing the valve as he responded to her on the radio. Investigators believed he died instantly.

The others had died when the fuel tank blew.

Only Yuri remained unaccounted for, but given that he

was diving at the time, he could have been rocked by the wave and washed out to sea. His weight belt and tank could have kept him from surfacing. Or he could have run into some other problem—whatever it was that had prevented him from responding to her on the radio—and already been unconscious, or even dead, at the time of the blast.

Jared was a professional. He knew how to manage both technical and scuba dives. It was his boat, his equipment, which the Navy was leasing for the excavation. But even experts made mistakes, and the incorrect gasket was identical in appearance to the correct one. It was plausible that he'd gotten them confused.

But what if he hadn't? What if the gaskets had been switched deliberately?

Everything about the explosion was a fluke, a horrific alignment of errors with tragic results.

She should have been at the bottom, with Yuri, but trouble with her tank had sent her up. Jared turned on the oxygen for her, and the world came apart.

"I've had a lot of time to think in the last two days," she said to Luke. "And one thought won't let me go. What if Yuri set up the explosion? What if he planned it all and swam away? What if Yuri is still alive?"

The rain was coming down sideways, making the porch little protection. Luke didn't want to step inside the cabin where he'd made love to her, so he nodded to his truck. This wasn't a conversation they could have at the restaurant across the street. "Grab your purse. We're driving to Forks while we talk."

"Why are we going to Forks?"

"You need a cell phone that works in Neah Bay and a better wetsuit."

"There's no dive shop in Forks. I looked."

"There's a whitewater rafting group that's closed this time of year. The owner is about your size, and she's got a European wetsuit like mine she's willing to sell."

Undine cocked her head in interest. "She has a C-Skin?"

"Yep."

"I've always wanted one," she frowned. "But my budget is shot right now. I was on paid leave including per diem until my ears healed. Once the doctor cleared me to fly, I was on my own for my hotel in Port Angeles. I'm pretty much living on credit now."

"The suit is used, so it'll be cheaper. And I assumed, given that you lost all your gear in a work-related accident, the Navy would pay for a replacement."

"I'm sure they will, but it'll take weeks to process the paperwork. You know the US government." She crossed her arms. "I'm nearly maxed out. I can't afford it, not right now."

He'd always assumed her father was wealthy, given his state of the art research boat and his high-tech institute, but she mentioned that he'd done the reality show for the money, and she really did seem concerned about finances. This shouldn't surprise him, but it did. "If the suit fits, I'll front you the money. It's a good deal, and I don't want to listen to you whine when we dive."

She shook her head. "Borrowing money from friends, enemies, and payday loan places tops my list of things to never do."

"Seems like screwing grade-A assholes should rank higher than that, but to each their own." He didn't know why her resistance irritated him. Maybe it was because he'd looked forward to seeing her rush of excitement when he told her he'd lined up a C-Skin for her. He was so fucking pathetic, the way he wanted to walk away from her and please her at the same time. "We'll go to Forks, and you'll try on the damn suit. If it fits, we'll figure out how you can pay me back." He crossed his arms and scanned her from head to toe. "I'm sure we can think of something."

She stiffened. "You're despicable."

"No argument there." He turned toward his SUV. "Let's roll."

She retreated inside her cabin just long enough to make him wonder if he'd baited her too much and she wouldn't join him, but then she stepped outside, and he noted that she'd changed out of her sweatpants into worn, hip-hugging jeans and brushed her hair.

Goddamn, she was sexy. He continually failed to understand this attraction; he'd just have to learn to live with it. He shifted in his seat and adjusted his erection in his constricting jeans.

He'd have thought sex would have gotten her out of his system, but it appeared to only have made his situation worse. He'd been told to expect to dive with her four or five times but was authorized for as many dives as it took to get the information they needed. Given that they could dive a maximum of twice per day—with at least six hours of off-gassing in between—they'd need a run of good weather to complete this nightmare in a reasonable amount of time.

All he could do was pray the sun god would take pity on him.

She tossed her coat into the backseat and slid into the front. He pulled out into the road before she even had her seat belt buckled. "Have you ever been to Forks?" he asked.

"No. But I hear the vampire infestation is way down."

"The boom is past. They only have one dedicated *Twilight* store now. I hear there were four at the peak."

They drove past the Makah Museum. "I don't suppose

there are any car-rental places in Forks?" she said. "I'd like to get one so I can go out to Ozette when it's too rainy to dive."

"I have no idea." He frowned. He knew she'd been stranded—thanks to him—and debated whether or not he should make a grudging offer. "There's not a lot to see—I mean, the beach is beautiful, but the village, the archaeological site, is gone. They removed it all with the excavation."

"I know. But I'd still like to see it. I've mostly done underwater archaeology, but Erica and Mara have convinced me that terrestrial sites are interesting too."

That brought to mind the question he'd wondered since he sat by her bed in the hospital. "What got you into archaeology? You seemed to love marine biology and were in a prime position to follow in your dad's shoes. I'd have expected you to be well on your way to being one of the most respected names in the field by now."

The crash of rain on the hood and the swipe of wiper blades across the windshield was her only answer. Finally she sighed softly. "It's complicated. I never planned to return to marine biology, but now it might be a possibility." She shrugged. "I love my job, though—for the most part. When my boss doesn't completely ignore the one thing I told him absolutely not to do."

He needed to come clean with her. "I had a long talk with my NOAA commander, and the truth is, they wouldn't have assigned me to this without my agreement."

She raised a pretty, arched brow. "That sort of kills your argument for being pissed at me."

He shook his head. "Oh no, sweetheart. I can always come up with reasons to be angry with you."

"So why did you agree?"

"Because I also believe the explosion was deliberate. Why else would someone be digging on the *Wrasse* wreck? And, like you, Yuri was my first suspect."

"It's too convenient, the fact that he disappeared *before* the explosion. If I had died, no one would know that. They'd think his disappearance was due to the explosion."

"Did the Navy ever run a check on Yuri Kravchenko?" he asked.

"I doubt they would have bothered. They ran one on Jared, certainly. It was his boat, and the Navy was leasing *Petrel* for the excavation, but Yuri, Loren, and Scotty were Jared's crew and were only scheduled to be on board for the setup phase. Five days at most. After we completed the prep, Navy divers were supposed to arrive and take over. They were the ones who would excavate. I was supposed to remain in a supervisory capacity, the representative from UAB." She shook her head. "Nothing about the USS *Wrasse* was top secret. It was an old sub that had been stripped for SINKEX. The only thing remarkable about it was the retired submariners who died unnecessarily. I doubt the Navy saw any reason to run a check on Jared's crew, because they wouldn't be on board when the Navy's elite divers were present."

"I called one of the investigators with the Coast Guard to confirm that no one used a cable trencher during the investigation."

Undine hugged her knees to her chest, a sure sign she was feeling vulnerable. He hated that he wanted to pull her into his arms even now, but there it was. "Greg asked that question too."

"Then you already know no cable trenchers were used."

She nodded. "They would have tossed boat fragments instead of finding them. I've only used one once, when the wreck was under several feet of sediment."

"So if there was nothing to be gained from excavating the sub, why is someone doing it?"

She shrugged her sleek, swimmer's shoulders. "I'm

baffled. I considered that maybe there was something on *Petrel* they were looking for, except…*Petrel* fragments wouldn't be under that much sediment."

"Not to mention they were collected or at least picked through." Luke veered around a rock in the roadway. The rains had caused rocks to fall from the hillsides that lined the coastal road. Normal for this time of year, but if the storm didn't abate as predicted, they could face a road closure that would cut off the town from the rest of the state. "The storm is supposed to break this afternoon. If the weather is okay tomorrow, Ray will take us out."

"The Coast Guard is going to lend us Parker Reeves as a backup diver to help Ray with the boat. We'll need to make sure Parker is available tomorrow."

Luke was well aware of all the details that had been hammered out without his input. "I already spoke with him. He's good to go whenever we are. His orders are to be on call. He's good, but not master diver certified."

"That's why we couldn't use him for my primary partner. The SecNav waiver requires master divers." She unfurled her legs and planted them on the floor. "Thank you for agreeing to dive with me again, Luke. I need to know what happened to *Petrel*."

"I want to know too."

"You might even be a decent human being." She spoke softly, making him wonder if she'd intended to say the words aloud.

"Only decent? I was thinking more along the lines of remarkable. Or wonderful. Even heroic comes to mind."

She shook her head. He'd bet she rolled her eyes, but he needed to keep his gaze on the road. "I figure anything above asshole is compliment enough," she said.

He laughed. "True." He turned down the wiper speed as

the rain decreased to a drizzle. "Tell me everything you know about Yuri."

*uri Kravchenko watched the couple drive out of town. She was with the former SEAL, the scientist who worked for NOAA. But if what he'd witnessed on the beach the other night was any indication, they were less concerned about the *Wrasse* than they were with getting it on, which worked for him. But still, Gray was a problem. The fact that she was still in town was a problem.

What were the odds she'd be thrown clear of the wreck? He'd needed her to make her decompression stop to trigger the explosion, but by his calculations, she should have been taken out by the oxygen line.

Yet here she was with the man who'd plucked her from the water. That a NOAA vessel had been nearby was a factor outside his control. Sometimes you have to roll the dice.

If only the Coast Guard helicopter hadn't been available for fast airlift. If only she'd suffered a stroke. With the excavation delayed indefinitely, no one else who cared would have dived on the *Wrasse* wreckage for months. Sea currents would have long since cloaked the evidence of his digging.

He'd considered disposing of her that first night she'd returned to Neah Bay, but another accident so soon after her dive would've raised too many questions. And odds were, if she saw evidence of his digging, at that point, she'd already told her boss. Killing her wouldn't serve a purpose; it would only raise suspicion.

But another dive would be a problem. He couldn't stop now, not when they'd finally located the hull. One, two more dives and they'd have it.

Now that she'd left town, he finally had an opportunity to

check out her cabin, to see if she was still in Neah Bay because she planned to dive on the wreck again.

It was risky. The couple might just be taking a short trip to Seiku, and anyone could see him enter the cabin, but last night, he'd managed to swipe the extra key from the office, and he might not get another chance.

There was no other option. Early on a weekday, no one was around. Only two other cabins were even rented, and no vehicles were parked out front. He climbed out of his truck, which he'd parked in front of the post office, and strode with purpose toward her unit. In moments, he was inside, fairly certain no one had seen him.

He went for her laptop first. Thankfully, she didn't use password protection to access her desktop. He wasn't computer illiterate, but he was no hacker either. Her mail program was built-in and her password was preloaded.

Sweat broke out on his brow when new emails loaded. Hopefully she wouldn't notice the download had occurred while she was out. He ignored the new messages and focused on her sent emails.

His bowels loosened when he read the email she'd sent to her boss with the subject: *Re: Yuri Kravchenko*. A quick read of the contents confirmed his worst fears. She'd seen the signs of digging and suspected him.

Worse, NOAA and the Navy wanted her to dive with the former SEAL—Sevick—to collect evidence of their digging. He'd seen enough and closed the program, being careful to leave the desktop exactly as he'd found it except for the additional emails.

He had no choice. He had to collect the weapon immediately. Fortunately, the weather was supposed to clear. Tonight it should be safe to dive.

But Gray and Sevick would undoubtedly see signs of his

digging when next they dove. They might see *M-357*. Would Gray recognize it? Or would she believe it was the *Wrasse*?

If he couldn't find the torpedo tube, if he couldn't remove the weapon before Gray and Sevick dove again, then the only way to delay the Navy from catching on and finding the device before he did was to take out the couple either before or during their dive.

As usual, the trick was making it look like an accident.

Or, even better, make sure the blame fell on someone else.

Chapter Eleven

"Yuri worked for Jared off and on for the last three years," Undine said. "He was born and raised in the former Soviet Union and left Ukraine about five years ago. I gathered Yuri was something of a local character here on the peninsula, a fisherman by trade. He didn't learn to dive until he moved here, but three years ago, he was experienced enough to start working with Jared, who has the best commercial diving vessel on the north coast." Undine paused and cleared her throat. "*Had* the best boat."

Luke dropped a hand onto her knee and squeezed. "Go on."

She closed her eyes. She could see Yuri so clearly in her mind. It was odd to feel betrayed—if, indeed, Yuri was behind the explosion—by a man she'd known for only a few days.

Grief was so strange. For a brief moment, when it first flashed in her mind that Yuri might be alive, she'd felt joy at the idea she wasn't the sole survivor of the accident. But that thought was quickly followed by the acknowledgment that if Yuri was alive, it hadn't been an accident.

"He grew up near Chernobyl," she continued. "Most of his family was killed in the meltdown. Only he and his younger sister survived. He made no bones about expressing his hatred for Russia and Russians. I only knew him for a few days, and in that time, he'd made sure I—and anyone who'd listen—knew exactly how he felt about the Crimean annexation. He was obsessed with the desire for Russia to be punished for sinking that passenger ferry last spring." She opened her eyes and took in the road ahead. "He was so vehement, more than once I wondered if he lost someone in the ferry incident. So much so that yesterday I asked my friend who runs Raptor to look into his background."

"Raptor? Is that the mercenary company owned by that senator from Maryland?"

Crap, she had another confession to make to Luke. Bad timing considering he was actually being nice to her. "Yeah. That's Raptor. Trina, a coworker at NHHC and one of my closest friends, is engaged to the CEO." She cleared her throat. "So, I have something else I need to tell you."

Not surprisingly, he stiffened.

"Trina is worried about me and something of a mother hen. I've been an emotional wreck since the accident, and she thinks the fact that you saved me has only made it—*me*—worse. She believes I've been hung up on you forever." She gazed out at the trees that lined the road. Anything was better than facing Luke. "Trina nagged Keith—her fiancé—to check you out."

"He ran a background check on me?" His voice was guarded.

"Yes. I'm sorry. I didn't know anything about it until it was too late. It was before—before we had sex. And just a preliminary screen, the kind they run when they're considering hiring someone."

"Meaning he looked at my military record—the parts that

aren't classified—and anything in public databases. Did he find any ugly secrets I should know about?"

"No." She cleared her throat. "If it makes you feel better, Keith said he wants to offer you a job."

"What's the pay like?"

She gave him a startled look. "Do you want to work for Raptor?"

His laugh held a hard edge. "No. Not even a little bit. I've got a commitment to the NOAA Corps. I'm working in my field again. I'm exactly where I want to be. Or at least I was, until your boss jerked me around."

She winced, but felt rather maxed out on apologies where he was concerned. She could only say she was sorry for other people's actions so much.

"What did Keith find out about Yuri?"

Relief settled over her that he was letting this latest affront slide. "Nothing yet. I'll email him and cc you, so he'll loop you in if he finds anything. That way you can ream him out for running a check on you. Or talk SEAL stuff. Whatever it is you former Navy guys do."

"Keith was a SEAL?"

She nodded. "He was a sniper."

"I guess I should be careful how much shit I flip him, then."

She laughed. Keith and Luke would probably get along just fine.

"Anything else about Yuri you remember?"

She shrugged. "He was an old-school Eastern European sexist bastard. He sometimes almost seemed to be a caricature—the crotchety Ukrainian. Scotty liked to bait him by calling him Russian—I gathered that was an ongoing joke that never got old for Scotty. But when Yuri wasn't being those things, he could be nice. Almost a grandfatherly type. Between losing his family in Chernobyl and some other things he hinted at, I gathered he'd suffered some horrors at the hands of the Soviets. I felt sorry for him when he wasn't being a pain in the ass. He was thirty when the Soviet Union fell apart. Old enough to have seen some nasty stuff."

"Those former KGB guys are still going strong under Putin, and they don't mess around. Do you know *why* Yuri came to the US?"

"He never said. But then, I barely knew him." She thought carefully about their conversations. "He ranted about Russia frequently but never spoke of how he felt about the US. He mentioned Canada a few times and, I gathered, took the ferry from Port Angeles to Victoria fairly frequently. I asked him about it, because it's a trip I'd like to make before I leave. I've never been to Victoria."

"What did he say about it?"

"He complained that they didn't serve vodka in the ferry lounge, and he always felt like he was being profiled at customs on both ends. He said he went there because he had Ukrainian friends who'd settled in Sidney, BC."

"That might be something to look into."

"I'll mention it to Keith in my email."

"You said he was a fisherman and worked for Jared off and on."

"Yeah."

"Did Yuri have his own fishing boat?"

She nodded. "He lived on his boat and moved around the coast."

"What happened to it?"

She shrugged. "I would imagine it went to his next of kin —his sister?—but she probably lives in Ukraine. But again, I only knew him a handful of days."

"Another question for Keith, then. Does he have access to that kind of data?"

"If he doesn't, then Erica's husband, Lee, could get it for us. He's good at making computers give up their secrets."

"You know, this can all be done legally. No need for hacking."

"Oh, Lee'll do it legal." She silently added, *this time*. They all knew Lee strayed into questionable territory now and then, but Luke was right, there was no reason for that here. "I could always ask Mara to brief Curt Dominick on everything. Curt can get the FBI involved. Given the military vessel, the explosion, and Yuri's Ukrainian background, there are at least a dozen different Federal laws this could fall under, and excavating *Wrasse* without a permit is an SMCA—Sunken Military Craft Act—violation, so we have a starting point, but it would help to get Curt's attention if we found conclusive evidence that the explosion was no accident, or that Yuri is alive."

Luke shook his head. "You could get the US attorney general involved in this with just a phone call? You do move in impressive circles, Ms. Gray."

"Well, his wife is my ultimate boss, even above Greg— she's the one who could get him involved. But yeah, Curt and I are friends. Although he works a hellish number of hours, so of all my friends' significant others, I probably know Curt the least well."

"Is he as cold as everyone says?"

"He's not cold so much as driven. He's a good man. Totally in love with Mara. It's really sweet how his eyes follow her around the room."

Undine was envious of their relationship. Actually, she was envious of the relationships all of her friends had. Not that she needed a man to be happy, but that the men she'd been with never elicited the kind of emotion she witnessed between Lee and Erica, or Curt and Mara.

She barely knew Cressida, but even she could see that her

boyfriend, Ian, was crazy about her. Just once she'd like to be the recipient of that intensity of emotion. Even if it didn't last.

"Have you ever been in love, Luke?" The moment the words were out of her mouth, she regretted them. What was she thinking, asking Luke Sevick, of all people, about love and relationships? They'd had meaningless sex just sixty-three hours ago. Not that she was tracking that or anything.

He glanced at her askance. After a long pause, he said, "Yeah. Once."

"What happened?" Instead of jealousy, she realized she felt sad on his behalf, that he'd loved someone and it hadn't worked out.

"The usual. I was deployed. She got fed up with me being gone all the time and cheated."

"That sucks."

He shrugged. "I'm neither the first nor the last guy that's happened to. I'm just glad it happened before I did something dumb like ask her to marry me—which I'd been ready to do." He paused. "What about you, Undine? Has there been anyone special in your life?"

"No. There've been plenty of relationships—Trina refers to my dating pattern as serial monogamy with a sixty-day expiration—but I've never been in love."

"Love is overrated. Sex is just as good"—he gave her a sidelong glance—"or even better without it."

Chapter Twelve

The couple returned in the early evening. From the deck of his boat, Yuri looked through binoculars and watched them unload a bag of groceries from the store in Forks, answering his question on where they'd gone.

Next Gray pulled a wetsuit from the back of Sevick's SUV. Shit. She was getting better equipped to dive. At least they wouldn't have mixed gases. They'd be limited—as he and his team were—to short bounce dives. No more than fifteen minutes at the bottom. The time restrictions and the need to search only at night had hampered Yuri from the start. But he had the location now. He would find the weapon in the next day or two.

Sevick closed and locked his vehicle. A sign he intended to stay the night?

A few minutes later, the occupant of the cabin adjacent to Gray's stepped off his porch and dumped a bag of coals in the portable grill in the parking area. He probably had a stringer of fish to cook.

The wind whipped up as the man poured lighter fluid on the coals, and he gestured as if he'd been splashed with the flammable liquid. His movements were sloppy, like a man who'd had too much to drink.

Yuri kept his binoculars fixed on the drunken fisherman.

Perhaps there was a way to stage an accident that would be believable.

*A*fter they returned to Undine's cabin, they spent hours going over the chart, planning the following day's dive. As they talked, Undine tied knots every five meters on a long rope they'd purchased in Forks. They would use the line as a leash and to measure any excavated areas they found.

"With this wind, the water will be choppy," Luke said. "It'll be harder for us to work our way down. We'll have less time at the bottom."

She nodded and tied a carabiner to one end of the line and held it up for Luke's inspection. "We'll hook this to the anchor line and leapfrog each other at the five-meter intervals. If we swim in a circle around the anchor, we should be able to cover a thirty- or forty-meter radius."

Her email chimed, and she turned to her laptop next to her on the bed. She and Luke had settled into an accord over the course of the day. Not friends, not enemies, hell, not even frenemies. Just coworkers. As Luke had said earlier, sex the other night had been simple biology.

She'd taken several classes in biology, and Luke held a BS in the subject. They both understood the science of attraction and sex.

She opened her Mail program. "Email from Keith," she said. "Looks like he was able to track down Yuri's boat."

"What did he find out?"

She scanned the contents. "His boat was moored at the marina here at the time of the accident. It was released to his next of kin—twin nephews—who, surprisingly, lived in Seattle. It was all handled with shocking speed, but he owned the boat without any liens, and his will stated clearly who the beneficiaries were, so probate wasn't necessary."

"Does he say where the boat is now?"

"No. If we find anything on our dive that indicates Yuri might have survived, I'm sure the Navy or the FBI will call on his next of kin. But until then, there's not much that can be done."

Luke nodded. "Anything on the victims of the ferry sinking? Is there a connection to Yuri?"

"Nothing so far, but the ferry manifest is incomplete. Much like it could take months to figure out who was on a Washington State Ferry if there were an incident." She stood up and stretched, then glanced at her watch, surprised to see they were deep into the evening hours. She grabbed the TV remote and hit the power button. "We should check the forecast." A local channel had satellite pictures with a ticker across the bottom providing predictions.

"Looks like we'll be good for tomorrow," Luke said. The image changed, showing an extended area, and the ticker offered a longer-range forecast. "But we could be facing a Pineapple Express. We may want to try to get two dives in tomorrow."

"We won't have enough daylight for that unless we go out at eight a.m."

"I'll talk to Ray and Parker. We *could* dive in the dark."

"You probably have much more experience with that than I do."

He nodded. "Diving as a SEAL is a helluva lot different. A lot less focus on the pretty fish. More of a commute, really."

"Do you miss it? The SEALs?" She couldn't help but stare at the muscles that proved he kept up with whatever exercise regime he'd maintained when he was in the service. She could stare at his muscles all day. And touching him, getting up close and personal with his perfect body? Sheer pleasure.

"Sometimes. The adrenaline. The team. They're my brothers."

"One of the guys who works for Keith at Raptor was on his SEAL team. And you can see it—all the guys are friends, but Keith and Josh…it's different."

Luke nodded. "If you don't have a lot of experience with night diving, tomorrow is not the day to start. We'll keep an eye on the weather and hope the storm will hold off for a few days." He stood. "I should head. I need to move out of the NOAA's research housing tonight. They've assigned another researcher to complete my project, and I need to vacate for him."

"Are you moving into one of these cabins?"

"No. I've got a reservation out at Hobuck, the cabins on the Pacific coast. Full-size fridge and a cooktop."

She'd wanted to book one of those cabins, but when she first made her reservation, it was on her own dime, and the ones on the bay were cheaper. "Jealous. I'm mighty sick of microwave meals, and the restaurant is getting old."

She could swear he was about to make her an offer, or even kiss her good night, when he rubbed the back of his neck. "Meet me at the dock at eleven tomorrow."

*L*uke had to leave. He shouldn't have allowed her to get comfortable with him. It was much easier when the anger crackled between them.

Except, of course, he'd screwed her brains out when amped up on anger. So maybe not. Maybe this…cooperation…or whatever it was would mean he could keep his hands off her?

Forget that he was angry, and, more importantly, she was vulnerable. He was an asshole, sure, but was he a complete asshole?

So far, yeah.

It was probably only a matter of time before her friend the sniper called for open season, and hell, the Raptor CEO had a mercenary army at his back. Then there was Stefan Gray, who already wanted to have Luke neutered.

Not that he was scared of either man or army. It was more about being able to face himself in the mirror, and he'd been having a problem with that since he'd slipped out of her bed the other night.

But damn, even now, he wanted her. He wanted angry and fierce. He wanted to ride that line of anger and lust all the way to home base again. And again.

He descended the wide porch steps and crossed to his SUV, his brain absorbed with thoughts of stripping Undine of the T-shirt and formfitting jeans, and screwing her for hours.

He pressed the unlock button on the remote key, when the scent of smoke penetrated his lust-infused mind. He glanced back at the row of cabins even as he pulled open the car door. A portable grill on the porch next to Undine's had an orange glow. The wind gusted, and the glow turned into a flame that licked at the wooden porch post. Sitting on the porch railing right next to the flaming grill was a line of small green propane canisters and a can of lighter fluid.

Shit.

He slammed his door closed and stomped up to the cabin. What sort of fool lit a barbecue on a wooden porch on a windy night?

A glance inside the bowl showed nothing but flame. The

guy wasn't even cooking anything. Luke grabbed the round lid by the handle—hot because the grill was over-fired—and dropped it on top. The vent was open and too hot to close with bare hands, but at least that would slow down the flame while he roused the fisherman.

He pounded on the door, and two minutes passed before a bleary-eyed man opened the door. "Wah…?" the man asked.

Luke reached inside and grabbed the fire extinguisher mounted next to the door, then entered the cabin and snatched a towel from the bathroom. Without a word, he returned to the porch, removed the lid with the towel, pulled the pin on the extinguisher, and doused the flames.

Once he was certain the fire was out, he turned to the gaping fisherman. "Hose it down and get it off the porch. Don't ever park a lit grill on a wooden porch on a windy night again." He shoved the extinguisher into the man's hands and stomped back down the steps, then crossed the small parking lot to his truck.

Chapter Thirteen

The sky was a crisp, clear blue. Undine wouldn't believe it was November, except for the chill. "The Washington coast is insanely beautiful in the fall—when it's not raining. Why did I not know this?" she asked Luke.

"It's one of those secrets within a secret," he said as they walked down the dock. "The rain in Seattle isn't nearly as awful as Washingtonians would have you believe, and the corner of the Olympic Peninsula is remote and wild and one of the most beautiful places in the world."

"I haven't been out to Cape Flattery yet. I hear it's like standing on the edge of the Earth."

"It's even better than that. Whales and sea lions play in the distance while waves crash against the rocky shoreline." He cast her a sly grin. "All mermaids should feel at home."

"Sounds like a place I should go."

"You should."

She didn't point out that she didn't have a car because he'd insisted on driving her to Neah Bay and there were no rental agencies in the area. He obviously hadn't decided yet if they were going to attempt anything resembling friendship during this time that they were stuck together.

He was so damn frustrating. She would take the bus to Port Angeles on the next rainy day and rent a car.

They climbed aboard Ray's boat. She greeted Lt. Parker Reeves with a hug. He'd been so understanding during her panic attack two weeks ago. She was thankful his pride hadn't been hurt when she'd been able to complete the dive with a different partner.

Luke greeted Parker with a handshake, and it was clear they knew each other already. Not surprising given the size of Neah Bay, and it sounded like Luke spent a lot of time in the community even though he lived in Port Angeles.

Parker was suited up and ready to swim, but he was really there to provide support for Ray on the boat. They hadn't needed backup on the first dive because it hadn't been a Navy-sanctioned and Navy-funded undertaking. It had been two private citizens chartering a dive boat. This was different, but even so, they were skirting the regs a bit.

Parker untied the lines while Ray took the helm, and they set out. Undine stepped down into the cabin to change into her new, used wetsuit. She was sort of in love with the thing and grateful to have it, even if it meant borrowing money from Luke. She would be far more comfortable in the water today.

Luke entered the cabin. She slid the curtain aside as she zipped the suit at her neckline.

"Need help with that?" he asked with a blatant leer.

"I think I can handle it." She scanned him from head to toe. Once again he'd only pulled his wetsuit over his hips, leaving his bare chest on full display. "What's the matter, Sevick? Forgot how to dress yourself?"

"And let you miss an opportunity to check out my guns?"

He flexed as he turned, and damn if his lats and delts didn't dance.

She rolled her eyes. "Suit up. Like lousy sex, I want to get this dive over with and move on."

His brow furrowed with confusion. "I wouldn't even know what that means."

She snorted. The sad part was, he probably didn't. At least, based on her limited experience of him.

She returned to the upper deck. Parker was on the back deck above the dive platform, inspecting the oxygen tanks to be used for the decompression stop. She dropped onto the bench seat next to Ray at the helm as he guided the boat to the coordinates of the wreck. She wrinkled her nose at the smell of cigarette smoke on his clothes, but could hardly complain. It was his boat; he could smoke if he wanted—as long as he didn't light up near the oxygen. "Do you dive, Ray, or just captain the boat?"

"Just captain. I used to dive, but years ago, I was diving with a friend and…things…went wrong. Bad air in his tank. I just…I never could stomach the deep after that. I snorkel sometimes, but no scuba."

"I'm sorry," she said. "Is that why Luke asked you to skipper for us?"

"I don't know. But it is why I said yes. You were smart to get back in the water again as soon as you could. Sometimes we need to face our demons head-on."

They reached the coordinates, and he hit the button to drop the anchor. After it reached bottom, he put the engine in idle and let the boat drift with the current, setting the anchor and pulling the line taut. "Strong chop today. You're going to have to fight your way down."

"Luke said the same thing."

"That's because I'm always right, honeycakes."

She turned to see Luke. "Keep that up and I'll end up with an injury from too much eye rolling."

Ray laughed.

"Ready?" Luke asked.

She nodded and left the helm to finish donning her dive gear.

"The radios don't work from deck to the bottom—it's too far," Luke said to Parker. "If we need you, we'll swim up until we're in range, which is probably five to ten meters below the decompression stop."

Parker nodded. No one expected him to have to get in the water. He fulfilled a checkbox on a form, nothing more.

The wind rippled across the water as she secured her tank on her back and cinched her weight belt. Luke checked her tank, hoses, and regulator. "You're all set."

She performed the same service for him, pausing to admire his body encased in neoprene. He looked like a super-hero. He'd be called Scubaman, or maybe Ichthyotor.

"Whatcha doing there, Gray? Can't get enough of my ass?"

She'd roll her eyes again, except it was true. "If I hadn't seen your chest bare, I'd think you're wearing a superhero costume with built-in muscles."

"Careful, or you're going to swell my ego."

She circled to his front and let her gaze slide down his body. "Impossible. Your ego is already mammoth."

He slipped a hand behind her neck and pulled her close, but stopped short of kissing her. He chuckled. "You noticed. But then, of course you did."

She shook her head and pushed at his chest, wishing her heart hadn't raced with anticipation for the kiss that didn't happen. "Please. I get more satisfaction from my shower massager."

He laughed and pulled on his mask. "Time to get wet, then," he said and slipped into the Salish Sea.

She followed and cursed as the icy water filled her wetsuit. At least the new suit would warm quickly and stay warmer at depth.

She swam to the anchor line and grabbed on. For this dive, they'd descend as quickly as possible by climbing down the line hand over hand. They hadn't bothered with that on the first dive, because then, there'd been no hurry. It hadn't been a job, it had simply been an exercise to get her back in the water, plus they'd gone slower to ensure her ears would clear. But this time she was diving with a purpose and would need every minute she could get at the bottom, which meant as fast a descent as possible.

Bubbles skimmed along her body as she breathed in a slow, steady rhythm following Luke down the line. The world closed above her, reducing the scope of her realm to the only thing she could see with any clarity: Luke. He moved smoothly, his muscles working as he pulled himself ever downward. He made it look easy. Graceful. For her, it was damn hard work. Her biceps burned with the effort to keep up with his pace.

"How are your ears, Gray?" he asked.

"Clearing fine."

They'd planned their underwater exploration carefully last night, to maximize the area they would cover. She had her premeasured leash line encased in the mesh bag at her hip. The rope was much longer than before, so they'd be able to view a larger area as long as they moved quickly.

They reached the bottom, and Undine used the carabiner to hook on to the anchor line. She scanned the seafloor, searching for landmarks that would tell her how far they were from the site of their first dive. She spotted what she suspected was the excavation trench in the distance. "To the east," she said to Luke.

His nod was barely perceptible in the large dive mask. "I'll follow your lead," he said.

She swam to the cleared area. Four knots on the leash. "Damn, Ray's good. We're only twenty meters from our target."

"He's the best," Luke said.

The storm had churned the sediment. Only a faint trace of the trench berm remained. There was no chance she'd find tracks from the trenching robot here. Discouraged that they wouldn't easily be able to document the disturbance to the site, she released another ten meters of line, extending the radius of the survey circle. She and Luke would swim in a circle around the anchor line, but at different radii. He was at twenty-five, while she was at thirty. From there, they'd leapfrog down the line, each taking the next five-meter interval knot away from the center.

She was on her second circuit, a full twenty meters out from her starting point, when she saw a furrow indicating another excavation trench. It too had been dug before the storm, with only a faint berm of the trench remaining. "Luke, I've got something."

"On my way."

He swam up the rope to her side, his light growing brighter in the dark water even at that short distance. She dropped the leash so she could photograph the ridges of sediment, then swam to the center of the excavation and probed the soft floor with a telescoping ruler. She hit something solid eight centimeters down and cleared an area with her hand. The loose sediment moved easily but clouded the water. Luke joined her, his spotlight piercing the haze and revealing a swath of encrusted metal.

With a flick of her wrist, she fanned the sediment to the side. The ease with which it moved argued that a trencher had blown through recently, but it was possible storm currents had churned the sediment. The exposed curve of the large sheet of metal hinted at one thing. "This could be *Wrasse*'s hull."

"Looks like it," Luke said.

She swam forward, fanning with her hand. The contour of the metal was narrowing to a point. "Holy shit. Luke, look at this."

She'd kicked up too much sediment, and they had to wait for it to clear before what she'd glimpsed was again visible. "There's a wrinkle there and there. And the nose is crushed."

"*Wrasse* crashed into something before she went down," Luke said.

Undine's light swept through the cloudy water. She'd seen the charts. All large rocks and other hazards that projected from the sea floor in this part of the strait had been mapped. There was nothing this far from shore that should have threatened the *Wrasse*. Not at periscope depth.

"Yeah, but what did it hit?" she asked.

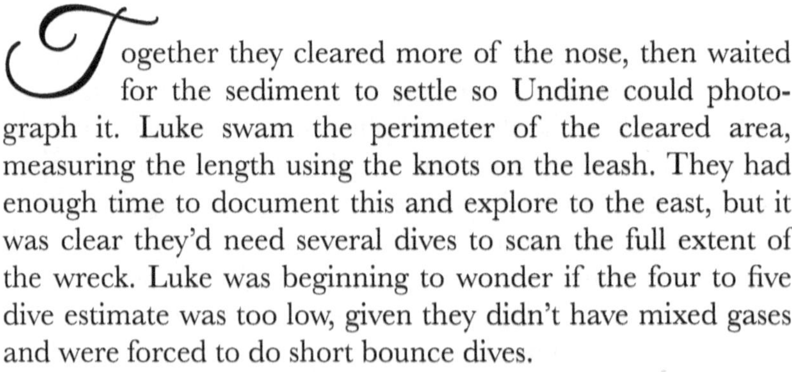

Together they cleared more of the nose, then waited for the sediment to settle so Undine could photograph it. Luke swam the perimeter of the cleared area, measuring the length using the knots on the leash. They had enough time to document this and explore to the east, but it was clear they'd need several dives to scan the full extent of the wreck. Luke was beginning to wonder if the four to five dive estimate was too low, given they didn't have mixed gases and were forced to do short bounce dives.

The Navy work order authorized as many dives as needed

to document the SMCA violation, which Undine had explained was the primary reason the Navy was expending the funds. With *Petrel*'s sinking having been ruled an accident, they weren't officially diving to investigate that wreck, even though the explosion was both his and Undine's motivation for being here. Finding out why someone had uncovered *Wrasse*'s nose could potentially explain why someone had blown up *Petrel*.

But the wreck was too deep to stay at depth for long. With more than a little dread, Luke wondered if Undine should—or even could—convince her dad to bring *Nereid* to the strait. The dive boat was an update of Cousteau's *Calypso*, and would have everything they'd need to safely explore the sunken submarine, including a remote-controlled unmanned submersible. There was something going on here, and quick bounce dives weren't going to cut it for long.

He pulled the leash taut to measure the excavation, when the line in his hand went slack. He tugged on the line, and it came to him without resistance. He glanced toward Undine, who was photographing the wrinkles in the sub nose. He pressed the button on his mask to speak. "'Deen, the leash came unhooked."

"Not possible. I used a carabiner."

"Then the carabiner came untied."

"No way. I tied it myself last night. I'm queen of knots."

She certainly had him in knots, but that probably wasn't what she meant. "We need to head to the anchor. We're low on time anyway." He swam, following the yellow line that lay on the sea floor. He'd gather it when they reached the anchor. A check of his dive computer indicated they had three minutes before they needed to ascend.

He reached the anchor and stopped short at what he didn't see. "Aww fuck." Probably good that he didn't hit the radio button for that, Undine would be freaked out enough.

He turned to face her and grabbed her gloved hand, then hit the button for the radio. "We have a problem."

She looked down at the anchor, then over his shoulder to where the line should be. She hit her radio button. "The boat lost the anchor. We have no line to follow up."

Chapter Fourteen

$\mathcal{U}$ndine was trying really hard not to hyperventilate. No anchor line. Nothing to hold on to during the decompression stop in a strong current. Would the boat even be there when they surfaced?

"Slow breaths, Undine." Luke's voice was calm. Controlled. He showed no hint of stress. "You can do this. You've had to do decompression without a line to hold on to before. That's why we have dive computers."

She nodded and focused on her breathing.

"Decompression will take longer without pure oxygen from the boat. We need to go now. Okay?" His calm, reassuring voice penetrated the fog of panic.

"Yes," she said firmly. "I can do this."

"I know you can, honey, or I never would have agreed to this." He used his dive knife to cut the leash line a meter from the end carabiner and clipped it to his belt. "Hold the line and my hand. We'll stay together. I'll set the pace. Remember, we want to stay behind our bubbles." He gently pushed off the bottom, and she followed.

Slowly they rose. "What…what do you think happened? To the boat?" she said.

"I'm sure the anchor line was frayed, and it snapped due to the current. Ray'll drop another anchor. He'll have drifted, but he won't be far when we surface."

She needed to hold on to that belief. "With *Petrel*, the first thing that happened was the anchor line broke." The dark waters above her head offered no hint of what awaited them at the surface.

"I know, honey. But this isn't *Petrel*. You're going to be fine. I won't let you get bent again. I promise."

She almost would have expected—and even welcomed— the cocky bastard with the huge ego, but Luke was all business. Calm, confident, and competent, the three characteristics she needed most. "I'm considering upgrading you from 'decent' to 'heroic,'" she said.

He chuckled, the sound distorted and breathy coming through the mask. "Let's wait until I've earned it. Right now, focus on your breathing and rate of ascent."

She focused, as instructed, on swimming, with just the slightest flick of her fins pushing her up and into the current. Occasionally she rose ahead of her air bubbles, but he slowed her with a tug on her hand.

He studied his dive computer. "We're drifting too far. We need to swim into the current a little harder. More horizontal than vertical."

If they got too far off, they might not find the boat when they surfaced, especially if the surf was high. Her breath came in rapid pants.

"Slow your breathing, Undine. You're doing fine."

She took a slow, deep breath, making sure there was no pause in her breathing either before or after. Skip breathing, or anything that required breath holding, was dangerous in scuba, and she wasn't a novice, even if she seemed like one in her panic.

God, Luke must think she was an idiot and be wondering why the Navy had ever given her permission to dive in the first place. "I'm not usually this…easily freaked out."

"At sixteen, you were one of the best divers I'd ever swam with, and you're even more experienced now. You got bent through no fault of your own, and you're scared because of what happened with *Petrel*. It's normal. Expected."

"We're going to be okay," she said, testing out the words.

"Yes. We will." His conviction was soothing.

It took forever to reach the decompression stop, but that was when things got even harder, making her wonder why she'd been eager to get there to begin with. They needed to maintain a constant depth while battling the current. They had weight belts to bring them down, and buoyancy compensator vests to float them, but nothing to keep them at that place in between except swimming into the current.

They both tried to remain as horizontal as possible so the pressure was equal across their bodies, and Luke tracked their depth and time with his dive computer. The computer gauged how long they needed to maintain their depth, but the numbers shifted as they fought the current.

Panic nipped at her fins. She couldn't see a shadow of the boat on the surface, and now that they were in range, they should be able to raise Ray on the radio. But he didn't respond to their hails.

"What do you usually do during decompression?" Luke asked.

"You mean aside from trying not to die?" Did her voice have an edge of hysteria? Probably.

"Yes," Luke said, with no hint of irony. "Aside from that."

"Read."

"What do you read?"

She knew what he was doing, and she wanted to resist.

She wanted to give in to the fear that had her whole body shaking, and either sink or surface. Because she was pretty sure her muscles were about to seize.

"You can do this, sweetheart. I know you can. Fifteen more minutes and we'll know what's going on at the surface. But right now, there's nothing—absolutely nothing—we can do about it. We *must* stay here. You are not getting bent on my watch."

She tightened her fingers around his wrist. She was probably cutting off his circulation, but she needed to feel him, which was hard through the neoprene gloves. "I like romance, usually with suspense." She braced herself for him to denigrate her choice of fiction. Maybe if she got a righteous anger going, she might forget about the arterial gas embolism that was in her immediate future.

"I've never read any romance. Who are your favorite authors?"

"There's one—Toni Anderson—who's a marine biologist. You'd like her."

"I'll check her out."

He was probably just humoring her, but she was okay with that. "What do you like to read?" she asked.

"Nonfiction mostly. But when I'm looking for a break, science fiction and fantasy."

A shadow passed overhead, and she looked up to see a large salmon, swimming in the current like a torpedo. Pure grace and speed. "Did you see that?" she asked Luke.

"Yeah. That's always been one of my favorite parts about decompressing. Being forced to just *be* in the water. Watching a salmon in the wild is nothing like seeing one in an aquarium."

"You don't read when decompressing?"

"Nope. Too much to see. Even in dark-as-hell water, there's always something."

Her teeth began to chatter, and she had to work to keep from floating up.

Luke rubbed her arm. "Dump some air from your BC."

She raised the hose, and bubbles escaped, and she settled without having to fight the rise.

His hand moved to her hip. "You got this, Undine. You're doing great."

"Liar. I'm within two heartbeats of losing it."

"Bull. Undine Gray doesn't lose it. Undine Gray can face down a grade-A asshole and convince him to take her diving. That took guts."

"That wasn't guts. That was desperation."

"Well then, dig down and find your inner desperation. Because you're going to need it for"—he checked his dive computer—"ten more minutes."

"Don't worry, my desperation is right at the surface." Her chattering teeth turned into shivering that spread from her belly outward. She focused on her breathing. On holding at the proper depth.

The minutes dragged on, and Luke stayed beside her, whispering encouragement. Holding her hand. Keeping her sane.

He also used the dive computer and kept them safe and on target, never showing a hint of the stress that she fought with every ripple of her fins.

Finally, Luke's computer cleared them for surfacing, and up they went.

They reached the surface, and she pulled off her full-face mask and took a deep breath. Luke did the same and slipped an arm around her waist and pulled her against him. He kissed her, quick but deep.

She cupped his face. "Thank you, Luke."

"Just doing my job, ma'am." He released her. "And I'm not done yet. Time to find Ray."

She scanned the water, waiting for a swell to lift her so she could see across the strait. A wave rolled over the surface, and up she went, seeing nothing toward the Pacific. Another swell, and she didn't catch sight of a boat to the east. "Luke?" she said, hearing the tremor in her own voice.

He put his mask back to his face and called to Ray on the radio. No response. She scanned in all directions. Looking toward the US, then Canada. A fully loaded freighter moved slowly in the distance. But no dive boat. No Ray.

Once again, panic threatened to suffocate her. She turned toward the Washington coastline. She was cold, exhausted, and more than a little terrified, but it was time to buck up. Luke had gotten her to the surface. She wouldn't drag him down now. She took a slow, steady breath, dropped her weight belt, and said, "Luke, you ready to swim?"

Chapter Fifteen

The nearest land, Waadah Island, which projected out from the breakwater that fronted Neah Bay, was two miles away. The swim would be brutal, cold, exhausting, and take at least an hour and a half. Luke knew Undine was scared. He'd seen—and felt—her trembling. But she'd held together like a champ on the world's longest decompression stop when she had to be on the verge of a PTSD-inspired panic attack. And now she'd turned and faced the next obstacle head-on.

He was impressed. And he would damn well get her to shore.

She was a strong swimmer, he knew, and they had fins. Their legs would do the work. The hardest part would be fighting the current. He gave thanks that she had the thickest, warmest wetsuit available. They had time before hypothermia set in.

He swam at her side, letting her set the pace. After a thousand yards, he stopped her and made her drop her empty air tank, inflate her BC vest, and float on her back. She was breathing heavily, and it was hard to know if that was due to the exertion or stress. Probably both, but she needed to ease up on the exertion and control her stress.

"We've got a long way to go," he said. "Let your fins do the work."

"I know. It's hard to hold back, though. To remember to pace myself, that we'll get there faster if I don't try to sprint."

"You always preferred sprinting over the distance swims, didn't you?"

"Go all out and done. Yep. That's me."

It was how she'd run the other night as well. Hell, it was how she'd lived, too eager to be an adult. And now that he understood her, it was a lot harder to hold that against her.

"Do you think…Ray left us?" she asked.

"No. The anchor was at the bottom; the line snapped. Ray wouldn't leave us. He must've had other trouble after the line broke, or he'd have been there."

She nodded. "He seemed…like a good guy." She still breathed heavily, but the rate was starting to even out.

"He *is* a good guy," he said.

"Someone might have sabotaged his boat." She turned her head to meet his gaze as she floated on the surface. "Someone could be trying to kill us. Kill me. Again."

He hated confirming that fear when the end result was still a possibility. An unlikely one, given that there was no way in hell he'd let anything happen to her, but he couldn't dismiss the fact that they still had a mile and a half to swim to the island. She physically had the strength, but panic was a dangerous factor, a wild card that could prevent him from quite literally keeping her afloat.

But placating lies could do more harm than good. She'd see right through it, and it would piss her off. "It's possible. Everyone at the Coast Guard knew we were diving today, and there's no telling who Ray might have mentioned it to. Neah Bay is a small town. Anyone who wanted to know what we were up to could easily find out, and we know someone is looking for something on the sub."

"But, killing us…wouldn't that just draw attention to the digging? It's too late to hide it."

He'd considered that—the slow ascent and long decompression stop had allowed for plenty of time to think—and he'd come up with only one reason that made sense. "It could be a delaying tactic. If something happened to us, the focus would be shifted to the boat—and to Ray—it would take days to get another pair of divers who could explore *Wrasse*." Her breathing had leveled out. "Time to go," he said. "Ready?"

She nodded, and again they were off, fighting the current, waves, cold, and fear. They took another break after five hundred yards, and the next after that at two hundred, the intervals getting shorter as she grew more tired. They'd only swum half the distance, and her energy was starting to fail.

She floated on her back, her breaths coming in shallow gasps.

"You've got this, Undine. As a mermaid, you *own* the damn sea."

"I'm not feeling"—hard gasp—"very"—another gasp—"mermaidish right now."

"I've always loved watching you swim," he said, trying another tactic.

"Bull. You're humoring me so you won't have to drag me to shore."

"True that I don't want to drag you, but I'm not humoring you. Watching you swim has always been a weird turn-on. I used to fantasize about having sex with you in the tank at the institute. Before I knew, I mean."

She sputtered out a laugh. "That would have gotten you fired even if I weren't the boss's underage daughter." Her breathing slowed a notch. "A couple did that once. They'd disabled the camera, and it was the middle of the night, so no one should have noticed, but my dad couldn't sleep, and his favorite thing to do when he can't sleep is…watch the fish in the big tank. I gather he turned on the underwater lights, and everyone got a huge surprise."

Luke laughed. "Was it anyone I know?"

"Nah, it was about four years after you left."

He couldn't help but stiffen at her wording. He hadn't simply left. But that was the problem with being around Undine. Too many triggers. Even in a situation as nutty as this was, swimming for their lives, he couldn't let it go.

Much as he wanted her—and he wanted her body more now than ever—there was no possibility for a real relationship. Not with the amount of baggage between them. And he might be an asshole, but he didn't think he was so depraved that he'd screw her again knowing that. She was just too vulnerable, and would be even more so after today.

"Let's do another two hundred," he said, and they set out.

They were down to hundred-yard intervals by the time they neared the island on the end of the spit, but once Undine had the destination in sight, she went full-bore, ignoring Luke's caution to pace herself.

She made it, but he figured she had nothing left by the time she stood up in the low surf and approached the beach on the eastern shore of the island. Cleared of the water, she collapsed and immediately cursed the cold sand at her back. "Washington may be pretty," she panted, "but sometimes, I hate it here."

He couldn't really argue with her on that as he collapsed next to her. His muscles burned. It had been forever since he'd had to do a swim like that—where it really mattered. At least swimming was low-impact or his injured hip would be throbbing.

In spite of his exhaustion, his adrenaline was pumping.

He wanted to pull Undine on top of him and kiss the hell out of her.

Okay, he wanted to do a lot more than kiss her, but the cold water had affected his…ego…so it would take him a few minutes. But he didn't act on the impulse. Didn't let the adrenaline win. Because he was a professional, and his job was to protect Undine's gorgeous ass and not fuck around until she was safe. And by the time that happened, the adrenaline would be gone and he'd be sane again and remember all the reasons he couldn't, shouldn't, and wouldn't.

They were both rising to their feet to begin the long trek across the island and over the spit, when two Coast Guard boats shot out of their harbor. A search party?

He and Undine stood and waved, not bothering to yell, knowing they'd never be heard over the roar of the engines and crash of the surf.

Both boats passed before one suddenly turned in their direction. They'd been spotted.

The boat slowed when it reached the tricky island coastline. The tide hid the shallow, treacherous rocks that were splendid tide pools at low tide. The narrow channels between rocks would be impossible for the vessel to navigate.

Undine let out a heavy sigh. "I guess it's back in the water for us." She took a shallow, graceful dive and moved through the channels with the ease of an eel.

Much as he wanted to admire her ass in that wetsuit, he followed and quickly reached the side of the boat, where Undine was already being pulled aboard.

Once on deck, they were given warm towels, and he asked what had happened to Ray and Parker.

"Not sure," the young Coast Guard boatswain's mate said. "We received a Mayday call just a few minutes ago. I gather there was both engine and radio trouble, but Lt. Reeves finally got the radio to work and let us know there were two divers down when the anchor snapped and the boat had drifted too far for you to see him when you surfaced."

"They're okay?" Undine asked.

"Yeah. And they were relieved when we radioed in that we spotted you."

"The Coast Guard will inspect Ray's boat for sabotage?" Luke asked.

"We're going to tow it into our marina. An investigator will be out tomorrow at the latest."

"Good," Luke said.

"We're going to take you to the station as well," the boatswain's mate added. "You can shower and get warm. We need to interview you, and the medic needs to check for signs of decompression sickness and hypothermia."

Luke nodded, knowing this was standard procedure.

He took a longer shower than he intended, but damn, it felt good to breathe uncompressed air while hot water poured down his back. He was toweling dry when Ray, Parker, and the boat arrived at the facility, and his clothes, wallet, and keys were returned to him.

They were all interviewed separately, which took time. He gathered that the sabotage on the boat was done well—individually, each problem could be an accident, or poor maintenance on Ray's part. The anchor line by itself could be an accident. Hell, he'd been on boats when that happened before, but he had a hard time believing Ray would screw up so badly and let a diesel engine run dry, and the fact that the radio went on the fritz at a critical time…that was highly improbable.

In all, three hours passed before a Coast Guard employee finally drove him and Undine to his truck in the tribal marina. Undine's cabin was just across the road, and she hugged the bag of her belongings to her chest and said, "I can walk from here. I'll let you know what my boss says after I talk to him about today's incident. He probably won't demand we dive again, and even if he did, we no longer have a boat. My guess is this is it."

Her sudden dismissal caught him completely off guard. "You're just going to walk away?"

"Oh. Um. I guess I should have said thank you. For saving my life. Again. You were heroic. I mean it."

For some reason, he hated hearing her repeat his egotistical tease in that dead voice. "I didn't mean you had to thank me. I don't want your thanks. I want to know why the hell you're walking away."

"Your responsibility to me is done. I asked if one of the Coast Guard guys could give me a ride back to Port Angeles tomorrow, and they said they could arrange something. You're off the hook. Free."

"What if I don't want to be free?"

She looked at him incredulously. "That's all you've wanted from the start."

"Well, I've changed my mind. I'm not done diving on the *Wrasse* wreckage. And you aren't either."

"Oh, yes I am."

"You need to dive there again for the same reason you did before. If you don't face it, it'll be that much harder to get in the water again."

Her nostrils flared, and he knew he had her. He didn't bother to ask himself why he was trying to convince her when she'd been right about him wanting to be free. All that mattered was she was scared. Scared enough to be willing to give up the thing that was most important to her. And he couldn't let that happen.

"The Navy won't authorize another dive for me at that depth after what happened today. We were already pushing the regs."

"So it won't be a Navy-funded dive. It'll be two private

citizens diving together. You're a civilian. They can't stop you."

She seemed to be holding her breath. When she finally met his gaze, her eyes were damp. "I'm scared, Luke. Someone tried to kill me. Kill you. All I want to do is fly home. I'd go tonight if it weren't too soon to fly after diving."

He stepped toward her and grabbed her biceps. "They tried, but they failed. You didn't get bent. You are just fine." He pushed her hair off her cheek and cradled her face with one hand. "As perfect as ever. And it would take a lot more to hurt me than what we did today. Hell, I had to face worse scenarios in SEAL training. You probably faced worse in Navy dive school."

"But in dive school, I didn't panic! I was a failure today."

"No, you weren't. Not even a little bit. You held it together, in spite of your PTSD. That was fucking amazing, how you pulled through when you had every reason to lose it."

"I want to go home," she said, her voice plaintive.

"Tough. I won't let you." He glanced at the row of cabins, her temporary home in Neah Bay. The burning grill on the porch last night didn't seem so innocent after what happened today. "And you aren't going back to your cabin either."

"I'm not?"

"No. You're moving in with me."

Chapter Sixteen

Undine put away her clothes in the loft bedroom of the oceanfront cabin. Luke had offered her the downstairs bedroom, but the ceiling was low over the loft. With his height, it would be difficult for him to escape bashing his head.

The whole situation was surreal. The cabin was small, cozy, and had a breathtaking view of the Pacific Ocean. The perfect romantic getaway, except that she was here because someone had tried to kill her, and a former SEAL had just declared himself her bodyguard. That he still traveled with a pistol shouldn't surprise her, but it did. He'd been keeping it locked in a rear storage compartment in his SUV, but from now on, he said it would be on the nightstand or holstered at the small of his back.

She wasn't squeamish around guns. She'd hung around with enough Raptor operatives in the last year—and even dated one—that she was familiar with men and women who wore them as part of their job. But Luke wasn't wearing it because his work required it. He was locked and loaded because someone had tried to kill them both.

She was having a hard time wrapping her brain around that, and an even harder time accepting that that person could well be Yuri, and the reason had something to do with the *Wrasse* excavation.

She hadn't been able to face calling Greg to give him the full update, so, coward that she was, she called Erica and gave her the details. Erica insisted they bring Mara into the conversation—which, admittedly, was probably who she *should* have called first. Sometimes she forgot Mara was head of NHHC and Greg was only in charge of UAB, but that was because Greg was determined to ignore Mara's authority, and in the grand scheme of things, Undine and Erica answered to Greg.

Mara alerted Curt, and Undine found herself passing the phone off to Luke, who briefed the attorney general on the security measures he was taking to protect Undine. Together, she and Luke shared what they'd learned from the Coast Guard, and Curt promised to press them for details on the investigation.

Now, with the important phone calls done, she unpacked and sat down on the bed, trying to catch her breath. Or her equilibrium. She wasn't quite sure. When her eardrums burst, she'd suffered vertigo. They'd healed, but she felt just as off-balance now as she had immediately after the explosion.

Sounds coming from the kitchen told her Luke was preparing dinner. She didn't know if she was hungry, or if she'd even be able to eat, but she was utterly humbled that he was taking care of her.

Talk about heroic. The guy should have a statue made in his honor. She glanced over the loft railing to see him chopping vegetables in exercise shorts and nothing else. The statue should be cast bronze, or maybe sculpted from marble. Definitely nude.

She descended the narrow staircase. "Shirtless cooking? Not that I'm complaining, mind you."

He grinned and flexed a bicep. "Someone insisted on putting the thermostat in the equatorial range."

"Oh. Uh, I guess I'm warm now. I'll turn it down."

"Or leave it. If you get hot, you could go topless. I won't mind."

She laughed. "Tempting. Can I help you chop?"

"Nah. Pretty much done. Just augmenting a bag of salad. Dinner will be simple. Sautéed veggies, salmon, and salad. Why don't you open the white wine I picked up in Forks? We'll sit on the porch and watch the sunset before I put the fish on the grill."

She opened the wine and poured them both glasses. She stood behind him and took a sip from hers as she admired his back.

"Just can't get enough of my ass, can you, Gray?"

"Never," she said, and slapped him on the butt. "The sun is getting low. Better get out there, or we'll miss the green flash."

"Good luck. I've been coming here on a regular basis for the last year, and have yet to see it."

She pulled on a thick fleece coat and stepped outside. The wind whipped her hair. She searched her coat pocket for a ponytail holder and felt lucky when she found one. She settled in a heavy plastic chair, and Luke joined her a minute later. Unfortunately he'd covered his body with jeans and a jacket.

They sat in silence sipping their wine as the sun descended toward the sea. After a while, he scooted his chair closer and draped an arm around her shoulder. She responded by leaning her temple against his shoulder.

She'd think about how weird it was to have this moment of harmony with Luke, but she didn't want to go there. She was *tired* of going there. "Thank you," she said, "for insisting that I stay. That I dive again. You're right. I need to do it. You're also right that we did fine today, and I need to remember that."

"I'm always right. Being right is one of my many talents." She laughed.

"Seriously, you did great. I was impressed."

"Thank you."

The sun hit the Pacific, and they were silent as they watched it disappear below the horizon. There was no green flash, but the hues of the sunset more than made up for it, as the sky transitioned from yellow to orange to pink and finally magenta. There were just enough clouds to hold the hues. The sunset was a gift, and exactly what she needed.

When the last drop of color disappeared from the sky, Luke stood. "I'll get the grill going."

The wind had whipped up, and Undine moved inside. It was nice to be in a cabin that had an actual couch, and chairs that weren't barstools. She'd liked her little place in Neah Bay, but it had been slightly more than a hotel room compared to this. Plus, she was grateful to have company.

When dinner was ready, she asked Luke if he'd like a second glass of wine. "Nope. On bodyguard duty. One glass is all I get."

"You really think someone could try again? Tonight? Here?"

"I have no idea, but I won't take chances by dulling my response time." He carried their plates to the table and held out a chair for her. She sat, getting a whiff of his warm musky scent as she brushed by him.

He sat across from her at the small, circular table. "I doubt we'll be able to line up a boat for tomorrow. We definitely won't have pure oxygen for the decompression stop without Ray. But I should be able to find a boat for the day after tomorrow."

"That's fine. I wouldn't mind having a day to mentally prep. And I've got a lot of calls to make tomorrow. I'm going to email Erica the photos I took of *Wrasse*. We may as well get started analyzing the scant information we have and see if we can figure out what the sub hit."

"I was thinking I could take you to Ozette or Cape Flattery, if you can spare a few hours."

She smiled and lifted her fork. "I'd like that."

As with everything when it came to Undine, the offer was impulsive. But he didn't regret it. She needed a break, and so did he. They settled into their meal and kept the conversation light. After dinner, she insisted on cleaning because he'd done all the cooking. He moved to the couch and pulled out his laptop to answer the afternoon and evening's accumulation of emails.

His boss had more questions about the potential for sabotage. Keith Hatcher, CEO of Raptor, emailed him privately to ask about Undine's mental state and asked Luke to call him. "I need to make a phone call," he told her and stepped outside for privacy.

Whoever had tried to kill Undine—and his money was on Yuri—so far had only gone for sabotage that could look like an accident, or straight-up opportunity, if the grill on the porch had been more than a drunken fisherman's carelessness. So he was likely safe from sniper shots on the porch, but he left the overhead light off all the same.

He dialed the number Keith had sent. Had Undine told her friend, the historian who was engaged to Keith, that Luke'd had sex with her the other night and walked away in the harshest way possible? If so, he was about to face shots from a different sniper, via the phone.

Keith's greeting was friendly enough. "Curt gave me a full update. Because this is a Coast Guard investigation, there isn't a need for him to get involved, but I understand he's reached out to the Special Agent in Charge in Seattle, to give her the heads-up that there could be an investigation coming across her desk. He's especially curious about the possible Russian/Ukrainian connection, and asked me to keep him in the loop with anything we learn about Yuri."

Luke dropped into the heavy plastic chair, shaking his head. Unbelievable that the US attorney general was monitoring the investigation. If Yuri Kravchenko really was behind the attempts on Undine's life, the man was in for a nasty surprise. "Is the FBI going to start digging into Yuri's background?" he asked.

"Right now, this falls under Coast Guard jurisdiction. Plus today you were diving on a Navy contract. The Navy will likely defer to the Coast Guard, but they will open their own investigation if they aren't satisfied with the Coast Guard's findings. But all that will take time, which is one reason Curt contacted me. I can cut some corners. Given that Undine engaged Raptor's services after your first dive—which wasn't a government-funded operation—and asked me specifically to look into Yuri Kravchenko, we can be involved. Basically we're operating as PIs on this, but I can also provide personal security for Undine if you'd like to be relieved of that duty."

And there they were, the real reason for this call. Luke was being given a gracious out. He glanced through the gap between the long curtains hung over the sliding glass door that fronted the cabin. Undine had settled on the couch with a tablet in her hands. The soft glow of the lights caressed her pale skin, and his heart rate picked up just looking at her.

When he went inside, he'd find a clip to hold the curtains

together at the center. Not for privacy, but for safety. Every-thing he did over the next few days would have that priority.

"No. I've got this," he said to Keith.

"I've read your service record—"

"Yeah. I heard." He said it with more amusement than anger. He'd been irritated at first, but appreciated the protec-tiveness Undine's friends had for her. He was starting to feel that way himself.

"Yeah, about that. I'd say I'm sorry, but I'm not. Trina was concerned about Undine's PTSD and her overall emotional state. Given that you two had a history, and Undine fixated on asking you to take her down again, Trina wanted to know what sort of person you are. If you hadn't checked out, she'd have insisted I send one of my skilled divers out to partner Undine. But one thing was clear when I checked your record—I don't have any guys who have close to your experience underwater. It was obvious Undine had chosen the best man for the job and hadn't picked you because she wanted an excuse to see you."

"That's also why I said yes," Luke said.

"Which told me you're a decent human being."

Luke suppressed the urge to suggest heroic as a better adjective. The ridiculous boasts were for Undine's amusement.

"So having read your service record, I know you've got the skills to protect her, but if you want out, I can send a guy."

"How can you afford this? I know Undine can't pay."

"I have a discretionary fund set up by the company owner for things like this. Clients who can't afford our services but whose safety we take a personal interest in—either due to personal relationship or for national security reasons. Undine is family, and the potential for Ukrainian involvement makes this a no-brainer."

"Is that why you were involved in Ian Boyd and Cressida Porter's exfil from Turkey?" Luke had read the news accounts at the time and noted Raptor's involvement, which had been a footnote in the reports. Undine had mentioned Cressida once or twice, and he'd gathered she now worked for NHHC.

"Exactly. Cressida and Trina are close friends, which put her situation on our radar." He paused. "If you give me three days, I can send either Sean Logan or Josh Warner. Both are former SEALs. Neither has your experience underwater, but you guys who were based in Pearl Harbor are hard to match. By the way, if you hear any of your old buddies are looking for work, send them my way."

"I'll do that." Keith was pushing hard the idea of Luke relinquishing protective duty for Undine, making him certain Keith knew some of the uglier details of his interactions with her. "Listen, I'm in this now, whether I want to be or not. She had a tough time today but she handled it like a champ. If I walk away from her, it would only set her back further. I won't do that to her."

"Good. As I said, Undine is family. I didn't want to have to get all protective on your ass."

"Yeah. I'd kind of like to avoid that too. Undine tells me you were a sniper…" He rubbed the back of his neck and searched for something to say. "So…you know the guy who shot bin Laden?"

Keith laughed. "No. You?"

"Nah. Dickhead."

"Yeah. Oath-breaking asshole."

Luke watched Undine through the gap and felt a sensation in his chest that was something other than lust. "I don't break oaths, Keith, and I won't let anything happen to her."

*L*uke seemed anxious when he stepped back inside the cabin. "Who did you call?" Undine asked.

"Keith."

Ah hell. Was this more meddling from Trina or genuine Raptor business? Undine loved Trina, she really did, and was touched that Trina cared enough to get involved, but harassing Luke was going too far. "He doesn't know," Undine said, "about the other night. I mean, I didn't tell Trina. So if he was a jerk, it wasn't because of that. And if he *was* a jerk, I'm sorry and I promise to kick his ass when I get home."

Luke paused before her and held out a hand. "C'mere."

She rose, and he pulled her against him, wrapping his arms around her waist. His big, broad body surrounded her in an all-encompassing hug. She tucked her face against his chest and wanted to melt with the pleasure of just being held.

When the embrace ended, she stepped back. "What was that for?"

"I just needed to hold you, I guess." He stroked her cheek. "Keith was fine. He just wanted to make sure I intend to see this through. My guess is he wanted to be certain our past wouldn't interfere with my ability to protect you. Honestly, that question didn't occur to me. I'm not thinking about the past anymore." He held her gaze, his eyes intent. "But I never asked you if you want me for your bodyguard. Keith said he could send an operative with dive experience. If you'd prefer someone from Raptor, say the word. I'll stick with you until they get here, then bow out."

Her heart squeezed. It would make sense if Luke wanted an out. "Is that what you want?"

"This isn't about what I want. It's about keeping you safe, and if you aren't comfortable with me, you won't be safe. You know the guys from Raptor. You might be more at ease with them."

"You didn't answer my question. Do you want out?"

"No."

Relief flooded her. Given their history, she'd held herself back from making a move on Luke. He had initiated every kiss and touch, which was unlike her. She preferred being the initiator, and it was time to stop being timid with him. She pushed him into her vacated seat on the couch and straddled him. She draped her arms around his neck as his hands closed on her waist. "Good, because you're the only person I want with me underwater or on land."

She kissed him, and there was nothing tentative about her kiss or his response. Their tongues intertwined and his arms tightened, pulling her closer. His hands slid up her back, under her arms. When he reached her shoulders, he pressed down at the same time he ground upward with his hips. His thick erection pressed against the juncture of her thighs, and she groaned at the sparks of pleasure the sensation triggered.

She could think of nothing better than having Luke inside her, of losing herself in the joining of their bodies. She wanted his mouth on her, and she wanted to go down on him. She sucked on his tongue, imagining the head of his cock in her mouth and how she'd tease him until she finally relented and made him come.

His hands moved to her breasts, and she pressed against him to let him know she approved of the action. She tugged at his shirt. She wanted to be skin to skin. To run her hands over his incredible body and let him know exactly how much she appreciated the hours he spent in the gym.

Luke leaned back his head and released her mouth, flinging his hands wide at the same time. "Shit, Undine. I can't do this."

All hell, here it was. He'd throw their history in her face again. Anger surged. She might have initiated it, but he'd been an active participant in the kiss-and-grope. "Dammit, Luke, I'm getting tired of you holding the past against me—"

"No! That's not what I meant." His hands closed around her hips when she made a move to scramble off his lap. "I meant it when I said I'm not thinking about the past anymore. I'd be happy to never think about it again."

"Then what's the problem? I want you. You want me. We're single, consenting adults."

"If I have no-strings sex with you now, today, while you're vulnerable, it would make me a complete asshole. We've already established that I'm an asshole, but that's going too far, even for me."

"I'm okay with no-strings sex."

"You're saying that because you're ramped up. I am too. I want to bury myself inside you and forget everything for a little while. But I won't take advantage of you that way. Not when all I can offer you is a no-strings, no-emotion fuck. We already did that, and you were pissed when I walked out. This time I *can't* walk out. I made a promise to protect you. So we'd be stuck together in a tiny cabin, and you'd start regretting tonight pretty damn fast."

His logic was solid, and she couldn't ignore the hint of hurt at the fact that he wasn't willing to consider anything beyond a no-strings fling, which meant that her emotions were already engaged.

No matter how much she wanted to deny it, it was too late for her to have emotionless sex with him. She climbed off his lap and rubbed her arms, feeling cold again even though the thermostat was still set high.

"I'm sorry, Undine."

She nodded. "I guess I need to be content that you don't hate me anymore, and leave it at that."

"If it's any consolation, turning you down right now is sort of killing me. I can guarantee I'll be jacking off later."

"Yeah, well, I hope the shower has a massage head."

He closed his eyes and let out a small groan. "Okay, now I know what I'm going to imagine while I jack off." He got to his feet and pressed a soft kiss to her lips. "I like the woman I've gotten to know these last few days. I'm glad that when this is all over, we can both move forward with peace between us."

His words made it achingly clear that there would be no friendship, no ongoing contact, and she felt bereft just thinking about it. Trina had believed Undine was hung up on Luke from the moment she shared the sordid tale. What would Trina say when Undine returned to DC and it became clear that this time she really had lost her heart to Luke Sevick?

Chapter Seventeen

"Time to get up, sunshine."

Luke's voice was entirely too cheery for… She glanced at the clock on the nightstand, then pulled her pillow over her head. It ought to be illegal to be that happy to be awake at any time before seven in the morning. "Go away."

"But we need to get our morning run in before we go to the gym. You don't want to miss the sunrise."

"Yes. Yes. I *do* want to miss the sunrise. I love missing the sunrise. It's my favorite thing to miss." She peeked out from under the pillow and fixed him with a one-eyed glare in the dark bedroom. "And for future reference, the only acceptable reason to wake me this early is for sex. Or fresh baked cinnamon rolls, and even then they better have frosting."

He laughed. Usually she found the sound pleasant, but now it made her want to smother him with her pillow, just until he quieted and let her sleep. She wasn't a monster.

"I take it you aren't a morning person," he said in that grating, cheery tone.

"I like mornings just fine. Morning starts at seven on workdays, and nine on non-workdays."

"Today it starts at six fifteen because I need a run. And after we run, we're going to the gym."

"So your plan is torture then?"

"How do you think I got this amazing body you admire so much? It takes work, sweetheart."

"Fine. Go work. I'll sleep. I'll be sure to admire your perfection when you get back. Everyone wins. Now let me sleep." She flipped over on the queen-sized bed, presenting her back to him, then pulled the covers higher.

The bed dipped as he settled beside her and pulled her close, until he nearly spooned her, but for the layers of blankets that separated them. He nuzzled her neck. "Maybe I should have started this way. Woken you slowly."

She wanted to purr, the caress felt so sweet.

He nipped at her shoulder. "But now's not the time for this," he murmured against her skin, "Because we need to go for a run."

He really was a bastard that he'd kiss her to cajole her *out* of bed. "It's really okay with me if you go for a run without me. In fact, I'll give you my Fitbit, and we'll both get steps."

"It doesn't work that way. And I can't run without you. I'm your bodyguard. Your body has to be with me, so I can guard it."

"Then don't run."

"But I *need* to. And sunrise on the beach is my favorite time to run. It's even low tide, so we'll have plenty of shoreline. C'mon, Undine. Don't you want me to keep in shape?"

She groaned. "You're really going to make me do this."

"I'll let you cop a feel of my ass."

She shook her head and laughed. "Do you seriously expect me to go to the gym afterward?"

"Yes. But after that I'll take you to the restaurant for breakfast. You can get a cinnamon roll. With frosting."

"What if I just go to the restaurant and get a cinnamon roll, while you maintain your magnificent shape?"

"No way. We're stuck together." He nudged her onto her back and slipped his hands around both of her wrists, pulling them above her head. He leaned down and nuzzled her neck some more. "Please, sweetheart? I usually get up at five thirty for my workout, but I waited until after six to wake you. I'm considerate that way. Don't you think my consideration should be rewarded?"

"Five thirty? Willingly? That's inhuman."

"It takes time to maintain this shape. Hours. Every day. Which means I get up early."

She wanted to pout, but the way he kept teasing her neck with his lips made it impossible. She groaned and said, "Fine. We can go for a run."

He kissed her, a soft brush of his lips against hers. "You won't regret this, sweetheart."

"I already do."

The morning run wasn't the most awful thing in the world. She actually liked running, just not before seven in the morning. The sky lightened as they ran along the Pacific Ocean, and eventually the sun peeked over the rocky hills that lined the beach. Out of deference to her, Luke maintained a pace that had to be aggravatingly slow for him, considering how smoothly his body ate the distance.

He wasn't kidding about his dedication to fitness, or the amount of time it took from his day. After the run they went to the gym, which was next to the general store, not far from her old cabin, and he did a "short" hour-long workout.

"You do this every day?" she asked as she watched him lift weights. She'd participated in the CrossFit-style workout for the first twenty minutes, but after her AMRAPs were done she decided to sit out the rest of the class. She was good for the day considering they'd started with a three-mile run.

"I try, but I don't always have time for the run."

Watching Luke exercise was something of an aphrodisiac, and she mentally cursed him for putting the brakes on their fun last night. Surely she could handle a little no-strings action?

But if she were being honest, she couldn't.

Meaning he was right again, damn him.

Workout complete, Luke took her to breakfast as promised, and she undermined her virtuousness in running by ordering a giant meal. She set down her fork after having cleaned her plate. Full to bursting, she wanted to go back to the cabin and take a nap, but figured she should be pragmatic. "While we're in town, let's stop by the museum and check on the electrolytic reduction on the metal case."

"Good idea. I want to stop by the Coast Guard and see if they'll send out a patrol boat during our next dive. Since our dive won't be for the Navy, this won't be an official request, but I think Parker will be on board with the idea."

"Okay. I like the idea of the boat having backup even more than having Parker available as a secondary diver."

At the museum, Undine was happy to see Annie, the tribal member who'd helped her set up the electrolytic reduction tank, was working at the admissions counter. Annie greeted her with a big smile. "I've been dying to take a look at what's in the tank, but the water is so clouded with rust, it's hidden."

"Can you take a break now?" Undine asked.

"Give me a minute and one of the docents can spell me."

Undine and Luke browsed the gift shop while the woman went to track down someone to take over the counter. A green shawl with a Coast Salish hummingbird motif caught her eye. She was completely broke, but it was beautiful and she could wear it in the cabin instead of setting the thermostat at eighty and making poor Luke wear nothing but exercise shorts. Although, she liked it when Luke wore nothing but shorts…

She set it back on the shelf. She really couldn't afford any extras right now. She still had to figure out how she was going to pay Luke back for the wetsuit.

"That'll bring out the green in your eyes," Luke said.

"My eyes are brown, not green."

"Your eyes have a lot of green in them. Especially when you're in the water, or wearing pale green shades, like that one." He plucked the shawl from the shelf and went to the checkout counter.

"What are you doing?" she asked.

"Bribing you."

"Bribing me?"

"I'm going to give this to you tomorrow morning when I wake you at five thirty so we can go for a run."

"You aren't really going to do that."

"I am. And you'll agree because you want this shawl more than sleep."

"There are few things I want more than sleep. You've denied me one of them, and I can promise, that shawl, much as I like it, isn't another."

"Six o'clock, then."

"Six o'clock, *and* I get the shawl?" She paused to consider. "Okay. But no gym."

"Oh no. If I'm buying you the shawl I get a run and gym time."

"There's something seriously wrong with you if you like working out that much."

He flashed a grin. "And yet you love the results."

Yes. Yes, she did.

Annie returned with a docent, and he purchased the item then handed it to Undine. "Don't worry, I'll still parade shirtless around the cabin if you want."

"I want," she said, utterly shameless. But not shawllless. She opened the package and pulled out the soft cloth.

Luke took it from her hands and draped it around her shoulders. "Yep. Beautiful." His mouth brushed against hers.

"Uh, you ready to go check out the conservation lab?" Annie asked with laughter in her voice. "Or can I convince you to buy Undine one of our silk scarves? They're a little pricier, but gorgeous."

"If you want to go jogging the day after tomorrow, I'm going to require silk," Undine said.

"I've set a dangerous precedent, haven't I?" Luke asked.

"Yep." She took his hand and headed for the front door. "Let's go see how your boon is doing."

In the museum conservation facility across the parking lot, Annie unplugged the power supply to the reduction tank, then Undine removed the negative and positive leads. She donned rubber gloves before dipping her hands into the opaque brown water in the medium-sized fish tank. Her hands closed on the case, and she paused. She loved this part of lab work, the big reveal.

Slowly, she lifted out the metal object, and Annie gasped and said in an excited tone, "The sides look almost new."

Brown water dripped off the much-cleaner metal case. Annie was right, the flat surfaces had cleaned well. Undine turned the case in different angles to allow the water to drain as she examined it. "There's still too much oxidation on the hinges, clasps, and seam to open it. They probably used a different metal alloy—one that was more prone to corrosion. But we can rinse it off and take a look at the top and bottom."

"Wow. It's *so* much better, though. I really doubted there was solid metal beneath all that rust," Annie said.

"The US Navy made things to last back in the sixties," Undine said. "This case was built like a safe."

She carried it over to the deep lab sink and set it inside, then turned on the faucet. The rust-colored water soon ran clear from what Undine guessed was a solid-steel case. Annie stood on one side and Luke the other as the flat surface cleared.

"Something is etched on the front," Annie said.

Undine had noticed the markings when she first pulled the case from the tank, and now directed the spray on the etching. "Letters under a star."

"Undine, are you sure this came from *Wrasse*?" Luke asked.

She shrugged. "What else could it be from?" She looked closer at the faint marking inside the star and gasped, understanding Luke's question.

"CCCP?" Annie asked. "What does that stand for?"

"It's not English," Luke said. "It's Cyrillic." He pointed to the star. "And barely visible in the middle of that star, is a hammer and sickle."

Chapter Eighteen

*Y*uri had pushed himself and his team to the limit to clear *M-357*'s tube. The Soviets had been so uncreative, giving their subs numbers instead of names. They should have let Tom Clancy name them. *Red October*, now there was a name. Yuri had taken to calling the Soviet vessel *Magnum*, which worked both for the M and the 357. His little pet name for his not-so-little pet project.

He'd located the torpedo tube the night before last, but by the time he had it, he didn't have enough bottom time to grab the contents. He'd been forced to resort to sabotaging Ray's boat, in case Gray and Sevick glimpsed *Magnum* during their dive. He'd hoped they wouldn't surface and be able to share their tale, but knowing the SEAL's skills, he'd hedged his bet by giving them something else to find. Hopefully they'd been too distracted by *Wrasse*'s crumpled nose to have ventured west of the US wreck.

Gray had to have freaked out, but Sevick had lived up to his reputation. Yuri would have shot them when they were on the beach at Wadaah, but the Coast Guard had shown up before he could get a decent line of sight. He wasn't a sniper. Odds were, he'd have missed.

After they'd shared their story with the Coast Guard, there'd hardly been a reason to kill them. Plus Yuri'd had to get his ass back out on the water as soon as the sun set to clean out the tube. Two nights in a row, he'd been forced to make two dives without a sufficient surface interval in between. But it couldn't be helped.

Now his joints ached. He'd fitted himself with an oxygen tank, like he had emphysema and would take it easy all day, letting his nephews pilot the boat and take care of him.

They'd wanted to spend the day celebrating with vodka. At times the boys could be complete dumb fucks. The twins were irritated by the need to take turns venturing into town, but it was imperative that they not be noticed, and a pair of Ukrainian boys showing up drunk in the dry community would certainly be noticed. As it was, Yuri couldn't set foot in the general store or any of the restaurants. Even with the beard, he was liable to be recognized. He was dependent on his nephews bringing him groceries.

Plus, it was too soon to celebrate. They still needed the keys.

They would have to dive again. But not tonight. No. Yuri needed to recover, and the dumb fucks had had too much to drink before Yuri could stop them. He'd dumped the vodka overboard and they were sobering up. They'd lay low, anchor the boat off the coast at Sekiu, and Yuri would breathe his oxygen.

Tomorrow night, he'd dive again. He'd find the key. Then he'd take his vengeance on Mother Russia and every country that turned their backs on the plight of his people.

"Cyrillic?" Annie asked. "What does CCCP stand for?"

"It's the Russian initials for USSR." Luke turned to Undine. "Is there *any* chance *Wrasse* was on a secret mission? That it wasn't really being brought out to the Pacific for SINKEX?"

"None. We'd have been warned if we were likely to come across anything top secret on the sub. And if it had been on a secret mission, the effort to find her would have been mammoth in 1962. After all, she went down in the middle of the Cuban Missile Crisis. The Navy would never have hired a contractor to set up the dive. Yuri wouldn't have gotten near this project."

He nodded, agreeing with her logic. He studied the corrosion around the seam of the case and along the hinges. What the hell was inside? They couldn't risk forcing it open when they had the means to remove the corrosion. "We need to get this back in the tank and finish the electrolysis." To Annie, he said, "You can't tell anyone about this. No one can know that this case is here."

"The curator knows," Annie said. "He's the one who agreed Undine could use the tank."

"That's fine. Make sure he tells no one. Until we know what this means, this has become classified."

"We need to call Curt," Undine said.

Luke nodded. He placed a hand on her forearm. "I'm sorry, honey, but you and I need to dive again today. This morning."

She paled. "Today?"

"Yes. Time is critical. If there's something else down there—something Soviet—we can't waste time. It's probably what Yuri's been looking for, and he may already have found it. We need to know what we're dealing with ASAP. You and I can do another quick bounce, get answers, then let the Navy take over. It'll probably be our last dive." He winced. Poor wording, but it was true. The Navy would send specialists if they found what Luke suspected they would.

"Plus, if we go immediately, there won't be an opportunity to sabotage the boat or our equipment," he continued. "Yuri won't expect us to dive today. No one does. I need you, Undine. No one else in Neah Bay has the skills to do this dive with me, and I can't do this alone."

A hundred different emotions flashed across her face, each one a variation of fear. "How ironic," she said with a weak smile.

He grunted out a laugh. "Yeah. But here we are. I need you to take me down. I was a SEAL. I'm here. I have the skills needed. I can't ignore what could well be a national security issue. We can have answers in less than two hours."

"Where will we get a boat?"

"We'll do this one simple. A speedboat. No pure oxygen for decompression. We can get Curt Dominick to ask the Coast Guard to send out a patrol boat. Because of the safety regs, this can't be a government dive, so we can't use a Coast Guard vessel—this'll be at our own risk. But that doesn't mean they won't stand by after receiving a little pressure from the US attorney general. So what do you say, will you dive with me?"

She squared her shoulders and nodded.

He hadn't doubted her answer, but the fortitude she showed in giving it impressed the hell out of him. But then, almost everything she did impressed him. He kissed her, a quick hard press of his mouth to hers. "Thank you."

"Call Curt. I'm going to photograph the case, then get it back in the tank."

Luke already had his phone out and found Curt's private cell number in the contacts list. The AG answered immediately and wasted no time with pleasantries. "What's going on, Sevick?"

"The FBI needs to track down Yuri Kravchenko's boat. We've reason to believe he's looking for something Soviet near where *Wrasse* sank." As he explained the find to Curt, Undine emailed the man photos of the case with a close-up of the etching.

After Curt viewed the pictures, he cleared his throat. "I can't ask you or Undine to dive on the wreck. I need to go through channels. My process would take time."

"I know that, sir. Which is why I asked my civilian friend Undine if she could take a vacation day and go for a swim with me. She said yes."

"She's a fighter, our Undine." There was affection in the AG's voice.

My Undine.

Luke kept his gaze on her as she cleaned out the reduction tank. Was he really going to be able to walk away from her when this was all over? He was no longer certain.

"We'll be swimming two miles out in the strait. It might be nice if the Coast Guard could do a drive-by. Maybe hang out, even. Nothing official, mind you. Maybe a routine patrol?"

"I'll make sure of it. What time?"

Luke glanced at his watch. He needed at least an hour to line up a boat. He had no doubt Ray would be willing to skipper. "Two hours. High noon."

"Got it. I'll call you when it's confirmed. Thank you, Luke."

"Just doing my job, sir."

"Once a SEAL, always a SEAL?"

"Something like that." He hung up. His heart pumped with excitement. When he was a SEAL, he lived for the next op. He'd had a long break, but this was it. The next op.

Complete with national security on the line. He loved his job with NOAA, and yet he hadn't realized how much he'd missed the adrenaline-fueled action of serving his country as a SEAL.

Who would have thought Undine Gray's desperate plea seven days ago would lead to running a mission in search of a Soviet connection?

*S*teely calm settled over Undine before she even slipped into the cold water. This was no longer about her personal fears, or even an SMCA violation. She knew in her gut exactly what they'd find when they reached the bottom. *Wrasse's* crumpled nose had been the first clue. And taking immediate action to confirm her suspicions was more important than her, than Luke, probably more important than anything she'd ever done in her life. She wouldn't let Luke down.

Again they descended with speed, pulling themselves down along the anchor line. Her arms ached from the morning workout. Luke's muscles must be screaming, but he descended with ease.

At the bottom, they didn't waste time with leash lines. They had dive computers to guide them and too big an area to cover. They could only hope what they were looking for had been conveniently exposed by Yuri.

They were down to four minutes left at depth when Luke spotted a ridge of sediment that indicated an area had been cleared. He jetted in that direction, and Undine followed, shining her spotlight on the floor. She reached the clearing and felt a pulse of adrenaline. The area had been cleared by a cable trencher, probably less than twenty-four hours ago. They might have seen this yesterday if they'd ventured into this area, but they'd been exploring *Wrasse* and stopped when they saw her crumpled nose.

This wasn't *Wrasse.*

No, this was the conning tower and hull of a small Cold War-era Soviet submarine.

"Twin guns mounted at the forward end of the tower," she said as she snapped pictures. "The Soviet Union stopped using deck-mounted guns in the late fifties."

"This is too small to be nuclear powered," Luke said.

"Plus none of their nuclear subs had deck-mounted guns. This must have been one of their coastal attack subs. Small and maneuverable."

"A Soviet coastal attack sub," Luke said, the awe in his voice audible even through the tinny speakers. "*Wrasse* rammed and sank a Soviet sub in US waters in October 1962."

Emotion flooded Undine as she turned to face *Wrasse*'s final resting place in the dark distance. "Her complement was seven retired sailors, led by an admiral who joined the service during World War I. They were unarmed and blind but for their periscope. And for over fifty years, no one knew they died in a Cold War submarine battle in the middle of the Cuban Missile Crisis."

Chapter Nineteen

"Last spring, the week after Russia sank the passenger ferry on the Sea of Azov and tried to make it look like Ukraine was behind it, Yuri Kravchenko changed his will, leaving his boat to his twin nephews. A month later, those nephews obtained work visas sponsored by a Seattle-based tech company and moved to the city." US Attorney General Curt Dominick delivered the information via speakerphone to a group settled around a conference table at the Coast Guard Station. That the attorney general was personally involved in the investigation wasn't lost upon Commander Brian Martinez, the Coast Guard Station's commanding officer, who seemed to sit at attention, not that Luke could blame him. He felt the same way.

"The tech company might be a front for several factions allied against the Russian government, including Chechen rebels and Ukrainian neo-Nazis. I've got investigators delving into the company now. It's possible it was set up by former-Soviet Bratva groups and may even have ties to Georgian and Azerbaijani Mafia," Dominick continued. "This has opened up a whole new avenue of investigation. As far as Yuri

Kravchenko is concerned, we know that prior to the ferry sinking, his heir was his sister—mother of his twin nephews—and we now have confirmation that she died in the ferry incident."

So Undine was right, his outrage over the sinking was personal.

"Where are the nephews and the boat now?" Undine asked.

"That, we don't know," Curt said. "The nephews moved out of their Seattle address the day they claimed the boat. No one has seen or heard from them since. In all likelihood, the name has been changed and the boat painted. They had weeks to get the boat ready to search for the Soviet sub while investigation of the explosion was underway."

"I'll send patrols to check every marina and dock between here and Port Angeles." Commander Martinez fixed his gaze on the window that overlooked the strait. "They could just as easily be putting in at Port Renfrew or somewhere else along the Canadian coast."

"Yes," Curt said. "I'd like you to contact your counterpart in Port Angeles and send photos of the vessel in addition to the ID photos of the nephews provided by INS."

"How long before the Navy or Coast Guard can get divers out to examine the Russian sub?" Undine asked.

"We're working on that. As you know, getting divers with the right expertise isn't easy. For now, the first priority will be to watch the site, see if Yuri and his team show up in the night to continue their excavation. I trust you have a plan to monitor the strait, Commander?"

"Yes, sir. We already have a boat in position to intercept. However, we don't expect him to show until after it gets dark. If we do catch him, I assume we're to hand him over to federal authorities?"

"Yes. Officially, he'll be charged under federal law with

the murder of federal employee Sandy Tyson and the attempted murder of Undine Gray, also a federal employee."

Beside Luke, Undine stiffened. He reached under the table and took her hand. She squeezed his fingers. She'd been cool, composed, and competent during every moment of the dive today and the lengthy debriefing process afterward.

"The US Attorney's office in Seattle will handle the case," Curt continued. "And in all likelihood, espionage will be added to any charges filed against Kravchenko." Curt cleared his throat. "On behalf of the US Department of Justice, I want to thank both Ms. Gray and Lt. Sevick for their assistance in volunteering to dive today. I know it was dangerous and not something that could have been accomplished so quickly if we went through government channels."

"It's always an honor to serve, sir," Luke said.

"I'm glad we were able to help," Undine said. "It's humbling to realize what the seven men aboard *Wrasse* must have done. I hope further excavation will bring the full story to light. I'd like to see those men honored for the heroes they were."

Luke had no doubt that would happen. He'd gotten chills when he looked at the Soviet sub—and the sensation had nothing to do with the frigid water.

After the meeting wrapped up, Luke draped an arm around Undine's shoulder and walked with her to his SUV. Their rinsed dive gear had been stowed in the back of his vehicle when they returned to shore. They were packed up and free to leave.

He turned on the engine, then paused before backing out of the parking space. "The Coast Guard, the Navy, and the Department of Justice all have what they needed from us. Odds are Yuri has no reason to come after you again—in all likelihood, he was trying to stop us from finding the sub. We're done with diving on *Wrasse* and with Neah Bay."

She nodded but said nothing. He'd bet if he touched the base of her throat, he'd feel her pulse racing.

"I can take you back to Hobuck to pack up, then drive you to Port Angeles tonight. In two days, you'll be fine to fly home."

Her gaze was intent. Reserved. "Do you want to take me back to Port Angeles tonight?"

"No."

Her spine stiffened, but she showed no other outward reaction. "Why not?"

Heat unfurled from his belly as he gave her the honest answer he'd promised himself he wouldn't. "Because I want to make love to you on every flat surface in the cabin, and up against two of the walls."

"Which two?"

"Bedroom and hall. Also, come to think of it, the stairs."

"I thought sex was out while I'm vulnerable?"

"Well, it turns out, I *am* a complete asshole. And this would just be a one-night thing. I still plan to drive you back to PA tomorrow. After we go for our morning run, of course."

"But if you don't need to be my bodyguard anymore, you can run without me."

"Yeah, but I bought you a shawl. So you've gotta run. A deal's a deal."

"But I just slow you down."

"So? I like running with you." He firmed his lips. "Okay, I told you what I want. What do you want? If you want to go back to Hobuck for the night but don't want me to touch you, that's fine too."

She lifted his hand from her knee and pressed his palm to her breast. He cupped her, then ran his thumb over her nipple, which he could feel was erect even through her bra and sweatshirt. He slipped his hand under the sweatshirt and bra cup so he could tease her nipple directly.

"Take me to the cabin," she said, a breathy plea that made him rock hard.

He leaned forward and kissed her, his tongue dipping inside her mouth for a quick but deep kiss. He needed to get out of the Coast Guard parking lot before they broke indecency laws. "I'm adding the shower to my list. I want to play with you and the massage head."

Luke stripped Undine the moment they were inside with the door locked and curtains closed. He then scooped her up and dropped her on the kitchen table. "Table first," he said, and spread her thighs. His tongue was on her, and her whole body shivered with the jolt of hot pleasure.

He stroked her clit with his tongue like she was his favorite ice cream and she was in serious danger of melting. "Oh God, Luke." She wanted to say something more compelling than that, but her mind had blanked out at the pleasure, leaving her only capable of clichéd pants and moans. He didn't seem to mind her lack of creativity.

She watched him, his mouth on her curls as his tongue stroked her and his fingers slipped inside her. The pleasure was so intense, it was hard to keep her eyes open, but the look of satisfaction in his eyes added another layer of ecstasy to the experience.

Her orgasm came hard and fast. She bucked against him as she cradled his head between her thighs and hoped she didn't hurt him with the violence of her body's spasms.

She was still panting when he dropped a kiss onto her fluttering belly and said, "Don't move."

He stepped back and stripped, then disappeared into the bedroom. A moment later, he returned with a box of condoms and pulled one out. He stepped up to the table and pressed his thick erection against her sensitive clit, causing her to jolt.

He chuckled and handed her the condom. She took it in one hand and his cock in the other. She stroked the shaft several times before releasing him to open the packet with both hands. She rolled the thin latex over him.

He pressed his sheathed prick against her vagina, sliding only the tip inside before retreating. She groaned and pressed forward, trying to prevent his escape. "More," she demanded.

He teased her by only entering an additional inch past the head.

She grabbed his ass and pulled him closer, but he resisted and pulled all the way out, then leaned down and took her nipple into his mouth. Pleasure shot through her as he sucked on her, then he practically made her come off the table when he slipped his hand between them and stroked her clit.

She grabbed his head, threading her fingers through his hair. "Luke, if you don't bury your cock deep inside me *now*, I'm liable to rip out your hair."

He scooped her from the table and carried her to the hallway. He pressed her back to the wall. She cinched her legs around his hips while he supported her with both hands under her ass. He thrust his cock inside her in one smooth motion, burying himself to the base. She whimpered at the intense thrill, then wrapped her hands around his neck and pulled his mouth to hers. "I think," she said between deep, sucking kisses, "your cock"—another deep kiss as he rocked his hips—"is the best thing"—her tongue slid against his while his penis stroked her inside—"I've ever felt in my life."

"Being inside you is fucking amazing." Another deep

thrust and she was on the verge of coming apart. "You are so tight and hot and slick."

She could drown in the sensation.

He kissed her again. "Come for me, beautiful."

"Not yet. I want to come *with* you."

He nuzzled her neck. "No. I want to feel you come." He adjusted his hold so he could support her with one hand, and stroked her clit. The sensation sent a lightning-like jolt of pleasure through her. "Yeah. Like that. Come for me."

The direct pressure on her clit and the fullness of his cock were too much, and she crested the wave and came apart. Her orgasm came in pulses timed to his thrusts, and she rode each one, clenching down on his cock.

"Aw. Babe…" His words became an incoherent tumble of endearments and curses as he buried his face in her neck and came.

He held her against the wall as his breathing evened out. "Give me a minute," he panted, "And I'll carry you to the couch. If I try now, I'm liable to drop you." He lifted his head from her neck and met her gaze. "You make me weak, babe. You must be my kryptonite."

She laughed and kissed him. "You're my catnip."

He slid an arm behind her back and pulled her tight, then walked to the couch, where he sat down with her straddling him. He was no longer erect, but he was still inside her, and he rocked his hips. "Without the condom, I'd probably be too sensitive to enjoy this. As it is, I can just take it, as long as you don't move. By the way, this counts as table, wall, and couch."

"Table and wall, sure. But you still owe me couch."

He rocked his hips. "Couch."

She clenched her vaginal muscles, causing him to jolt.

He kissed the corner of her mouth. "That's cheating."

She did it again.

"That's it," he declared and flipped her to her back. He

pulled out of her even as he kissed her. "You need to give me a break, because we've got all night, and I'm nowhere near done with you."

"Why don't you lie here and recover while I make dinner?"

"Depends. What's for dinner?"

"I was thinking corn flakes."

He laughed. "Can you cook at all?"

"Sure. But I'd rather have sex."

He nibbled on her chin. "What part of recovery time don't you understand?"

She ran her hand down his body, slipped off the condom and stroked his cock. Amazingly, he thickened. "I can work with this."

"Yeah, but it's not enough for me. Let's play with the shower massager, then I'll cook."

Chapter Twenty

uke was in a deep sleep when the alarm went off at five thirty. For the first time in forever, he shut it off, pulled the beautiful, naked woman in his bed against him, and decided to skip the run. He intended to go back to sleep, but once his hand landed on her hip, he just had to keep touching her.

He woke her slowly, his mouth on her neck as he cupped a breast. She smelled like the shampoo he'd lathered in her hair last night. She made a purring sound and pressed her ass against his erection.

He could get used to this. "Time to wake, sweetheart. The last one to finish the run makes breakfast."

She groaned. "Are you really going to make me run this early?"

"No. I was thinking I'd make love to you instead. Unless you'd rather run."

She reached between their bodies and wrapped her hand around his erection. "I'll take this, please," she said. His cock thickened as she stroked him from base to tip and back.

He chuckled and slipped two fingers between her thighs, and she let out a sexy gasp. "I'm all yours."

He played with her body until she was panting, wet, and demanding. His erection bordered on painful by the time he slid inside her. Her tight body took him as he braced himself on his forearms and looked down on her face. Goddamn, she was beautiful. And he loved this. Being with her, inside her. Watching her. He even liked being with her and watching her when he wasn't inside her.

But being inside her, skin to skin, the stroke and slide of sex, this was more than he expected. More than two people releasing stress and adrenaline. Somewhere along the line, his emotions had gotten involved, and he wondered if he'd really be able to drop her off at a hotel in Port Angeles later today and say good-bye to her for the last time.

A cell phone rang, waking Undine from her morning post-sex nap. She rolled over to face Luke. "Yours or mine?"

"Yours, I think. Mine's in the living room."

She groaned and reached over him to grab it off the nightstand. Only a handful of people had this number; she'd bought the phone only a few days ago in Forks. She frowned when she glanced at Caller ID and wondered if she should pick up.

"Who is it?" Luke asked.

"My dad."

He stiffened. That fast, she felt the wall form between them.

She climbed out of bed. Tension had already ruined the moment. Might as well take the call. It felt weird to talk to her dad while nude and with Luke watching, his eyes brimming with anger, so she stepped into the bathroom and grabbed a towel as she greeted her father.

"Deenie, I have good news."

She cinched the towel around her, relieved he sounded cheerful. Maybe this call wasn't about her at all. "Did National Geo agree to do the three-part documentary?"

"No. Even better."

In the living room, she pulled the cord for the blinds. She'd heard the rain start in the middle of the night, but now she could see the forecasted storm was even fiercer than predicted. "That could take out the road," she murmured. The storm a few days ago was nothing compared to this Pineapple Express-driven rain. The ocean, which should be visible just across the grass strip that separated the cabin from the sandy beach, had disappeared in a haze of dark gray sky and gray rain.

"The storm is hitting you now?" her father asked.

"Yes. If I don't leave soon, I might not be able to get to Port Angeles today."

"That's why I'm calling. To stop you from leaving."

She pulled the phone from her ear and checked the number. Yes. Definitely her father, who hadn't wanted her diving this soon after the explosion at all and then had tried to convince her to fly south and dive with him in Monterey. "You don't want me to head back to DC? But I'm done here."

"I got a call from your boss early this morning, he was authorized to bring me in the loop because UAB wants to hire *Nereid* to examine the *Wrasse* wreckage."

The back of her knees hit the couch, and she flopped down. "You aren't an archaeologist."

"No. But you are."

Yeah, and he'd been furious when she changed fields.

"I don't understand. What did you do?"

"Greg explained the situation with the…other thing you found. I know I'm not supposed to disclose details until that matter has been handled."

Meaning the matter remained classified until whoever had tried to kill her—twice—was arrested. She frowned at the stormy ocean. No way would Yuri have attempted a dive last night, meaning he hadn't revealed himself and was therefore still at large.

"The Navy is eager to bring up *Wrasse* and explore that other thing. The story, when presented as a whole, will make a great documentary and garner some well-deserved recognition for the fallen sailors. After the current investigation is done, it will fall to UAB to explore the wrecks and determine what happened, and they want every part of the process filmed for an eventual documentary. UAB needs a dive boat equipped for technical dives and small robotic submersibles. I've got everything except the archaeological excavation skills. That's where you, dear daughter, come in. This is your chance to run the dig. It'll make your career. And I'm giving it to you."

Just like her dad to take credit for presenting her with an opportunity she didn't want or need. "Dad, I already work for UAB. I was already *on* the excavation. Luke and I are the ones who found the frigging…other thing."

"Yes, but you were just the UAB advisor on the dig. Now you're going to be the woman in charge. You'll be sidestepping Erica in seniority, equal to Greg on this. The star of the documentary."

"I don't *want* to sidestep Erica, and I sure as hell don't want to star in any documentary. I'm content where I am. I need to work my way up through the ranks like anyone. Jesus, this is one of the reasons why I got into underwater archaeology, so my famous father couldn't meddle in my career. So no one could say I got where I am because it was handed to me."

"That's not the reason you gave when you quit your job at the institute."

"I said it's *one* of the reasons. The other reason still stands. I won't dive with you again."

"But you'll dive with Luke?"

She stiffened at his tone. "Hell yes, I'll dive with Luke." She glanced up to see him standing in the bedroom doorway. God, what must he think of her?

"Well, tough. I told UAB they could have *Nereid* for the excavation as long as you run the project. I'm bringing the boat north as soon as the storm breaks. You'll have at your disposal an integrated side scan sonar, a multibeam sub bottom profiler, and the latest in magnetometer technology to examine the wrecks for the Navy, Coast Guard, and Attorney General's office. And you and I are going to dive on the wreck for the opening shot of the documentary."

His words were a sucker punch to the gut. "You would really hold the investigation hostage just to force me to dive with you again? Have you forgotten that they're investigating why someone tried to *kill* me?"

"I'll do all the remote sensing without your cooperation, but I won't let the Navy use the boat for more than that unless you dive with me."

"It's really that important for you to win? One forced dive won't change a damn thing. You were wrong about Luke twelve years ago. You're wrong about him now."

"I wasn't wrong then or now. It's time for you to take your childish blinders off and see him for what he really is. He saw a vulnerable young girl who was heir to the institute. You were his ticket into the business. He *used* you, Undine."

"No, Dad. It's time for you to take *your* blinders off. You felt betrayed because you were as impressed by him as I was. He was the son you never had, and that warped your view of what happened. Getting involved with me was the fastest way to the exit, not to the top. And he resisted every step of the way, but I *pushed*. Because I was young and stupid and selfish."

Luke's expression was shuttered as he listened to her side of the never-ending argument with her father.

They'd both been able to forget the past, for a few days at least, but with her father heading north, returning to that happy place would be impossible. And dammit, she was emotionally invested now. Probably even in love. She couldn't be sure what she felt when it came to Luke, but it was something far more significant than lust.

"He didn't know it would get him kicked out of the institute or he'd lose his scholarship. He's a snake, Undine. Accept it and move on as I had to do. He's damaged our relationship enough."

"No, Dad. *You* damaged our relationship with your insistence he's more to blame than he was." She met Luke's gaze, and a tear escaped, which she immediately wiped away. "Luke Sevick is every bit as amazing as we both thought he was twelve years ago. I betrayed him, and you kicked him in the face and stole his dreams. But he turned around and joined the Navy and served his country as an elite operator, and then he joined NOAA so he could work to study and protect the very resource *you* value the most, so get off your high horse and stop judging him. He's saved my life two, possibly three, times, and he helped me get back in the water when I feared I'd never dive again. So back. The fuck. Off."

She'd never cursed at her father before, although she'd been sorely tempted over the years. And always, Luke had been the center of their argument, their once-tight father-daughter bond irreparably damaged.

She took another deep breath. "I have no control over

whether or not you come north and map the wreck. All I can say is it's the right thing to do, and I would be ashamed of you if you refused over something so petty as our ongoing disagreement. But I also don't know if I'll be here when you arrive. I'm done and want to return to DC. It's time for me to get back to my life. But, if I am here, and if Luke is here, you will greet him with respect. You will shake his hand. You will thank him for all he has done for our country and for me. If you can't do that, if you say so much as one disparaging word about Luke to anyone at NOAA, the Coast Guard, the Navy, the film crew, a cab driver, or even a waitress at IHOP, I promise you, I will never set foot in the institute again, and I sure as hell won't be in your damn documentary."

She punched the End button and threw the phone on the couch, then took a deep breath and swiped at her eyes again. On shaky legs, she stood and passed Luke on her way to the stairs. She climbed to the loft, grabbed her suitcase, and began dumping her clothes inside.

"What are you doing?" Luke asked from the staircase.

"I want to go to Port Angeles now, before the road closes."

He ducked down and moved to sit on the foot of the bed behind her. "I don't care if the road is open. We're not driving in this storm. Rocks will be sliding down the embankments along the coastal road. It's too dangerous."

"Fine. Then take me back to the cabins in town. I can't afford one of these by myself." She waved a hand to indicate the loft and the nearly full-sized kitchen below.

"You don't want to stay here with me?"

She swiped at more tears as she emptied another drawer. "Please. I just gave my dad the ultimatum I've been trying to avoid for twelve years. I don't have it in me to fight with you too." The towel around her chest slipped, and she grabbed it before it could fall. She might have a bit more dignity if she weren't hunched over under the low ceiling, packing while wearing nothing but a small hotel bath towel.

Warm hands landed on her waist, and he pulled her onto his lap. "Why would we fight?"

"Because it's my fault he ruined your life, and he's bringing *Nereid* here. And he's such a stubborn ass, he's bound to be horrible to you, and you'll start to hate me again, and I can't face that."

Not when I'm crazy in love with you.

Aw, hell. What a moment for her feelings to become crystal clear, even if she only said it in her mind.

Luke ran a thumb over her right cheek, spreading her tears across a cheekbone. "First, my life was changed, but not ruined. I've had a pretty damn amazing life so far. Joining the Navy wasn't my original, intended path, but it was where I was meant to end up, and I wouldn't give up my years of service for anything. Maybe I should thank your dad."

She glared at him. "Don't joke about that. It's not funny."

One corner of his mouth curled in a smile. "The strangest part is, I'm not joking. And it might be fun to freak Stefan out by telling him how grateful I am that I lost the scholarship and was forced to look elsewhere for a career." With his other thumb, he wiped away the tears on her left cheek. "And there's nothing Stefan can say that will make me hate you again. Your father has no part in what's between us now."

He pressed his mouth to hers, lips closed, sweet and gentle. "I'm not going to lie and say I know or understand what I feel for you, but I can promise you, it's not hate."

She held his gaze, at a loss for what to say. She wasn't entirely certain if her heart was breaking or opening. Breaking because this was a temporary thing between them that would end when either of them left Neah Bay, or opening because he'd admitted to having feelings for her, he just wasn't sure what they were.

"As far as Stefan goes, with this storm, he won't be here for a few days. When he gets here, we'll face him together."

"You're staying? You aren't planning to go back to your life in Port Angeles before he gets here?"

He glanced toward the front window. "No one's going anywhere in this storm. But even if we had crystal-clear blue sky, I'd stay. I have more than a week before NOAA is expecting me back, and if you aren't rushing back to DC, I can't think of anything better than spending the next few days making love to you. I still owe you bedroom-wall sex."

She pressed her nose into his chest, taking in his musky, masculine scent. Their early morning sex still lingered on his skin. She ran her tongue over his pectoral muscle and licked his nipple. "I'd like a do-over on the couch."

"That can be arranged." He bounced his butt on the bed. "Right now I'm thinking we haven't tried loft sex yet."

Chapter Twenty-One

The storm lasted for three days, and it took out power along with the coastal road. On the second day, the cell tower went out, severing their final tie with the outside world. They'd stocked up on groceries and condoms on the first day, and Luke purchased a camp stove and several canisters of propane, which he set up on the covered porch for cooking and heating water for bathing. Their cabin was a perfect haven during the deluge, and they stayed warm by sharing body heat.

"When this storm's over, you're going to owe me a ten-mile run," Luke said as he ran his tongue down her belly late in the afternoon of the third day.

"It's not my fault it was raining too hard to run three mornings in a row."

"It's barely raining now. We could knock out three miles, then you'll only owe me seven tomorrow."

She enjoyed running with him, but enjoyed teasing him even more. "How about I go down on you instead?"

He shook his head. "I'm still enjoying the memory of you

going down on me an hour ago. I don't want to replace it yet."

She closed her eyes and replayed in her mind the encounter that had started out as a sponge bath. Power outages were a helluva lot of fun when stranded with a hot former SEAL in an oceanfront cabin that was made for sex.

"C'mon, babe. I need to run."

"You don't need me to go with you. You said Yuri's not a threat anymore now that we've exposed his secret."

"But I like being with you. Tomorrow the sun's gonna shine and the power will come back on and the world will intrude. I don't want to give up even one minute of this time alone with you. Even for a run."

She threaded her fingers through his hair. "When you put it that way, how can I say no?"

They set out in the sprinkling rain an hour before sunset. She wasn't as avid a runner as Luke, but she wasn't a hater either. It was an inexpensive form of exercise and took less time than walking. She loved this, though, running by his side.

She had no idea what she was going to do when this was over, because she had no doubt she'd fallen hard. She knew he cared about her and would even miss her when they said good-bye, but he'd been careful to make no promises, offer no hint that this was anything other than a fling.

This ended when they left Neah Bay. Those were the rules she'd agreed to. And she'd abide by them. But damn, Trina was going to be pissed when Undine came home with a broken heart. Cressida at least had the decency to return from her nightmare with Ian.

Everyone had planned to rally around Cressida, but in the end, she didn't need the emotional support because she and Ian were working through the trauma they'd faced together. Having been gone for most of the summer that

Cressida interned at NHHC, Undine didn't know her well, but according to Trina, she'd come back with an inner strength she'd lacked before. Tempered steel.

Undine had a feeling she'd return from Neah Bay a needy mess, much worse off than she'd been when she left. What was the opposite of tempered steel? Aluminum foil?

But then, she'd been fine when she left DC, having faced zero attempts on her life at the time and not having been the sole survivor of an explosion that killed four coworkers and which may have been rigged by the fifth.

She'd also never been in love before. Not when she was sixteen with Luke. Not when she was twenty-four and dated Trey, her dad's right-hand man at the institute. And not in September, when she'd broken things off with the latest in a string of boyfriends before heading to Washington.

But she was in love now, and it was a euphoric heart-breaking feeling she didn't know what to do with. These last days with Luke had been the euphoric part. If she could just forget they had no future, she could enjoy each moment for the perfection it was.

She'd never realized how much happiness was tied to hope. How much thoughts of the future contributed to enjoying the moment, until she was trying desperately to hold on to the thrill of the moment and forget the bleak future.

She'd ruined any possibility of a future with Luke when she was too young to understand what she was doing.

⁂

Yuri watched the couple run down the beach, not a care in the world. Gray had lost four coworkers, and she treated this like it was a romantic vacation for two. Selfish bitch. People were dying in Ukraine, and Americans reneged on their promise to train Ukrainian soldiers. The Canadians were balking as well. No one cared unless oil was involved. They were all selfish.

Yuri wasn't a killer; he was a soldier serving his country. Jared, Loren, Sandy, and Scotty had been casualties of war. Their deaths would serve a bigger purpose, and Yuri had disposed of them with the same level of remorse Lt. Sevick and all special operators of his ilk gave the enemy combatants they injured or killed.

Yuri considered himself a special operator and as such hadn't enjoyed the killing, nor had he celebrated the deaths. It was simple necessity. Like lancing a wound or setting a broken bone. To heal, to get stronger, first, one must hurt.

To win a revolution, one must accept the burden of killing. He would give his all to his people, if not his country, and knew that to see this mission to the bitter end, he would likely make the ultimate sacrifice. His death, like Jared's, would be a necessity.

But now that he was certain Gray and Sevick had found *Magnum* and had shared the story with local and federal authorities, it was starting to feel a little personal. Gray needed to understand his pain. His loss. Her particular suffering might not be a necessity, but it would be…satisfying.

Media hound Dr. Stefan Gray didn't sneeze without alerting the media. Convenient for Yuri, because he'd set up a Google alert on the man's name the moment he'd realized Undine Gray planned to dive on *Wrasse* again. Thanks to the alerts, he'd learned Gray was bringing his research vessel to Neah Bay. It gave Yuri the perfect opportunity.

The timing was perfect. It was all coming together.

Dr. Gray never missed a photo op, and Yuri could make sure the attention-hungry reality TV star would have the ultimate moment in the limelight. The world would witness his grief.

It was a bitter pill that Undine Gray's death would

likely receive more attention and outrage from Americans than his city of Chernobyl had received. Her death would garner more sympathy than the ferry sinking that had taken Iryna.

But so be it. He'd use that too.

The twins had agreed this was a better plan than going after Moscow. Either way, Moscow would burn. Eventually.

The device would go off in the middle of the strait, when the boat was over a fault line. Hundreds, even thousands might be killed from the initial blast. But hundreds of thousands, even millions, would be taken out by the resulting earthquake and tsunami.

Then the US and Canada would finally understand they shouldn't have turned their backs on the soldiers they'd promised to train. If they weren't with *all* Ukrainians who fought against pro-Russian separatists and Russian annexation, then they stood with the invading army. The factions and distinctions didn't matter. Russia and their allies—both passive and aggressive—would suffer the same fate as Chernobyl.

❀

The power came on that night, and the following morning dawned crisp and clear. Undine frowned at the bright, sunny morning. Their happy, secluded respite was over. And today Luke was going to make her do CrossFit in addition to the run.

He was far too cheery about the coming workout as he bribed her by delivering her tea in bed. "I think we need to break up," she said as she sipped her tea.

"I'm too much of a morning person for you?" he asked.

"Too much of a fitness nut. Plus, I need butter in my diet."

He straddled her legs on the bed and cradled a cup of coffee in his hands. "No one needs butter."

"When was the last time you had real butter? Have you forgotten how amazing it is?"

He laughed. "Probably."

A loud knock on the front door heralded the end of their respite from the world. "Maybe it's the resort manager," she said hopefully. They'd left a note on the management office door saying they were fine without electricity and didn't need assistance during the outage. Being midweek and with the storm making surfing dangerous, the two adjacent beachfront cabins were empty, as were most of the ones that lined the road and faced the water. Even though there were a few guests at the resort, it had felt like they were the only people for miles.

He leaned down and kissed her. "I'll check while you throw on some clothes."

He climbed from the bed. Shirtless, he wore only his favorite exercise shorts. He closed the bedroom door, and she slipped from the bed and grabbed underwear, bra, T-shirt, and sweatpants from the drawer. It was seven thirty in the morning, just after sunrise, early for a drop-in visitor.

She'd just donned her panties when she heard her father say, "I'd like to talk to my daughter."

*L*uke went cold the moment his gaze landed on Stefan Gray's brown-green eyes. So like Undine's, and so full of loathing. For a brief time, the man had been a mentor. A father figure who'd filled a void created when Luke's dad drank himself to death.

Luke had worshiped Dr. Stefan Gray, and he'd been gratified to be the recipient of Stefan's praise and attention. He'd been aware he was viewed as the new golden boy at the institute, and he'd believed his own hype. His own infallibility.

Standing next to Stefan on the porch was Trey, a man Luke remembered from the months he'd lived and worked at the institute. He knew Trey was now Stefan's second in command—the job everyone expected would one day be Undine's.

Trey flashed Luke a smug grin, and Luke had no idea why, but he was struck with the urge to deck the man. And he didn't usually go for unprovoked violence with virtual strangers. But then, Trey had always rubbed him the wrong way.

Luke leaned against the doorframe, making no move to invite the pair inside. Instead he glanced over his shoulder and shouted, "Sweetheart? You dressed? Your dad's here."

He turned back to flash his own smug grin, well aware that was the most childish thing he'd done since he was twelve years old. He might as well have said *I'm fucking your daughter.* He took in the vein throbbing at Stefan's temple and tried to find remorse but came up empty.

He'd only feel bad if his words pissed off Undine. She didn't deserve to have to pay the price for his baiting of her dad.

She stepped out of the bedroom, disheveled and beautiful but clothed, and walked up to Luke. She kissed his cheek before she met her father's gaze. Okay, she'd picked her side. Luke slid an arm around her waist, feeling even more smug satisfaction.

"Hi, Dad. Trey. What a surprise to see you." She made no move to hug or even shake either man's hand.

He hadn't realized how worried he was about this moment until it had arrived. He wasn't sure why, but he'd feared she'd abandon him in the face of her father's scorn. Stefan Gray had a magnetic personality. It was one thing to reject him on the phone, but quite another to face him down in person.

"May we come in?" Stefan said in a stiff voice.

She looked to Luke for permission.

He leaned down and brushed his lips over hers. He was being a total dick but couldn't seem to stop himself. "Your call, babe."

She rolled her eyes. "You are such an ass sometimes."

"Yes. I am. I really am."

She shrugged. "But he has it coming." She faced her father. "Fine. You can come in."

That Stefan hadn't said a word disparaging Luke meant the man had taken Undine's ultimatum seriously. He had to give Stefan credit; the man did love his daughter. "Coffee or tea, Stefan? Trey?" he asked.

"Coffee, please," Stefan said. Trey requested the same.

Luke filled the coffeemaker and set a fresh pot to brew.

"How did you know where to find me?" Undine asked.

"There are only a few motels and resorts here. We drove around until we spotted Luke's SUV."

He didn't explain how he got Luke's vehicle description, but no doubt he had friends willing to divulge that information.

Stefan frowned. "You didn't mention you'd checked out of your room at the Cape."

"We made the decision when it was clear someone had tried to kill us. Because I'd been targeted twice, it seemed wise to keep my name from any registry. I didn't mention it to you because I figured you might stroke out. I'd have given you the heads-up today, but you didn't call first."

"The cell tower is still down."

She gave a sharp nod. "Is *Nereid* here?"

"No. Trey and I caught a flight to SeaTac yesterday. We

spent the night in Port Angeles and drove here after the road opened this morning."

"How bad was the road?" Luke asked. It was rare for the coastal road to be closed for more than a few hours.

"Fine now, but there was a mudslide before Sekiu and another one between Sekiu and Neah Bay. Crews had to clear one before they could even get to the other."

"Which explains why they haven't been able to fix the cell tower," Luke said.

Stefan cleared his throat. "I'd like to speak with my daughter in private."

Luke met Undine's gaze. She shrugged. "Why don't you and Trey take a walk?"

He nodded and stepped into the bedroom to grab a sweatshirt. He slipped on his running shoes and stepped outside. It was a bright, perfect morning with patches of blue sky peeking through the clouds. At least, the day had started perfect when he'd figured he'd get to enjoy a run with Undine and then maybe make love to her again before they went to the gym.

But instead he was stuck walking on the beach with Robert Kilpatrick III, aka Trey, while Undine's dad tried to convince her Luke was pond scum and taking advantage of her.

He was both of those things, but that didn't mean it didn't still rankle.

"You didn't waste any time," Trey said, his voice full of self-righteous disdain.

"On the contrary, Undine's been legal for ten years now. I've wasted a lot of time." The taunt slipped out, and yet, at one point yesterday, the thought had occurred to him. Not that he should have pursued her as soon as she was of legal age, but that maybe, if they'd met again when she was in her early twenties, their paths would have been different. He'd have been able to let go of the anger sooner.

"You know you're just her rebellion. A way to piss off Stefan. So if your plan is to use her to get back into the institute, think again. Besides, Undine never sticks with anyone for long. I give you six weeks, tops. "

Something in Trey's tone tipped Luke off. "Six weeks? Somehow I doubt you lasted even that long. I bet you were pissed when she dumped you. And there you were, hoping it would seal the deal with you as Stefan's right hand."

"She told you that?" Trey's tone was defensive.

Luke laughed. "Hell no. She's never mentioned you at all."

Trey went silent. Luke could practically see gears in the man's head turning as he searched for words to put Luke in his place. But there was nothing he could say that could hurt Luke. Trey was the one with dreams of being the next Stefan Gray. Trey was the one who gave a damn about receiving the man's praise. The only person who mattered to Luke was Undine.

The thought was a revelation of sorts. She mattered to him. He was still unclear how, and he had no delusions there was a future for them, but he cared about her and suspected he always would.

Chapter Twenty-Two

"*H*e's using you to get to me," Undine's father said as he paced in front of the couch.

"Bullshit, Dad. You aren't that important in his life, so get over yourself." She crossed her arms. "I don't understand how you can harbor so much animosity toward the man for twelve damn years. And even if he were to blame for seducing me—which he's not—I'm *fine*. The only psychological damage that occurred came from your reaction. I'm not saying what I did was okay, but it didn't break me or warp me. I get that you are and were looking out for me, but let it go. For the love of God, please *stop*."

"You say you're fine, but you've never had a relationship that lasted very long. You're afraid to get close because you were used as a means of professional advancement when you were sixteen. You never gave Trey a chance, because even though you were older, the fact that he's in line to take over the institute was too similar."

Undine flung up her hands, exasperated. *This* was what her father had believed all these years? "I didn't give Trey a chance because he's a smug prick. If anyone has ever dated me to get in your good graces, it's Trey. And I've never dated a man longer than a few months because I don't believe in wasting my time when I can tell the relationship isn't working, not because of some deep-seated trauma stemming from what happened with Luke. All my trauma, every damn bit, stems from you calling the prosecutor and pushing for Luke to serve time for what *I did*. I was devastated when you took away his future. Yes, Luke's loathing crushed me, but I could deal with it because I knew I deserved it. Because I knew it was my fault. I owned what I did."

She wanted to pace, but her father stood in the only good pacing area in the small cabin, so instead she tapped her foot. "We're done discussing this. I don't need your psychoanalysis. I don't need your shaming. I'm *happy*, Dad. In spite of everything that's happened since *Petrel* blew up, I'm happy. Probably happier than I've ever been in my life. If you can't see that, if you can't be happy for me, then get the hell out of this cabin and my life, because the one thing you should want for me is to be happy. Isn't that what parents are supposed to want for their children? But your coming here and disparaging Luke and bringing Trey—when you know how I feel about him—is a blatant attempt to ruin my happiness."

"You love Luke, don't you?"

She gave a sharp nod. She'd been eager to tell someone— that someone being Luke—and had considered confessing to Trina when phone service returned. Ironic that her father was the first person she'd told.

"He'll break your heart."

She shrugged. "That's my problem." She glared at him. "And as my father, you damn well shouldn't be wishing for that outcome."

He went silent. Finally, he said, "I never want to see you hurt. Ever." He sighed. "And I had no choice but to bring Trey. He knows technical diving better than anyone at the institute after me. But he wouldn't be second in command if you'd come back. His job is yours if you want it. It always has been."

"And Trey knows it, which is why he asked me out to begin with. And once I realized his agenda, I broke it off." She'd been twenty-four and felt utterly used. A few months out of grad school, she'd moved back home and was trying to decide if she'd been wrong in turning her back on the institute, if maybe she should give up her penance and go back to the field that was her first love. But Trey's pathetic courtship had pushed her in the other direction, and she'd taken an internship at NHHC, which later became a permanent position.

Of course, that worked in Trey's favor too, as he'd taken out Undine as competition for the institute's top spot. Of all her relationships, Trey was the only man who made her skin crawl.

And her dad loved him like a son.

It was no wonder her friends in DC had become a surrogate family. Her real family sucked.

I wonder what kind of relationship Luke has with his family?

She pulled herself back, full stop, from that line of thinking. It didn't matter what his relationship was with his mother and brother, because odds were, she'd never meet them.

"*Nereid* should arrive around noon. The film crew wants to get some setup dive shots, stock footage to sprinkle throughout the documentary. The weather is perfect today. Blue sky in November is rare along this stretch of coast. Are you available this afternoon?"

"I don't want to be in your documentary, Dad."

"It's not *my* documentary. It's UAB's. The Navy's going to get a lot of mileage from this."

She shook her head. "Seven people died when *Wrasse* sank."

"They died heroes, and you'll make sure everyone knows it."

"And four—maybe five—died on *Petrel.* Is that going to be part of the documentary?"

"Only if it becomes important to the narrative. That's a separate investigation. The film crew will want to interview you about that to splice it in if needed. But including it will depend on what's learned in the investigation and what the Justice Department wants to keep classified."

"I won't parade my experience in front of cameras for the sake of added drama. I won't sensationalize the deaths of Jared, Scotty, Loren, and Sandy that way. But the documentary will be dedicated to them, or I won't participate at all."

"Done," her father said.

"I won't dive with Trey. I will dive with Luke, but only if he's willing to participate. You won't pressure him." He'd already been forced to dive with her by UAB once.

"Fine." Her father cleared his throat. "Will you dive with me?"

She stared at him as she considered the question. Twelve years ago, she'd given her ultimatum: drop his attempts to prosecute Luke and reinstate his scholarship, or she'd never dive with her father again. She'd never wavered on that ultimatum and hadn't gone scuba diving with her father since she was sixteen.

Now they'd need a time machine for Stefan to retract the complaint he'd filed with the district attorney or to give Luke his scholarship back. "I'll dive with you on one condition."

"And that is?"

"You need to shake Luke's hand, thank him for saving my life, and tell him you were wrong."

"I thought your father was going to dive with us?" Luke said as he donned his wetsuit.

"I did too. But apparently, he couldn't bring himself to meet my terms," Undine said.

"What were they?" he asked. She'd been quiet when he and Trey returned to the cabin and hadn't even groused when he dragged her to the gym after their run.

She shrugged. "It doesn't matter."

For the first time, Luke found the limits on their undefined relationship constricting. If they were a true couple, he could push her to open up. But a temporary fling held no such rights. She could cut herself off emotionally, and he had no room to complain.

He pulled her against him. "How serious was your relationship with Trey?" She'd told him once that she'd never been in love. Had she lied? And why did the idea that she might have cared for the prick grate so much?

"On my end, not serious at all. On his end, he said he loved me. But only because he was worried I'd return to the institute and steal his job."

"Asshole," Luke said.

"Yep. He actually did the thing my father accuses you of, and my dad turned a blind eye."

"Because you were older."

"Yeah. But to me, what Trey did was far worse than anything you did."

"That's because I'm amazing, while he's a dickhead."

He got the laugh he was hoping for, and she rose up on her toes and kissed him. "You're amazing drenched in double chocolate awesomesauce."

"Careful. You know what that does to my ego."

She smiled. "I'm counting on it."

Thank God for cold water, because otherwise the documentary would have some ridiculous footage given the snug fit of his wetsuit.

"Let's get this over with," she said.

They grabbed their remaining gear to meet with the film crew, including the director, Diego Ojeda, who'd been filming Stefan Gray's work for fifteen years. Diego and his cameraman, Mario, were probably as knowledgeable about marine biology as anyone on the boat.

Diego wanted a series of water shots first, with both Undine and Luke fully outfitted for scuba. They didn't dive below twenty feet, so there was no need for recompression. As Stefan had promised, all they wanted were random clips of them both in the water. B-roll shots taken while the light was good.

Back on deck, Diego asked them to answer a few questions, speaking directly in the camera while they froze their asses off in their saturated wetsuits. "It's because you look too damn good in a wetsuit, Sevick," Undine said with a snicker. "If you ate more butter and cut down on the exercise, they wouldn't want you for cutaways."

Luke couldn't resist and grabbed her by the waist and pulled her onto his lap. He kissed her neck and whispered in her ear, "No way am I getting rid of these guns you love so much."

"You two are dating?" Mario asked. "That's cool. Can we include that in the documentary? Viewers love it when things get personal."

Undine stiffened against Luke. "No," she said firmly as she pushed up from his lap.

He was left feeling irked but had no idea why. He shouldn't want their temporary relationship documented in a permanent film any more than she did.

"*W*e should check on the case at the museum. It might be openable now," Undine said as they walked down the dock.

"We'll probably need to break the lock."

"I told Greg that. He said as long as we photograph everything first and film the opening, we're fine." They'd discussed shipping the item to DC right after they discovered the Soviet submarine, but no one wanted to interrupt the electrolytic reduction process to ship it back. Aside from it being fragile due to the corrosion, there was always the possibility that whatever was inside shouldn't be shipped at altitude.

Of course, electrolytic reduction had halted during the power outage, but at least it had remained submerged in the tank, preventing it from drying out and turning brittle before the corrosion was washed away.

The curator had given Undine a key to the storage facility and the alarm security code at the end of their last visit, allowing them to bypass finding an employee to admit them. When they reached the door, Undine punched in the code before using the key, as instructed.

The control panel flashed as if nothing had registered. No tones accompanied the buttons as she pressed them.

She tried again. Nothing on the panel changed.

"The power outage may have fried the system."

She glanced at the main museum building. "I hope it's just here, and not the whole museum. I'd hate to think of all those artifacts unprotected."

He nodded in agreement and said, "Try the key anyway. If it sets off the alarm, all the better."

She twisted the key in the lock, and the door swung free without resistance or noise.

Undine wrinkled her nose, and Luke caught the acrid

scent a moment after she did. She took a step forward, but he held out a hand to stop her. "I go first." He pulled his gun from his back holster and entered the room. He rounded the corner to the area where the tank was set up and stopped short. Annie, the enthusiastic tribal member who'd helped them before, was slumped over the tank, her head facedown in the brown water.

Chapter Twenty-Three

A cold, terrifying numbness infused Undine as Luke checked for Annie's pulse, knowing from the smell he'd find none. The scent of singed electronics hinted that Annie had died at the beginning of the storm, before the power went out, while the water was still electrified.

Someone must have turned up the voltage to the tank, prior to pushing her head under.

Federal law dictated that with some exceptions, homicides on Indian reservations fell under FBI jurisdiction. That would certainly be the case in this instance, given the tiny police force that likely only handled misdemeanors and low-grade felonies. From conversations with Curt in the past, Undine also knew prosecution for major crimes committed on tribal lands would fall to the local US Attorney's Office, which in this instance was the Western District of Washington, in Seattle, so instead of calling 911 to report the murder, she called Curt, who contacted the FBI.

He requested they not inform the local police, as the small population on the reservation meant word would spread quickly, and inexperienced officers might not maintain the integrity of the scene. Instead he asked that Luke guard the body with assistance from the Coast Guard. Given the remote location, it would take several hours before the FBI's crime scene investigators would arrive. Parker was called for this purpose, and he and Luke took up posts outside the building.

While the two men guarded, Undine sat with the museum curator in his office in the main building. Upon learning the news, he'd closed the museum, using the excuse that the alarm system was offline and electricians needed to access the display cases. Other museum employees accepted this story, as the system really was down.

The FBI had asked that no one be informed of Annie's death until they arrived. After all, they still needed to confirm the victim's identity, which wouldn't happen until she was removed from the tank.

In a small tribal town like Neah Bay, everyone was family. Word would spread quickly once the first family member learned the news, and the curator told Undine he feared his ability to remain quiet if he went home to his wife and children. So he hid in his office, in silence with Undine.

"Did you tell anyone about the case?" she asked, her voice barely above a whisper.

"No. Of the museum staff, only Annie and I knew you'd set up the reduction tank. It was hardly significant at first, and later, you asked that we remain silent. I don't know if Annie told anyone, but I don't think she would have."

They lapsed back into silence.

She didn't even know if the metal case was still in the opaque water. Luke had touched nothing but Annie's neck at the crime scene. But of course, her gut said it would be missing when the tank was finally emptied. What else could Annie's murderer have been after?

Conspiracy theories ran rampant in her mind as she

waited. Had the mudslides that closed off the town been caused by something other than the storm? The power outage had somehow taken out the museum's generators, frying the alarm system. That was unusual. And finally, the cell tower's loss of power, that was rare. She'd learned land-line phones were the first to go, but she'd been unaware of that because the cabins at Hobuck didn't have landlines.

With the road closed and the water too rough for boats to make port, Neah Bay had been completely cut off from the rest of the country for two full days. For Undine, it had been a magical, thrilling romantic respite, and now she wondered if it had been done to delay notifying the outside world of Annie's murder, and guilt and shame clogged her throat.

The curator had told her Annie lived by herself in a small cabin on a dirt road outside the boundaries of the town. During the bigger storms, the tribal member would check on her homebound neighbors and deliver food and fuel for generators. When she didn't show this time, people must have assumed she was hunkered down herself. Or maybe they did note her absence, but there was no way to call and check on her.

Guilt weighed heavy on Undine's conscience.

"It's not your fault, you know," the curator said, breaking the long silence. "The storage building is a curation facility. It made sense for you to leave it with us."

She met his gaze. His dark skin had the sallow undertone of grief. She could swear the lines around his eyes had etched in a little deeper in the last hours. "I could say the same to you."

"Usually, I'm the one who closes down the museum and storage facility when a big storm rolls in, but Annie volun-teered because she knew I didn't want to miss the Seahawks game." He shook his head. "The satellite dish went out before halftime, and the power twenty minutes later. I should have come back. I should have checked. I'd received the text from Annie that everything was fine, but still, I should have checked."

"It's possible Annie was electrocuted and didn't die from drowning. In which case, she was dead before the power went out. Even if you had come back to check, it could have been too late."

He gave a sharp nod. She reached across the desk and took his hand. His fingers curled around hers. It was a strange thing, to attempt to comfort a stranger, when there was no comfort to be found. This must be how the doctors and nurses had felt when she was in the hospital right after the explosion. But this man's grief was so much more profound. He'd lost a coworker who was also family.

Her pathetic attempt at comfort made her all the more thankful that Luke had been at the hospital when she woke. He'd been a virtual stranger as well, and yet deep in his core, there'd been a familiarity. He'd known she'd need that familiarity and accepted the job of being both the bearer of horrific news and comforter. He'd held her, which she'd needed desperately, and she wished this man before her could go home to his wife and receive the embrace he must need.

At last, the FBI arrived. She was interviewed. The agent had already been briefed on the case and its importance by no less than Curt himself, so the interview went quickly, as she filled in only the smaller details.

When she and Luke were finally free to leave, they went back to the cabin that had been such a lovely haven, sheltering them from the storm. Darkness had fallen, but they didn't bother with turning on lights. They sat on the couch in the dark, she crawled on his lap, and they held each other. Too nauseated to eat, too numb to cry, too distraught to make love.

Eventually, he carried her to the bedroom and set her on

the bed. She emerged from her grief-ridden haze long enough to brush her teeth and don a T-shirt. She slipped under the covers and he joined her, pulling her back to his chest and tucking his knees behind hers.

Hours later, she woke to the feel of his lips on her neck, his hand cupping her breast. She turned and faced him. He brushed a soft kiss over her lips. "If you don't want to make love, I understand."

She stroked his cheek. "Are you wanting something life-affirming?"

She felt his nod in the dark. "I've seen a lot of death. I've even caused it. It was always part of the job. The mission. Protecting my brothers on the team. Protecting Americans who had no idea what we were doing, how far we were pushing ourselves physically, mentally, to be the best of the best, so we could kill on their behalf. I've seen a lot of the ugly shit humans do to other humans in war zones.

"But Annie, she wasn't in a war zone. She was just a bystander. Like you. Like the others on *Petrel*. Shit, Undine, all I could think was that could have been you. I feel horrible for Annie. For the tribe. For her family. And yet deep down, I'm selfishly grateful it wasn't you. And I want to make love to you, if only to confirm on a stupid, selfish, psychological level I don't even understand, that you're still here with me." His hands slid up her back, under the T-shirt. A caress, but not a demanding one. "But if you aren't in the mood, if sex is the last thing you want, that's fine. I can be content with holding you."

She threaded her fingers through his hair and pulled his mouth to hers, testing to see if he could arouse her. She kissed him tentatively, no promises. Her tongue touched his with a gentle swipe. Slowly, the heat between them built, a simmer at first, which grew hotter with each silent touch of hands or mouths.

T-shirts and underwear were discarded, and they were skin to skin. Their bodies knew each other well at this point, but this was different, this utter silence. Even their breathing was muted, as if the devil were listening and they didn't want him to know they were seeking comfort in lovemaking in the wake of his atrocious act.

The silence and darkness added a special element. They had to rely on touch, and touch alone, to know the other was pleased. The tremor that passed along his hips as she took him in her mouth. The wetness of her vagina as he slipped two fingers inside her.

I love you.

The words repeated in the silence of her mind. A chant. A mantra. A truth she didn't dare speak.

When she couldn't take the intensity any longer, she pushed him to his back. She sheathed his penis with a condom and straddled him. His erection slid inside easily. She rocked on his hips, loving the feel of his cock as his pelvis thrust upward from the bed. The abrasion of her clit against his pubic hair. His hands cupped her breasts, and still, they made not a sound.

I love you.

She tilted her head back, holding her breath against the pants and moans and words that wanted to break free. This silence was like scuba without full-face radio masks. The darkness was the water, the air a cold current against her bare skin. She didn't need to close her eyes in the complete blackness of the room, but she did anyway.

I love you.

Luke touched her clit as he thrust and she rocked, and her body coiled with pleasure, on the cusp of what was destined to be an intense orgasm. From the way his body tightened between her thighs, she knew he was close as well. His thumb stroked her clit, and she crested. The rhythm of his thrusts changed as she clenched around him, and she knew he was coming even though he made no sound.

She let out her breath with an audible gasp as another pulse of pleasure hit her, her orgasm increasing in intensity, not decreasing. She collapsed on his chest, breathing heavily. Wave upon wave of orgasm pulsed through her as he continued grinding his pelvis to hers.

Luke chuckled, the first sound he'd made, and rolled over, still nestled between her thighs.

The darkness of the room, the feel of his body, the intensity of the orgasm, they all cocooned her. Without thought or even the knowledge she was about to speak, the words she'd chanted in her mind broke free. "I love you, Luke."

Undine pushed against his chest and swore. He locked his arms tight around her back, preventing her from fleeing, even though he wanted to let her escape. Only a complete asshole would pretend he hadn't heard her declaration, and while Luke was certain he was on the far end of the asshole spectrum, he hoped he wasn't that much of a prick.

"Forget I said that," she said as she tried to escape his hold.

"I can't." But he wanted to. God, did he want to. He wanted the bliss of three heartbeats ago, when he'd ejaculated and was caught up in the heat and sensuousness of being inside the body of a beautiful woman who meant…*something*…to him.

But she'd said the words. This was the point of no return, and he had no idea where to go with this moment. Once, he'd spoken first and had believed he'd said them to the woman he'd spend his life with.

He'd been wrong. So horribly wrong.

Twice, he'd received the words, and they'd been the hopeful declarations of women who loved the idea of being with a SEAL far more than the reality. He'd recognized the fantasy for what it was and ended both relationships.

But with Undine, he was at a loss. Did he love her? It was hard to say, given the tangle of emotions she triggered. All he could do was give her the honest truth. He kissed her first, to stop her frantic attempts at retreat. It didn't work. "Honey, settle down."

"Settle *down?*"

From her tone, he guessed that was the worst thing he could have said. He stroked her cheek and slipped from inside her. He had about ten seconds before the condom would start to itch on his flaccid penis. Better settle this quick, because he had a feeling getting out of bed and cleaning up—as he'd done when he was in full asshole mode after sex a week and a half ago—would trigger bad memories.

Women had no idea how much men's reactions after sex were triggered by bodily discomfort. When his cock itched or was otherwise engaged in pleasure or pain, he'd have trouble giving his name, rank, and serial number. It was one reason torture aimed at the genital region was so damn effective. He might have been a SEAL, but his resistance training had lapsed years ago.

And he'd never been trained to face a moment like this. All he could do was be honest. "I care about you, Undine. But I don't love you."

Shit. He should have gone with something more vague, like *I don't know how I feel.* It was the truth and less harsh. This was a six-cylinder situation and his post-orgasm brain was at best a one-cylinder engine.

She tried to leave the bed, but he pinned her in place. "No. Stop. *Dammit.* I…shit. Please?"

She stopped fighting him, but he felt the tension in her body. "Please what?"

"Please understand that I'm a dumb fuck. But you should have figured that out by now."

"True." Her body remained tense.

"Let me try again. I care about you. But I don't know where this is going. The original rules—this ends when we leave Neah Bay—are still in play for me. I can't make any promises for more." He wished he could see her face but at the same time was afraid. Maybe the dark was better. Yeah. It had to be.

"Let me go, Luke. *Please*. Let me go."

He rolled off her, and she slipped from the bed. "Undine…"

He heard her searching for clothing in the dark. She opened the bedroom door. Light from the nearly full moon flowed through the high windows and gave the room a milky glow. He slipped off the condom and rose from the bed. He dropped it in the bathroom trash.

She was a dark, half-dressed shadow as she passed him in the hall and crossed the kitchen to the sliding glass door. The comforting sound of crashing waves entered the cabin when she opened the door and slipped outside.

Much as he wanted to give her space, going outside when a killer—who'd twice targeted her—might be on the hunt wasn't smart. He couldn't even give her that.

He returned to the bedroom and plucked his shorts from the floor then followed her outside. "Undine, you can't—"

"I'm just going to sit on the porch," she said as she dropped into one of the heavy plastic chairs.

"I need to be with you. To protect you."

"I'd rather you didn't." She pulled her knees to her chest, planting her bare feet on the seat.

"Tough." He sat, and cold plastic met his bare back. He

should have grabbed a blanket or shirt. Stupid. But that was nothing new. Undine had had him in knots since she showed up at his door in Port Angeles.

She loves me.

The thought triggered a warm sensation in his belly.

She loves me.

He'd never been truly loved by a woman before. And with Undine, it sure as hell was real, or she never, ever would have said it.

The warmth in his belly spread.

She loves me.

This might not be a bad thing.

It might even be the best thing that had ever happened to him. If only he didn't fuck it up. Except, he probably already had.

The night was crisp with low clouds on the horizon, but the sky above was open and clear, revealing a brilliant canopy of stars over the moonlit ocean. The bright moon gave enough light to see waves break both on the shore and in the distance.

He was freezing his ass off, however, in the chill wind. He stood and plucked Undine from her seat. "Luke!"

He moved to the porch steps and sat down, facing the ocean with Undine on his lap. He leaned against the upper step and looked at the stars now that they were no longer under the porch roof. She settled against him, the tension in her body leaving her by slow degrees.

He inhaled the salty, fresh air. Listened to the crash of the waves. "So. You love me."

She made a noncommittal grunting sound in reply.

He tightened his arms around her, so thankful for this moment. This beautiful night. This beautiful woman. He buried his face in her neck. "Cool," he whispered.

Chapter Twenty-Four

"We couldn't get a decent side scan sonar image on the *Wrasse* before because it was covered by too much sediment," Undine said to her father. "Fifty years in the strait can do that."

Undine, Stefan, Trey, and Luke sat in a semicircle around a table on the *Nereid*, colorful charts laid out on the surface. A camera was rolling. The information she imparted wasn't for Stefan's benefit so much as it was for documentary viewers.

Luke fidgeted in discomfort, wondering how the hell he'd gotten himself roped into this. He was a SEAL, trained to avoid the limelight, yet here he was at the table, in front of cameras. Even worse, this wasn't being forced on him. Like an idiot, he'd volunteered.

When he agreed to swim with Undine in the cutaway shoot yesterday, it had been nothing more than a fun way to needle Stefan. He'd never planned to stay on for the actual excavation and filming. But then he'd found a woman's body in a tank of electrified, rusty salt water, and now he couldn't walk away.

Diving on *Wrasse* and the Soviet sub might be the fastest

way to figure out Yuri's plan, to know what he was searching for in the deep, and why he'd wanted the case badly enough to kill for it. And so once again, Luke's plans to leave Neah Bay were foiled by conscience and a quest for answers.

He'd been granted leave from his NOAA duties until the excavation was complete, because his bosses at NOAA were delighted with the idea of him having a role in the documentary, complete with his Navy SEAL background and current NOAA credentials below his name whenever he answered questions and spoke directly to the camera. It would look good for the agency, and everyone believed the story of seven retired sailors taking down a Soviet sub during the Cuban Missile Crisis would garner much deserved attention. There was already talk of a big screen release, not a straight-to-TV run.

The thought made his eye twitch.

His SEAL buddies were going to have a field day, calling him a glory hound and teasing him for going Hollywood.

"This is the magnetometer reading that was taken a year ago," Undine continued, "after the *Wrasse* was first located. Magnetometers can tell us when something is present, but they can't provide more than positive or negative data. In this instance, it indicated iron or other metals were present on the seafloor, but no hint as to the actual configuration." She pointed to a figure-eight-shaped red patch on the paper in front of her. "The reading was a big red blob, which now makes sense knowing there are two subs down there."

Undine and Stefan sat in the middle of the semicircle. Luke was to Undine's right, her father to her left. Trey sat to Stefan's left. The seating was cramped, but there was plenty of space between father and daughter. Her body language conveyed the rift between them to anyone who bothered to look. But at the same time, it was clear father and daughter cared about each other very much. A heartbreaking dynamic, if Luke could view it without bringing his understanding of the rift into focus.

Luke knew Undine's mother had essentially abandoned her when she was six. Similarly, Luke's dad had suffered chronic pain. When Luke was a boy, his father had escaped into a prescription drug and alcohol addiction, where he stayed until the day when Luke was fourteen and his dad crawled into a bottle and never came out.

He'd never been able to forgive his father for not finding another way to cope. For not choosing his sons over pills. Luke treated his body like a damn temple as a result. He drank alcohol, but rarely, and never, ever to excess.

When the doctors said he would suffer persistent pain in his hip from the combat injury that had ended his tenure with the SEALs, he'd been shaken, fearing going down the path his father had taken. But he hadn't taken a prescription painkiller in three years, two months, and sixteen days. Instead he worked out, until the pain in the rest of his body eclipsed that of his hip. When that failed, he meditated. And on the rare occasions when the pain fired up and it was so bad he was tempted to seek a stronger painkiller, he'd call his mother or his brother. He'd hear their voices and know they were enough reason to stick around. To not take the easy out that could lead him down the road to uncontrolled addiction.

His family was that important to him. They were his reason for facing the pain head-on, for fighting his way through with nothing more than mind over neurons.

Much as Luke hated Stefan, seeing Undine's painful estrangement from the only real family she had triggered a disturbing ache, akin to the one in his hip, but more focused in the chest region, which meant he was going to have to come to some sort of accord with the bastard. Everyone estimated the excavation would take a full month, and he was committed to the bitter end.

Undine shuffled the papers, bringing up the original side scan sonar image from a year ago, which showed almost nothing of interest, just a bump that was likely the conning tower of the USS *Wrasse*. "Now that there has been some clearing of the Soviet sub"—she purposely left out information on how and when that clearing had occurred, as this was for the camera—"I think we might be able to get a decent side scan image."

"Worth a shot," Stefan said. "We'll do some magnetometer readings as well. Maybe we can get more refined data with the new equipment we've just installed on *Nereid*."

Stefan, Luke had learned, had used his TV money to buy some new toys, equipping RV *Nereid* more like a treasure hunting—or underwater archaeology—vessel rather than a scientific research boat.

Had Stefan been trying to lure his daughter back into the fold? Why did he need to?

While he understood better than anyone the rift between the two, he didn't understand why Undine, who loved the ocean and studying the living organisms within it as much as Luke ever had, wasn't working in the field of her heart, especially when her father could pretty much hand it to her.

Stefan prattled on for the camera about the sonar system and how it would provide them with enough information to develop a grid for the excavation. Then Undine took over and explained why having a framework for examining the Soviet sub was important, because admiralty laws protected the vessel in the same way US vessels were protected in foreign waters.

"Excuse me," the director, Diego, said off-camera. "Are you saying Russia retains sovereignty over this vessel even though it sank in US waters, and likely engaged an unarmed US submarine in battle before both sank?"

"Yes, exactly. We can dive on it and examine it, but we

can't harm the integrity of what remains at the bottom of the strait. Presumably there are human remains aboard, and we need to treat the Soviet submariners who died with the same respect we wish for our men who've been lost in foreign waters. However, we can and need to examine the wreck, in an attempt to determine what happened to both vessels in October 1962. External evaluation won't violate admiralty law."

"Will the remains of the US sailors be recovered from the USS *Wrasse*?" Diego asked. He knew the answer; they all did. This was again for the documentary-viewing public.

"Yes," Undine said. "But their recovery will not be filmed."

Diego gave the hand signal indicating that was a wrap, and she slumped against Luke's shoulder now that the cameras weren't rolling. Because he was a sucker, he kissed her temple.

"You handled that like a pro, Undine," Diego said. "No one will believe this was your first time in front of the camera since you were sixteen."

Luke frowned. Undine hadn't been in any of Stefan's documentaries since then? Luke had spent the last dozen years avoiding watching the institute's regular films—which once upon a time had been his favorite thing to watch—because he hadn't wanted to catch a glimpse of her or her esteemed father. Did she quit working for the institute imme-diately? He understood her not wanting to work for her dad, but he still didn't understand why she didn't pursue her own career in one of the many marine biology-related fields.

He slid out from the bench seat, releasing her from her imprisoning position. She stood and stretched. "I need some fresh air. Join me on deck?" she asked Luke.

"I'll be up in a minute," he said.

"'Kay." She stretched up on her toes and kissed him.

Yesterday he'd have thought the action was to piss off her dad, but he had new perspective today, given her admission in the middle of the night.

She dropped down, but he wrapped an arm around her waist and deepened the kiss before letting her go. He, however, *did* do that to piss off her dad. Or at least, that was what he told himself.

As soon as she disappeared up the steps, he turned to Stefan. "Why did Undine leave marine biology?"

Stefan scowled and glanced from Diego, who was conferring with Mario, the cameraman, mere feet away, then back to Luke. "You know why."

"I know why she left the institute. That's not what I'm asking. I want to know why she holds an undergrad degree in archaeology and a master's in nautical archaeology. When she was sixteen, she was well on her way to a bachelor of science in marine biology. Why did she change majors?"

Stefan cleared his throat and glanced at the other three men in the cramped cabin. "Would you mind giving us a moment of privacy?"

"No problem," Diego said. He and Mario retreated to the upper deck, but Trey remained.

"You too, Trey," Stefan said, before Luke uttered the same words. After what Undine had told him, he itched to punch the man. Discussing her in front of Trey was dangerous to his self-control.

As soon as they were alone, Stefan let out a heavy sigh. "She didn't tell you?"

"I wouldn't be asking if she had."

"Then maybe I shouldn't either."

"Cut the crap, Stefan, and tell me."

"It's your fault, you know. She was brilliant. Is brilliant. She'd be running the institute already if she hadn't changed majors."

Luke squeezed his hand into a fist. Yeah, it was a good thing Trey wasn't here, because he wanted a punching bag right about now. "How could her changing majors possibly be my fault?"

"When you lost your scholarship and I ensured no one in the field would hire you even to mop their floors, she gave me an ultimatum. She said she'd never dive with me again if I didn't make things right for you."

He shrugged. He'd guessed something like that had happened from the phone conversation he'd heard. "That's not what I'm asking."

"When I refused, she told me that as long as you can't work as a marine biologist, she wouldn't either. She said that if you couldn't have the career you love, she should be punished the same way. After all, she claimed—and believed—you didn't know. She gave up a brilliant career for an asshole who lied, manipulated, and used her."

The breath had whooshed out of Luke as Stefan's first statement sank in. Undine had punished herself in the only way she could—in a manner that equaled Luke's punishment. And all this time, he'd had no idea.

She couldn't make things right, so she'd made it fair.

During all his years of being angry, he'd thought she'd never paid a price. In his mind, she was Princess Undine, who could lie, seduce, and ruin without penalty.

But that wasn't the truth at all. She'd paid dearly with the loss of the close bond with her dad. And she'd given up studying a subject she loved.

"So you see why I hate you, Sevick," Stefan said. "You ruined her future. You walked into my institute, and I treated you like a son. Hell, you were so smart and passionate about our research, I might even have wanted you for her—someday—when she was older. But you couldn't wait. She was sixteen and on the cusp of so much, and you took and destroyed."

"I didn't *know*, Stefan," Luke said, the words hoarse in his throat. "I never would have touched her if I'd known she was only sixteen."

"Bullshit. You *did* know. And the one thing I protected her from was breaking her by telling her exactly how you used her. I was hoping she'd figure it out for herself when she was old enough to handle it, or that Trey would tell her. But he didn't, and I couldn't deliver that blow."

"What do you mean, 'Trey would tell her'? What the fuck are you talking about?"

"I'm talking about the fact that Trey *told* you she was only sixteen. He told me how he warned you to back off, that she was too young. And you ignored him."

A dozen years ago, he'd constructed a mental dam to contain his rage. He'd survived SEAL training by knowing the limits of the dam. He'd channeled the anger into long, brutal workouts, letting the rage release in a controlled flow, like water filling a reservoir. He'd mastered the rage so it wouldn't sneak up on him when he was underwater or on a mission. But now, that dam fissured, and he had no control over the flow.

The object of his rage had a face, which, for the first time in twelve years, didn't belong to either Stefan or Undine.

He turned to the man he'd admired, the man who'd taken away his future. At least now he understood Stefan's unrelenting fury. His utter lack of remorse. Even the reason he'd never held Undine responsible. It all made sense. "You stupid fuck. You believed Trey? That asshole never told me a damn thing."

Luke closed his eyes as memories came flooding back. Trey's jealousy over Luke's growing role at the institute and his animosity when Stefan promised Luke a prized spot on an upcoming research expedition.

"You've kept a snake by your side all these years." He shook his head. "Was he the one who told you? About Undine and me? Did you ever think that for him to know we'd had sex, he would've had to follow us to the cove? So ask yourself this, if he followed us, if he was *watching*, why didn't Saint Trey stop us before it was too late?"

Stefan blanched, but Luke didn't much care. The fissure widened. The dam crumbled. Luke had a target to find.

He left Stefan and bounded up the stairs. On the deck, he whirled in a circle, looking for Trey. He was on the bench, being interviewed by Diego. Sitting in the same spot where Luke had pulled a soaking-wet Undine onto his lap the day before.

He stalked toward Trey, vaguely noting the camera was recording, but he didn't have enough control left to care. He grabbed Trey by the collar and pulled him to his feet. "You gutless, spineless, rotten bastard. You lied." He wanted to strangle the man, but found just enough control to avoid homicide.

"What the hell are you talking about, Sevick?" Trey glanced nervously at the camera.

Luke slapped him across the cheek. Not too hard. Just enough to get his attention. Like this was an interrogation. The quick kind, like when the clock was running down during an op, and the informant turned out to be playing both sides. "You get a slap every time you lie."

Trey tried to push him off, but Luke didn't budge. He had twice Trey's muscle mass and full knowledge of how to use it.

"I don't know what you mean!" Trey said.

Luke slapped him again. The other cheek this time. "Lie."

"I never lied to Stefan."

Luke hit again with his right hand. "You lied twelve years ago. You're lying now. It's time for the truth."

"You mean when I told him about you and Undine? I didn't lie. You had sex with her."

Luke checked his swing. Truth. "Keep going."

"I never—"

Slap.

"I can keep this up all day." He couldn't prompt Trey. The man had to say it on his own, or he'd claim Luke had fed him the words.

"I don't know—"

Slap.

His fingers itched to go for the throat. His slight grip on control was slipping.

Deep breath. Focus.

"Say it, dammit." He raised his hand again as if to strike.

Trey flinched, then slumped when the slap didn't come. "I told Stefan that I'd warned you Undine was underage. I told him you knew."

"And?" Luke asked, hand poised.

"It was a lie."

Luke took him by the scruff of his neck and made him face the camera, barely seeing the shocked bystanders who'd gathered behind them. "Say it into the camera, Trey. Tell everyone what you did."

"I lied. So Stefan would take away your scholarship and have you blackballed. I lied. But you're still the asshole who had sex with an underage girl."

"And I'm guessing you're the prick who watched it happen and didn't do a damn thing to stop it."

"Why should I have when you were giving me the perfect opportunity to get rid of you?" Trey broke out of Luke's grip and took a swing.

Luke let it connect with his jaw and didn't even feel the

sting. It gave him the perfect excuse to do what he'd been burning to do. He pulled back and popped Trey in the jaw. Trey's head snapped back, and he tumbled backward over the rail, hitting the water with a satisfying splash.

Luke turned back to the audience that had gathered on deck. Stefan, Undine, Diego, Mario, and the four others who made up Stefan's staff. He knew his eyes had to be downright feral. Punching Trey didn't lessen the rage. If anything, he was more ramped up. "I'm out," he said. "I can't work with that asshole."

He needed to get the hell out of here. He hadn't suffered a rage incident like this since the early days, before he learned how to channel it, before he built the mental dam. He jumped to the lower deck. Thank God they were still at the dock; otherwise, he'd have to swim to shore.

He disembarked without looking back. As he marched toward the road, he heard Mario help Trey from the water. He fought the urge to turn around and shove the man back in the icy bay.

Did Trey's lie even matter?

Would Stefan have backed off without it?

The fact remained that Luke was the one who slept with Undine. He'd fucked up his own life in screwing around with the boss's daughter. He might not have known her age, but he knew damn well how close she and Stefan were.

He'd envied their relationship and had viewed Stefan as a father figure. Not a surprising transference given his sorry excuse for a dad. Had he wanted Undine simply because his subconscious saw a way to secure Stefan as a father-in-law? Had he been interested in her back then because she was a means to an end?

Was he actually guilty of the one thing Stefan had believed about him?

And what the fuck was he doing with her now? Was he

seeking revenge? There was no doubt that getting involved with her—*getting her to fall in love with me*—was a fine revenge on both Undine and Stefan.

The rift between father and daughter was bigger than ever, and everyone involved knew Luke would just break Undine's heart.

The pumping rage that drove his feet down the dock whispered the ugly truth: If his goal was revenge, he couldn't have planned it better.

Chapter Twenty-Five

Undine watched Luke bolt down the dock and was torn between giving him space and tearing after him. She realized now how much he'd been holding himself in check in the beginning, when their past kept slapping them in the face. The angry sex that first night as he battled anger and attraction made sense. It was a wonder they'd been able to move beyond his pent-up rage at all.

But for a few magnificent days, their present hadn't been overshadowed by the past, and they'd forged something new. Something real.

Until her father and Trey had brought it all back.

Luke marched out onto the main road and made a beeline for the gym. She let out a sigh of relief. He'd find an outlet that wasn't Trey's face. She wouldn't mind throwing a few punches at Trey herself, but Luke's strength combined with his anger could easily kill the man.

"I never lied to you, Stefan. I just wanted Luke to stop." Trey's voice was shrill and anxious. "I was afraid for my life!"

She had no doubt he was afraid, but she also had no doubt he was lying to her father again, trying to undo the damage. How had he managed to convince her father to keep his lie a bitter secret all these years?

Deep down, she knew. Her mental state after the blowout had been yet another weapon in Trey's arsenal. Stefan had probably believed that if he broke her faith in Luke once and for all, she'd feel used, violated, leaving a scar on her young psyche. It was true she'd struggled with the fact that Luke had hated her. So her dad had sacrificed their bond by never explaining his steadfast determination to destroy Luke.

Her heart broke for her dad then, what he'd given up in the name of protecting her. But she was also pissed at him for not having faith in her. He'd treated her like an adult in every way, but when she got into a very adult mess, he'd treated her like a child far younger than she really was.

It wasn't like she was twelve. She'd been just a few months shy of seventeen, for chrissake, and taking junior-level college courses while teaching scuba safety and acting as an assistant research scientist at the institute. She had a professional and academic life most people didn't have until their early—or even late—twenties. And her dad had been so proud of her for all of that.

Until she'd ventured into another adult area he wasn't ready to deal with.

She'd recognized long ago that on one level, he'd been right. She hadn't been ready for sex or the emotional complications—at least, not with someone so much older. But that didn't change the fact that her father had expected her to live in an adult world of his creation, unintentionally isolating her from peers her own age. There was no one in her world with whom she could safely explore relationships and sexuality.

Then poor Luke showed up. He didn't stand a chance when he unintentionally broke through her emotional isolation. "Dad," Undine said. "Like Luke, I'm out. I can't work with Trey. Have fun making the documentary without us."

Trey's eyes turned feral—as wild as Luke's had been. "You bitch! This is all your fault. You and that stupid jarhead jock."

Laughter bubbled up. "He's a frogman, not a jarhead, moron."

"He's a bully," Trey continued. "I haven't done anything wrong, and you're trying to fuck me over. You're jealous of my relationship with your dad, so you want me out."

She looked at Trey in shock. "So this is all about *you*? You lie to my dad for twelve years, allow our relationship to be destroyed, and ruin a man's life, and it's all about *you*? How precious." She glanced around the boat and remembered her role in this operation. This wasn't a Stefan Gray documentary. This was UAB, and she was in charge. Her dad had it written into the contract. "You know what, I take it back. I'm staying. You, however, are fired."

"You can't do that. This is your dad's boat. Your dad's institute."

"You're fired from the documentary. You have ten minutes to gather your personal belongings from this vessel and leave."

Trey looked to her dad, who'd been silent throughout the exchange. "Are you going to let her do that, Stefan? She knows nothing about *Nereid*."

Her dad let out a heavy sigh. "No."

Trey lit up. "Thank God. I knew you'd—"

Her dad's fist shot out and connected with Trey's jaw. He tumbled over the side again. Stefan leaned over the rail and waited for Trey to surface, then said, "You don't even have ten minutes. Your belongings will be delivered to the dock. You have two days to move out of your quarters at the institute. You're fired."

✳

*T*hirty minutes into Luke's workout, after most of his rage had abated, the two youths who'd been watching him lift weights approached him. "We heard a rumor that you were a SEAL," the first one said.

Luke grimaced as he lifted the barbell to shoulder height. His hip burned, but no more than the rest of him. Once he had the heavy weights resting on his chest, he said, "I was," then pumped the bar above his head and held it.

"You know the guy who shot bin Laden?" the other one asked.

Luke lowered the bar in stages until it was on the mat, then faced the boys. They were probably seventeen or eighteen; both had wiry builds, much as Luke had at that age. Their dark hair, complexions, and facial features indicated they were Makah tribal members. He'd seen them in the gym several times since he started coming here.

"Nah. I wasn't on Team Six. I was on the team that focuses on water-based operations."

"Me an' Jimmy," the first one said, "we want to join the Navy. We want to go through Basic Underwater Demolition/SEAL training and become SEALs. We're doing a mock physical screening test in a few months."

Luke presented his hand. "Luke Sevick."

"Daniel Ferguson," the first one said, shaking his hand. "Ray's my uncle," he added, before Luke could ask.

"Jimmy Houser."

"Nice to meet you both," Luke said as he shook Jimmy's hand.

"Do you have any tips, or advice? We've been working out. We're in good shape, but we've been watching you, and it looks like we've got a long way to go."

"I've been out of the SEALs for over four years. My workout is different. I injured my hip in combat and can't do the harder, longer endurance training—not without a lot of pain. So instead I lift weights to increase swim strength and have more muscle mass now than I did as a SEAL. To get through BUD/S, you need endurance and functional strength." He glanced down at the barbell at his feet. "Forget lifting. Sure, I can deadlift four hundred pounds now, but I can promise you, I never needed to do that as a SEAL. What I needed—what you'll need—is the endurance you build with ruck marches and long runs. You need to be able to run five miles just to get to the chow hall at the end of an intensive day of swimming and workouts on the grinder. Fifty-mile bike rides are good prep for BUD/S. Grinder physical training—calisthenics—is key. Also pull-ups and kettlebell workouts, those will get you ready for the mock PST. How many miles can you run?"

"We've both completed a half marathon," Jimmy said.

"Good. You'll need to be able to do ten on sand in addition to a road half marathon. Fortunately, you've got some great beaches around here to practice on. But the most important thing when it comes to making the cut is attitude. You've got to want it more than you've ever wanted anything in your life. You've got to believe the training is actually going to kill you, and want it enough to keep going. Nothing can quite prepare you for that."

"Would you be willing to…work with us? I mean, you're here working out anyway. Maybe show us your grinder PT routine, and we'll follow?"

"I'm no fitness instructor," he said. "I'm not qualified to give advice. I don't know how to assess your limits. But if you want to follow my lead and adjust as necessary to suit your level, I'm cool with that."

What started off as a calisthenics workout morphed into sparring lessons as others in the gym joined in and the boys wanted a demonstration of fighting techniques.

He knew what happened to Annie probably wasn't far from their minds, and wasn't surprised the gym was busy the day after a shocking murder that must have rocked the tiny community.

Ninety minutes into his workout, the rage was gone and he was flying high on a different sort of adrenaline. Uncomplicated human interaction. Guys bonding.

Only this wasn't him working out with his team. Here he was the mentor, a role he enjoyed. This was the break he'd needed. Better than meditation.

He was on the mat working with Daniel, demonstrating a hold. His grip was loose so as not to hurt the boy, as he showed arm position and leverage. The front door to the gym opened, and he glanced over to see the beautiful water nymph who was slowly but surely stealing his heart.

He paused, just taking her in, the way her brow furrowed and her lips opened in surprise as she took in the scene that surely looked like Luke was beating up on a young tribal member.

An elbow gouged him in the ribs, and a moment later, he was flat on his back, with Daniel's foot on his chest. Daniel had used Luke's distraction and taken the advantage in the sparring match. Smart boy.

Luke grinned up at him. "Big mistake with placing your foot there." In slow motion, he showed how to hit the back of the knee and grab the ankle, throwing the boy off-balance. He brought Daniel down and took the power position.

Face thusly saved, he left Daniel on the mat and approached Undine. He was coated in sweat and had to smell worse than a locker room, but she didn't flinch. She wrapped her arms around his neck and planted her mouth on his for a long, deep kiss.

He slipped his arms around her waist and lifted her. Kissing her with exuberance after the emotional upheavals of the day. There was so much left to settle between them, but this…this was real. Whatever it was that initiated it might not matter, because the chemistry between them was a tangible thing.

"I really hope you know her," Jimmy said.

"Dude, what body spray do you use?" Daniel asked.

Undine laughed, and he set her down. She faced the group of gaping boys, who'd just witnessed the too-intense-for-public kiss. "Nope. We've never met. But it's not the body spray, it's the muscles." She made a face. "Although body spray or deodorant might be a good idea, now that you mention it."

He laughed. "I'll hit the shower, then we'll head to the cabin?"

She nodded. "I'll wait."

"You missed your workout today. You could get thirty minutes of cardio in while I clean up." He flashed a grin to let her know he was teasing.

She rose on her toes and whispered in his ear, "I have a different workout in mind. I hope you haven't overworked your quads."

He nipped at her neck and murmured, "That sounds like I'm going to do the work, not you."

She shrugged. "So you'll wear my Fitbit."

"I really think someone needs to explain to you how a Fitbit works."

She slapped him on the butt. "Hit the shower. You can explain on the drive home."

He headed into the locker room, entirely too pleased at the sound of the word home in reference to their cozy rental cabin on the ocean.

"I want to be clear on one thing," Luke said as he settled in the driver's seat of his SUV. "I didn't push for Trey to confess for your father's benefit. I don't give a damn if Stefan believes me."

"I figured you just wanted to hear him say it," Undine said, surprised that this point was so important to him. "You've owned your part, I've owned mine. But Dad and Trey have never owned theirs."

"I suppose that's part of it, but that wasn't why either."

"Then why did you?" she asked. A water droplet gathered at the end of the wet hair at the nape of his neck, forming a short, thin ducktail. She reached out and ran her fingers through the swatch, dispersing the moisture and tickling his scalp. He'd barely taken the time to towel dry his hair after his shower. In a hurry to get home or eager for this conversation?

He caught her wrist and brought her damp fingers to his lips. He sucked her index finger into his mouth. This argued that he was eager to get home and start Undine's workout.

"I did it for you," he said. "I couldn't bear the idea that you might believe the lie. That you might think I knew all along. That I used you."

The emotion in his voice made her breath catch. He might not love her, but he damn well did care. For now, that was enough. She pulled his hand to her lips and kissed the knuckles that had punched Trey. "It doesn't matter if my dad had come forward with that claim twelve years ago, six years ago, or today. I never would have believed it. I *knew* you, Luke. And don't forget, I saw your face when you learned the truth. You were shocked. Horrified. Repulsed. I never would have doubted you. Ever. I'm sorry my dad couldn't see you as clearly as I did. I'm sorry he believed Trey."

Luke shrugged. "I'm not sure what your father believed mattered. But what you believe matters to me. A lot."

She'd already told him once. There was no point in holding back now, especially when she had a feeling these were words he really needed to hear right now. "I believe I love you. And it's okay that you can't say it back. I get that. Just know it's true for me."

He leaned over and kissed her, soft, sweet, just a little bit of tongue, but packed with emotion. "Cool."

She rolled her eyes and laughed. "Let's go home, Cyrano."

"Nobody will ever say you love me because of my way with words."

"No. It's totally that you're a badass scientist."

"I thought it was my body?"

"Nah. Your body turns me on, absolutely, but the fact that you're a scientist has always been the sexiest thing about you."

She cradled his hand in her lap as he drove and told him Trey had been fired from both documentary and institute. "I understand if you don't want to be in the documentary with my dad. Unfortunately, I can't fire him."

"I don't know what I want. You and I were fine until your Dad got here. I thought I was done with all the anger and resentment. I wasn't thinking about the past at all until it smacked us in the face, reminding me we were in a bubble that isn't the real world. I felt a kind of rage today I haven't felt in years, and it scared me. I didn't like me very much."

She also heard what he wasn't saying. The reason he couldn't commit to her beyond Neah Bay. She—their history —was a trigger for him. As long as her father was part of her life, he couldn't forget the past, not when it was closer to the surface than he'd ever imagined.

Chapter Twenty-Six

The following day, Luke dropped Undine off at the marina with a kiss. Her task for the day was to refamiliarize herself with *Nereid*, and review the side scan sonar data her father had collected the day before.

Luke would keep busy by checking in with the Coast Guard, who'd finished the inspection of Ray's boat and were in the loop with the FBI on the murder investigation. After that, he planned to return to the gym and work out with the boys. Mostly he was killing time because he wasn't ready to face Stefan. He feared the rage that had engulfed him yesterday.

At the Coast Guard Station, he learned they'd found definitive evidence of sabotage of Ray's boat. Not that this was a surprise, but it had been necessary to verify. Commander Brian Martinez—Coast Guard Station Neah Bay's commanding officer—requested an update on the excavation plans. The Coast Guard would do periodic sweeps of the area when *Nereid* was anchored above the subs. Luke shared what he knew of the schedule without mentioning that he might not be part of the project.

He didn't like the idea of Undine diving without him, especially on technical dives, which meant she'd be on the bottom longer. Mixed-gas dives were a complicated venture. Much as he was glad Trey had been fired, the man was also the institute's mixed-gas expert. Stefan would now have to remain on deck to run the hoses, meaning Undine would be paired with a less-experienced diver.

All of Stefan's staff were versed in mixed-gas, but Luke had a hard time trusting anyone but himself when it came to Undine's safety.

When Luke's meeting with the Coast Guard adjourned, Parker asked if he'd like to grab lunch at the station cafeteria. Considering they had much healthier fare than could be found in town, Luke accepted the invitation. During lunch, he quizzed Parker on his technical diving experience. The guy might make a good dive partner for Undine. He was in the uniformed armed services and knew how to handle a weapon. Not that that was necessary underwater, but Luke figured the threat remained, and he'd like someone on deck with the right skills.

"I heard there was some excitement on *Nereid* yesterday," Parker said.

"Scandal travels fast," Luke muttered with a grimace.

"No. It's more that Trey Kilpatrick showed up here and asked if we could help arrange a ride for him to Port Angeles. It seems that Dr. Gray expected the man to walk."

"What did you do?"

"*I* suggested he hire a taxi to fetch him."

Luke laughed. "Good Lord. I don't want to think about how much that would cost."

"Yeah," Parker snickered. "Unfortunately, one of the others told him about the bus line." Parker's eyes twinkled. "You know anything about the bruises on his face?"

Luke shrugged. "I hear he ran into a door."

"And I hear there was camera rolling when the door hit him."

"If he sues the door, the door is so fucked."

"In my experience," Parker said, leaning forward conspiratorially, "if someone is dishonest enough to lie in one area, he's dishonest in other ways as well. I've been wondering for the last three years why Dr. Gray had to resort to reality TV to fund his institute. Yesterday, Kilpatrick said something that perked my interest. He's been second in command at the Gray Oceanographic Institute for four years."

"He received the promotion, and then Gray's finances took a turn."

"Exactly. I bet you dollars to donuts you never hear a word from Kilpatrick or his lawyers. He's going to quietly disappear because he's been shut out before he can cover his crumbs, and that boy had his hand in the cookie jar."

Parker's suspicion had merit, enough that Stefan should probably have someone secure the institute's financial data in case Trey had set up a back door, but Luke also realized this could be wishful thinking. He was bitter enough to enjoy the irony of Gray listening to the wrong man twelve years ago, and his trust in Trey had cost him both his daughter and the respect of the scientific community. Because the reality TV show had certainly harmed his reputation.

"You follow Stefan Gray's life that closely?" he asked Parker.

"I've been a fan since I was five years old. Some boys go through a dinosaur stage, some boys like trains. For me it started with whales. It morphed from there into a fascination with the whole damn sea. Gray's documentaries fed my obsession as a kid. Love of the sea is why I serve in the Coast Guard today."

Luke nodded, having undergone a similar childhood

phase that turned out not to be a phase at all. "If I didn't get into NOAA, I'd have tried for Coast Guard."

"With your background, you'd have been a shoo-in. I'd love to have you out there on patrols. But dealing with drunk tourists who shouldn't be at the helm of a boat is a far cry from fighting terrorists." Parker leaned back in his chair. "So, you know the guy who shot bin Laden?"

✵

Luke picked up Undine at four, as dusk was just beginning to settle over the bay. Clouds were thickening as well. A rainstorm was rolling in. Back at the cabin, he made dinner, a vegetarian quinoa dish he was pretty certain she wouldn't like, but he needed his amino acids, and his hip needed the anti-inflammatory properties. He'd make it up to her by giving her butter to go with it.

After dinner, he stood and stretched. His hip was stiffening. He'd overdone it in his workouts these last two days, pushing endurance instead of focusing on lifting. But exercising with the local teens had been fun and a good outlet. Today he'd had six boys and two girls in his improvised class, one of the newcomers had mentioned that Annie was his aunt. Another named her as cousin.

They were frightened, young, full of aggression, and needed an outlet. The regular trainer at the gym had pulled Luke aside and thanked him for working with them, as Luke broke up the routine at a time when it was sorely needed. They respected Luke. Admired him. Stories of his exploits as a war hero had already begun to circulate. He shook his head at that. Jokes with Undine aside, he was a quiet professional and would never claim hero status for doing his job.

But far better that these boys and girls show up at the gym rather than turn inward, and for them he'd pretend to be a badass SEAL who'd single-handedly liberated an entire village from the Taliban, if that was what they needed to see. The reservation was dry, but poverty was readily visible and there were enough handwritten signs warning of the dangers of drugs posted throughout the neighborhoods to know they were fighting an ongoing battle with drug and alcohol addiction out here at the remote northwest edge of the country.

So Luke had overworked his hip to impress a group of teens with his badass SEALness. At thirty-four he might not be old yet, but he clearly wasn't seventeen anymore. "You ever do yoga?" he asked Undine.

"Exercise that sometimes includes taking a nap? Yes."

He laughed. "You've gone to sleep while doing yoga?"

"I went to a few classes with this one instructor who always had a warm-down meditation that put me to sleep. He was my favorite instructor, but my Fitbit wasn't impressed with him."

"I need to stretch my hip. Join me?"

"Quinoa and yoga? You do know how to woo a woman." She winked at him.

He forgot all about his hip five minutes into the workout when Undine assumed the Downward Dog pose. Her ass in the air pretty much wiped all thought from his brain.

Ahh, the healing powers of yoga.

Or libido.

Unfortunately, there was a knock on the door, interrupting his intention to interrupt her workout. Even worse, the visitor was Stefan.

Luke invited the man in and offered him a drink. Water with lemon. Luke had manners, but he wasn't about to open a bottle of wine. Stefan accepted and sat on the couch. "I wanted to stop by last night but figured you weren't ready to see me."

Luke nodded and handed him the glass. He turned a

kitchen chair to face the couch, while Undine took a seat on the end of the couch closest to the door.

"Thanks for the tip about locking down the finances. I had my tech guy change all the passwords, and my accountant has an assistant who will go through the transaction files."

"It wasn't my idea. Parker Reeves mentioned it. But I thought it had merit, given the lengths Trey was willing to go to secure his spot at the institute."

Stefan sat forward and leaned his forearms on his knees. "There is something I want to tell you, if you're willing to listen."

Luke paused, doing a gut check for a surge of anger. None came. But then, he was being given a choice in this and appreciated the consideration. "Go ahead."

"Twelve years ago, the night after I tossed you out of the institute, Undine had me convinced I needed to let the matter drop. She'd explained how she was the instigator, that she'd lied. And I believed her. I couldn't hold you accountable when you were as much a victim. Honestly, if she'd actually been nineteen, I would have warned her of the dangers of dating a coworker and explained to her that things not going well in the relationship weren't grounds for firing, so she'd have to tread carefully, and then I would have stepped back and tried not to get my hopes up that my favorite daughter was dating my favorite employee."

Undine caught her breath. Her hand slipped across the space between herself and Stefan, and she took her dad's hand in hers. All while Luke was finding it a bit difficult to breathe.

"But she wasn't nineteen, and I couldn't condone the relationship, no matter how fond I was of you, Luke. The firing would have remained—all of us working together would have been difficult, but odds were you'd have been rehired after she turned eighteen or went off to grad school. I'd planned to return your scholarship and to keep the drama private between us. No blackballing.

"But then Trey visited me in my office. As you guessed, he was the one who originally told me of your relationship, so it was natural for me to tell him the decision I'd just made. He then told me that he'd warned you Undine was underage, and that you'd laughed it off. And I'm ashamed I believed him. And so the dominos fell."

"With all due respect, sir, the dominos didn't simply fall, you kicked them."

Stefan nodded. "I did. I kicked them. I felt betrayed. And I needed to protect my daughter from a viper who would do that. And I didn't see I'd let the good man get away and held the true viper close. I'm sorry, son. For everything I did. For what my daughter did. When I think that you could have gone to jail…I just… I know sorry doesn't cover it, but it's all I have to offer."

Luke took a deep breath. Days ago, he'd told Undine he didn't want her apology, and when she'd offered it anyway, he'd rejected it.

He'd never imagined Stefan Gray would apologize. He cleared his throat. "Thank you, sir."

"I know you've got a good position with NOAA, but, well, a job just opened up at the institute…"

Luke couldn't help but smile as he shook his head. "No, thank you." He shrugged. "I'm in the Commissioned Officer Corps. It's uniformed service and not a job I can simply quit. Nor do I want to."

Stefan nodded. "I understand. But I hope you'll consider returning to the documentary."

"Dad, no. You agreed not to pressure him." Her tone was scolding but affectionate. Luke was glad the rift had begun to heal.

His gaze slid over Undine. Her thick mahogany hair had slipped in front of her eyes, and she batted it away, an action she did frequently. A tic, both familiar and endearing, which revealed her eyes. Right now her wide, brown-green eyes were damp, and her long lashes glistened with unshed tears. Taken separately, some might think her nose was a bit too long and her chin a bit too short, but the end result was utterly perfect. And damn if he wasn't crazy about her.

He'd planned to offer up Parker to be her dive partner. The man could handle the deep, and with Stefan running the gas lines, she'd be fine. But no way could he hand her off to another dive partner any more than he could hand her off to any other kind of partner.

While they remained in Neah Bay, she was his, in water and on land. "Sweetheart, there's no way I'm letting you go back to the deep without me."

❈

That night, they made love with the lights on. Luke watched her come as he brought her to orgasm with his mouth and again when he was inside her. He only closed his eyes as his own orgasm overtook him, holding her tight as he pulsed with release in her welcoming body.

Afterward, he lay beside her, tracing circles on her back, as he knew she liked. The lights were still on, but she was half-asleep. He should turn them off and let her rest, but he couldn't stop looking at her.

Finally he realized why he was so energized and couldn't take his eyes off her. "I forgive you," he blurted.

She rolled over to face him, her eyes no longer lazy with satisfaction and contentment. "You do?"

He ran a finger down the length of her nose. God, how he loved her imperfect nose. "I do. I forgive your father too."

"How can you…?" There was wonder in her voice. "How can you even do that?"

"Because when you love someone, you don't want to see them in pain. And holding on to the past hurts you. I can't do that, not when it no longer matters."

"Wait. You…love me?"

"Yep. I love you."

Her lips widened in a broad smile. God, he loved her smile, the way it lit her brown-green eyes and revealed an ever-so-slightly crooked front tooth. Imperfectly perfect. Just like the rest of her. "Cool," she said.

He laughed and pulled her against him, feeling lighter than he had since…forever. Who knew that forgiveness would be this freeing? This utterly good. Jesus, all the years he'd wasted with anger. He should have tracked her down when she was twenty.

He was energized. Fired up. He needed to move, to burn the energy, or he'd never sleep. "I love you so much, I'm not even going to insist on you going for a run with me."

"You're going for a run, now? It's nearly midnight."

"It's only a few days since the full moon. It's bright with the moon reflecting off the water. I'm feeling pumped right now. A run along the ocean is just what I need."

"You're crazy, you know that right?"

"Yep. Will you come with me?"

She hesitated. Then she shook her head. "I think your kind of crazy is infectious, because a run in the moonlight sounds kind of good to me too."

He kissed her perfectly imperfect nose. "You won't regret this, sweetheart."

They stopped to rest when they reached the stream to the north that cut off the beach. He'd set too fast a pace, and she needed to catch her breath. He gazed up at the one bare stretch of sky that had a smattering of stars. The November

Leonid meteor shower had begun, but they wouldn't see much of it with the cloud cover.

The sand at his feet was littered with sand dollars. He reached down and scooped one up. It was bleached white, long since dead. Ancient legend said sand dollars were coins lost by mermaids. He smiled and held it out to her. "Was this one yours?"

She laughed and accepted his offering. "No. But I'm keeping it anyway. I still have the one you gave me the very first time we made love."

He slipped his hand behind her neck and pulled her to him for a deep kiss. "I'm glad."

He didn't know if he and Undine had a foundation to build on for the future, or if loving her merely shut the door on the painful past. He wasn't ready to face the question of whether they'd try to make this work beyond Neah Bay, and didn't think she was either.

She lived in DC. He lived in Port Angeles. She had friends in DC who'd taken on the role of family. He couldn't quit his job, and he didn't believe she wanted to quit hers. "Your dad told me you left marine biology because he forced me out."

She nodded.

"Why didn't you tell me?"

"It was my punishment, and it was only fair, but it didn't change things for you. It didn't feel right to tell you, as if it was some noble gesture, because that wasn't what it was about." She sighed. "And the truth is, I almost went back on it, after grad school. I moved back into the institute while I was looking for a job. It's when I dated Trey." She shivered, and he draped an arm around her. "The fact that I almost caved proved it was *always* a choice for me, while it was never a choice for you. So it wasn't equal. When I was offered an internship with NHHC, I jumped at the opportunity, both because it was a job I wanted and it meant I wouldn't have to go back on my vow. The internship led to a permanent position with UAB, so I never had to face that choice again."

"Now that I'm working in the field again, would you consider going back?"

"I don't know. I never really thought about it. Maybe? But…I really love my job, and it's damn hard to get a steady employment as a nautical archaeologist. It would be hard to walk away."

He nodded. She was tied to DC as much as he was tied here. "We should head back. We need to sleep if we're going to dive tomorrow."

"Walk or run?" she asked.

He entwined his fingers through hers. The run had dispelled his energy. He was no longer amped. Just content. "Let's walk. Unless you're cold and in a hurry to get back?"

"No hurry." Her fingers tightened around his, and she leaned her temple on his bicep. "This is nice."

He released her hand and draped his arm around her shoulder. "This is perfect."

They'd walked a half mile when he caught a whiff of smoke in the wind. The arc of the beach meant he couldn't see the cabins or the RV park, but he could see an orange glow. "Awww, shit."

Undine gasped. "Our cabin."

He set off full-bore, with her by his side. She dropped back, and he slowed so she could stay with him. He couldn't leave her alone. The glow grew brighter as they rounded the curve of the beach. At last, their cabin was in sight.

And fully engulfed in flames.

Chapter Twenty-Seven

Theirs was the only cabin that burned. The porch of the empty cabin to the right also caught fire, but the volunteer firefighters managed to contain it before more than the side stairs were destroyed. It was eight the following morning when Undine and Luke collapsed onto the bed of one of the smaller cabins that faced the beach.

The manager expressed concern the arsonist would strike again even as he gave Luke the key. "We'll just be here for one more night. Then I'm taking her to Port Angeles."

The man nodded.

Luke's biggest concern now was the question of whether or not the arsonist had known they were outside the cabin, or if this had been yet another attempt at murder.

Was it pure luck they were still alive?

The one consistency in the timing of the fire was that the excavation of *Wrasse* and the Soviet sub had once again been delayed. But of course, if Undine had died, the excavation would be put off indefinitely. No way would Stefan Gray stick around with his fancy dive equipment and run an excavation when his daughter had just perished, and the Navy would have to scramble to get a dive team up here to investigate.

The thought had Luke pulling her tight to his side. He'd already spoken with the Coast Guard, the FBI, and Curt Dominick, and they all agreed the target was most likely the excavation. Someone wanted to keep him and Undine out of the water. Which was why he would dive this afternoon, after he'd slept for a few hours. He'd been trained to work ops short on sleep, but Undine hadn't, so Stefan, who hadn't been told of the fire until an hour ago and therefore had a full night's sleep, would be Luke's dive partner.

Stefan's crew was qualified to manage the mixed-gas hoses, but for added security, Parker would be aboard *Nereid*.

Thank goodness Luke's dive gear had been on *Nereid*, not in the Hobuck cabin.

Soon they'd have answers. His only wish was that he had backup from his old SEAL team. This had become an op, and he could no longer think of it as a favor for the Navy or an old acquaintance.

Likewise, the bubble with Undine had been broken. The only reason he shared her cabin now was to protect her. No more distractions. No sex. No talk of love or the future. All that had fogged his mind and allowed him to turn soft and sloppy.

He was an operator again. A man fighting for his country and, in this instance, fighting for his woman. He wouldn't let the Navy, the FBI, the Coast Guard, or the attorney general down. But most of all, he wouldn't let Undine down.

He would sleep for four hours, then wake up and begin his mission. He closed his eyes, and, like the trained operator he was, he immediately fell asleep.

*U*ndine didn't like being on deck while Luke and her dad were at the bottom together. They hadn't been able to get the direct communication link that worked with the mixed-gas hoses to work, so they wouldn't be able to talk to anyone on the surface until they were back in radio range at the decompression stop.

The silence from below was unnerving.

Dad and Luke weren't using scuba. The gas was fed down tubes that ran directly from the boat, as the pure oxygen had been for decompression on her other dives. Both the mixed gases and the means of transmission to the divers meant they could be on the bottom longer. Coldness was a factor, because mixed gases caused divers to lose body heat and the longer period at the coldest depths only made it worse, but *Nereid* had hoses that pumped warm water directly into their wetsuits, further extending the amount of time they would be at the bottom.

All this meant an extended decompression stop, which meant more waiting for Undine, as the two men she cared about most in the world were on the bottom of the sea.

This sucked.

They were both extremely capable and experienced divers, but given the sabotage that had occurred at every stage, bringing them to this situation, she was still afraid. All she could do was monitor the hoses and make sure no one did something stupid, like hooking the monoxide outlet to one of their gas hoses.

Time moved slowly as she checked the dials for the hoses yet again. All the numbers were within the target range.

"It's good to have you back, Undine."

She smiled at Annabelle, a woman who was just a few years younger than her dad and had worked for the Institute since Undine was seven. Annabelle had been a surrogate mother in her younger years, and Undine hadn't realized how much she'd missed Annabelle until she arrived on *Nereid*. "It's good to be back."

"Are you planning to stay? Now that…well, everything." Annabelle gestured toward the anchor line where Luke and her father had disappeared below the surface. She flashed a grin. "Luke is more attractive now than he was twelve years ago. Maturity looks good on him."

Undine smiled back. "The muscles do too."

"It's nice seeing you two together. Like a jigsaw puzzle that was missing pieces, finally complete."

She nodded and tried not to think of the questionable future or the shock of the scary night. Everything was unsettled, and she and Luke as a couple was the least of it.

Someone had burned down their cabin. That someone could well have believed they were still inside.

"I'm glad Trey is gone," Annabelle continued. "I almost quit several times in the last few years after Trey took over the number two job."

Undine was glad to be pulled away from her thoughts. "Why didn't you take the job? Didn't Dad offer it to you?"

"He did. But I'm a scientist, not management. I'm not saying I couldn't do it. But I didn't want to. I still don't. You know Stefan is going to ask you to return."

"He already did. I said no. To answer your original question, no, I'm not back—with the institute—permanently. I have a life and a job all the way across the country."

"Bummer. But I understand." Annabelle checked her watch. "In five minutes, they'll start ascending for decompression."

"This wait is killing me."

"By tomorrow, the submersible should be back online. No more sending people down when we can use Marvin."

Undine couldn't help but smile. She'd nicknamed the

minisubmarine Marvin after reading *The Hitchhiker's Guide to the Galaxy* at the age of eleven. In spite of it being less robot and more remote controlled, the name had stuck. "That'll be a relief."

She and Annabelle settled into silence as the older woman returned to her task of prepping the pure oxygen line for the decompression stop.

At last, Luke's voice carried over the radio, informing them they'd reached decompression depth without incident. Parker relayed this news to the Coast Guard vessel waiting a hundred meters away. Undine glanced across the choppy water and gave the boatswain's mate on the deck a thumbs-up.

Luke is okay. Dad is okay.

I can breathe again.

Far too many minutes later, Luke finally climbed on the dive platform, followed by her dad. She didn't hesitate and ran forward and kissed Luke. The cold, salty water dripped from his BC vest and gear, saturating her.

He kissed her back, but his response was reserved. Something was wrong. Her gaze flew to her dad, but he looked unharmed and not even upset that his daughter was making out with Luke yet again. But then, he seemed to have moved on as if the last twelve years had never happened. Luke was back in the fold.

Undine knew it wouldn't be such an easy transition for Luke, even with apologies and forgiveness and love.

She met Luke's gaze, and his eyes were shuttered. He gave her a quick shake of his head, then glanced toward the deck where Annabelle and the film crew waited. "We need to go to the Coast Guard and call Curt. Now."

What the hell did they find at the bottom of the strait this time?

"From the markings you can see in these photos and the chipping of the corrosion on the inside, it's clear the torpedo tube was cleared out recently, within the last week, possibly even before the storm," Luke said. He'd opted for the expedient hose down instead of a full shower, and Stefan had done the same, so they'd settled into the conference room within thirty minutes of surfacing, and his hair was still damp.

He pointed to the photo that was projected on the screen. "By the time we located the tubes, we were down to just a few minutes left on the bottom, so we took as many photos as we could but didn't have a chance to explore further."

The attorney general's curses emitted from the speaker at the center of the table. Luke had emailed the photos to him before the conference call began. "Undine, what can you tell us about the sub?" the AG asked.

"From studying the photos Luke and I took of the deck gun and conning tower last week and our measurements of the length of the hull, I believe we have a Quebec-class sub. They were small, maneuverable, coastal attack submarines. Only the earliest versions had deck guns. There are photos of one such sub, *M-305*, online, to give you an idea of size and configuration. The Quebec-class subs had four twenty-one inch torpedo tubes in the bow. One tube was recently cleared out. One still has something inside, but it's so rusted over, it's hard to be certain what it is. It doesn't look like a torpedo. It appears the other two tubes were emptied before she sank."

"Did Quebec-class subs carry nuclear missiles?" Curt asked.

"No. They weren't first-strike subs capable of carrying MIRVs—but that doesn't mean they couldn't be retrofitted to transport a nuclear warhead. It might be a good idea to bring Trina—NHHC Cold War historian Dr. Trina Sorensen," she added with a glance at the men in the Coast Guard conference room, "—into the conversation. She knows much more about what the Soviet Union was developing at the time than I do."

Within minutes, Curt had Dr. Sorensen—Keith Hatcher's girlfriend, if Luke remembered correctly—patched into the conference call. Curt explained the top-secret nature of this conversation and explained to those listening in Neah Bay that Sorensen had high-level security clearance through her job at NHHC. Then the attorney general repeated his question. "Is there any evidence Quebec-class subs carried nuclear torpedoes?"

"No direct evidence," Sorensen said, "But that doesn't mean it's impossible. In 1961 and '62, the US was manufacturing the W54, our smallest nuclear warhead. We aren't entirely certain how small Soviet bombs got, but at the same time we were developing the W54, all sides were experimenting with nuclear artillery. It's possible an early scud might have been small enough to fit into a Quebec-class torpedo tube. Worth noting, however, is that if they only placed the actual nuclear device, without the necessary shell or missile housing, the bomb itself could be compact but powerful—more powerful than our W54s."

"So we can't rule out that whoever was digging on the Soviet submarine didn't recover a nuclear device?" Curt confirmed.

"It's possible," Sorensen said.

"How soon can we get a Geiger counter down there?" Curt asked.

"My remote-controlled submersible should be back online tomorrow, and it can take a Geiger reading," Stefan said, "in addition to giving us a better view of what's down there. If Marvin isn't ready to go, Lt. Sevick and I will dive again to get the reading. We need at least a six-hour surface interval, or we'd dive again today."

"Okay," Curt said. "I'm about to brief the secretary of state, so she'll be prepared to open a dialogue with Russia if we get a positive reading on the radiation. I need to remind everyone that this issue is classified. We don't want to create a panic when this could be nothing of the sort."

Luke studied the people around the table. Stefan, Undine, Commander Martinez, Lt. Parker Reeves, another lieutenant named Boyle, an ensign named Taylor, and Shales, the boatswain's mate who'd rescued them from the beach. Most of them—including Undine—didn't have the security clearance of even Dr. Sorensen, but they'd been involved from the start or, like Stefan, had been brought into the loop out of necessity, and so they were part of the core team.

Each person acknowledged the attorney general's orders, and the meeting adjourned. Luke leaned back in his chair as he met the gazes of the various Coast Guard men. From their grim expressions, he knew they were thinking the same thing he was. Yuri had gone to a hell of a lot of effort to extract something from that torpedo tube.

When Ukraine split from the Soviet Union, they'd ended up with the secret underground Soviet submarine base in the port town of Balaklava on the Crimean Peninsula. The massive hidden fortress had a great deal of information that detailed Soviet submarine activity during the Cold War. Not even the Kremlin had copies of some of the paperwork that ended up in Ukrainian hands.

It was entirely possible Yuri Kravchenko had access to those papers and knew exactly what happened on that October day in 1962. He might well have been searching for the Soviet sub since he arrived in the US five years ago. No way in hell would he have gone to all that trouble for a simple torpedo. Ukraine had a stockpile of those.

Luke figured that after fifty-plus years resting at the bottom of the strait, the Geiger counter reading of the empty torpedo tube would be off the charts.

Chapter Twenty-Eight

Undine had lost count of how many times she'd had plans to return to Port Angeles, only to have the trip put off. Since the fire, she was ready to leave Neah Bay, to be anonymous in a big city. She would happily go to Seattle to hide for a few days, just until she got her equilibrium back.

But they needed to know if there was radiation in those torpedo tubes, and Luke needed to be on hand in case Marvin wasn't up to the job. And no way in hell was she leaving Neah Bay while Luke remained.

And so they spent another night in a beachfront cabin, just a hundred meters from where the sweet cabin that had been their haven—the place where she'd fallen in love for the first time—had once stood. Luke didn't make love to her. He said—and she agreed—they couldn't afford to let their guard down. Instead, he held her while she slept, and she had a feeling his sleep was light—ready to spring into action should a threat appear.

The following morning, she parked herself next to the control station for Marvin on the back deck as her dad reattached the remote-controlled camera's wires. "What happened to Marvin?" she asked.

"When money got tight, I had to let Jose go."

Undine felt shock slide through her. Jose was a mechanical wizard who handled the technical repairs for the institute's most delicate equipment. "Why did money get so tight? I mean, letting go of Jose—that's pure penny-wise, pound-foolish."

Her dad's jaw clenched. "I know. It was a combination of things. I overbought on technology and upgrades to the boat. Some of those upgrades were a failure. Then IMAX was having their own problems and closing theaters, and they decided not to move forward with 3D theater showings of that documentary we'd filmed for wide release. They wanted to show superhero movies instead."

Undine grimaced. She'd seen the last three Marvel movies in 3D at an IMAX theater, but had yet to watch her dad's last documentary, which had released straight to DVD without even the National Geographic label that added a deserved layer of prestige. But she *had* bought the documentary, at least.

"So you don't really think Trey was embezzling," she said.

"I honestly don't know what to think. It's possible Trey took a bad situation—one that I'd created—and found it was the perfect cover for his actions. I didn't delve deeper into the money, even though I should have, but I do know that by the time I realized the extent of the institute's financial mess, it was far worse than I'd expected."

"And so you agreed to *Sink or Swim*."

"Much as I hate that reality show, it's kept the lights on. Last week, I signed the contract for season three. We've got permission to film some of it in Palau." Her dad's gaze fixed on Luke, who was on the other end of the deck conferring with Annabelle, who would pilot Marvin and operate the Geiger counter. "You know, viewers would love your SEAL if he stepped into Trey's role as the competition organizer."

She shook her head with a smile. Her dad was correct, viewers would swoon and Luke's background would be a huge draw, bringing in new viewers. But she couldn't imagine any scenario in which Luke would agree to become one of the faces of her dad's reality show, even if the underlying competition involved bringing a better understanding of the sea to TV viewers. "Yeah, I don't think so."

"Me neither. But damn, he'd be perfect. As would you—"

"No, Dad."

"Hear me out. If you aren't willing to be a regular, maybe you could show up in one episode as a celebrity judge."

"I'm not a celebrity—"

"You have name recognition, and after the explosion, people know your face. Filming for season three will start when the *Wrasse* documentary is in postproduction. Appearances on the show would be a good tie-in for the documentary. Promo for NHHC."

As much as she wanted to shoot down the idea, it had merit—presuming they actually produced the *Wrasse* documentary to begin with. Right now, with the questions about the Soviet submarine, that was doubtful. "I don't know, Dad."

"How about this… My publicist reminded me that as long as I'm here, I should attend the black-tie party on the ferry that runs between Port Angeles and Victoria this Saturday. The British Columbia premier and the governor of Washington will be on board to sign the agreement for the International Salish Sea Management Plan. It will be done with great pomp and circumstance. The agreement sets up a plan to expand both the US and Canadian marine wildlife sanctuaries into the strait. There'll be lots of press. The event is a perfect fit for my brand, and a great opportunity for some mild, positive promotion for *Sink or Swim*."

She shook her head, hearing her dad speak of his life's work as a brand. But like him, she wholly supported the cause of extending the sanctuaries and had been following the negotiations for the management plan with anticipation. It was the first such agreement between state and province and long overdue, even if it wasn't actually binding. "How can the state even afford to host a black-tie event like this?"

"I didn't mention the best part—the party is being paid for by a Seattle tech-company billionaire who's made the seas his pet cause. I've been courting him for donations to the institute for years. Hell, I'd rename *Nereid* for the right donation."

She'd heard more and more nonprofits were selling naming rights in the same way stadiums did. But in his heart, her dad was as superstitious as most sailors, and she couldn't imagine him blithely renaming *Nereid* or any boat. "I take it the billionaire will be there."

"Yes."

"And you want me to go with you to the party and talk him up?"

Her dad nodded. "Along with reporters covering the event. Because of *Petrel*, you're a person of interest. People want to know how you're doing."

Talking about *Petrel* with reporters didn't sit right with her, but it would help her father and the institute, and deep down she hoped the institute's finances could get back on track so he could dump the damn reality show.

"I could get Luke added to the guest list. People would love to see you two together, especially after he saved your life after the explosion."

He'd saved her life at least twice, but the tabloid-watching public would never know about any of that. "It's on Saturday?" she asked.

"Yes. It's an evening cruise on the Blackfish Line's MV *Chinook*, after the regularly scheduled runs from Port Angeles to Victoria are done for the day. It'll be a quick round trip. We won't even disembark in Canada."

Saturday was five days away. Trina could overnight her evening gown to Port Angeles. It wasn't *impossible*. "I'll think about it."

He finished hooking up the cables and flipped the power button. The screen on the control console came to life and displayed the deck and marina at which the camera on the submersible was aimed. "So far so good."

Undine moved the joystick that aimed the camera, and the image shifted as the camera repositioned. The image froze when she directed it to the straight downward position, the optimal angle for viewing the seafloor.

Her dad cursed and checked the camera mount. "The camera is moving. We lost the video feed." He disconnected the wires and started over. A half hour later, Marvin was up and running and they were no longer losing feed when the camera hit a sharp angle within the housing. They would send Marvin down to get a reading of radiation levels on the Soviet Quebec-class sub. Luke and her dad would dive only if Marvin failed.

Luke had gone over the charts with Annabelle, who could drive the submersible better than a twelve-year-old playing Mario Kart. Over the years, she'd developed the instinct for maneuvering through currents and obstacles that couldn't be anticipated. She'd once battled an octopus and won—without hurting the poor creature. She had the touch to get Marvin to the bottom in one piece, and the skill to find the tubes and get the reading.

It took her thirty minutes to maneuver Marvin to the

bottom, then, with Undine, Stefan, and Luke's help, they directed her over the two sub wrecks and finally located the empty torpedo tubes. In the meantime, they got better video of both vessels than had been previously acquired.

Marvin was a miracle for collecting data.

Two hours later, they gathered around the Coast Guard conference room table to share the results of Marvin's reconnaissance mission. They had photos and video. Marvin had even captured exterior markings on the sub—meaning it might be possible to identify the exact submarine that had engaged with *Wrasse*. But the most important thing they'd learned was at the top of the agenda: the item missing from the torpedo tube had been radioactive.

*L*uke had expected it, but still, confirmation that a nuclear device had been taken from the Soviet sub was shocking. Scary. He wanted to drag Undine home and make love to her and then set out to find Yuri and rip the SOB's head off.

But instead he was stuck in a meeting where calmer heads prevailed. They needed to find Yuri and the bomb, but it had to be done in a way that would protect the secret and prevent panic.

Curt Dominick brought the secretaries of Homeland Security and state and the directors of the CIA and FBI into the telephone conference. They'd each brought along experts to aid the discussion—the CIA had an analyst who'd been studying Ukraine and Russia for years, while the FBI had an expert on Russian Bratva, Ukrainian neo-Nazis, and the Georgian and Azerbaijani Mafia.

The bigwigs all shared Curt's office at the Department of Justice, while Luke shared the table with Station Neah Bay

Commander Martinez and the rest of the Station employees who'd been involved from the start. The new member at the Neah Bay table was Annabelle, whom they'd had to tell because she'd operated Marvin.

From the grim looks on the faces around the Station table, the excitement and awe of having direct dealings with the AG had transformed to disbelief at the level of the threat, utter shock at the importance of the investigation that had stemmed from a simple dive to fend off PTSD.

Luke's gaze met Undine's. Her personal struggle had uncovered a massive threat to US security—much more than a footnote to the Cold War, which was what the sinking of *Wrasse* would have become.

"We've got a team of investigators heading your way," the FBI director said. "We'll have people crawling all over the coast to find Yuri Kravchenko and Alexei and Ivan Lutsenko."

Undine cleared her throat. "We know Yuri was upset about the sinking of the ferry on the Sea of Azov as it was crossing the Kerch Strait from the Crimean Peninsula to Russia. Today my dad reminded me of something that…has been nagging at me, and I've only just realized why. There's a black-tie event on Saturday night on the ferry that runs between Port Angeles and Victoria. Both the Washington governor and the BC premier are going to be there, and local media should be in attendance. The ferry itself is an international passenger-and-car ferry—just like the Kerch Strait ferry line. Yuri has ridden that ferry a lot—he told me he had friends in Sidney, BC, but he could have been scoping the boat. If he's looking for attention for his cause, this event is the perfect target."

Luke sat up straight, a frisson of excitement running through him. In his gut, he was certain Undine was right, and from the looks on the faces of the Coast Guard officers, they agreed.

Silence had settled in the wake of her theory; the CIA analyst finally broke it. "Everything we've been able to compile on Kravchenko tells me that Ms. Gray is correct. It fits his profile. He'd target the ferry. I also think he's crazy enough to set off the bomb."

Chapter Twenty-Nine

"At this point, the best way to allay suspicions and gain information is for Dr. Gray and Undine to accept the invitation to the event," Curt said.

Beside Undine, Luke stiffened. "No."

She dropped her hand to his knee. "Accepting doesn't mean we'll go. Both the governor and the premier consulted with Dad about the proposed boundaries for the marine sanctuaries. If he *didn't* issue a press release saying he's attending the event while he's in town, it would look suspicious to Yuri."

"That's exactly what I was thinking," Curt said. "In fact, I think Dr. Gray should stress the fact that Undine is going as well, to make sure we have Yuri's attention."

"My publicist will handle everything," her dad said. His gaze shifted to Undine. "One way to do that is to offer details like the name of the designer you're going to wear."

"I was planning on going with Helly Hansen or maybe Carhartt."

Her dad shook his head. "Your mother will be mortified.

I'll call her and have her set you up with something appropriately amazing and disgustingly expensive."

Just what she needed, her former-model mother to finally show interest in her awkward tomboy daughter. How long before she complained that Undine never had the nose job? She groaned. "If you want expensive, I can go with Filson."

Luke laughed. "You aren't actually going to the party. It won't matter."

"What do you think about adding Lt. Sevick to the guest list?" Her dad directed his question to the speakerphone. "As Undine's date, the former SEAL who saved her life would garner a lot of attention."

Luke stiffened.

"Yes," the CIA director said. "Given the media coverage he got after pulling Undine from the strait when the *Petrel* sank, it will up interest in the event. Yuri will be thrilled—which might make him sloppy."

Undine flashed Luke a grin. "Don't worry, honey, you aren't actually *going*."

"Touché," he said through stiff lips.

"Welcome to my world, babycakes."

"It sounds like we need to focus the search for Kravchenko and the Lutsenko twins in Port Angeles," Commander Martinez said. "Have you been in contact with the commander there?"

"We have," the secretary of Homeland Security said. "The Coast Guard and Border Patrol have photos and descriptions of Kravchenko, his boat and his nephews."

Parker flipped through the slides on the PowerPoint projector and brought up the driver's license photos of Ivan and Alexei Lutsenko, fraternal twin brothers. Undine had studied the photos many times since they'd initially received them, and she was certain she'd never seen either man before.

"With five days' lead time," the secretary continued, "we'll find all three men before the ferry sets out on Saturday, and if we don't, we'll put a halt to the sailing. The governor can have her photo op another time."

"So what's our next step?" Luke asked.

"We need to stop all underwater investigation on the *Wrasse* and Soviet sub," Curt said. "This is no longer an NHHC investigation but an active threat to national security. You, Lt. Sevick, get a vacation. Go back to Port Angeles if you'd like. Undine and Dr. Gray, we need you both to stay in Washington, to make it appear you're going to the event on the ferry, but there is no need for either of you to stay in Neah Bay if you wish to leave. When this is resolved, NHHC might move forward with the documentary, but for now, all pretense of filming should stop."

The meeting adjourned not long after that, and Undine found herself swept forward with the group, who agreed to go out to dinner at the largest restaurant in town. They took over the small, one-room diner and talked loudly about the hold on the documentary due to Navy funding not coming through. Boatswain's Mate Shales was smooth in laying the foundation without being heavy-handed in getting the misinformation out.

Luke was quiet throughout the meal, but he had a hand on her knee or his arm around her shoulder the entire time. A few days ago, she would have written his touches off as designed to piss off her dad, but Stefan showed no tension at Luke's blatant claiming of her. In fact, he seemed to welcome it.

My, my, how things can change.

After dinner, she said good night to her dad, Annabelle, and the Coast Guard contingent, and Luke drove her home to their Hobuck cabin. They sat in his SUV in silence, staring at the dark cabin in the largely empty resort. It was Monday night, and the place had cleared out of surfers and week-enders on Sunday afternoon.

Something was off with Luke, and she had no idea what it was. He loved her. She loved him. And yet, something had happened in the last few hours; some sort of barrier had formed. All at once, the problem slapped her in the face. "We're going to Port Angeles tomorrow."

He nodded.

"And this—between us—is Neah Bay only."

He nodded again.

"Because I live in DC. You live here. And neither of us are willing to change that." But even more than that…she was a trigger for him. He might have forgiven her and her father, but letting go of twelve years of anger wasn't some-thing that could be done in a day.

"I *can't* quit, Undine. And I don't want to. Don't ask me to give up my world for you. I already did that once."

She sucked in a breath. She had to find a way to let him go that they could both accept. "I would never. And I…don't think I can give up mine. In DC, I'm not Stefan Gray's daughter. I have friends. A job. A life." She shifted in her seat to face him. "I love you, Luke, but I don't see a future for us. The fact that there's peace between us means the world to me. It's a gift, a freedom I never expected to have. If that's all I take home from Neah Bay, it will be enough."

*F*reedom. His love meant freedom to her. She wasn't willing to give up her job and move. She wasn't willing to sacrifice that piece of herself for him. But then… like him, she'd already done that. Maybe hers had been deliberate, voluntary, but that didn't make it any less real. And maybe that's all this was for her, a chance for redemption. Forgiveness.

He believed one hundred percent that she loved him. But maybe it was a different kind of love. Not the burning, aching, I-need-to-be-with-you-until-the-end-of-time feeling he had so much as the peace of the past being put to rest. A deep, abiding feeling that meant she could let the guilt go and move forward. Without him.

She loved him. But maybe not enough. "I'd like to amend the rules."

She raised a perfect, crookedly imperfect brow.

"While you're in Port Angeles, I want you to stay with me." It had irrationally bothered him that she'd wanted their relationship kept out of the documentary. He refused to be her dirty secret again. "And I want the press release about the party to state we're a couple. Even if this ends when you get on the plane for home, I want the world to know you're mine right now."

"I think…" She inhaled deeply, her chest rising and staying high as she held her breath. Tears gathered in her eyes. Finally, she exhaled. "Staying with you would only make it harder when it's time for me to leave. I'm a rip-the-bandage-off sort of woman." She grimaced. "Face PTSD head-on and dive on *Wrasse*, even if it means asking the one man on the planet who hates me for help."

"I don't—"

"I know." She took his hand and cradled it in hers. "I'm in love with you, Luke. And because of that, I can't spend time with you in Port Angeles and still say good-bye without falling apart. The original rules still apply. This ends when we leave Neah Bay. We have tonight, but tomorrow morning, I'm going to catch a ride to Port Angeles on *Nereid*."

Her words were a blow. But it was his own damn fault for setting the rules to begin with. He thought of a thousand protests, but they all came to the same conclusion—all he could ask for was another week, not a lifetime. She was right to rip the bandage off now, because in another week, he might not be able to let go.

Chapter Thirty

Undine didn't think anything in her personal life could be worse than saying good-bye to Luke. But that was BC. Before Charlene. She'd never considered what it would be like to face her mother as she nursed a breaking heart.

Charlene Gray arrived in Port Angeles Tuesday night, a mere twenty-four hours after Stefan informed Charlene that Undine intended to venture into the public eye for the first time, and just four hours after *Nereid* made port in the north-coast town. A former model who'd never quite hit the big time, Charlene had seized on the opportunity to grab a little limelight. It didn't hurt her aspirations that it would also be Undine's first public appearance since being the sole survivor of an explosion that had made national news.

So now, here Undine was, driving a rental car to Seattle with her estranged mother in the passenger seat, on a mission to buy a dress she didn't want for a party she didn't really plan to attend. All while feeling like her heart had been ripped out of her chest because she'd ended things with Luke to protect them both.

The day was dark, rainy, windy, and pretty much sucked as far as Undine was concerned. She counted to ten as her mother nitpicked her appearance and suggested she purchase bigger breasts for the third time.

Why did Seattle have to be so damn far? And why did she agree to go dress shopping in the first place?

But she knew the answer to that one. She'd hoped the day trip would prevent her from calling Luke and telling him she was desolate and would take whatever she could get, no matter how painful the good-bye would be later.

It was also true that part of Undine had looked forward to the mother-daughter outing. It was a month of reconciliations for her. Maybe her mother's arrival would make it a hat trick. Plus, she hadn't gone shopping with her mother since she was fourteen—before her unsatisfactory breasts had even fully developed.

But an hour into the drive and she was wondering how she could have forgotten there was a *reason* she hadn't gone shopping with her mother in half a lifetime, a reason she'd whittled her visits down to one lousy weekend every other year, and the odds against a miracle hat trick were forty kabillion to none.

Charlene was self-absorbed and never considered Undine's feelings as she blathered on about her life, denigrated Undine's choices, and complained about her accommodations on *Nereid*.

In short, Undine's resentment was riding high, and she wished she'd opted to stay with Luke, even if it meant having quinoa and kale with every meal. "Mom, can we...not talk for a while?"

"Typical. I come all this way to help you out, and you're nothing but critical of me."

Undine took a deep breath and asked herself if she had it in her to fight this battle or if she'd ignore her mother's comments, like she always did. But her patience snapped. "I'm sorry I have Dad and Grandma Gray's eyes, and I got Dad's nose, and that I don't have your figure or your grace, but I happen to think I'm okay, in spite of the fact that I'll never be a supermodel. There is more to life than being photogenic. There's an entire world that goes on while you're posing for attention."

"You don't have to be insulting. Your father should be ashamed of how he spoiled you."

"He may have spoiled me, but at least he was there."

Charlene let out a sharp gasp. "You had a choice. You could have chosen *me*. But you chose him."

They were back to that again. "I was six, Mom. What sort of parent leaves it up to a six-year-old to choose, then resents the child for her choice for the rest of her life? Stop punishing me for choosing Dad. *You* never should have given me that choice. You could have demanded fifty-fifty custody, but you didn't want the burden of being a mother for half the year."

"That's not true! I was devastated when you chose your father. I cried for weeks."

She found that hard to believe, considering Charlene had abandoned Undine at six and rejected her again at sixteen. "Yeah. You say that, and maybe it's even true, but again, I was *six*. I chose the parent with the cool boat. The one who seemed to want me."

She drove in silence as her mother stewed over that. At last, she pulled into the Bainbridge ferry terminal parking lot and parked the rental car. They had at least thirty long, excruciating minutes until the ferry would leave, then a thirty-five-minute crossing. Then shopping in downtown Seattle.

She'd take a two-hour CrossFit workout over this. "Screw it," she muttered. "You know what, Mom? I didn't ask you to come. In fact, the one time I really needed you—right after the explosion—you were on vacation and couldn't be bothered to cut it short to come visit me. Dad was here within twelve hours. Erica came for a week. Trina came for the following week. But you? You called and left a message. So you aren't allowed to gripe that you're doing me a favor now. I thought maybe, just maybe, we'd have fun today, but if you're going to spend the day telling me all the ways in which I've disappointed you in looks and personality, you can just take a taxi to SeaTac from downtown Seattle."

Her mother's eyes widened. "You'd send me home? You wouldn't even let me go to the party after I came all this way?"

Undine leaned back in her seat. "Why do you want to go to this party so badly, Mom? You don't even give a crap about the marine sanctuaries or the management plan."

Her mother pursed her lips.

"Careful, or you'll get wrinkles," Undine couldn't help but say. Then she sighed and reached for her mother's hand. "What's going on?"

"Andre left me."

"Andre was a shallow prick. Let me guess, he's taken up with a woman my age?"

A tear slid down her mother's cheek. Undine knew her mother had liked her…consort? Sugar daddy? Keeper? Whatever the term was, Andre had financed all the extras in Charlene's life, from diamonds to luxury cars to vacations that couldn't be cut short for traumatized daughters, and her mother had cared for the man as much as she was capable of caring for anyone, Undine supposed.

"Yes. Only she's even younger. Perfect, perky breasts. No stretch marks on her perfect, flat belly. I'd hoped…if this party makes the news, Andre would see me with you and your father. Happy. On my feet. And he'd be sorry."

"That's not how Andre is wired. And frankly, I pity his

new mistress. But then, I pitied you. Have you ever considered trying to find a partner you truly loved? Someone you want to be with?"

"I tried that with your father, and look where it got me."

"It got you a daughter and a life on a boat traveling around the world."

"A boat! It's not like the *Nereid* is a luxury yacht! There were no cocktails at sunset. No dinner out with other couples met in port. No. It was all boring research. Work."

"And you didn't love Dad—or me—enough to make it work. To maybe try to enjoy, learn, and grow from the travels. You just resented that there wasn't enough booze."

"He should have loved *me* enough. He should have given up the travels. Stayed in one place."

"He did! He built the institute, hoping you'd be there when he returned from research expeditions."

"The institute was even worse than the boat. The only people who ever visited were more science types. They made sure to talk slowly and use small words when they talked to me. And when Stefan was home, he was always working. I was so lonely, Undine. I had no one to talk to. No one who respected me. No one who saw me as anything other than Dr. Stefan Gray's dumb trophy wife."

Undine's breath left her in a rush. She and her mother had experienced the same loneliness at the institute and similar discrimination. Her mother because she was beautiful and presented a shallow front, and Undine because she was young, a nuisance, and her only credential for taking up valuable space at the institute or on the boat was that she was Stefan Gray's daughter.

She'd forgotten her mother had actually lived at the institute for a time. Undine had been so young when her father broke ground; her memories were vague at best. When Charlene left, Stefan had set off on a two-year research expedition, taking Undine with him. Those expeditions had been the reason Undine had to be homeschooled. By the time she was fourteen, she'd begged her father to stay home—probably much as Charlene had—so she could go to high school. Be normal. But then she'd taken tests that showed she'd mastered the high school curriculum, and the next thing she knew, instead of being a normal high school freshman, she'd been an abnormal college freshman.

Would she change it all now if she could? Insist on going to high school for the experience, if not the education?

Would Luke give up being a SEAL if he had a time machine and could go back to the moment that had irrevocably changed his future?

Her mother had wanted her father to give up his life aquatic, failing to recognize that Stephan Gray, without his travels and studies, would never be happy and wouldn't be the man she'd fallen in love with.

And now, Undine couldn't help but wonder if she'd glommed on to an excuse to end things with Luke because she was scared of what he would say if she told him she loved him enough to want to find a way to make a relationship work. Could she give up her career for him? Would she still be herself without the professional life she'd worked so hard to build?

What if he didn't want her for the long term? After all, he'd been the one to insist their fling was temporary.

So she'd reverted to her old pattern of serial monogamy with a sixty-day expiration—but she hadn't even given Luke the full two months. Which made sense, given that she'd spent her adult life rejecting men at the moment a relationship was on the cusp of getting serious.

Her dad had blamed her dating pattern on Luke, but she suspected it had a lot more to do with her mother. She'd asked

Charlene, when all hell broke loose at the institute, if she could live with her until her eighteenth birthday. She'd even applied for a transfer to the University of Arizona. But her mother refused, saying Andre didn't want her around. The rejection at a time when she desperately needed a mother had cut deep.

Undine's head throbbed, and she closed her eyes against the pain. She might have screwed things up with Luke, but she had an opportunity here. All she had was the present, this exact moment with her mother in a rental car, sitting in a parking lot and arguing while waiting for a ferry to arrive so she could spend a lot of money she didn't have on a dress she didn't want or need.

There were no time machines. She couldn't change the past. But maybe, just maybe, she could have a mother. "Mom, I already asked my friend Trina to overnight a gown for Saturday. I only agreed to today because I thought we might have fun, but the truth is I don't want to go shopping. I hate shopping even more than I hate okra. But the aquarium in Seattle is one of my favorites. I know you don't love looking at fish so maybe we can make a deal. If I show you the aquarium, you can show me something you love. Let's spend the day doing things we each enjoy. Seattle has a great art museum."

"I'm sick of art museums. Andre considered going to museums an acceptable activity. But I always wanted to do the Underground Tour. Whenever we visited Seattle on Andre's business trips, he said the tour was too grimy. Philistine. I think he believed I didn't know what philistine meant. He was such a pretentious ass."

Undine smiled. "I can't think of anything better than topping off the aquarium with the Underground Tour. Maybe after that we can go to a bar in Pioneer Square, and I can teach you how to flirt with philistines."

"Your dad said you have something going with that handsome SEAL who saved you."

She shrugged, unwilling to explain the situation to her mother. "*I'm* not going to flirt. I'll be your wingwoman. You can even tell people I'm your little sister. Just like old times."

Her mother laughed. "No. Let's tell them you're my daughter." She winked at Undine. "No one will believe us anyway."

*L*uke pulled on his running shoes and stretched, wishing Undine were with him for this morning run.

It was five thirty a.m., one week before Thanksgiving, the sun wouldn't rise for another two hours, and it was pouring rain. She'd gripe about the timing and conditions, but he wanted her by his side because she'd make the misery fun.

And afterward, he'd make love to her for hours.

Less than two minutes after she said good-bye and boarded *Nereid*, he'd begun to question why he'd insisted their fling end when they left Neah Bay, or why he'd ever called it a fling to begin with.

He knew he'd reached a pathetic low when he started trying to come up with excuses to call her. He hadn't invented an excuse to call a girl since he was fifteen.

He was a former SEAL. He'd raided terrorist strongholds. He'd rescued hostages hours before they were slated to be executed. He'd swum into enemy territory in the middle of the night and helped remove a warlord from power. Surely he could call a woman on the phone and say… What?

I'm an idiot for letting you go. I want to find a way to make this work.

But what if she'd meant it—the peace between them gave

her freedom to move on with her life? What if for her, their relationship was closure of sorts?

He hated the word closure. Especially if it meant Undine was done with him.

He crossed his apartment to the front door. A lonely run in the cold rain would be fitting for his mood. He grabbed his apartment key and yanked open the door.

Undine stood in the hall, her hand poised to knock.

He stared at her in shocked silence, wondering if this was a dream, if the alarm clock hadn't gone off yet.

She flashed a tentative smile. "I have the strangest urge to go for a run, but it's too dark to go by myself. I was wondering if you'd join me?"

His heart pounded, but he managed to find a cocky smile. "I'm not sure. It's a bit early, and you tend to slow me down."

Her smile widened. "I was afraid you'd say that, so yesterday, when I was at the aquarium, I bought you a bribe." She reached into a tote bag and pulled out a silk tie decorated with dozens of tiny blue tangs. "They didn't have shawls, and I thought this would match your eyes."

He couldn't hold back his grin. "So, if I take that tie, I have to go running with you now?"

She nodded. "And tomorrow morning too."

He slipped an arm around her waist, pulled her inside his apartment, and closed the door quietly, in deference to his sleeping neighbors. Then he scooped her up and pressed her back to the door. She dropped the tie and tote bag and wrapped her legs around his hips and arms around his neck.

His lips were a scant inch from hers, but he didn't kiss her. "What if I don't want to go running in the cold, dark rain? What if I want to make love to you instead?"

She threaded her fingers through his hair. "We can do that, if you prefer, but no tie until after you take me running."

"Fair enough," he said. "But what happens after we run? Will you go back to *Nereid?*"

"If you want me to. But I'd rather stay here with you."

"That can be arranged." He ran his lips over her jaw, then kissed her throat. "But you should know I don't do flings." The fingers in his hair tightened, and he smiled against her neck.

"You don't?" she asked in a husky voice.

"Nope. Not anymore. Because I've fallen in love with you, and now that I have you back in my arms, I'm never letting you go."

Chapter Thirty-One

Friday afternoon, Undine was plastered to Luke's chest, enjoying a post-sex cuddle, when his landline rang. She rolled off him so he could answer it, but he made no move to grab the phone. "I prefer this moment just as it is." He slid a hand over her hip and cupped her ass.

"No argument from me," she said. "I'd be happy to pull the blinds and turn off the lights and pretend we aren't home forever." They'd deftly avoided talking about how they were going to make this relationship work. So far, they'd only acknowledged they both wanted to try, and she'd been content with that.

He nipped her earlobe. "At some point, we'd run out of food. And my landlord would demand rent. I suppose I'd have to go to work eventually."

She ran a hand over his chest, then slid farther south to trace the indentations between his abs. "We'd also run out of condoms."

"Which means you'd almost certainly get pregnant, and then we'd have a baby with brown-green eyes and a beautiful smile like Mom to take care of."

He said it so casually, as if having a baby together wasn't a scary prospect. As if he liked the idea. She touched his chin. "Or gorgeous blue-tang eyes and an adorable chin cleft like Dad."

He slid down and kissed her belly, and she knew he was imagining her stretched out with his child. The weird part was, it didn't freak him out, or her, for that matter. She'd figured she was years away from her biological clock going off, but all at once, she felt it tick.

He met her gaze, his eyes intent. The air in the room seemed to thicken as she drew in a heavy breath.

"I was thinking I would put in a request to transfer to the DC area," he said softly. "There are always open billets in Silver Spring."

Her heart thumped hard against her breast.

The phone started ringing again. Luke cast a glare over his shoulder at the offending item on the nightstand.

"You would do that?" she asked. The suggestion triggered more fear than the thought of having his baby, which was nutty.

"There's no guarantee, and even if it did come through, it would take months. We'd be apart for a long time while the request is processed. But I'm willing if you want to stay in DC."

The answering machine picked up. This time, the caller stayed on to leave a message. The male voice carried from the answering machine in the kitchen through to the bedroom. "If you're home, Lieutenant, pick up. There's been a development in the search for Yuri Kravchenko."

*H*e'd been dangerously close to telling her he wanted it all—her, marriage, a baby—but pulled back at the last second, remembering there was an interim step. And then the stupid phone had interfered before he could get her answer.

This wasn't a fling for either of them, but they had yet to discuss *how* they were going to make it work. One of them would have to sacrifice, and now that he'd made the offer—and she hadn't ecstatically accepted—he couldn't help but wonder if she was having second thoughts. Was this just a final stop on her road to freedom?

And why the fuck was he focusing on that and not the fact that Yuri's boat had been found?

He needed to get his head on straight. He pulled open the closet door and opened his gun safe. A SWAT team was, at this very minute, gathering to raid the boat. It was entirely possible there could be a nuclear standoff in the marina just a few miles from his apartment within the next thirty minutes.

His request to be included on the SWAT takedown team had been denied. It was the right call to make—he didn't know the team and had never trained with them—but being left out after being the man on scene from day one still rankled. He'd been given the heads-up on the raid as a courtesy.

"Call your parents. Ask them to take you to Seattle." He wanted her far away from what could become ground zero.

"Where are you going?" she asked.

"To the Coast Guard Air Station. I'm one of a handful of people who knows exactly what's going on and who has the training to deal with the situation. I'm going to offer my services as backup on the water. Yuri won't escape that way."

"I can probably convince my dad to take Mom to Seattle again." Her mother was completely unaware of the situation, and they were all determined to keep it that way. "But I won't go with them. Not without you."

"You can't come with me to the Station."

"Why not?"

"You aren't and have never been active duty."

"But I know Yuri. No one else there does."

"No, Undine." He paused. "The thought of you anywhere near Yuri, anywhere near the bomb, scares the hell out of me. If you're in potential danger, I'll be distracted, and I need to be focused on the full scope of the mission, not just your safety."

"I'm just as scared for you. You don't have to go to the Coast Guard Station at all."

"Don't ask that of me. I may work for NOAA, but it's still uniform service. I took an oath to defend the constitution from enemies foreign and domestic. I need to honor that oath and do everything in my power to get that bomb back and protect my country."

"I took the same oath as a federal employee."

"But you aren't trained like I am. I know what I'm doing. I can help. And I intend to be on a Coast Guard boat, making sure Yuri doesn't escape."

Her chest rose with a deep breath. "I'll stay here, then. I'll make dinner. And wait for news." She wrapped her arms around her shoulders. "While you're gone, I'm going to turn up the heat to the equatorial range. I don't know how you live in this chill."

He smiled. "The thermostat is programmed. I'm not usually home this time of day during the week."

"Promise you'll call as soon as you know anything."

He stepped forward and put his arms around her. "I will. We were having a conversation earlier that I very much want to finish." He reached down and stroked her belly, holding on to the insane notion that someday, she'd carry his child.

"Me too."

He released her and donned a holster. "Dare I hope for something more exciting than corn flakes for dinner?"

She smiled. "I was thinking of wrapping sticks of butter in bacon and deep-frying them."

He laughed. "That'll go great with the Brussels sprouts in the crisper."

"You would ruin bacon with Brussels sprouts."

He slipped an extra magazine into his pocket, then pulled her against him again. "I have a recipe that will. Blow. Your. Mind. I'll make it when I get back."

"For Brussels sprouts?"

"No."

"I'm afraid to ask what you think is mind-blowing. Kale-wrapped yams?"

"No. But that sounds awesome."

She groaned. "What torture do you have planned?"

He flashed a grin. "Bacon-wrapped tater tots. With cheese."

Her eyes widened. "Oh my God. I think I just came."

"And you will again as soon as I get home. And then you'll have bacon-wrapped tater tots."

*Y*uri's boat was empty. He'd been there—recently, if the food waste on the counter was any indication —but not in the last several hours.

The Geiger counter indicated the bomb had been on the boat too.

Luke turned to Parker—who'd been assigned to Port Angeles along with the other Neah Bay personnel who'd been actively involved with the investigation from the start. Once the boat had been cleared by SWAT, Parker had finagled permission for Luke to explore Yuri's fishing boat. From the look of things, the twins had lived on the boat as well, sharing the v-berths in the front, while Yuri lived in the small captain's cabin.

"No hint as to where he went?" Luke asked the FBI agent managing the scene.

The man's gaze swept Luke from head to toe. "Who are you, and why are you here?"

"Lt. Luke Sevick."

"Sevick. The former SEAL?"

"Yes, sir."

The man offered his hand. "Thank you for your service, before, and in the past weeks. I've been briefed on the sequence of events."

Luke gave a sharp nod, glad he wasn't about to be booted from the vessel.

"We haven't been able to process enough data to determine where Kravchenko went, but everything indicates he knew we were coming." The man swept his hand wide. "He's only left behind what he wanted us to find."

And that didn't include a Cold War-era Soviet nuclear bomb.

* * *

This was where it could all go wrong. Or it would be the moment when five years of searching paid off. Yuri used the stolen key fob to raise the gate to the parking garage and parked in the designated space. The government would have realized he'd abandoned the boat by now. It was a shame to give up the vessel, but there was no other way. It had served its purpose. As Yuri would serve his.

He or his nephews might die today. Death wasn't his intention. Not yet. He wasn't the suicidal sort. He wanted to see the results of his labor. But even so, he'd taken the necessary precautions. The plan would continue in his absence.

He glanced at his watch and nodded to Alexei. It was time. They didn't have long. The SEAL would return home after the search was complete.

And then the game would begin.

Chapter Thirty-Two

$\mathcal{U}$ndine's heart hammered as she tucked herself in the closet, next to Luke's locked gun case. She should have asked for a gun. But then, she'd never fired one. Luke would have refused on safety grounds. And he'd have been right.

But then, they'd never expected Yuri's nephew, Alexei Lutsenko, to show up here. Had never imagined she was still in danger, but she'd seen him through the peephole in the door. He'd looked straight into the circle—much the same as she had nearly three weeks ago—and demanded she open the door. He'd brandished a gun, and she'd bolted backward, tripping on the shoes piled by the front door, including the high heels his mother had left behind on her last visit, which he'd placed next to the door as a reminder to mail them to her.

She'd made a noise when she tripped. Alexei knew she was here.

But still, she'd tiptoed away and searched for a place to hide. *A place to die.* Because sure as hell the man was here to kill her.

She grabbed her purse from the table on her dash through the dining room. If she hid, maybe she'd buy just enough time to place a call. From the bedroom nightstand she'd grabbed Luke's landline, she'd use that to call 911. She'd use her cell to call Luke.

She slid down into the smallest, deepest corner of the closet as the 911 operator answered. "Nine-one-one, what's your emergency?" a woman said in a flat voice.

"This is Undine Gray," she whispered even as she pulled up Luke's cell number with her other hand. "There is a man with a gun at the door. He's a Ukrainian terrorist."

Luke's phone rang.

"This is part of the raid of the marina by the SWAT team," she continued. "The terrorists are here." Her eyes teared. *Please, Luke, pick up.* "The SWAT team is in the wrong place."

"Undine? What's going on?" Luke asked.

"The SWAT team needs to come here," she whispered into both phones. "Alexei Lutsenko is here. I'm hiding in the closet. Help me. Please, Luke. Help me."

⁂

*L*uke's stomach plummeted at Undine's desperate words. "I'm coming, honey. I'll bring the team." To the men on the boat, he said, "Alexei Lutsenko is at my apartment. Now. With Undine." He bolted for the deck and grabbed Parker and a SWAT officer. "I need back up."

Into the phone, he said, "Undine, is he inside or in the hall?"

"Not—"

He heard a muted bang, and she let out a sharp squeal of fear.

"He just shot the lock, I think." Her words were interrupted by trembling breaths.

The dead bolt would require more than one bullet. Sure enough, more thumps sounded over the connection. The apartment walls were thin enough that the sound carried all the way to the bedroom closet and over the phone line.

The SWAT officer directed them to a patrol car positioned at the end of the dock. Parker and Luke jumped into the backseat, while the SWAT officer directed the uniform to drive them to Luke's.

Within seconds, they were racing down the waterfront street, Luke providing directions. On the police radio, a dispatcher announced there were reports of shots fired in an apartment building. Luke's address was given. A second report indicated they had a 911 call from a woman claiming a terrorist was at the same address.

"He's inside now, Luke!" Undine whispered urgently.

"We're coming, sweetheart. Tuck the phone in your pocket. Keep the line open. Do everything he says. Even hand over the phone if he demands it. I'm coming."

"I love you, Luke."

"I love you too, Undine. I'm coming, sweetheart."

They rounded a sharp corner at speed. One side of the vehicle lifted, but the officer handled it with the skill of practice.

"He's in the living room."

"Hide the phone. I can see my building. We're five blocks up the street. Can you hear the siren?"

"Yes." A pause. "He's in the room." Sound became muffled. She must've tucked the phone away.

Muted, indistinguishable words. Her voice. Then a man's. The muffling got worse. The phone was being jostled. Undine let out a shriek.

The loud pop of a gun firing.

He gripped the phone so tightly, he was in danger of crushing it.

She screamed louder.

The phone thumped some more. "Bitch! You think I didn't guess you'd have a phone?" The voice had a heavy accent, Ukrainian, he'd bet, but to his untrained ear it could easily be Russian. The man spoke directly into the receiver. "You want your woman, Sevick? I will give you her *and* the bomb for ten million dollars."

Luke stared at the phone in shock. No way in hell were these men after a simple ransom for the weapon. Yuri Kravchenko was a zealot who'd spent years looking for this bomb. He didn't want a payoff; Luke believed in his gut Yuri wanted nothing less than a world war.

But maybe Alexei hadn't gotten the same memo?

"Where the hell am I supposed to get ten million dollars?" he said, just to keep the man talking. Four blocks to go. Sirens surrounded them. Everyone was closing in, but the traffic between them and the building was a mess as drivers panicked upon seeing a wave of police vehicles in their rearview mirrors.

"Dr. Stefan Gray can pay," Alexei said.

Luke seriously doubted Stefan had that kind of cash on hand, but he wasn't about to tell the Ukrainian that. He relayed the ransom demand to the SWAT officer, who relayed the information over the police radio. Parker spoke to his commander on his cell phone.

Keep him talking, Parker mouthed.

Luke nodded. "How do we get the money to you?"

"You'll receive instructions. Wait for my call."

The line went dead.

"What can you tell us about your building?" the SWAT officer asked.

Luke focused inward. He wasn't a NOAA lieutenant

tonight. He was a special forces operator, and this was an op. He couldn't think about Undine in danger. He had to think like the operator he was. "Underground parking. The best way to get her out would be to have a vehicle in the garage."

"How many exits?"

"Two. One on the north side, one on the east."

The SWAT officer radioed the information to the rest of his team. Vehicles sped past them into position.

"He won't get away," the officer at the wheel said. "There are only three of them. We have an army."

"But he has a hostage. And a nuclear bomb."

⁂

*N*othing about this felt right.

Ransom?

Undine found it hard to believe Yuri had gone to all this trouble only to pull a Dr. Evil-type super-villain move and demand money.

Money he *knew* her father didn't have. He'd sneered at her father's solution to fund his struggling institute enough in the week they'd worked together.

But Alexei was convincing, making her wonder if he didn't know Yuri's real agenda.

She struggled against him as he dragged her toward the front door of the apartment. He slapped her. "You scream, and I will shoot anyone who crosses our path. Man. Woman. Child. They will die." He studied her with the cold, hard gaze of a sociopath.

She nodded.

He pressed his gun into her lower back and pushed her out the door. "To the stairs."

Thankfully, they came across no one on the short trip to the stairway. Luke's neighbors were all likely hunkered down in their closets after the shots were fired, just as Undine had done.

Sirens echoed in the stairwell. From the noise, she could believe every police car in Port Angeles was closing in on the building.

Luke is coming.

They went down two flights before Alexei yanked her into a hall. They were on the second floor of the building, the first level of condos. He dragged her down the hall, passing two apartments before he shoved open the door to unit 206. Was he going to take another hostage?

Inside, she came face-to-face with Yuri Kravchenko.

Chapter Thirty-Three

They weren't in his apartment and hadn't left through the garage or any of the exits. Her phone was still on, but the GPS hadn't moved. And the phone wasn't in his apartment.

Which left only one option: they were still in the building.

Four floors. Sixteen apartments per floor, except for the first floor, which had business offices and shops that had already been evacuated. A convenience store on the waterfront side. A wine bar. A dentist office. There'd been no sign of Undine and Alexei in any of the businesses. The apartments were now being evacuated one floor at a time.

They would find Undine. They had to. But what condition would she be in?

Why had Yuri chosen this for his stand, when the ferry had appeared to be the perfect target? It should have been irresistible for the angry zealot.

But instead Yuri had fixated on Undine. A different sort of statement, but it made a kind of sense. Undine had exposed him. He'd spent years searching, and she'd triggered the series of events that would have ended his plot before it could get off the ground. So Yuri had gone for the personal target.

That it made sense didn't help. Luke never should have left her. He should have insisted she go with her parents to Seattle. He should have protected her as he'd vowed he would to Keith Hatcher.

He stood in the lobby as another family was led out the door. He nodded to his neighbors, who looked terrified at the chaos that had become of their comfortable condominium community. He doubted his landlord would renew his lease when this was all over.

Not that he gave a fuck. He just wanted Undine back. He marched across the lobby and headed for the stairs. He'd join the search of the apartments. He had to do something.

He stepped onto the second-floor hallway and nodded to the SWAT officer who guarded the stairs. If Luke were making a stand here, he'd choose this floor—low enough to escape through a window if necessary, and a decorative lip circled the building just below the second-floor windows, providing a wide ledge for walking.

This was the floor. Sixteen apartments. Were any vacant? He turned to the SWAT officer. "What's the word on this floor? Any vacancies?"

The man radioed his boss, who was with the building manager, to relay the question.

A moment later, the reply came. "We have a vacation mail hold on 201, and 206 is vacant. For sale."

"Is the unit number included in the real estate listing? And do the photos show the unit without furniture, obviously vacant?"

The officer relayed the question; the response was immediate. "Yes and yes."

The officer in charge of the manhunt followed up with orders for Luke and the officer. "I'm sending the search team to you. We're placing priority on 206 and the other two vacant units with a public listing, but only 206 has photos that show an empty condo, making it our first priority. We need to evacuate the adjacent apartment—quietly. Guard the entrance to 206, but do not move on the unit unless you have reason to believe the hostage will die without immediate intervention. The hostage negotiator is en route as we speak."

Undine. The hostage has a name.

He didn't dare say the words aloud.

Luke positioned himself to the side of the door, out of the peephole's view. He listened but heard no voices. Given the thin walls, if they were in there, either they were in the bedroom, or they were being amazingly silent. Even low sounds would echo off the empty apartment's walls.

The SWAT team arrived and confirmed the adjacent apartment was empty. It was a weekday afternoon, and the building had gone into lockdown before five o'clock. The apartment was on the same side of the elevator as Luke's apartment, meaning that like his, these were the one-bedroom units. Most families—people who were more likely to be home on a Friday afternoon—lived down the hall, on the other side of the elevator, in the two- and three-bedroom units.

He knew the layout. The door would open directly into the dining area, which flowed directly into the living room. The living and dining rooms were essentially one long rectangle that stretched the length of the apartment from hallway to street side.

To the left of the dining room was the open kitchen. Next to the kitchen was the bathroom, next to the bathroom the only bedroom. The bathroom had two doors: one opened into the living room, one into the bedroom. The main bedroom door opened directly into the living room. A simple, efficient design, without wasting space with an unnecessary hallway, the entire unit was a rectangle. The bedroom and living room shared the north-facing exterior wall, and both boasted wide windows that overlooked the strait. The kitchen and dining room shared the south wall that spanned the corridor.

He signaled to Officer Blakely, the SWAT team leader he'd met on Yuri's boat what already seemed like ages ago, but in reality was ninety minutes at most. They walked toward the stairway, away from 206. "I might be able to confirm they're in there and even where they are in the apartment."

"If you can perform that miracle, and we get orders to storm the place, you're on the team."

A minute later, he and Blakely and a third officer silently entered the living room of the adjacent apartment. He pulled out his phone and dialed Undine's number.

Her ringtone played clear as day through the thin wall.

✳

*Y*uri's gaze jerked toward Alexei. "You idiot! You kept her phone?"

"Why does it matter? They know we're in the building. This way we can arrange the ransom without using our own phones."

Undine breathed shallowly, silently, determined not to draw attention to herself in the stark bedroom. She tucked herself into the corner. Her hands and feet were bound, but there was nothing in the bare apartment to tie her to, leaving her free to scoot and roll.

"Your job isn't to think, Alexei." Yuri's voice echoed off the walls. "Your job was to grab the girl. Her phone could be used as a bug. They could be listening to us now."

Yuri dropped her cell phone on the wood floor and

slammed the heel of his boot into it. He glared at his nephew. "Flush it down the toilet."

"Why not toss it out the window?"

"They're watching the windows, fool. Trying to pinpoint where we are in the building. Once they know, they'll put snipers on the rooftop of the restaurant in front of us. This apartment doesn't have curtains. We'll be easy targets. The longer it takes them to find us, the better chance we have of escaping with our lives."

Ivan entered the room and spoke in rapid Ukrainian. At least she assumed it was Ukrainian. He pointed to Undine, and she guessed he cursed at both men.

"It doesn't matter if she can understand us," Yuri said in crisp but accented English. "Because she won't be able to tell anyone. The hostage negotiator will broker the deal. Our safe passage for the bomb, but she will come with us, our insurance. They want the bomb so badly, they'll give her up without a fuss. The bomb is more important than any one woman, and everyone—including her—knows that."

Ivan argued in Ukrainian, his face turning red as he spoke to his uncle. He pointed at Undine again and then gestured in frustration.

"We'll tell them that if they provide us with a lifeboat, we'll put her on it once we're deep in the Pacific. They'll have no choice but to accept the deal, or the Olympic Peninsula will know the pain of Chernobyl."

Yuri's plan crystalized for Undine. They would demand a boat stocked for the long ocean crossing so they could flee to allies in Russia, likely intending to toss her overboard when they no longer needed her. There were so many flaws with the plan—for starters there would almost certainly be tracking devices on the vessel. The US military could and would hunt them to their deaths. But with her as a hostage, they would have a strong bargaining chip. The military would be forced to hold back. Yuri was a skilled seaman. He could pilot the vessel across the ocean to a Siberian port. His allies might even have a ship or a submarine awaiting them.

It was unlikely he worked for the current Ukrainian government, as they were generally allied with the US. Threatening Washington State with a nuclear bomb would only harm their cause. He must be with one of the splinter groups—the neo-Nazis or some other faction—a group that was taking a page from ISIS's playbook, using terror to destabilize and grab power.

"Why, after years of searching, are you giving up the bomb so quickly?" she asked, her voice a dry rasp.

Ivan swung to face her, offering a frigid glare, while Yuri shrugged, unconcerned. He answered Ivan in Ukrainian, then turned to Undine. "Your government will figure it out soon enough. Aside from the fact that you made it impossible for me to bring the bomb back to Russia to set it off in Moscow, I don't have the keys to activate it. We had to stop diving on *Magnum* before we could find the key box because the Coast Guard had patrol boats guarding the site twenty-four hours a day."

"You don't have the key box?" she asked. Was that what Luke had found on their first dive? But then, if it were, Yuri would have gotten the box when he killed Annie, so it must not have been it. Then she shook her head, realizing what Yuri had just said. *He can't initiate the bomb.*

This whole abduction was a bluff. He had a nuclear warhead he couldn't move and couldn't use. So he was trading it for a big payday and a ride out of town.

He couldn't kill Undine and expect to walk out of this apartment alive, and he couldn't set off the bomb.

If only Yuri hadn't destroyed her phone. There was a chance the FBI had used it as a listening device. Mara had told her how Raptor had done exactly that, back when

Raptor was owned by Robert Beck. If the police knew which apartment they were in and knew Yuri couldn't activate the bomb, they could storm the place. She might be hurt in the crossfire, but she had a helluva better chance at survival than she did if she were hauled off by Yuri and his nephews as their hostage.

Chapter Thirty-Four

Luke met Blakely's gaze, blessing the cheap construction he'd once cursed. Yuri had backed himself into a corner, intending to bluff his way out, but then unknowingly showed his cards to the very people he needed to dupe.

Luke and Blakely left the third officer in the apartment with a notepad and whispered instructions to write down everything he heard. Their advantage would last until Yuri realized they knew where he was. If he disclosed more, they needed to know every word.

They returned to the hall and sent a second officer in to act as runner should they overhear something vital. Both men had their radios turned off. No noise from police communication would tip off Yuri that they'd taken up a position that allowed them to listen in.

Pacing quite a distance down the hall from 206, Blakely radioed his boss and told the man to get a sniper on the roof across the street immediately, then relayed the vital piece: the bomb was a bluff. Both Luke and Blakely were ordered to return to the ground floor, where they could discuss the situation with the just-arrived hostage negotiator.

The lobby was orderly mayhem as patrol officers escorted out terrified-looking families clutching scant few belongings in small groups.

The police had taken over the manager's office, where Luke met with the hostage negotiator and the captain in charge of the evacuation. It was decision time. Yuri didn't know they'd pinpointed his location, but he had to know they would be closing in soon.

Luke paced while the powers that be discussed options. He'd done what he could. Much as he wanted to, going in alone Rambo-style wouldn't help Undine. He was just another soldier here, and a lowly one at that, given that he didn't know how this team operated.

The negotiator was solid and had handled dozens of situations, but even he admitted this was beyond his experience. He'd handled home invasions, domestic disputes, one bank robbery gone wrong, but ninety-five percent of his calls were due to mental illness, where hostage-taker and hostage were one and the same.

This was a zealot who wanted to start a world war. Yuri and his nephews wanted to live, wanted to walk away from here, but the bottom line was all three men had known going in that they might die, and had accepted that. The best negotiator in the world wouldn't be able to convince them to surrender. With surrender off the table before they'd even started, what was the strategy?

Skip negotiation and raid the apartment? Or go through the motions to lull Yuri into complacency?

The lights were off in 206, but snipers on the opposite rooftop could discern movement inside thanks to night-vision scopes and the wide picture windows that lacked curtains.

Luke blessed the condo owners who'd had the old drapes removed when they moved out.

They'd spotted Undine huddled in the back corner of the bedroom, and relayed the information that she was alive and appeared bound but uninjured.

Thank God.

Three men crossed back and forth in front of the bedroom window. All three were armed. One pointed his pistol at Undine several times as he argued with the man they'd identified as Yuri. The one who was described as volatile and an active threat to Undine.

The moment Yuri learned they knew which apartment they were in, they'd avoid the windows as much as possible. Or they'd plant Undine in front of one of them at all times.

The need for immediate action settled the plan. There would be no negotiation.

*T*he wide front windows rattled under the assault of wind that whipped off the strait. Undine shivered in her corner. It was so cold, if there were light in the room, she was certain she'd see her breath. She didn't like being in the bedroom with Ivan and Yuri. Alexei, who was in the living room—presumably guarding the door—might have dead eyes, but he didn't point his gun at her as often as Ivan did.

The cold apartment gave her an idea. The men had to be as uncomfortable as she was. "Can we turn on the heat?" she asked. Her teeth chattered, underscoring her point.

Ivan said something in Ukrainian to Yuri. Much more than a simple yes or no. Those words she would have understood—Yuri had taught her them when they'd worked together a lifetime ago.

Yuri argued back.

They volleyed for a bit, then with what was almost certainly a curse, Ivan stood and left the room. This apartment was the exact floor plan of Luke's. The thermostat would be in the living room. She'd hoped they'd send her to adjust it, and she could flick the light switch mounted next to it. Maybe she'd get out an SOS before they could stop her.

Curses streamed from the living room. She gathered that Ivan didn't understand the computerized system. "I know how to work it," she said to Yuri.

"Fine. Go help him."

"I can't walk with my feet bound."

"Then crawl."

She sighed. With her hands bound, her movement was more scooting than crawling, but she wasn't going to press her luck. When she entered the living room, trepidation set in. Ivan would be right next to her at the thermostat. Unlikely she'd have time for an SOS. But he'd be temporarily blinded by the light, which was a plus.

She reached the wall and climbed to her feet.

Ivan stood close to her. Too close.

Why hadn't she ever taken a self-defense class? Lee's stepbrother, JT, had a private gym in DC where all the guys worked out, and Lee and Curt, who both held ridiculously high belts in karate, had offered to give her lessons numerous times at Erica's urging. But Undine wasn't a fan of that kind of exercise, and so she'd stuck with running and the occasional yoga class.

When she got back to DC, she would learn to kick ass.

Until then, she'd have to improvise.

She finally got to her feet and flipped open the cover on the thermostat box. She frowned and reached for the light switch, flicking it up before Ivan could react.

He said something sharply in Ukrainian and slammed the light off.

"I need to see the buttons!" She flipped the light on again and elbowed him back with the same movement, knowing the action could be suicide.

Yuri came running into the room. "Turn it off!"

The front window shattered, and Ivan and Yuri both dropped to the floor.

Behind her, the front door slammed against the wall, and men in SWAT gear poured through the opening.

Dead-eyed Alexei raised his gun but dropped to his knees before he squeezed off a shot.

Before she could take in the chaos, warm arms surrounded her, and she melted into Luke's firm chest.

His mouth covered hers, and she kissed him back, then tucked her face into the heat of his body. Her shivering eased.

"Next time I want you to go with your parents to keep you safe, promise me you'll listen."

She gave him a sharp nod and said, "I will," then faced the chaos of SWAT team and terrorists. All three men were down and being searched. An all clear was given, and paramedics entered the apartment.

She glimpsed Ivan between officers. He'd taken a head shot. The paramedics passed him on the way to Yuri, who'd been shot in the chest and still had a chance. They also attended Alexei, who appeared to have been shot in the gut.

Another medic approached her. She shook her head. "I'm fine. Just cold." She gave Luke a wry smile and held up her hands. "And bound."

He cut the rope at her wrist with a knife, then freed her ankles. She ran her hands over her wrists, rubbing the sore spots. Watching as medics loaded Yuri onto a stretcher.

"It's over," she said, feeling the wonder of the moment. "It's really over."

"Not quite. We still need to find the bomb."

She smiled. "No. You don't. It's in the bedroom closet."

She led him into the bedroom. Two officers followed. In the room, she approached the double sliding doors next to the bathroom doorway, then slid one panel to the side. "Yuri was so proud, he showed it to me right after Alexei brought me here. Yuri told me all about it."

She crossed her arms and studied the corroded four-foot-tall bomb that was still strapped to a heavy-duty hand truck. A cylinder just shy of two feet in diameter, it was a warhead without the missile. It had been designed to fit within the Quebec-class sub's torpedo tube, but it hadn't been fitted with a rocket or other propellant. Shaped like a giant bullet, it was pointed at the top, while the base resting on the lip of the hand truck was flat. She waved toward a panel Yuri had opened when he showed off his new toy. "Under there is a timer. The bomb is initiated with keys—by hand—and the timer gives the person who activates it ninety-nine minutes to escape. It was designed to last years underwater, which probably stretched to decades thanks to being in the torpedo tube this whole time."

"Did Yuri say how he knew about the sub, the bomb, and the timer?'"

She nodded. "The bomb came from the Soviet underground submarine base at Balaklava in Sevastopol. According to Yuri, Balaklava had its own arms factory. They made this bomb there and fitted it into one of *Magnum*'s torpedo tubes." She paused, then added, "Yuri named the sub *Magnum* because it was the *M-357*."

She faced the doorway, looking toward the room where Yuri lay in his own blood. "He said that near Sevastopol, the Soviet Navy had top-secret underground headquarters and a massive bunker—Yuri called the bunker Object 221. In 1992, a Russian mobster bought the entire complex and gutted it. Yuri's compatriots purchased much of the paperwork relating to Balaklava from the mobster, and they've spent over two decades going through those records.

"Six years ago, they found documents detailing the final mission of *M-357*. Yuri was given the job of recovering the bomb. He said the sub was supposed to go to Seattle and plant this device near West Point. The fourth torpedo tube held a boring machine, which would have been used to drill a hole for the bomb. The launch keys were to be planted with the device, in a metal case built to withstand years underwater. When the Kremlin ordered it, an agent would don dive gear and start the ninety-nine-minute countdown." She stared at the heavily corroded device and shivered. "It was essentially a first-strike weapon they'd intended to bury along our own shoreline."

"But the seven men inside USS *Wrasse* spotted them and sank the sub before they could get to Seattle," Luke said.

She nodded. "Who knows if other, similar missions were successful? I can't help but wonder if there are old nukes buried all along the Pacific coastline."

"Russia will have to come clean on that. At least they can blame Khrushchev."

"Yuri said he didn't have the keys."

"I heard that part," Luke said, nodding toward the wall. "Thin walls."

She dropped her jaw. "Wait. The phone rang—"

He nodded. "We heard everything after that point. Even that you were going to adjust the thermostat. You took a perfect amount of time getting from one room to the other. It gave everyone time to get into position."

"That wasn't by design. It was because Yuri was an ass and wouldn't untie me. Yuri said you'd be watching the windows. I was going to attempt Morse code."

He slipped an arm around her. "We got lucky tonight."

She stayed within the circle of his arm and turned to face

the SWAT officers, who'd followed them into the room to secure the nuclear weapon. They'd been listening to her story with rapt attention. "Why don't we call the attorney general and everyone else in the chain of command and figure out who can take this nightmare out of here?"

More police, Coast Guard, and other military officers began streaming into the apartment bedroom.

Luke pulled her tightly to his side. "There's been a team equipped to take control of it in Port Angeles since Tuesday. They're probably on the stairs heading up now."

Another medic stepped forward. "Ms. Gray, we'd like to examine you."

"I'm fine," she said. "They didn't hurt me."

She had no idea who would be in charge here, so she tugged at Luke's hand and made a beeline for Brian Martinez, the Neah Bay Coast Guard Commander. He, at least, was the authority she knew. "Let's get the debriefing over with. I want to crawl into bed and have you hold me for at least the next sixteen hours."

"Sounds good to me," Luke said.

Chapter Thirty-Five

*L*uke flipped between morning news programs. Both local and national covered the story of Ukrainian rebels who'd taken a hostage in a Port Angeles apartment building in an attempt to highlight their cause, necessitating an apartment-to-apartment search, but all mention of a Cold War-era nuclear device had somehow been kept from the media.

Thank God.

Even Undine's name as the hostage had been kept out of the reports. The powers that be at the FBI and Homeland Security were working on their cover story, as officials within the State Department prepared to open talks with Russian officials to find out if other bombs had been planted along US coastlines.

It was going to be a tense few months between the US and Russia, but as long as the truth was kept from the media, it could be handled with diplomacy and wasn't likely to be catastrophic.

Undine's tea finished steeping, and he poured her a cup, placing a slice of lemon on the side in hopes of swaying her to give an affirmative to his all-important question. But then, with Undine, if he wanted to butter her up, he probably should use actual butter.

He should have called room service and ordered her a cinnamon roll. With frosting.

He crossed the living room of the expensive hotel suite he'd booked late last night after they were finally done with questioning. It was the only room he could get at the last minute, because his entire building was officially a crime scene, with dozens of displaced residents. But after the day Undine had, she deserved a little luxury, so he hadn't balked at the price of the suite.

Luke set the teacup on the nightstand and slipped into bed with her. He pulled her against him and kissed her slowly along the neck, then her ear. Her cheeks. And her perfect nose. She smiled and kept her eyes closed as he moved to the other side of her neck.

"I made you tea, sweetheart."

"Don't tell me. You want to go running."

"How did you guess?"

"Because you're the only man on the planet who kisses a woman to get her *out* of bed."

"Please will you run with me? I don't want you out of my sight all day. Possibly never again…but I *need* to go for a run."

She smiled, and her eyes finally opened. God, her eyes were beautiful, especially in the morning when she was sleep-saturated. But also in the evening, when she was sex-saturated. Basically, her eyes were beautiful always, particularly when she looked at him just like she was doing right then. "I'll run with you."

"That easy? No bargaining or complaining?"

Her smile widened. "That easy. Because I secretly love running with you."

"It wasn't exactly a secret." He kissed her again. "You never answered my question yesterday——"

She placed a finger over his lips. "I'm still reeling from yesterday and need time to think. I'm afraid of being rash because we were both frightened. Afraid we'll make promises we can't keep. Today, I just want to be. To enjoy. To know we made it through. Tomorrow we can talk about the future, but today, I just want to live in the moment."

He nodded. Her request was reasonable, even though he couldn't help but wonder what she meant about promises they might not keep.

After their run, they took a shower together, and he made love to her up against the cold tile wall. Living in the moment wasn't such a bad thing.

She was taking a post-run, post-sex nap when her father called. "I'd rather not wake her," Luke said, still feeling a jolt of surprise that Dr. Stefan Gray was so utterly okay with the fact that he and Undine were together.

It had been nine weeks since Luke had plucked her from the water, and three since she'd showed up at his door. In that time, his world's polarity had flipped. He couldn't get her out of his life fast enough three weeks ago, and now he was desperate to keep her here.

Insane.

"Is there a message I can pass on to her?"

"Her mother wants to know what time we're heading to the dock tonight. Charlene has no idea Undine was the hostage in question yesterday. She still thinks we're going to the party."

Luke frowned. They'd had no intention of going to the party when there was a chance it could be Yuri's target, but now Yuri and Alexei were in custody and Ivan was dead. The bomb was contained. They actually *could* go.

The powers that be would probably even encourage their

attendance. Proof of business as usual if rumors were to start up. So many people had learned about the bomb last night. The story could well be impossible to contain. But all acts that smacked of normalcy would undermine rumors. "I'll ask her if she wants to go when she wakes up. If we have to, we can tell Charlene my apartment building was the one evacuated last night, and we're tired from the ordeal."

"I'll wait for your call before I say anything."

Undine came padding into the kitchen area as Luke hung up the phone. She walked up behind him and slipped her arms around his waist. "What did my dad want?" she asked with a yawn in her voice.

"Your mother still thinks we're going to the party tonight."

She groaned. "I suppose it's not a terrible idea."

"I was thinking the same thing. We can check in with Curt, see what he'd like you to do. Security will still be tight on the boat given the VIPs who will be there. You being front and center, bruise-free and smiling as you chat up Seattle reporters, would go a long way to quashing rumors should they start."

She sighed. "Yeah. We probably should go. At least I'll get to see you in your dress uniform."

"And I'll see you in something that's not made of neoprene or Gore-Tex."

"Ha! That's what you think."

He laughed and turned so he could kiss her nose. Good Lord. He was going to a black-tie event with Dr. Stefan Gray, Gray's ex-wife, and his daughter.

When his SEAL buddies got wind of this, they were going to be utterly shocked. They were among the few who knew the full story, who knew exactly what the cause of his rage was all those years ago. He couldn't wait to see the look on Joel's face when he asked him to be his best man.

*L*uke and Undine went to his apartment to retrieve her gown and his dress uniform. When they returned to their hotel suite, she locked him out of the huge bathroom so she could get ready. Charlene had offered to style her hair and do her makeup, but she declined, wanting to look more natural than her mother would allow.

Now she second-guessed that decision. She wanted to look pretty for Luke, and one thing her mother knew how to do was sparkle.

Her gown, at least, was gorgeous. Made by a designer she'd never be able to afford new, the gown had been a bargain when she bought it at a DC consignment store to wear to a fund-raising event at the National Geographic Society.

Bronze satin with a low bodice that—with the right bra— highlighted her usually scant cleavage, the gown had bead-work on the bodice and waist and a straight skirt that just revealed her toes peeking through low, beaded heels. The dress was the most elegant thing she owned, and she hoped Luke would think she did it justice.

As it was, if any portion of the party occurred on the upper or front deck of the ageing ferry, she'd freeze her tits off, even with the soft, faux-fur wrap. Evening wear was not meant for November in the Pacific Northwest.

Hair properly coiffed—tied in a simple twist at the nape of her neck—and makeup complete, she slipped on the gown and shoes, then took a deep breath and unlocked the door.

"Holy shit," Luke said when she emerged from the bath-room. He was in the process of donning his shirt, and his hands fell slack as his eyes followed her. "I've always known you're beautiful, but...*damn*. You're stunning in that dress."

She stopped before him, her heart melting into an indis-

tinguishable lump as warmth spread from the no-longer-func-
tioning organ outward. She smiled and twirled, so he could
see the low back, and he caught her as she faced him again.
"Stop. You're blinding me."

She laughed. "Thank you. I take it you approve."

"I don't know why you even considered going shopping
with your mother when you had this in your arsenal."

"Temporary insanity. But I ended up having a nice day
with Mom. And it was so much fun to take her to a dive on
Pioneer Square—"

He held up a hand. "I never, ever want to hear stories
about you flirting with other guys when I'm not there to
establish my claim."

She shook her head and laughed. "I didn't flirt."

"You always flirt."

"I used to. And I was really good at it. But strange thing
was, I didn't want to. At least, not without you there to stake
your claim." She stepped closer and put a hand on his chest.
"But it was fun, going out with Mom. She's been playing the
role of Andre's perfect companion for so long, it was nice to
see her be…someone different. She drank beer. From a *can*.
And she danced to live music that wasn't played by an orches-
tra." She pressed her lips to the base of his throat, smiling at
the smear of lipstick she left behind. Staking *her* claim. "But I
wished you'd been there. I want to dance with you. In a bar. I
think…I want to go out on an actual date."

His hand settled at the small of her back, and she leaned
against him. "Doesn't tonight count?"

"I suppose it does. But double-dating with my parents
isn't exactly what I have in mind."

"Do you think…something is going on between your
parents?"

She shrugged. "Before Andre came into the picture, I
think they used to hook up when their paths crossed. They

did love each other once, and that love never turned to hate. My mom was just lonely, and eventually the love faded."

She met his gaze. "That's what I'm afraid of, Luke. Trying to make long distance work but in the end feeling nothing but lonely. You've been through that, and I've seen it fail firsthand."

"Sweetheart, you're nothing like your mother, nor are you anything like my ex-girlfriend. I have no doubt in my mind we can make this work until I can get a transfer."

"But what if you transfer to the DC area, and then we discover this…isn't real? After all, our situation has been utterly unreal. What if the emotions stem from something that can't be sustained in the day-to-day?"

"Then we'll deal. But we won't know unless we try." He kissed her nose. "I need to finish getting ready." His mouth dropped to her lips, and his tongue slipped between them for a deep, toe-curling kiss. He raised his head and smiled. "And you need to fix your lipstick. We're supposed to be at the dock in twenty minutes."

She left him to fix her makeup. She'd offered him an out, and he didn't seize it. The knot of fear that had been building from the moment he offered to transfer to DC started to unravel. The last thing in the world she wanted was for Luke to make changes in his life for her, and then be unhappy. She would give him up before she'd be the cause of life-changing strife for him again.

"I think," Undine said as Luke parked near the ferry terminal, "you should wear your dress uniform in the Men of NOAA calendar."

"But then you can't see my guns."

"Yeah, but all I want to do when I see you in that uniform

is open your fly and screw your brains out. Is it bad to have sex while in uniform?"

"All public displays of affection are out when I'm in uniform, but behind closed doors and off duty is a different story."

"No public displays of affection tonight, then? Does that mean we can't even dance?"

"This isn't a duty uniform. Dancing is okay, but we'll have to keep it PG," he said as he climbed out of his SUV.

"I suppose that's reasonable, as long as I can have my way with you when we get home."

The idea of Undine straddling him and taking him deep while she still wore that gown gave him an instant hard-on. Damn, this party was going to be torture. Three hours. They'd only be on the boat for three hours.

The *Gilligan's Island* theme song popped into his head. But they wouldn't get lost on the Strait of Juan de Fuca, and in three hours, they'd be back at the dock. Then they'd return to the hotel, where they had a plethora of new surfaces to christen.

He planted his hand on the small of her back as they waited to cross the street to the terminal. A Seattle news satellite van pulled into the ferry lot, where it stopped as a bombsniffing dog was led around the van. By the time they'd crossed the intersection, the van was driving into the ferry tunnel, a reminder of how very public this party would be.

Three hours. He could handle three hours. Then the real celebration would begin. Yuri had been captured. The bomb had been retrieved. He would convince Undine they had what it took to make long distance work. He wouldn't be satisfied with healing old wounds and closing the door on the past, and there was no way in hell he'd be content if she walked away. Now he only looked toward the future.

They entered the ferry terminal. Unlike the regular ferry

crossing, all the guests, even the governor and the premier, were walk-on passengers. Only catering—and apparently news—vans would be loaded on the car deck. Metal detectors had been brought in to screen the passengers, which was unusual for this crossing. Border Patrol had required it of the Blackfish Line for this event.

Luke had requested and been granted permission to wear his service weapon, even though it wasn't usually worn with the Dinner Dress Blue uniform. He left Undine's side to be screened separately, by none other than Lt. Parker Reeves. "Don't they ever give you a day off?" he asked the lieutenant.

"They wanted a few of us on board who were in the know…just in case."

Luke glanced at the other uniformed Coast Guard officers, spotting Commander Martinez and Boatswain's Mate Shales. "I'm glad for it," he said. "It's why I asked for permission to carry."

Parker nodded. "The threat may be over, but we aren't going to take chances."

A large hand dropped onto Luke's shoulder, and he turned to see Ray Ferguson. He startled at the sight of the always-casual tribal dive boat operator in a tux. "Man, they'll let anyone attend these things," Ray said.

Luke laughed. "I hear my date's dad is some sort of VIP. How'd you make the cut?"

"Tribal VIP. I was the Makah liaison for the marine sanctuary where it abuts the reservation."

Luke hadn't noticed Ray's name on the guest list, which had the hair on the back of his neck prickling, but he could hardly invent those credentials.

Undine cleared security and greeted Ray with a hug. Parker let out a low whistle at seeing her, causing Luke to drop an arm around her waist and pull her tightly to his side, completely disregarding all rules about public displays of affection while in uniform. "Mine," he said with a grin.

"You're a lucky man, Sevick." He winked at Undine. "If only you'd been able to dive with *me* that day…"

She rolled her eyes. "Right, as if my complete freak-out was the least bit appealing. But you're sweet to pretend otherwise." She took a deep breath. "My dad just called. He and Mom are already aboard, and they want us both pronto for an interview with KING 5. You ready?"

"Let's get this over with," Luke said.

*E*very part of Yuri hurt. A bullet in the chest was no small thing, but he was alive, so he wouldn't complain. He'd asked the nurse the date and time, but she'd said nothing. He was handcuffed to the hospital bed, and from the tubes he saw coming out from under the covers, he gathered he'd had surgery.

He'd been shot, but what about the others?

The image of Ivan dropping, red sprouting on his forehead, came to him. Ivan was dead. What about Alexei?

He stared at the monitor he was attached to, trying to make sense of the numbers and lines. He needed to know the date. The time. But couldn't quite place why.

The upper corner of the monitor said his name. Followed by numbers. The date? He stared at the screen, and it came to him. Today was the date he'd been waiting for. His sacrifice had paid off, and his reward had been granted against all odds. The party on the MV *Chinook*. The numbers next to the date also made sense. It was just after eight p.m. In less than thirty minutes, the real party would start.

Chapter Thirty-Six

*L*uke handed Undine a glass of champagne. They clinked glasses, then she took a sip. "The interviews weren't so bad. I liked meeting the governor. I was surprised she could hold her own talking about the sanctuary."

"She means it when she says taking care of Washington waters is a priority for her," Luke said. "It's why I voted for her."

"I thought you'd only lived here for a year?"

"This was my home port when I did my three years of service on a ship. I spent a lot of time in Washington when I was a SEAL—we do a fair amount of training in these waters —and knew this was where I wanted to be stationed, so I made it my official address."

She couldn't help but flinch at that. He wasn't in Washington by default. This was home for him. "Are your mom and brother still in California?"

"Mom's in Oregon. She bought a house on the water in Astoria. Beautiful place. Ryan is in northern California, Eureka."

"Also on the coast."

"We Sevicks love the ocean."

He was a West Coast man through and through. He might hate DC. In time, he'd resent her. She sipped her champagne. When had she turned into such a pessimist?

Her gaze landed on the governor, who was chatting with the premier of British Columbia and his wife along with the tech billionaire her father was eager to secure as a patron. She nodded toward the governor. "Do you think she knows about the *Wrasse* and *Magnum*?" She realized she'd taken to calling the Soviet sub by the name Yuri had given it.

"I expect she does, but her expression was convincingly blank when we were introduced. She's got a good poker face."

They stood near the back of the forward cabin. Rows of seats were bolted down, facing the front windows. The VIPs were in the open space at the front, where a table had been set up for the signing of the management plan when they reached the international border in the middle of the strait. The signing was more ceremonial than binding, but she appreciated the attention both governing bodies were giving to the Salish Sea and was thankful to the benefactor who'd put his support behind the action. As an underwater archaeologist whose first love was marine biology, she heartily approved all efforts made by governments to coordinate marine life protection and preservation.

She turned back to the side windows, looking west down the strait, toward Neah Bay. "I wonder if the full story of what the *Wrasse* submariners did will ever be able to come to light, or if it will be classified along with what happened yesterday."

"Hard to guess," Luke said.

"It makes me sad, the idea we might not be able to tell the world what those seven men did. Think about what they stopped—the Soviets might have succeeded in planting"—she glanced around, ensuring no one was within earshot, but still she whispered—"that *thing* on the Seattle shoreline. And we have yet to find out if they did succeed elsewhere." She took another sip of her champagne as she gazed out the window. They'd gotten lucky with the weather. It had rained earlier in the day, but the night was crisp and clear.

"They were going fifteen knots and were two hours into their sail when they dropped to periscope depth," she said. "They hadn't reached Sekiu yet. Too far from Neah Bay to have spotted *Magnum* already. I wonder why they dove?"

"A bunch of retired sailors who'd finagled a joyride in a sub that was so important to them, they'd traveled to Bremerton just to say good-bye to her? I bet you anything it was a lark," Luke said. "Because they could."

She nodded. Like Luke, she'd known enough sailors to recognize the ones who really loved the vessels. Sailors attached to their boats and subs in the same way pilots bonded to their aircraft. And he was right, the men who'd attached to *Wrasse* enough to want to say good-bye before SINKEX would have relished one last dive in the old girl.

She held up her champagne glass. "To the *Wrasse* seven. May the world someday learn of their sacrifice so they can be honored as heroes."

Luke clinked his glass to hers. "To the *Wrasse* seven."

They stood in silence, gazing out at the strait and sipping champagne. When her glass was empty, Luke said, "There's dancing under the heat lamps on the upper deck. Will you dance with me?"

"You're okay with missing the ceremony down here?" She nodded toward the table and press corps.

"Sweetheart, I've been to enough bullshit ceremonies to last me a lifetime. I'd much rather hold you in my arms in the moonlight, because that dress is amazing on you."

She smiled. Dance in the moonlight at a black-tie event with the man she was crazy in love with? *Yes, please.*

On the upper deck, she wasn't surprised to find her parents dancing cheek to cheek. She wouldn't waste energy on the hope they were starting something that would last. She'd given up those fantasies when she was nine. But she did want both her parents to be happy in the same way she'd demanded her father wish happiness for her, and right this minute, her parents looked happy, which was frosting on a cinnamon roll as far as she was concerned.

Luke took her in his arms, and they swayed together to a classic jazz tune that had been new when MV *Chinook* first crossed the strait in 1959. She leaned against him and breathed in the scent of his aftershave mixed with the fresh sea breeze. Under the heat lamps and pressed against his body, she was plenty warm and never wanted the moment to end.

"I'm crazy in love with you," Luke whispered, his lips brushing her ear.

She linked her fingers together behind his neck and met his gaze. "Cool," she said.

He laughed.

She loved the way his face lit up when he laughed. The way he held her gaze when he made love to her. Even the way he dragged her on three-mile runs and paired bacon with Brussels sprouts, although that should be a bacon abomination.

She rose on her toes and pressed a soft kiss to his lips. "I don't want you to move to DC."

He stiffened against her, and his brow furrowed. "Can we please not discuss this now?"

"—because I think I should be the one to move."

He stopped swaying to the music, but the hand on her back held her snug against him. "What?"

"I want to live here. With you. You already had your life and career upended because of me. If we're going to make this work, it's my turn to give up something for you."

"What about your job?"

"There's a fair amount of coordinating that needs to be done between UAB and the Olympic Coast National Marine Sanctuary. Between that and the *Wrasse* excavation, I could be busy for a while. And when that work runs out… I don't know. Maybe I'll go back to school and get a master's in marine conservation, or phycology."

"You want a master's degree in seaweed?"

"Okay, maybe fisheries biology. My point is, there's lots I could study, and I have a feeling my dad would help out with a scholarship if I made a few appearances on his TV show." She grinned at him. "If *you* appeared on the show, maybe he'd pay for my PhD."

He laughed. "You'd pimp me out that way?"

"Hell yeah. If you go shirtless on TV, I can brag to everyone that those guns are mine."

"I always thought you were more impressed with my ass."

"A-plus all the way, but Dad's sponsors probably don't want you to drop trou on TV."

He flashed his cocky smile. "Mistake on their part. My ass could sell a lot of product."

She laughed. "It could. It really could." She took a deep breath. "So. What do you think?"

"About you moving here or pimping me out?"

"The moving part."

"Yes. I want—"

The engine noise grew louder as the boat slowed. They must have reached the international border. It was time for the ceremony. "Should we go down?" she asked.

His hand on her back cinched her tightly against him. "You aren't getting out of this conversation that easy."

"I don't want you to leave Washington. And my dad's in California. It makes more sense—"

A boom from a lower deck halted her speech. Undine slammed into the couple next to them as the boat lurched starboard. A second boom and they rolled to port. The boat rocked so hard, a man by the rail nearly fell overboard.

She gripped Luke's wrist as she tried to stay on her feet. She glanced around the crowded upper deck, almost expecting the boat to disintegrate under her feet.

They were in the middle of the strait—forty-five minutes from shore in either direction. All at once, there was another boom, this one muted compared to the first. The boat rocked, but not as much. The loud hum of the ferry engine cut out.

They were dead in the water.

Chapter Thirty-Seven

*L*uke shouted instructions for everyone on the upper deck to gather at the center. The boat could list if forty people all rushed to one side at the same time. Perhaps because he was in uniform, the passengers listened to him.

"Are we sinking?" Charlene Gray asked.

The boat rocked and lurched, but he had no idea if they were taking on water. They weren't listing at the moment, which was a good sign.

"Your attention please," a firm male voice said over the loud speakers. "Life vests are stored in the benches on the upper deck and in overhead bins at both ends of the vessel. Please don a life vest and wait in place. Do not proceed to the passenger assembly areas. Blackfish Line crew members are assessing the situation, and will provide further instructions shortly."

"Stay here with your parents," Luke said to Undine. "I'm going to find Parker and Commander Martinez."

"I want to go with——"

He pressed a fast kiss to her lips. "You promised yesterday you'd do what I say in these situations."

"Aww. Shit. I did. But I didn't think it would ever actually happen."

"Neither did I." He clenched his jaw. "I'm starting to think Yuri's takedown was a little too easy."

"It didn't seem easy when Ivan was pointing the gun at me."

"Wh*at*?" Charlene said, adding a shriek to the end of the word.

"He backed himself into a corner," Luke said. "He knew he'd never walk out of there."

"But we got the—" She paused and let out a fake cough, cutting off what she'd been about to say as she cast a sheepish glance at her mother and the other passengers, who were paying close attention to their conversation.

Luke had a horrible feeling Yuri had known what he was doing all along. "Pass out life jackets to everyone. I'll go find Parker."

He pulled on the gloves that were part of the dress uniform and, facing outward, braced his hands on both rails of the steep outdoor stairs that led to the lower deck and slid down on his hands in a rapid descent. He landed on the promenade with a thump.

He wanted to pull his weapon, but party guests inside the galley area could easily assume he was a terrorist and charge him. He entered the cabin through the rear door. People shouted questions to the Blackfish Line attendant who was dutifully passing out life jackets. Some passengers displayed fear, while others only showed annoyance. It was easy to see who thought this was simple engine trouble, and who suspected something far worse.

He hurried through the cabin toward the front of the boat, looking for someone from the Coast Guard, given that the Blackfish employees were all busy calming guests. He was stopped by several people, each asking if he knew what was going on. He guessed they flagged him because of the uniform. Dress or not, it indicated authority.

He shook his head in frustration. He could be going up against terrorists and he was in his damn Dinner Dress Blues. Parker and the others were in their Coast Guard winter blues, but those were service uniforms. Functional. At the very least, he wished he had a radio in addition to the gun, but it hadn't occurred to him he'd need one. They weren't exactly standard for formal occasions.

He yanked off his bow tie as he crossed the center cabin toward the front. At the doorway, he pressed himself against the frame, drew his weapon, and peeked into the room where the ceremony had been underway. He swore. The reporter was front and center with the governor and premier, giving what had all the earmarks of a live-on-the-scene special report.

Shit. There would be no containing this story.

He tucked his weapon back into the holster and strode into the room, determined to put a stop to what could well be feeding information directly to Yuri's cohorts.

He'd bet everything he owned this was Yuri's last play.

Godamnmotherfuckinghell.

He didn't have enough words to express how fucked up this situation had gotten in less than thirty seconds.

Be the SEAL. An operator. You're on an op that just went FUBAR. Adapt. Adjust. Think. Survive.

If necessary, kill.

He wasn't a scientist right now. He wasn't a NOAA lieutenant. He was a badass SEAL, and some motherfucker had just attacked his country, his state, his home, and his woman.

These assholes were going to pay.

He marched up to the reporter who was excitedly

reporting on breaking news. She had no fucking clue how much danger she was in and was making the most of her moment in the spotlight after being assigned to cover what would have been a footnote on the eleven p.m. broadcast. He slammed the camera to the floor with one hand and yanked the microphone from the reporter's hand with the other. "Cut," he said, his tone lacking irony. He was too pissed for that. He faced the reporter. "Why don't you just tell the fucking terrorists our social security numbers while you're at it?"

Her eyes widened. "No one has confirmed—"

"I don't give a fuck what has been *confirmed*. You need to assume it's an attack first and act accordingly, not assume it's a damn engine malfunction and feed intel directly to the people who've disabled this boat. If I'm wrong, yay. I'll buy you a new camera. But if you're wrong? We're all fucking dead."

His gaze scanned the room, spotting Boatswain's Mate Shales, pinned in the corner by anxious passengers. Luke nodded for Shales to meet him at the door for the promenade.

The man extracted himself, and they stepped outside. "Good job getting the reporter to shut the hell up. I tried but—"

"I have nothing to lose. Right now, I'm a NOAA scientist. You're on duty."

"Exactly."

"What's the word?" Luke asked.

"There's a hole in the side of the car deck, and the engine seized. No word on why yet. Commander Martinez is on the bridge, the others are on the car deck, searching for planted explosives and the person who set them."

"We've got tangoes on the boat?"

"No one knows. The charge could've been on a timer."

Shales nodded to the water. "*Adelie* is on her way with a bomb-sniffing dog aboard, but it'll take the cutter at least fifteen minutes to get here. For now, we aren't taking on water, at least."

Luke rubbed a hand over his face. "Why aren't we evacuating passengers onto the lifeboats and life rafts already?"

"Orders are to stay in place until we know if we've got tangoes aboard. If they're hiding among the passengers and we help them escape…"

Luke nodded. He'd suspected as much.

"When *Adelie* gets here, we'll probably start tendering passengers to her. Each guest will be thoroughly screened."

"I need a radio so I can help with the search."

"They have extras on the bridge. I'll radio the commander and tell him you're coming."

"Thanks." Luke vaulted over the gate that blocked the employees-only stairs to the bridge and hurried up the steps.

Commander Martinez unlocked the door to admit him. "It appears we were wrong about Yuri, Lt. Sevick."

"If you give me a radio, Commander, I'll join the others in searching for tangoes."

Martinez pressed a two-way into Luke's hand. "We need to find them quickly. A Ukrainian neo-Nazi group has claimed credit for disabling the boat." He waved toward a TV monitor mounted to the side of the helm. Dread surged through Luke as he viewed CNN's bold red headline: BREAKING NEWS: TERRORISTS SEIZE US/CANADIAN FERRY WITH WASHINGTON STATE GOVERNOR ABOARD.

They didn't yet have live helicopter feed of the ferry in the middle of the strait, so naturally, they aired the one piece of film they did have—Luke's angry approach just before he broke the camera. It aired in a loop, replaying on the right side of the screen, while an anxious news anchor spoke directly to the camera on the left. On the bright side, maybe this would crush Stefan's desire to put Luke on the TV show.

The ferry captain turned up the volume.

"Again, if you are just joining us, breaking news from the waters that separate the US and Canada in the Pacific Northwest. Terrorists have seized an international ferry that was hosting a private party attended by the governor of Washington. We've just gotten word the premier of British Columbia is aboard as well. A Ukrainian neo-Nazi group, upset by the US and Canada's decision not to train Ukrainian troops engaged with Russia to reclaim the Crimean Peninsula, have claimed credit for the taking of the vessel. They have stated that if any US or Canadian Navy or Coast Guard vessels get within a thousand yards of the stranded ferry, they will begin killing passengers."

Luke's stomach clenched. "Do we believe their claim?" he asked. "Are they on board the boat?"

Martinez gave a sharp nod.

"One of my crew is missing," the ferry captain said. "Either he's the one who disabled the engine—which I don't believe for a second—or he encountered a terrorist in the engine room."

Luke turned for the door. "I'll join the search."

"One more thing, Lt. Sevick," the commander said. "The timing of the explosion was precise. The bomb went off the exact moment the governor and premier were about to sign the agreement. If the bomb was set off with a remote, the terrorist must've been in the cabin at the time. Which means at least one terrorist was on the guest list."

"And another was already in place in the engine room," the ferry captain said. "The engine went offline seconds after the blast. So we're dealing with a minimum of two individuals."

ndine hadn't wanted to carry an evening bag and now was grateful for the discreet pocket in her faux-fur wrap, because she *did* have her cell phone. With a great feeling of accomplishment, she pulled out her phone. She could call Curt, except his line would probably be busy, so she'd call Luke and find out what he'd learned. Or she'd call Keith. Someone, anyone, who was in the loop and could tell her if the boat was about to sink or be invaded by Ukrainian neo-Nazis.

The mood on the top deck was anxious after the prolonged silence from the bridge. There'd been no further announcements. Nothing. Passengers grumbled about wanting to go to the main cabin, but she argued, insisting their orders were to stay in place. For whatever reason, they listened to her. Probably because Luke's inferred authority had transferred to her in his absence. She had to believe that if there were terrorists aboard the boat, it wouldn't be wise to have the passengers all clustered in one place. Why make it easy for them?

But still, she told herself it could just be an engine malfunction.

She unlocked her phone in hopes of calling someone who could tell her what the hell was going on and discovered the flaw in her plan: they were in the middle of the strait; she didn't have service. She stared at the circle with the slash through it, the symbol that said in no uncertain terms: *Give it up, bitch.* She didn't even know her phone had that symbol until she'd arrived in Neah Bay.

She'd had to buy four phones since arriving in Washington two and a half months ago. The one she arrived with blew up on *Petrel,* the next one didn't work in Neah Bay, then had burned in the fire, the third she'd bought in Forks but it had also burned with everything else, the fourth had been smashed by Yuri, and now this one, which she'd bought this afternoon when they ventured out to grab her gown, failed in the middle of the strait.

What was it with Washington and cell phones? Or was it an Olympic Peninsula thing?

She sucked in a sharp, painful breath, irrationally upset over the very least of her problems.

Damn Yuri for so many horrible things. For killing her coworkers. For trying to kill her. If Luke or her parents were harmed tonight, she'd march straight to his hospital room and rip open the sutures from his surgery and then she'd taser his open wounds.

Or maybe she'd just shoot him.

She gazed across the deck. Where was Luke? Had he found Parker? Or was he in danger?

He's a former SEAL. He can take care of himself.

He might be a former SEAL, but he'd gone alone—without knowing what he was stepping into—down to the heart of the boat. His cell was probably as useless as hers. He'd had to find the Coast Guard contingent without the aid of radios. And there could be—probably were—people on board who would shoot first.

The ferry was in the middle of the strait. That much she knew. In the long minutes Luke had been gone, Coast Guard vessels had raced toward them and…stopped.

The boats were too far to swim to without a wetsuit.

It was as if they had orders to stand down, come no closer.

Which brought to mind the question…what was the penalty for breaching the buffer zone that surrounded the ferry? The silence from the bridge was worrisome. Did they have control of the bridge? Were terrorists aboard, or were they operating remotely?

How far away could someone be and still set off a bomb? *How far to set off a nuke?*

Did Yuri's compatriots have a better cellular provider in this black hole of coverage? What was the carrier of jihadists or anti-Russians, or neo-Nazis or whomever the hell they were dealing with?

"Luke will find them and take them out," her father said.

She nodded even as she said, "He's not Superman." It wasn't that she didn't have faith in his abilities; it was that he wasn't invincible. Bullets wouldn't bounce off him. She was terrified something would happen to him.

"The Coast Guard is on board. He has backup."

"Why aren't the other boats getting any closer?" her mother asked. "We could be evacuating to the other boats, or getting on the life rafts if the ferry is in danger of sinking."

"They must have orders not to come closer," Undine said. "I think we're dealing with a hostage situation."

"You think they've taken the governor hostage?" Charlene asked. "How terrifying."

Undine shook her head. She watched the circle of boats bobbing in the waves. "No. Not just the governor." She turned to glance across the deck. At least forty people milled about, orange life vests around their necks, reluctantly following the rules. "I think we're all the hostages."

Chapter Thirty-Eight

Luke scanned the car deck with his gun out. This deck was usually monitored by ferry personnel and off-limits when the ferry was underway, but this run was different in every way, starting with the fact that there were hardly any cars, just three catering vans and two satellite news vans.

The obvious culprit would be the caterers. But none other than the secretary of Homeland Security had said the caterers and absolutely everyone with access to the party would be screened. Which meant either someone had magnificent cover, or they'd straight up stolen ID. Luke was inclined to believe in the stolen ID. Nothing elaborate when simple would work.

He'd entered the deck from the aft stairs on the port side and could only see the port half of the tunnel, which was split down the middle by a center divider. The divider housed more stairs that led up to the passenger deck, as well as access to the engine room and other maintenance rooms. An archway by the center stairs connected the port and starboard tunnels.

"Sevick?" Parker called out from the other side of the divider. "I need backup."

Luke hurried to the archway and cursed when he rounded the corner. Ray Ferguson stood with his back to the metal partition with his hands up. He glared at Parker, who had his gun pointed at Ray's heart.

"Good timing, Sevick. Look who I just found in the storage locker. Tell us what you were doing there, Ray," Parker said in an irritated tone.

"I already told you, *brah*. I came down to the car deck for a smoke." Ray might have used Hawaiian slang, but his usual laid-back demeanor was long gone. Luke didn't blame him.

"You came down here for a smoke? The place that's off-limits?"

"I couldn't smoke on the upper deck where the heat lamps are, because that's where everyone is dancing. It was cold on the promenade but warmer in the staircase. After I finished, I thought I heard someone yell, and entered the deck to see if anyone needed help. Then the bomb blew, and I was hit by a piece of shrapnel." He pointed to his leg. His trousers were sliced open at the calf. "I hid in the locker for protection in case there was another blast. I was just about to come out so I could take care of the cut when you found me."

"Wait. The bomb blew inward?" Luke asked. He turned to scan the gaping hole in the middle of the starboard side of the ferry. It cut through the car deck and into the underdeck. A few feet lower and they'd be in danger of taking on water.

"Yeah," Ray said. "It blew from the outside. Two blasts in rapid succession."

Luke cursed. Given that Yuri was likely the mastermind of this assault, he'd known charges set by scuba divers was a very real possibility. But this meant that if there were more, they were also on the boat exterior, and Luke didn't have scuba equipment to search for them. Not to mention he couldn't check the entire hull by himself in the next thirty minutes. He crossed the deck toward the hole to look at the jagged edges. As Ray had said, the metal had bent inward.

He turned to Parker. "Let him go."

"No. He could be the one. He could be working with Yuri. He might be the one who set the charges."

"Ray? He doesn't dive. Everyone knows that."

"So he drove the boat. Dammit. It makes sense. Only a handful of people knew about the case, and Ray was one of them because he saw you bring it up. He killed Annie and grabbed the case."

"Annie was my *cousin*," Ray said through gritted teeth.

"Ray knew about the case," Luke said, "but he didn't know it was at the museum."

"He could have guessed—where else would you do electrolytic reduction in Neah Bay?"

"I didn't *know*," Ray said. "And even if I did—why the hell would I give a damn about the case? Enough to kill my cousin? You aren't making sense, Parker."

"The sabotage on the boat, when Luke and Undine were left stranded at the bottom, that would have been easy for you to rig."

"I could say the same for you," Ray said. "The radio was working when we left, but once you got your hands on it, things went haywire."

"Stop it," Luke said. "You're wasting time, Parker. Ray, go back to the upper deck and see to that cut. And quit smoking. It's a disgusting habit."

"I know, man." Ray limped up the stairs.

"You could be making a mistake," Parker said. "Everyone is a suspect."

Luke shrugged. "It's not Ray."

"How can you be so certain?"

"He was recovering from surgery in September when *Petrel* exploded. He wasn't even in Neah Bay—he was staying with his niece in Seattle for almost all of October."

"Oh," Parker said. Then he took a deep breath. "Just because he couldn't have been part of the initial—"

"We're looking for neo-Nazi Ukrainians. Not Makah Indians."

"And Russians. You can't rule them out."

"Fine," Luke said. "Have you seen any Russians on the car deck? And where the hell are the other Coast Guardsmen? Why are you down here alone?"

A noise from the door that led down to the engine room drew Luke's attention. Two uniformed Coasties emerged carrying an unconscious man between them. "That the missing crew member?"

"Yeah. After they found him, I came up here to finish searching—and found Ray—while they provided first aid to stop his bleeding." To the others, Parker said, "He breathing?"

"Barely. We're taking him up. There must be a doctor among the passengers."

Parker nodded and stepped aside, letting the men pass to get to the wide stairwell.

"It's just you and me until they get back, Sevick. We need to search the storage lockers along this side, the utility rooms, and the vans. And then finish searching the engine room. This damn boat has a hundred hiding places on this deck alone."

"Sweep the lockers and bins first. Then we'll double up on the utility rooms," Luke said.

Parker nodded, and they set to work, clearing the life jacket storage and life raft storage containers first. They were large enough to fit a person and for safety reasons were never locked, making them the obvious choice for a man eager to hide.

They were also empty of anything other than the safety devices they were meant to house.

The ferry was quiet—eerie for being in the middle of the strait—without the noise of the engine. The tunnel curved, with cars exiting to the starboard side instead of straight out the front like the Washington State Ferries, so wind didn't blow straight through the space either, but rather entered through the back and glanced off the bow.

If the wind had been blowing, Luke never would have heard the click of a hammer being pulled back or the snick of the lock being turned.

He paused and studied the door marked "Crew Only" and nodded to Parker, silently asking if it had been searched.

Parker gave a quick shake of his head.

They moved as one, a team. Luke yanked open the door, and Parker took aim. A man charged, and Parker fired.

The man kept coming at Parker, carried by either momentum or sheer will. He had a pale object in his hand— a gun. Luke tackled him, diving forward and knocking him to the side as he pulled the trigger.

The gun fired. Luke felt the hiss of the bullet along his bicep, but not the sting. He knocked aside the weapon and punched the man in the face. Another blow to the chest where Parker's first bullet had hit him, and the fight left the man.

He lay slack on the deck, eyes open and breathing labored. He wore a tuxedo. As they'd suspected, he'd hidden among the guests.

"How many of you are there on the boat?" Luke asked.

The man coughed blood. "There could be one or a dozen. It doesn't matter. The bomb is counting down. You have no escape."

"What bomb?" Luke asked, the dread that had been with him from the moment of the first explosion bursting into full-on choking horror.

Blood coated the man's teeth, and the liquid pooled at the corners of his mouth. "The second bomb Yuri took from *M-357*. The timer is counting down. You can't shut it off."

"Where is it?" Parker asked as he scooped up the man's gun from the deck.

The man shook his head and closed his eyes.

"Shit. This fucker was 3D printed. That's how he got it through the metal detector."

"He walked on, then," Luke said. "With the other passengers." Not surprising, considering his attire.

"He could have hidden the bullets in the heel of his dress shoes. I knew we should have insisted on inspecting the shoes."

"Did you see who he was with? When he came aboard?"

"I don't remember him," Parker said. "He might've boarded when I was checking your weapon."

Luke searched his clothing and found a Canadian passport in the name of Ned Taylor. He vaguely remembered seeing the name on the guest list but couldn't remember if a companion had been named. "Radio the captain," he said to Parker. "Canadian authorities need to track down the real Ned Taylor and find out if he came alone. And someone needs to question Yuri Kravchenko. Now."

Parker relayed the information as Luke hurriedly bound, then searched the fake Ned Taylor as the man gasped for breath. His lung was probably collapsing. Even without a collapsed lung, he would bleed out without medical aid. There was probably a doctor and a heavy-duty first aid kit aboard. Luke knew advanced first aid and had more than once provided field dressing for gunshot wounds, but his to-do list tonight was full.

He had a motherfucking nuclear bomb to find and somehow disarm.

He would leave Taylor to die, except the man could provide more intel. Like where the bomb was and how, exactly, to shut it off. "I'm taking him to the passenger deck, to find a doctor."

"I'll search the vans and wait for backup to finish searching the maintenance rooms."

"I'll send the other Coasties down to help you."

Luke plucked the man from the floor and threw him over his shoulder, not bothering to be careful of his wounds. "I hate these suicidal assholes."

"He's getting blood all over your uniform."

"Dammit. These things are expensive." He headed for the stairs but paused at the foot of the stairs. "Thanks, Parker. Nice shooting."

"It's the first time I've ever fired my gun outside of training."

"I'm glad you had my back."

On the upper deck, he carried Taylor into the front cabin, where the VIPs were gathered. There was bound to be a doctor among them. A few people screeched and backed away when they saw him.

"This man needs a doctor."

A woman in a red gown nodded toward the front. "The governor's husband is patching up the other guy already."

"Who is he?" another passenger asked as he crossed toward the front of the ferry.

"Did you shoot him?"

"What happened?"

"Is it over, can we get off the boat now?"

The questions came rapid-fire, one on top of the other. Luke dropped Taylor on the floor in the middle of the aisle and said, "He's part of the group who planted the explosive.

Lt. Reeves shot him. We need him to live because he has intel." He looked to the governor's husband, who left the side of the now-conscious ferry worker.

"That's the guy who hit me," the crew member said. "In the engine room."

"What have we got?" the governor's husband asked.

"Probably a sucking chest wound."

The doctor cursed and ripped open the man's shirt. His wife, the governor, grabbed a large first aid kit bearing the Blackfish Line logo from the floor and brought it to her husband. She knelt across from her husband. "Tell me what to do."

"We need plastic—a rubber glove will do—to seal the hole."

She dug out a glove from the kit and handed it to her husband.

"You're going to ruin your gown, Governor," the tech company billionaire that Stefan had been hoping to woo said as he knelt next to her.

She cast the man a wry smile, "Then I guess it's a good thing Lt. Sevick broke that camera. This is not my best photo op."

"Hold this while I inflate his lung," the doctor said.

The governor didn't hesitate and pressed the rubber glove over the hole in the man's chest. Luke turned. They had the situation under control. "If he regains consciousness and speaks, report every word he says to Commander Martinez."

The billionaire nodded. "We'll do that, Lieutenant."

Luke turned for the door, catching sight of the woman in the red gown again. She had her hand in her purse, at an odd angle. Something pale flashed.

The same type of pale as the weapon Taylor had carried. Another 3D-printed gun. Luke didn't hesitate and lunged at the woman. Her eyes widened when she saw him coming, and she pulled the trigger.

Her shot buzzed past his ear, another close call, and he slammed her back against one of the mounted chairs, smashing her wrist against the inflexible arm. She screamed as her wrist snapped and the gun fell from her slack fingers. A stream of what could only be Ukrainian curses fell from her lips.

Yuri didn't bother to contain his glee when the FBI Special Agent in Charge marched into his hospital room with an entourage. Right on time.

"Where the fuck is the second bomb, Yuri?" the woman asked.

"Your super SEAL hasn't found it yet?" He made a tsking sound. "He must be slipping."

"Cut the bullshit. Where is the bomb?"

Yuri glanced at the clock on his monitor. "If Mykhail was on schedule, you have…eighty-five minutes to find it."

"How do we shut it off?"

"You can't. Not without the keys. Which Mykhail has surely thrown overboard." Mykhail and Irina were well trained and as dedicated to the cause as Yuri. Their visas had been sponsored by the same tech company that had sponsored Alexei and Ivan, and they'd been waiting for tonight nearly as long as Yuri had.

The woman fixed him with a fierce glare. "Why are you doing this? For ten million dollars?"

"No. I don't want money. I never wanted money. I want war."

"Your war is with Russia."

"You Americans and Canadians promised to help us,

then you refused to train our troops. You reneged on our deal. You let them steal our Crimean Peninsula. I will take your Olympic Peninsula. Vancouver Island too."

"We refused to train neo-Nazis! We didn't refuse to help Ukraine."

"You seized on any excuse. In so doing, you've allied yourselves with Russia. So now I will use a *Russian* bomb to kill you. So you will know the treachery of your allies. So you will feel the pain of Chernobyl." He tried to sit up in the bed, but the restraints held him down. Pain pierced his chest. "Do you know how many days my family lived and worked near Chernobyl after the meltdown, before the Russians told them of the disaster? How many days my little brother played in radioactive air?"

"*We* didn't cause Chernobyl."

"You have turned your back on us too many times. You have tacitly accepted what Russia did to us. To the people of Chechnya. They support Assad in Syria, and you do nothing. They shoot down a plane, and you do nothing. They sink a ferry, and you do nothing. You have the might to stop Russia, but you don't." He formed a fist, the only motion he was capable of in his bound state. "Do you want to know why I chose the ferry?"

"Because of your sister who died on the ferry in the Sea of Azov."

"Yes. But there is more than that. The nuclear weapon… it is small. It would take out Port Angeles, but not the Peninsula. It wasn't big enough to make my statement. But the strait…she has many fault lines. One little nuclear explosion above a fault will ripple outward. You will have a massive quake and tsunamis. Canada can say good-bye to Vancouver Island. The US can say good-bye to the Olympic Peninsula. And, if the right fault is hit, good-bye to your Seattle."

Chapter Thirty-Nine

*L*uke stared at the bomb. It was identical to the one Yuri had left in his building, complete with the encrustation that proved it had sat in a torpedo tube for over fifty years. Parker had discovered it in the news satellite truck, in a locker where one of the technicians said they usually stored backup equipment.

Given the amount of electronics in the van, it was the perfect hiding place. Between the electronics and the salt encrustations, the bomb-sniffing dog could easily miss the signature scent of the small explosive that would set off the fission reaction. And bomb-sniffing dogs weren't capable of detecting radioactive materials.

Luke wouldn't be surprised if someone in Yuri's organization had gotten a job working security for the TV station. Both the man and the woman had excellent IDs, and according to the intel they were now receiving, their neo-Nazi group had strong ties to various organized crime groups. They knew their way around the system.

Commander Martinez had a satellite phone and spoke

directly with one of the technicians who'd spent the last twenty-four hours studying the device that had been collected from Luke's apartment building. Luke watched as Martinez opened the panel Undine had pointed out on the other bomb. Sure enough, it revealed a mechanical clock, rolling down the minutes to detonation.

Eighty-two minutes remained.

The standard fail-safe had been built in; any attempt to disable the clock was a sure-fire way to detonate the bomb.

They didn't have time to dick around trying to disarm it. They needed to get the bomb the hell away from here.

"Can we just drop it in the strait?" one of the Coast Guardsmen asked.

"Too many fault lines," Luke said. "The strait is riddled with them. This thing goes off here, and it could set off the big one."

"Can we take it out to the Pacific?" Parker asked.

"We'd have to get it past the Cascadia subduction zone," Luke said. "If it hit there, we'd have tsunamis in the US, Japan, China…even Siberia."

Yuri may have found a way to hit Russia after all.

"How far do we have to go to get it past the subduction zone?" Parker asked.

"From here, probably a hundred and seventy-five nautical miles if we go due west."

"At thirty-five knots, that would take five hours," Parker said. "It's impossible."

"The Navy can send out an Osprey. Pick up the bomb, fly it out past the zone," Luke said.

"I don't know if any Ospreys are in the area. It'll take twenty minutes to scramble a Seahawk. The nearest one is probably on Whidbey. Maybe we could get a Blackhawk from Joint Base Lewis-McChord," Martinez said.

"If we load the bomb onto an Interceptor, we can start heading west," Parker said. "The Seahawk or Osprey can catch us down the line. That will buy us a few minutes."

"What's the max speed on the new Interceptors?" Luke asked.

"Forty knots. We won't be able to make it to the ocean, but we can at least get the hell away from the most heavily populated areas."

"Commander," Luke said, "The governor needs to initiate the tsunami warning system for all of Washington. People need to get to high ground, just in case. Same for the BC premier."

The commander gave a sharp nod. He pulled out his radio and hailed the Coast Guard Cutter *Adelie*. "Launch the Interceptor II and bring her to the aft car deck entrance."

"Orders were no boat can approach *Chinook*," the captain replied.

"Belay that, Captain. We believe we've captured all terrorists aboard *Chinook*, but even if we haven't, if we don't get the Interceptor, everyone on this boat—and all the boats in the vicinity—are going to die anyway."

While the captain made arrangements for the boat, one of the Coasties slid into the driver's seat of the van. "I'm going to back it closer to the edge."

"This could be a one-way trip, Luke," Parker said. "If a Seahawk or Osprey can't reach the boat in time, whoever is piloting the Interceptor will have to keep going. This is a one-person job, and that person is me."

"With two people, one can drive the boat and the other can work to disarm it."

"Do you know how to disarm a nuke?" Parker asked.

"No. But I know how to disarm explosives, and this contains a basic explosive to initiate the fission reaction."

"You want to open that thing up? While on open water, on a tiny boat?"

"Do you have a better plan?"

"Drive like hell for the ocean, and wait for a helicopter/plane to swoop down and pick me up."

"Have you ever been in a boat that was picked up by an Osprey before? Do you know how to hook up the cables, or what it's like to fly dangling by a cable from a small airplane? I have. This is a two-person job, Parker. Hell, it's a five-person job, but I don't want to risk anyone else."

Parker's insistence on going alone didn't sit right with Luke. There was an eagerness and an irritation that seemed…off. Luke was the first man to stand up for his country, but he wasn't eager to die, and this was almost certainly a suicide mission.

Yet Parker's tone held no fear that would lace even the bravest special forces operator's voice. Operators weren't brave because they felt no fear. It was the opposite. They feared but took the mission head-on anyway. They worked through the fear. Even with it. They never lacked it.

Something was off. And the thing that was off was Lt. Parker Reeves.

Yet he was volunteering to take a live nuke out to sea to save the world. It didn't feel right or wise to give Parker sole possession of the live nuke.

As Luke and the Coast Guardsmen maneuvered the bomb onto a hand truck and positioned it on a ramp to deposit into the Interceptor, his suspicion grew.

Commander Martinez secured an Osprey for the pickup, relaying the situation to admirals, secretaries of government departments, hell, for all Luke knew, the man could have a direct line to the president. But they didn't have time for others to discuss the situation and come up with solutions. It would take the Pentagon a month to formulate a plan, and the State Department six weeks to implement it.

Luke had to act now or watch everything he loved be destroyed.

Which could be how Parker felt too.

It was never a question of whether Luke would volunteer for this. It was the only way to make sure Parker disposed of the bomb. The only way to be certain Undine and even his mother and brother, both living in coastal cities, would be safe.

"I can do this alone," Parker said.

"No. You'll drive. I'll defuse. We'll have about thirty minutes before the Osprey picks us up, and if that fails, I'll keep trying while we're in the air. Letting the bomb drop is the last resort." And he'd stay with the bomb until the final moment. He wouldn't give up. He couldn't.

"You just can't let someone else be the hero, can you, Luke?" Parker asked. But his tone was congenial. Friendly. Even if a bit irritated.

"Nope. But I'm willing to share the glory."

The Interceptor reached the ferry. Luke turned to Boatswain's Mate Shales. "Find Undine on the top deck and bring her down."

The man gave a sharp nod and hurried up the steps. A loading ramp was stretched between ferry and Interceptor and the Coasties maneuvered the bomb into the bow of the small boat.

"Thank you for volunteering, both of you," Martinez said to Luke and Parker.

They both nodded. Luke could share his suspicions about Parker with the commander, but not only would that waste time, it would mean the commander would have to order someone else to go with Luke, and if Parker was willing to die for this, why ask someone else? For himself, there was no question that he'd perform this service.

He'd promised Keith he'd protect Undine, and he wasn't an oath breaker.

He was in it to the end. He always had been.

Parker fixed Luke with a steady gaze. "I want you to know, this isn't a suicide mission for me. I have every intention of making it back alive and basking in the glory of being a hero."

"I do too," Luke said. He turned toward the sound of footsteps in the stairwell. Breathtakingly beautiful in her knockout evening gown, Undine entered the car deck. "I have everything to live for," he added.

✳

*U*ndine wanted to beg Luke to stay, to let someone else volunteer, but that was not only selfish of her, it wouldn't be Luke. He'd never make that choice, and he'd only resent her for asking. No way in hell would she mar this good-bye with resentment.

She gripped the lapels of his blood-soaked uniform. "I'm going to be so pissed if you don't come back."

He smiled. "You know I can't let Parker be the only hero."

She let out a laugh even as a tear spilled. "You're not an asshole, you know. You never were."

"Shhh. Don't tell anyone. I have a reputation to uphold." The arm around her waist cinched her tightly to his chest. "I love you, Undine. I'm not going to die tonight. I'm coming back, and I'm going to marry you. I want to go scuba diving with you every day and make love to you every night. I want to be the father of your children. We have a whole lifetime ahead of us, and it starts tonight."

Her heart fluttered in an erratic beat. "Was that a proposal?"

"Yep. So how about it?"

She swiped away another tear. "Are you going to want me to go running with you every day?"

"You can have weekends off."

"What about when I'm pregnant?"

"We'll walk."

"Will you always ruin bacon with Brussels sprouts?"

His smile widened. "As long as I don't have to give up Brussels sprouts, you don't have to give up bacon."

She could live with that. "Where do you stand on red meat in general?"

"You can have it all you want, but I limit myself to prime rib on major holidays."

She pulled his face down to hers. "Okay. I'll marry you." She kissed him. Tears rolled down her cheeks and her heart pounded. This was strangely like the panic attack she'd experienced weeks ago with Parker, but instead of wanting to flee, she wanted to crawl into a dark space with Luke and never let him go. "I love you," she said against his lips.

"I don't have a ring to give you. For now…" He unpinned one of the medals from his uniform. "Keep this." He pressed it into her palm and wrapped her fingers around it. "You're mine, Undine Gray. And I'm coming back for you."

She nodded and let him go. She stepped back as he walked to the edge of the car deck and jumped into the boat with Parker. In the breadth of a heartbeat, he transformed from lover to special forces operator. Instructions were given and received. Lines were released, and the boat shot out into the Salish Sea. Luke didn't smile. Didn't wave. Didn't so much as look at her.

She understood why.

He was an operator on a mission that required every ounce of focus.

She opened her hand to see the medal in her palm. She'd been mistaken. It wasn't a ribbon or an award; it was his trident, the insignia he'd earned when he became a SEAL. She closed her fist around it and held it against her heart.

Now the waiting would begin.

Chapter Forty

The Interceptor took the wave head-on, dropping hard in the trough. Luke gripped the rail, but his ass flew off the bench and slammed down hard. The bomb, at least, was tied down and not in danger of flying overboard. Luke, not so much.

Water splashed over the gunwale and filled the bow. He was fucking freezing, but at least he'd donned a survival suit right after they set out, so he was mostly dry. He cursed into his headset. "Take it easy, Parker. I'm trying to operate on a nuclear bomb here."

"Sorry! It's hard to see the chop with your fat head in the way."

Luke couldn't help but smile. Suspicions aside, Parker reminded him a lot of one of the guys who'd been on his SEAL team.

The screwdriver slipped as he tried to fit it into the shiny new Phillips-head screw that held the lower panel in place. Yuri had replaced the screws, meaning this had to be the access point for initiating—and hopefully deactivating—the timer. "What's the ETA on the Osprey?" Luke asked. He hoped to hell he could get this thing defused before they had to go for a flight. Dangling from a plane that could fly like a helicopter wasn't his favorite thing in the world. At least they'd be pulled inside so the Osprey could fly at airplane speeds to get them past the subduction zone.

Luke's work studying the effects of sonar on marine mammals' ability to navigate meant he'd spent a lot of time on a boat out in the subduction zone. Even beyond the horrors of the potential for earthquakes and tsunamis, he felt dread at the idea of what a nuke would do to sea life. He could envision the destruction, and just the thought brought bile to his throat.

There were dog people and cat people. Luke was more of a seahorse person. He treasured everything aquatic. It was no wonder he'd fallen in love with a mermaid.

All at once, the engine cut off. Luke looked up sharply, meeting Parker's gaze through the windshield of the tiny cabin. "Is the Osprey here?" he asked using the radio. He didn't hear the telltale whirr of an Osprey engine.

"They're ten minutes out," Parker said.

Luke cursed, looking at the timer on the bomb. They had less than an hour. "Why are we stopping, then?"

"I have an idea for how we can turn off the bomb."

Luke stiffened. "An idea?" He clicked his mic when his voice didn't carry and realized Parker had shut off the radio at the console. Unease slid down his spine. "Why is the radio off?"

"More than an idea." Parker left the small cabin and joined Luke in the bow. The way he moved, the way he spoke, even the look on his face sent up red flags everywhere.

"What's going on, Parker?" He inched his hand toward his holstered pistol.

Parker had his gun pointed at Luke before he touched the

grip. "I didn't want to do it this way. If you'd just let me come out alone, we'd have been *fine*."

Luke's hand tightened around the screwdriver. He could disarm Parker and ram it into his jugular. Parker had no idea how skilled Luke was in hand-to-hand combat. "I'm not going to let you set off this bomb, Parker."

"I don't want to set it off. My orders are to disarm it at all costs. Even if I have to kill you."

"Your orders."

"Yes. My orders."

"Not from Commander Martinez."

"No. I have a different superior."

"Ukrainian?"

"No. Russian."

"**B**ring in a TV. Let me see the news," Yuri said. "Then I will talk."

"No," the FBI agent said. "We're not going to feed you. But you should know that both the man and the woman on the ferry were caught."

Yuri shrugged. "They knew the risks. My guess is Mykhail destroyed the engine, stranding the ferry, and Irina set off the charge to get everyone's attention, or you wouldn't be here. Even now, your Navy and Coast Guard are gathering around, news helicopters flying above. The whole world is watching the beginning of the end."

"The bomb is no longer on the ferry."

"Making a run for the ocean? That is even worse." He grinned. "The subduction zone is an even better target."

"How did Mykhail turn on the bomb, Yuri?"

"With a key."

"No. The bomb is covered in corrosion. The keyholes

aren't even visible. To use keys, the corrosion would've been chipped away. The holes would be obvious."

He'd expected this question. He would have used keys if he had them, but the paperwork from Object 221 had offered another way. He'd give them the truth…of a sort. "There were two bombs in *Magnum*'s torpedo tube. Do you know what they were for?"

"You told Ms. Gray the Soviet plan was to plant them off West Point, in Seattle."

"That was the plan for one of the bombs, yes. The other was…trickier. When *Magnum* first set out, she had a tracked vehicle attached to her back, the kind that can ride up on shore. Tracks of similar vehicles were found years ago in Scandinavia and presumed to be from Soviet incursion during the Cold War. They made similar incursions here.

"The first bomb was to be buried underwater, but the second was headed for the Seattle World's Fair science exhibit. The exhibit closed that very week, and the Soviets had a worker in place who was part of the breakdown crew. He would have planted the bomb amongst science exhibit materials, the items that were going into long-term storage as they transitioned into a permanent science museum. It would have looked like a very elaborate prop—1962 world of tomorrow at its best."

"*And?*" the FBI agent asked impatiently.

Yuri kept the smile from his voice. This was useless information by now. It would merely distract them as the bomb counted down. "Because the second bomb wouldn't be planted underwater, it was designed to be activated by radio signal."

"*Y*ou're going to have to shoot me before I'll let you touch this bomb, Parker. And I'm just as lethal with a screwdriver as I am with a gun."

"I don't want to shoot you. We're on the same side."

"If you've been spying on the US for Russia for several years, we're *not* on the same side."

"I reported nuclear sub movements through the strait. Data that can be gleaned from the Internet, but for some reason, my superiors wanted it firsthand."

"So you sold out when you were stationed at Neah Bay?"

"No. I was stationed at Neah Bay because I am a Russian operative in deep cover."

Sonofafuckingbitch. They'd had a Russian at the table at every single meeting. And on the boat when he dove with Undine. And—

Luke lunged for Parker, taking him by the throat.

Parker didn't expect the move, and his gun dropped from his hand. Luke had him pinned in the puddle that filled the bow and squeezed his throat. "This is for Annie."

Parker thrashed beneath him, but he was no match for Luke's strength or rage. The glow of the light mounted to the front of the cabin gave just enough light to see Parker's eyes bulge and his face go from red to blue.

"Kkkggeeee." It was more noise than formed word, and the only sound Parker could make. "Kkkkkgggg…"

Luke loosened his hands. He still needed this asshole's help if they were going to get this boat past the subduction zone. He'd have to hold a gun on him the entire time and forget trying to disarm the bomb.

"Key…" Parker gasped. "I have the keys. We can turn the bomb off."

Luke kept his hands on his throat. "Where did you get the keys?"

"From the case, but I didn't—"

Luke's hands closed again.

"….kkkkgggg."

Parker clawed at his wrists, shaking his head. "Dddddnzzz."

Luke let him take a shallow breath. "Didn't kill," Parker said as he bucked upward.

Luke released his throat. If Parker really had the keys, it was a bad idea to kill him before getting them. He could kill him after. "Where are the keys?"

"In my pocket. Get off"—he took a heaving breath—"and I'll show you."

Luke inched off him, retrieving the screwdriver and holding it in a clear threat. "If you didn't kill her, then how is it you have the keys?"

"She wasn't there when I took the case. The museum was still open. It was before the storm. Yuri must have heard about the case and that it was at the museum after I took it. He killed Annie when he didn't get it."

Luke sat back, and Parker pulled two small stainless steel keys and what looked like a coin from his pocket. "The case had these two keys and this coin in it. My contact at the GRU tracked down information on the two bombs, once we knew what Yuri was looking for."

Luke knew the GRU was Russia's largest foreign intelligence agency. Parker had access to information directly from the source. "You *knew* there were two bombs."

"Yes. It's why I insisted on being on the ferry detail tonight. I knew it wasn't over."

Luke would have been happy to strangle the man again. "You might've given a heads-up. This whole nightmare could have been avoided."

"My job is to make sure the bomb doesn't go off, not to blow my cover and spend the rest of my life in a US prison."

"You're a real fucking hero, Parker. Or whoever you are."

"My real name doesn't matter. I've been Parker Reeves for more than half my life."

"Cry me a fucking river. Now let's shut off this bomb, then I'm hauling you back to your station mates so they can tear your ass apart."

"I'm not going back with you. If you'd just let me come out here by myself, this could have been avoided."

"Shut up and give me a damn key. We turn them at the same time, I assume."

"Yes."

"Where are the keyholes?"

"There are two panels—one on each end, on opposite sides."

"How the fuck were you going to turn them both yourself?"

"I would've told the Osprey crew I found the keys inside and had one of them help me," Parker said.

Luke found the first panel and used the flat-edged screwdriver to pry it open. The rusted metal snapped and shattered, but eventually, he got it open.

And swore.

The entire mechanism had corroded inside. He had to chip away at the corrosion to find the keyhole—and pray the lock mechanism still worked. He did the same with the second panel, not trusting Parker to wield the screwdriver, even though it wasted precious minutes.

"I need to radio the Coast Guard," Parker said. "They'll be wondering why we stopped." He returned to the helm and used the built-in radio—which Luke couldn't access through his dead headset. "Lt. Sevick had an idea for disarming the bomb, but it required we stop. If it doesn't work, we'll continue on course to meet the Osprey."

The lie came so smoothly, and yet that shouldn't surprise

Luke. He'd been lying for so long, the truth would probably be far more difficult.

Luke had no choice but to keep working on the keyholes. He'd deal with Parker later. Once both keyholes were cleared and ready, Luke checked the countdown. They'd been stopped in the strait for ten minutes.

If this didn't work, those ten minutes could cost thousands of lives.

He and Parker took their positions and counted down, then turned their keys simultaneously. Luke checked the timer. Nothing happened.

"*Fuck!*"

"Do it again. Maybe our timing was off."

By their fifth attempt, sweat was pouring down Luke's face, and he was in the middle of the damn strait on a cold November night. "The keys are useless. It's too corroded. It sat rotting in the sea for over fifty years. It's a wonder the timer even works at all." But then, Yuri had been able to rewire that part of the mechanism. He'd probably had schematics for the bomb all along.

"Go back to trying to disable the timer," Parker said.

"Wait. Let me see the coin."

Parker shrugged and handed it to him. There was writing on each side. One side had "150" etched above "4-2-5" and the other said "3" above the letters "CCCP". He knew what the letters stood for, but the rest was a mystery. He tucked the coin in his pocket. "Fine, I'll work on the explosive, you get us farther down the strait."

He took his seat again and resumed his efforts to remove the lower panel with fresh screws, hoping the surgery wouldn't blow them all to hell. He'd just removed it when the Osprey was overhead. The tiltrotor aircraft was in helicopter mode so it could hover.

"Turn the radio back on, Parker!" he shouted. "I need to

talk to the pilot." No way could Parker hear him over the noise of the Osprey.

Even so, his radio came to life. "Interceptor to Osprey," Parker said, "We're having trouble with our radios. Lt. Sevick's is down. Over."

Luke clicked at his mic, and sure enough, he could hear but not speak. Parker had managed to jam him while Luke worked on the bomb.

"Copy that, Interceptor. Attach the cables, and we'll bring you in. Over."

"Negative on bringing us in. Sevick has discovered the bomb is atmospheric pressure-sensitive. It was designed for high-pressure depth. The low pressure of high altitude may cause it to detonate. Over."

Luke's jaw dropped at Parker's smooth lie, but then he wondered if the man was telling the truth—had he learned from his GRU sources that the bomb couldn't be transported at high altitude except in a pressurized aircraft that simulated air pressure at sea level?

"If we can't fly high, we can't haul ass," the airman above said.

"We're staying in the boat and will keep trying to defuse the bomb. Over," Parker said.

"Copy that. If you don't have it defused in twenty minutes, we'll have to chance atmospheric pressure decrease, or we'll never make it past the subduction zone. Over."

"Drop harnesses for Sevick and me, over."

Luke didn't waste time arguing with Parker and hooked up the cables to the Interceptor. He donned the harness that would prevent him from falling from the flying boat, and hoped to hell he wouldn't need it.

They lifted from the water, and the Interceptor took flight.

Luke stepped inside the tiny helm. He needed to talk to

Parker, and there was no way he'd be heard over the rotor downwash. "You need to hook up my radio, Parker!" he shouted. "We need to be able to communicate to defuse the bomb."

"I won't go up in the Osprey. I know what will happen— and I won't be taken into custody."

"Did you lie about the effect of high-altitude pressure on the bomb?"

Parker didn't answer. Finally he said, "We'll give it twenty minutes, like the airman said. We're wasting time."

"Unjam my radio."

Parker gave a sharp nod. They had no choice but to work together.

Defusing a nuke while dangling a hundred feet below an Osprey flying a thousand feet above the Strait of Juan de Fuca? No problem.

Luke planted himself back in front of the bomb and radioed the pilot. "The countdown is forty-nine minutes."

"We'll never make it," the pilot said. "We're a hundred and sixty miles from the safety zone. We'd have a chance in turboprop mode, but with you and a nuke hanging, we need to keep the rotors vertical."

Luke rubbed his hand over his face. Twenty minutes was too much given the distance. "Give me ten minutes. If I fail, we'll risk the air pressure."

"Ten minutes. That's all."

Parker glared at him but didn't object. Luke figured he'd toss the asshole overboard in nine minutes if he had to, but right now, he needed his help. He'd unscrewed the lower panel but hadn't had a chance to see what Yuri had done to the mechanism. He shined a flashlight into the opening.

Parker dropped down next to him and shouted, "What can I do?"

Even with headphones on, it was difficult to hear under the Osprey rotor wash.

"Find out how the Ukrainians initiated this thing," he shouted back. "They didn't use keys. However they turned it on is how we need to turn it off."

Luke studied the wires—corroded old ones mixed with new—as Parker was patched into the FBI SAC who was grilling Yuri. She said Yuri claimed to have activated the bomb using an ultra-low-frequency radio signal. The bomb activated when it received a specific Russian Morse code transmission.

Luke stared at the inner workings and spotted the radio receiver. Smashed to hell.

Sonofabitch. The guy on the ferry must have started the timer, then disabled the receiver. No wonder Yuri had answered the question. Aside from not having the actual code, they'd never get the receiver to work.

He moved the broken receiver aside and saw something that looked like an old sonar transponder. All at once it hit Luke what Yuri *hadn't* told them. "That lying sack of shit," he said. He pulled out the coin. "The coin is a key."

He glanced across the bomb at Parker. Over the man's shoulder, he saw the Olympic Mountains and rocky coastline as they neared the Pacific. The wind whipped his face as they flew at nauseating speed in a flying boat that was something out of Peter Pan's nightmares. In spite of the chill wind, he was sweating as he gripped the coin that was their lifeline.

"What do you mean?" Parker shouted. He looked a little green, but then, even seamen could get seasick in flying boats.

Luke nodded toward the cabin, and they both moved inside, where they could hear each other slightly better. "There were two bombs. One was meant to be above ground, the other underwater. Which meant they had to be initialized in two different ways. Ultra-low radio for above ground, but sonar for underwater." He showed Parker one side of the coin. "Three is a pretty damn low frequency, and CCCP is simple Morse code. The other side is the sonar frequency. You can't do Morse code with sonar, because all you get is a ping, no long or short sounds, so numbers work better. One-fifty is a standard sonar frequency."

He glanced at the boat. The Interceptor had to be outfitted with a multibeam sonar transducer. Luke had been working with sonar for years—both when he was in the Navy and his work for NOAA involved studying the effects on marine mammals. He was certain he'd found a very old sonar transponder inside the bomb.

"The transponder in the bomb will be forced to respond if we ping it at a frequency of 150 kilohertz with the combination four-two-five. The forced response will shut off the clock."

"Easy peasy," Parker said sarcastically. "How the fuck are we going to do that from here?"

"All we need is a transducer and some water." Damn, if this were a SEAL ROV or if he were outfitted for a SEAL mission, he'd have a handheld LIMIS unit. He radioed the Osprey and asked if they had one on the aircraft. The response was negative. "We'll have to use the one on the Interceptor, then."

"It'll be on the bottom of the hull," Parker said.

Aw hell. It looked like he was going to need the damn harness after all. And they were going to burn a lot more than ten minutes from the countdown clock.

Chapter Forty-One

They informed the pilot of the insane plan and the need for more time. They would be pushing past the limit. If they weren't pulled inside the Osprey in the next few minutes, they'd never clear the subduction zone.

Attempting this left no room for failure.

Less than two minutes after forming the plan, Luke was dangling over the side of the boat, following the sonar cable. He had an ax in one hand and a screwdriver in his pocket. Tools to save the world.

He didn't look down, to the side, or anywhere but at the small dark round hunk of metal attached to the hull. His target.

He swung the ax at the base of the boat, creating a handhold to pull himself toward the transducer. Finally he reached it and unhooked the cable. "Reel in the cable, Parker," he shouted into the radio.

The cable disappeared over the side of the boat. Parker would position it next to the bomb while Luke collected the transducer.

He didn't have time to finesse this job and used the ax

again, being careful not to damage the device. It was almost free when the ax slipped from his fingers. He looked down at the water below him, watching the ax disappear into the darkness. He felt the wind on his face. Moisture in the air.

He was dangling from a Coast Guard Interceptor over the Pacific Ocean, and he was going to die if he didn't get the damn glorified fish-finder up into the boat in the next ninety seconds. He pulled the screwdriver from his pocket and wedged it in the gap he'd made with the ax and pried with one hand while gripping the transducer and the hull with the other. No way in hell was he dropping this baby.

It broke free with a snap, and he pulled it to his chest, like a wide receiver making the game-winning catch. He swung erratically from the side, no longer holding himself steady with one hand. "Pull me up, Parker. I've got it."

Parker proved to be no slouch, lifting Luke's deadweight until he was able to get a grip on the side ladder. Luke climbed one-handed, then passed the transducer over the gunwale.

Back inside the boat, Luke checked the countdown.

They'd officially missed their window. They'd never clear the Cascadia subduction zone now.

If this didn't work, their only option was to go up.

If this didn't work, he'd killed them all.

Parker had gathered what they needed for their makeshift ocean for transmitting the pings. They planned to fill one of the dry bags with water from the bilge and bottled water he'd found in the small cabin. The bag was placed next to the bomb.

Now came the fun part. Luke needed to pick up the four-hundred-plus-pound nuclear warhead and drop it inside the dry bag. After the water was added, the transponder could receive the sonar pings.

Luke's job was to lift. Parker's was to get the bag under the bomb.

He strained with the weight, hugging the bomb to his chest with his feet planted wide. It would be easier if it had handholds. And if he weren't lifting from the rigid hull of a flying boat. He grimaced, thinking of his advice to the boys in the gym at Neah Bay. For the first time in his career serving his country, he was grateful he could deadlift four hundred pounds. This lift was less than that but the conditions pushed him to his limit.

The only easy day was yesterday.

"Got it!" Parker said.

Luke lowered the bomb and swiped his forearm across his brow as sweat blew into his eyes.

Parker set about filling the bag with water from the bilge. Luke snapped the top off a water bottle and poured.

At last they were ready. He put the transducer, which they'd hooked back up to the cable, in the water.

This would work.

It *had* to work.

Parker returned to the cabin, where the controls were for the sonar. Luke had already isolated the frequency.

He gave Parker a thumbs-up. "Start pinging."

The numbers sounded, four pings, then two, then five. Given the proximity of transducer to transponder, the reaction should have been instant. Luke watched the timer on the bomb.

Nothing happened.

He felt his blood drain to his feet. Nothing could have prepared him for this moment. This failure. This horrific disaster.

They were all going to die.

To the pilot, he said, "We need to go up. And fast." His voice barely made it past his lips.

"Not yet," Parker said. "We'll keep trying. Give us a few more minutes. Maybe I paused too long between numbers. Or not long enough."

"Don't stop until the bomb goes off," Luke said. He opened the panel and checked the sonar transponder. The wires were corroded, along with everything else. What if it wasn't firmly attached to the mechanism?

"Parker, I need replacement wire. Yank one from the boat console."

A moment later, Parker was by his side with a fistful of wires. "Take your pick."

Luke grabbed a wire stripper from the tool bag and cleaned the ends. Instead of replacing the wire, he attached it to both ends, paralleling the original.

The clock had rolled down to ten minutes.

Ten minutes left to live, and they were directly above the subduction zone. If this failed, they would have to go up, as high as they could. The atmosphere would fill with nuclear radiation, but there wouldn't be tsunamis below.

"Try again," he said to Parker.

Back in the cabin, Parker resumed pinging. Four. Two. Five.

Luke stared at the clock. The ten began to roll upward. The zero was followed by nine on the wheel. It stuttered, then froze in place.

Chapter Forty-Two

"They stopped it," Martinez said to the VIPs and military personnel who'd assembled in the command center of Coast Guard Air Station Port Angeles. Undine let out the breath she'd been holding for the last hour and fifteen minutes and burst into tears.

The governor draped an arm around her shoulders, and the comforting touch by a virtual stranger just made her cry harder. Fortunately, no one insisted she stop. The governor's husband simply handed her his handkerchief.

Thank goodness for tuxedos with handkerchiefs.

Undine's father had been invited to the gathering as well, but she'd insisted he take her mother to higher ground. Every cell in her body was focused on Luke and what he'd been attempting to do, and she couldn't deal with her mother's questions, or even her attempts at comfort. So she'd paced the room without her family, clutching Luke's trident and feeling so terrified she could barely breathe.

If the bomb hadn't been stopped, everyone in the command center would have been airlifted to a tsunami safety zone. They'd been within two minutes of heading to the airfield.

She swiped at her tears and cleared her throat. "They're on their way back?" she asked.

Commander Martinez nodded. "They're going to pull the bomb and Lieutenants Sevick and Reeves into the Osprey, then secure the boat so they can fly at top speed. They'll be here in thirty minutes."

She resumed pacing, no longer able to focus on the words. Luke was coming back.

Her Luke. Her hot, badass scientist.

The man who'd been able to forgive her for the unthinkable. Who loved her and wanted to marry her. Who'd just risked his life to save her and everyone on the western Pacific coast.

By the time the Osprey came into view, she was beside herself with anticipation. She darted outside into the frigid dark, ahead of the others who were also eager to greet the heroes of the night.

But no one was more eager than she was. The Osprey landed on the airfield like a helicopter, with just a soft bounce before settling in. Luke climbed out first. She waited at the perimeter of the launch pad, as she'd been instructed to do, but it wasn't an easy thing when waiting to kiss the man she intended to spend the rest of her life with, starting right now.

Luke jogged toward her in his now-tattered, bloody uniform. When he was close, she darted forward—screw the rules—and flung herself at him. He scooped her up and swung her around, and the whole world faded when he set her down and planted his mouth on hers.

His body was chilled, but his mouth was hot. His tongue slid against hers with all-consuming heat.

When their kiss ended, she said, "So much for no PDAs in uniform."

He laughed. "I have a feeling tonight I'll get a pass." His arm tightened around her waist. "Thank God you didn't change out of the gown. I was worried."

She laughed, and his lips bounced along her forehead. "Really? That's what worried you the most in the last two hours?"

"No, but in the last thirty minutes, it topped my list. I have plans for you in that dress."

"I can't wait. Although I suppose we have to sit through another grueling debriefing."

He flashed a cocky grin. "I can sum it up in a sentence. I'm the world's greatest sonar jockey."

"I can't wait to hear what that means."

"If you're afraid of heights, you don't want to know." He frowned. "I suppose I need to give Parker credit for the actual pinging."

She glanced behind him and scanned the crew of the Osprey. "Where is he?"

"He…grabbed a parachute from the Osprey and bailed while the boat was being secured. We won't be seeing him again."

She furrowed her brow. "Why did he do that? What happened?"

Luke turned but kept his arm around her waist and started walking toward the building. "Parker was—*is*—a Russian agent. He's been stationed at Neah Bay for a few years, tracking the movement of nuclear subs to and from Bangor. When *Petrel* exploded and Yuri went missing, he knew something was up. He explained a little before he grabbed the parachute and made a break for it.

"Do you think he…survived? I mean, there was no one to pick him up, and the water is cold as hell."

"He was wearing a survival suit and we were close to the Canadian coastline. There's a good chance he made it to land. The truth is I could have stopped him, but didn't. Disarming the bomb was a two-person job, and he knew it was likely a suicide mission. It doesn't excuse what he did, but I'm learning to let go of the past and move forward."

"Even when the past is…last week?"

Luke kissed her nose. "Yep. Especially then. If you didn't forgive me for being an ass that first night in Neah Bay, where would we be?"

"There was nothing to forgive. It was hot. You were hot. A-plus all the way."

"I was also an asshole."

"Stop calling yourself an asshole. You were honest. And I agreed. I wanted you. And I took just as much as you did." She brushed her lips against his. "I love you, Luke Sevick, and I'll embrace every step it took for us to get here, because here is where I want to be."

"You love me?" he asked, burying his face in her neck.

"Hell yeah. You're the hot, badass scientist of my dreams."

"Cool," he murmured against her skin.

Epilogue

Five months later
Port Angeles, Washington

It arrived in a plain manila envelope, but the humble packaging in no way diminished Undine's excitement. Trina could have scanned the copies and emailed the PDFs, but she'd been perverse and insisted on mailing hard copies. Because she knew it would kill Undine to wait. And also that it would look better on film if they recorded her receiving it and reading it for real—no acting involved. Ever since they'd pulled the airtight box from the sediment inside *Wrasse*, she'd known in her gut what would be inside.

One of the sailors had written an account of their encounter with *Magnum* that October day, and at last she held his words in her hands.

The smile she flashed for Mario and the camera after plucking the envelope from the mailbox was honest, and she didn't plan the way she clutched the envelope to her chest. It was simply her genuine reaction.

"Are you going to read it now?" Diego asked.

She'd planned on it, but it would be weird to read it without Luke but for the camera. He was at work and wouldn't be home for two more hours. "Not yet."

Diego gave the hand signal for cut and fixed her with a fond but irritated stare. She was used to that stare, having earned it often when they filmed the excavation of the *Wrasse*. This was supposed to be the final scene. The rest of the film was in postproduction already.

"Sorry, guys. I just can't without Luke."

Diego let out a heavy sigh. "Are you going to let us be there when you read it?"

She frowned. She really wanted this to be a private moment with Luke, but the documentary would benefit both her father's institute and NHHC—both organizations she'd given her heart to, and it would honor the sacrifice of seven men. She gave the director a sharp nod. "We won't read them without you filming it."

Diego's smile shifted to more fond, less irritated.

She called Luke at work and warned him that they would be filmed that evening. "Hurry home if you can, I'm dying to open the envelope."

"Will do, sweetheart."

Her fingers went to the pendant at her throat, a habit she'd developed soon after Luke gave her the necklace. A tiny silver sand dollar, it had three numbers etched into the back; the combination that had saved thousands—possibly millions —of lives.

The sand dollar and numbers served as a reminder to be grateful for every twist of fate that brought her and Luke together at the right place and time, after having met in the wrong place and time a dozen years ago.

The problem was she'd met him too soon. Then fate— and Yuri Kravchenko—fixed that, pressing the restart button twelve years later. Yuri, his nephew, and the two Ukrainians captured on the ferry were in federal custody, awaiting trial on espionage and terrorism charges. They would never see the outside of prison.

Parker Reeves had disappeared. Before he jumped, he'd admitted to Luke that he was the one who set fire to their cabin. He'd seen them leave and felt it was the perfect opportunity to spur them into action. He'd suspected Yuri had already recovered the bombs, but feared delays in the documentary filming would mean they'd miss the window of seeing the cleared torpedo tube. He'd known how Luke would react, that he'd choose to dive immediately. Proof Parker was very good at reading people, as a spy must be.

She wondered if he was alive. She didn't wish to see him again but found she didn't bear him ill will either. If he hadn't taken the case from the museum, Yuri would have gotten it and Luke would have died along with thousands of others that night.

Her parents were dating, which was strange, but not in a bad way. Her relationship with her dad was back on track—nearly as close as they'd been all those years ago. With her mother, things were strained, but improving. It was enough.

Luke's mother, however, had proven to be a warm, amazing woman. Undine told Luke more than once that she was marrying him for his mother.

The wedding was set for August, and her friends from NHHC were flying out to be her bridesmaids. She missed them terribly on a day-to-day basis but had zero regrets about her decision to move to Washington. Her home was, and would always be, where Luke was.

He finally walked in the door of their small rental house, and she threw herself at him. He scooped her up and swung her around, a habit he'd developed the night he saved the world.

She kissed him deeply. Then groaned, "No time for a quickie before Diego and Mario get here."

He flashed a grin. "Just as well, because I'm not in the mood to be quick."

Mario and Diego arrived, and they settled on the couch with the manila envelope between them. Diego asked a few scene-setting questions, then she opened the envelope.

The first words made her laugh out loud.

Oct. 20, 1962 - Sighted Soviet Sub Sank Same

"Can you explain why that's funny, Undine?" Diego asked off-camera.

"It's one word longer than a famous transmission sent by a pilot early after the US entered World War II. 'Sighted sub sank same.'"

"Is there more?" Diego asked.

"Yes." Undine began to read for the camera.

Because I retired with the lowest rank, the others have voted me scribe. They said it's in my name, and I suppose it is. They're selling it as an honor. Lazy bastards.

Now they're telling me I should say more, although sighted Soviet sub about sums it up...

It has been an honor to serve my country during WWII and with these sailors today. If anyone ever reads this, it will be a miracle, but we all hold out the hope that someday, people will learn what happened here.

It started when Avery dared the captain to take Wrasse down to periscope depth one last time. That got everyone excited. Even the admiral was on board. And so we dove, and that would have been it, but after we'd been underway at that depth for quite some time, we started to surface and caught sight of a glint of something at two o'clock. A Soviet sub was surfacing. The captain's son is an Air Force pilot whose job is to spot Ruskie subs, and he'd seen enough pictures to identify this one without hesitation. He said it's one of the ones that has the problem with oxygen evaporation, which could cause it to surface in a hurry. That had to be the reason their conning tower was riding the waterline in the Strait of Juan de Fuca.

They spotted us and fired a torpedo—that thankfully missed. Then they dove. A Ruskie in US territory is a bad thing on a good day, but with the Soviets trying to put bombs in Cuba, this is an especially tense week. That sub is up to no good.

We had no weapons to return fire, and they were dropping fast. They would get away. We could barely navigate with just the periscope.

The admiral suggested we use the only weapon we had—Wrasse herself—to take out the Soviets. And so we did. We rammed them, then we lost all power. We took on water, and we started to dive for real.

Avery tells me the proper word is "sink." I said if he prefers his wording, he can write the damn report...

The control room, where all seven of us are, remains air-tight, but the impact has bent the portal. It won't budge. We can't escape without having to swim through sections that have flooded. We'd drown before we could open a hatch, and if we made it that far, odds are we'd get bent surfacing and would never make it to shore in this cold water.

We're blind down here. We've heard banging through the hull. The Soviets are in the deep with us. They too have sunk. We'll share this grave and die knowing we succeeded in stopping them.

No regrets. It was the right thing to do. We are honored to serve our country and gladly give our lives to defend our shores.

Tell my beloved children how proud I am of them. I will be seeing my beautiful wife very soon.

Yours truly,
Lieutenant Commander Francis Wright, USN, retired

Other letters were included in the packet, but this was the only account of the sinking. The other notes were addressed to loved ones, saying good-bye, as Lt. Commander Wright had done at the end of his. Tears flowed down Undine's cheeks as she read the love notes. She met Luke's gaze. "You did the same thing, in the same place. You accepted a suicide mission without hesitation and might never have come back. I can easily imagine how those wives must have felt, but they had no idea of the heroic sacrifice their husbands made."

All the spouses had died years ago, but the *Wrasse* seven's children and grandchildren had since learned the truth. And it would all come out in the documentary, including the full story of what *Magnum* had carried in her torpedo tube.

Luke stroked her cheek. "I understand why they did it without hesitation. And I bet you anything, while Wright was writing this letter, the other six were trying to figure out how to stay alive, trying to hook up radios, anything. Even tapping out messages on the hull to the Soviets. But it was a different time, and what they had at their disposal was inadequate."

Undine wiped away her tears, remembering the camera was running, and there was one scripted line she was supposed to add. "These letters, along with other items collected from the *Wrasse* excavation, will become part of a permanent Cold War exhibit in the Smithsonian Museum of American History in Washington, DC. The *Wrasse* seven will posthumously receive the Medal of Honor, and the men will be buried with full honors in Arlington National Cemetery this coming Memorial Day. The *Wrasse* seven are the first US military personnel to receive our nation's highest military decoration for engaging with the enemy during the Cold War."

After a long beat, Diego said, "Perfect, Undine. That's a wrap."

She slumped back into the couch, clutching the letters to her chest while the two men packed their equipment. The documentary was done. Her final assignment for NHHC. A bittersweet moment.

After they walked Mario and Diego to the door and said good-bye, she flopped back onto the couch. "I think this means I'm unemployed now."

"And so you are," Luke said, pulling her onto his lap. "But

we'll worry about that tomorrow. Right now, I just want to hold you."

She snuggled into his lap, enjoying the moment. This wasn't the end. It was another new beginning.

"You aren't the only one to receive something interesting in the mail today," Luke said. "I received a card at work."

"A card?"

"Yeah. At first I thought it was from your dad, because the envelope was postmarked Palau and inside was a picture of Jellyfish Lake."

"Dad won't be in Palau until next month."

"Yeah, I remembered that after I turned it over. On the back it said '4-2-5' and nothing else. Parker Reeves is alive."

Author's Note

It is a burden, having readers who insist on meticulous research, but in the name of accuracy I diligently stayed at Hobuck resort in November to make sure I got the details right. The power did indeed go out, my cell phone has no service in that corner of my state, and I can confirm the sunsets are insanely beautiful.

If you ever find yourself lucky enough to visit Washington and can make it out to the Makah Reservation, I highly recommend visiting the museum to view the Ozette collection and hiking the Cape Flattery Trail. Staying in a cabin at Hobuck is a special treat. I can't wait to return.

The encounter between USS *Wrasse* and *M-357* was fictional, as are both submarines, but there are some similarities to actual events. Of particular note, USS *Bugara*, a Balao-class submarine, was being towed to the Pacific for SINKEX when she took on water and sank off the coast at Cape Flattery. No submariners were aboard *Bugara*, and no one on the tow vessel was injured when the cable slipped from the brake and ran free.

The bombs described in this story are also fictional,

however many countries experimented with nuclear artillery and the US developed "backpack nukes"—fifty-pound nuclear weapons that could be carried in a soldier's pack, many of which were more powerful than the bomb dropped on Hiroshima. Special Forces units, Navy SEALs, and some Marines were trained to carry these small devices. One documentary stated SEALs were trained to plant these nuclear weapons underwater.

This book would not have been possible without input from my husband, who worked for UAB at Naval History and Heritage Command in the late nineties, and like Undine, holds an MA in nautical archaeology from Texas A&M. He shared details both small—underwater archaeologists do indeed read paperback books during decompression—and large—there are accounts of US sailors hearing tapping by sailors trapped in sinking vessels. It is also true that notes written by trapped submariners have been found when the wreckage was later examined.

About the Author

USA Today bestselling author Rachel Grant also writes thrillers as R.S. Grant. She worked for over a decade as a professional archaeologist and mines her experiences for storylines and settings, which are as diverse as excavating a cemetery underneath an historic art museum in San Francisco, survey and excavation of many prehistoric Native American sites in the Pacific Northwest, researching an historic concrete house in Virginia (inspiration for her debut novel, CONCRETE EVIDENCE), and mapping a seventeenth century Spanish and Dutch fort on the island of Sint Maarten in the Caribbean (which provided inspiration for the island and fort described in CRASH SITE).

She lives in the Pacific Northwest with her husband and children.

For more information:
www.Rachel-Grant.net
contact@rachel-grant.net